SCIENCE FICTION ODDITIES

Groff Conklin, one of the most highly regarded anthologists in the field of science fiction, has put together an SF anthology that is truly different. He has selected nineteen science fiction stories, which are unusual and entertaining—and a little strange. Just how strange, you will find out . . .

Included are stories by Isaac Asimov, Avram Davidson, Fritz Leiber, Frederik Pohl, Alan E. Nourse, and many others.

Science Fiction
ODDITIES

EDITED BY

Groff Conklin

A BERKLEY MEDALLION BOOK
published by
BERKLEY PUBLISHING CORPORATION

ACKNOWLEDGMENTS

Alan Arkin, "People Soup." Copyright © 1958 by Galaxy Publishing Corporation. Reprinted by permission of the author and Artists Agency Corporation from *Galaxy*, November 1958.

Isaac Asimov, "What Is This Thing Called Love?" Copyright © 1961 by Ziff-Davis Publishing Company, Inc. Reprinted by permission of the author from *Amazing Stories*, March 1961, where it appeared under the title, "Playboy and the Slime God."

Stephen Barr, "Callahan and the Wheelies." Copyright © 1960 by Mercury Press, Inc. Reprinted by permission of the author from *Magazine of Fantasy and Science Fiction*, August 1960.

R. Bretnor. "Mrs. Poppledore's Id." Copyright © 1952 by Mercury Press, Inc. Reprinted by permission of the author from *Magazine of Fantasy and Science Fiction*, February 1952.

Avram Davidson and Sidney Klein, "The Teeth of Despair." Copyright © 1961 by Mercury Press, Inc. Reprinted by permission of Scott Meredith Literary Agency from *Magazine of Fantasy and Science Fiction*, May 1961.

G. C. Edmondson. "The Galactic Calabash." Copyright © 1960 by Mercury Press, Inc. Reprinted by permission of Robert P. Mills from *Magazine of Fantasy and Science Fiction*, May 1960.

H. F. Ellis, "Space-Crime Continuum." Copyright © 1954 by Mercury Press, Inc. Reprinted by permission of Ben Roth Agency from *Magazine of Fantasy and Science Fiction*, September 1954, which in turn reprinted it from *Punch* with the permission of the Proprietors of *Punch*.

Charles L. Harness, "The Chessplayers." Copyright © 1953 by Mercury Press, Inc. Reprinted by permission of the author from *Magazine of Fantasy and Science Fiction*, October 1953.

R. A. Lafferty, "What's the Name of That Town?" Copyright © 1964 by Galaxy Publishing Corporation. Reprinted by permission of the author from *Galaxy*, October 1964.

Fritz Leiber, "Rump-Titty-Titty-Tum-TAH-Tee." Copyright © 1958 by Mercury Press, Inc. Reprinted by permission of the author and the author's agent, Robert P. Mills, from *Magazine of Fantasy and Science Fiction*, May 1958.

Robert Lory, "Rundown." Copyright © 1963 by Galaxy Publishing Corporation. Reprinted by permission of the author from *IF Science Fiction*, May 1963.

Edward Mackin, "The Trouble with H.A.R.R.I." Copyright © 1957 by Hamilton & Co. (Stafford) Ltd. Reprinted by permission of the author and his literary agent, E. J. Carnell, from *Authentic Science Fiction*, 1957.

BERKLEY MEDALLION EDITION, NOVEMBER, 1966

BERKLEY MEDALLION BOOKS are published by
Berkley Publishing Corporation
15 East 26th Street, New York, N.Y. 10010

Berkley Medallion Books ® TM 757,375

Printed in the United States of America

CONTENTS

Introduction

Not so many years ago, when the otherwise quite independent words "molecule" and "biology" were being more and more often associated in the scientific press, a questioning student is said to have asked one of his professors—no doubt a cynical type—what, exactly, "molecular biology" was.

The professor is rumored to have answered, undoubtedly with a knowing smile, "The best definition that I can formulate for you on a moment's notice is that it is the content of any paper that appears in a journal having the phrase 'molecular biology' in its title."

This, it so happens, is analogically an excellent way to describe the contents of the present collection of curious literary objects. The stories are science fiction because each and every one of them appeared in some magazine having the words "science fiction" in its title or subtitle.

Other than that, these tales for the most part follow their own vision, and adhere to no established pattern or concept or definition. They are better described by the word "oddities" in the title of this book than by the first part of the phrase. Odd most of them are, and delightfully so. Science fiction (at least according to the standard definitions by the more erudite students of the subject) the large majority are not.

It is true that two or three representatives of the genre in its rigidly classical sense have been included, but that is only because I personally was enamored of them. On the whole, however, the stories you are about to encounter in this volume are solely intended to please, not to fit some pre-tailored straitjacket defining what science fiction should be. So—forget categories, and simply enjoy yourself!

GROFF CONKLIN

People Soup

ALAN ARKIN

The kind of comedian I like is one who knows how to *act funny*—not just *act himself*. Too many comedians are simply exhibitionists, and their work is as much a comment on their characters as on their inadequate acting abilities.

Alan Arkin is obviously a genuine comic actor: otherwise he would not have been able to write such a quietly insane bit of science nonsense as "People Soup." His stage acting speaks for itself: his hilarious doings in the Broadway stage hits, "Enter Laughing" and "Luv," his earlier work with the famous Second City improvisational group, and, most lately, his starring role in the 1966 movie hit, "The Russians Are Coming, The Russians Are Coming."

Unfortunately, Arkin has limited his "acting of the pen" to the classic bit that follows, plus one other *Galaxy* tale, "Whisk-Boom"; but he also wrote the music for an Off-Broadway play in which he had the lead part, and has on hand a "brilliant" (his word) "unproduced" (also his word) movie script.

Bonnie came home from school and found her brother in the kitchen, doing something important at the sink. She knew it was important because he was making a mess and talking to himself. The sink drain was loaded down with open soda bottles, a sack of flour, corn meal, dog biscuits, molasses, Bromo-Seltzer, a tin of sardines and a box of soap chips. The floor was covered with drippings and every cupboard in the kitchen was open. At the moment, Bonnie's brother was putting all his energy into shaking a plastic juicer that was half-filled with an ominous-looking, frothy mixture.

Bonnie waited for a moment, keeping well out of range, and then said, "Hi, Bob."

" 'Lo," he answered, without looking up.

"Where's Mom?"

"Shopping."

Bonnie inched a little closer. "What are you doing, Bob?" she asked.

"Nothing."

"Can I watch?"

"No."

Bonnie took this as a cue to advance two cautious steps. She knew from experience how close she could approach her brother when he was being creative and still maintain a peaceful neutrality. Bob slopped a cupful of ketchup into the juicer, added a can of powdered mustard, a drop of milk, six aspirins and a piece of chewing gum, being careful to spill a part of each package used.

Bonnie moved in a bit closer. "Are you making another experiment?" she asked.

"Who wants to know?" Bob answered, in his mad-scientist voice, as he swaggered over to the refrigerator and took out an egg, some old bacon fat, a capsuled vitamin pill, yesterday's Jello and a bottle of clam juice.

"Me wants to know," said Bonnie, picking up an apple that had rolled out of the refrigerator and fallen on the floor.

"Why should I tell you?"

"I have a quarter."

"Where'd you get it?"

"Mom gave it to me."

"If you give it to me, I'll tell you what I'm doing."

"It's not worth it."

"I'll let you be my assistant, too."

"Still not worth it."

"For ten cents?"

"Okay, ten cents."

She counted out the money to her brother and put on an apron. "What should I do now, Bob?"

"Get the salt," Bob instructed.

He poured sardine oil from the can into the juicer, being very careful not to let the sardines fall in. When he had squeezed the last drop of oil out of the can, he ate all the sardines and tossed the can into the sink.

Bonnie went after the salt and, when she lifted out the box, she found a package containing two chocolate graham crackers.

"Mom has a new hiding place, Bob," she announced.

10

Bob looked up. "Where is it?"

"Behind the salt."

"What did you find there?"

"Two chocolate grahams."

Bobby held out his hand, accepted one of the crackers without thanks and proceeded to crumble the whole thing into his concoction, not even stopping to lick the chocolate off his hands.

Bonnie frowned in disbelief. She had never seen such self-sacrifice. The act made her aware, for the first time, of the immense significance of the experiment.

She dropped her quarrel completely and walked over to the sink to get a good look at what was being done. All she saw in the sink was a wadded, wet Corn Flakes box, the empty sardine tin and spillings from the juicer, which by this time was beginning to take on a distinctive and unpleasant odor. Bob gave Bonnie the job of adding seven pinches of salt and some cocoa to the concoction.

"What's it going to be, Bob?" she asked, blending the cocoa on her hands into her yellow corduroy skirt.

"Stuff," Bob answered, unbending a little.

"Government stuff?"

"Nope."

"Spaceship stuff?"

"Nope."

"Medicine?"

"Nope."

"I give up."

"It's animal serum," Bob said, sliced his thumb on the sardine can, glanced unemotionally at the cut, ignored it.

"What's animal serum, Bob?"

"It's certain properties without which the universe in eternity regards for human beings."

"Oh," Bonnie said. She took off her apron and sat down at the other end of the kitchen. The smell from the juicer was beginning to reach her stomach.

Bobby combed the kitchen for something else to throw into his concoction and came up with some oregano and liquid garlic.

"I guess this is about it," he said.

He poured the garlic and oregano into his juicer, put the lid on, shook it furiously for a minute and then emptied the contents into a deep pot.

"What are you doing now, Bob?" Bonnie asked.

"You have to cook it for ten minutes."

11

Bobby lit the stove, put a cover on the pot, set the timer for ten minutes and left the room. Bonnie tagged after him and the two of them got involved in a rough game of basketball in the living room.

"BING!" said the timer.

Bob dropped the basketball on Bonnie's head and ran back into the kitchen.

"It's all done," he said, and took the cover off the pot. Only his dedication to his work kept him from showing the discomfort he felt with the smell that the pot gave forth.

"Fyew!" said Bonnie. "What do we do with it now? Throw it out?"

"No, stupid. We have to stir it till it cools and then drink it."

"Drink it?" Bonnie wrinkled her nose. "How come we have to drink it?"

Bobby said, "Because that's what you do with experiments, stupid."

"But, Bob, it smells like garbage."

"Medicine smells worse and it makes you healthy," Bob said, while stirring the pot with an old wooden spoon.

Bonnie held her nose, stood on tiptoe and looked in at the cooking solution. "Will this make us healthy?"

"Maybe." Bob kept stirring.

"What will it do?"

"You'll see." Bob took two clean dish towels, draped them around the pot and carried it over to the formica kitchen table. In the process, he managed to dip both towels in the mixture and burn his already sliced thumb. One plastic handle of the pot was still smoldering, from being too near the fire, but none of these things seemed to have the slightest effect on him. He put the pot down in the middle of the table and stared at it, chin in hand.

Bonnie plopped down opposite him, put her chin in her hands and asked, "We *have* to drink that stuff?"

"Yup."

"Who has to drink it first?" Bob made no sign of having heard. "I thought so," said Bonnie. Still no comment. "What if it kills me?"

Bobby spoke by raising his whole head and keeping his jaw stationary in his hands. "How can it hurt you? There's nothing but pure food in there."

Bonnie also sat and stared. "How much of that stuff do I have to drink?"

"Just a little bit. Stick one finger in it and lick it off."

12

Bonnie pointed a cautious finger at the tarry-looking brew and slowly immersed it, until it barely covered the nail. "Is that enough?"

"Plenty," said Bob in a judicious tone.

Bonnie took her finger out of the pot and stared at it for a moment. "What if I get sick?"

"You can't get sick. There's aspirin and vitamins in it, too."

Bonnie sighed and wrinkled her nose. "Well, here goes," she said. She licked off a little bit.

Bob watched her with his television version of a scientific look. "How do you feel?" he inquired.

Bonnie answered, "It's not so bad, once it goes down. You can taste the chocolate graham cracker." Bonnie was really enjoying the attention. "Hey," she said, "I'm starting to get a funny feeling in my—" and, before she could finish the sentence, there was a loud *pop*.

Bob's face registered extreme disappointment.

She sat quite still for a moment and then said, "What happened?"

"You've turned into a chicken."

The little bird lifted its wings and looked down at itself. "How come I'm a chicken, Bob?" it said, cocking its head to one side and staring at him with its left eye.

"Ah, nuts," he explained. "I expected you to be more of a pigeon thing." Bob mulled over the ingredients of his stew to see what went wrong.

The chicken hopped around the chair on one leg, flapped its wings experimentally and found itself on the kitchen table. It walked to the far corner and peered into a small mirror that hung on the side of the sink cabinet.

"I'm a pretty ugly chicken, boy," it said.

It inspected itself with its other eye and, finding no improvement, walked back to Bobby.

"I don't like to be a chicken, Bob," it said.

"Why not? What does it feel like?"

"It feels skinny and I can't see so good."

"How else does it feel?"

"That's all how it feels. Make me stop being it."

"First tell me better what it's like."

"I told you already. Make me stop being it."

"What are you afraid of? Why don't you see what it's like first, before you change back? This is a valuable experience."

The chicken tried to put its hands on its hips, but could

13

find neither hips nor hands. "You better change me back, boy," it said, and gave Bob the left-eye glare.

"Will you stop being stupid and just see what it's like first?" Bob was finding it difficult to understand her lack of curiosity.

"Wait till Mom sees what an ugly mess I am, boy. Will you ever get it!" Bonnie was trying very hard to see Bob with both eyes at once, which was impossible.

"You're a sissy, Bonnie. You ruined the opportunity of a lifetime. I'm disgusted with you." Bob dipped his forefinger in the serum and held it toward the chicken. It pecked what it could from the finger and tilted its head back.

In an instant, the chicken was gone and Bonnie was back. She climbed down from the table, wiped her eyes and said, "It's a good thing you fixed me, boy. Would you ever have got it."

"Ah, you're nothing but a sissy," Bob said, and licked off a whole fingerful of his formula. "If I change into a horse, I won't let you ride me, and if I change into a leopard, I'll bite your head off." Once again, the loud *pop* was heard.

Bonnie stood up, wide-eyed. "Oh, Bob," she said, "you're beautiful!"

"What am I?" Bob asked.

"You're a bee-yoo-tee-full St. Bernard, Bob! Let's go show Melissa and Chuck."

"A St. Bernard?" The animal looked disgusted. "I don't want to be no dog. I want to be a leopard."

"But you're *beautiful*, Bob! Go look in the mirror."

"Naah." The dog paddled over to the table.

"What are you going to do, Bob?"

"I'm going to try it again."

The dog put its front paws on the table, knocked over the serum and lapped up some as it dripped on the floor. *Pop* went the serum, taking effect. Bobby remained on all fours and kept on lapping. *Pop* went the serum again.

"What am I now?" he asked.

"You're still a St. Bernard," said Bonnie.

"The devil with it then," said the dog. "Let's forget all about it."

The dog took one last lap of serum. *Pop!* Bobby got up from the floor and dejectedly started out the back door. Bonnie skipped after him.

"What'll we do now, Bob?" she asked.

"We'll go down to Thrifty's and get some ice cream."

They walked down the hill silently, Bobby brooding over

not having been a leopard and Bonnie wishing he had stayed a St. Bernard. As they approached the main street of the small town, Bonnie turned to her brother.

"You want to make some more of that stuff tomorrow?"

"Not the same stuff," said Bob.

"What'll we make instead?"

"I ain't decided yet."

"You want to make an atomic bomb?"

"Maybe."

"Can we do it in the juicer?"

"Sure," Bob said, "only we'll have to get a couple of onions."

What Is This Thing Called Love?

ISAAC ASIMOV

Did you ever stop to wonder what a couple of thoroughly alien life forms from some unimaginably distant star might assume was the nature of human reproduction, if all they had to read was (to use Isaac Asimov's nice rephrasing of the real magazine's title) "Recreationlad"? Our author has given the matter some concentrated thought, and has come up with the following delightful bit of fun. It is based, of course, on the practical limitations on explicitness which the postal regulations impose on mailable magazines of wide circulation. . . .

Incidentally, this tale was originally published in *Amazing Stories* under the title "Playboy and the Slime God."

"But these are two species," said Captain Garm, peering closely at the creatures that had been brought up from the planet below. His optic organs adjusted focus to maximum sharpness, bulging outwards as they did so. The color patch above them gleamed in quick flashes.

Botax felt warmly comfortable to be following color changes once again, after months in a spy cell on the planet, trying to make sense out of the modulated sound waves emitted by the natives. Communication by flash was almost like being home in the far-off Perseus arm of the Galaxy. "Not two species," he said, "but two forms of one species."

"Nonsense, they look quite different. Vaguely Perse-like, thank the Entity, and not as disgusting in appearance as so many out-forms are. Reasonable shape, recognizable limbs. But no color patch. Can they speak?"

"Yes, Captain Garm," Botax indulged in a discreetly disapproving prismatic interlude. "The details are in my report.

These creatures form sound waves by way of throat and mouth, something like complicated coughing. I have learned to do it myself." He was quietly proud. "It is very difficult."

"It must be stomach-turning. Well, that accounts for their flat, unextensible eyes. Not to speak by color makes eyes largely useless. Meanwhile, how can you insist these are a single species? The one on the left is smaller and has longer tendrils, or whatever it is, and seems differently proportioned. It bulges where this other does not. —Are they alive?"

"Alive but not at the moment conscious, Captain. They have been psycho-treated to repress fright in order that they might be studied easily."

"But are they worth study? We are behind our schedule and have at least five worlds of greater moment than this one to check and explore. Maintaining a time-stasis unit is expensive and I would like to return them and go on—"

But Botax's moist spindly body was fairly vibrating with anxiety. His tubular tongue flicked out and curved up and over his flat nose, while his eyes sucked inward. His splayed three-fingered hand made a gesture of negation as his speech went almost entirely into the deep red.

"Entity save us, Captain, for no world is of greater moment to us than this one. We may be facing a supreme crisis. These creatures could be the most dangerous lifeforms in the Galaxy, Captain, just *because* there are two forms."

"I don't follow you."

"Captain, it has been my job to study this planet, and it has been most difficult, for it is unique. It is so unique that I can scarcely comprehend its facets. For instance, almost all life on the planet consists of species in two forms. There are no words to describe it, no concepts even. I can only speak of them as first form and second form. If I may use their sounds, the little one is called 'female,' and the big one, here, 'male,' so the creatures themselves are aware of the difference."

Garm winced. "What a disgusting means of communication."

"And, Captain, in order to bring forth young, the two forms must cooperate."

The Captain, who had bent forward to examine the specimens closely with an expression compounded of interest and revulsion, straightened at once. "Cooperate? What nonsense is this? There is no more fundamental attribute of

17

life than that each living creature bring forth its young in innermost communication with itself. What else makes life worth living?"

"The one form does bring forth life but the other form must cooperate."

"How?"

"That has been difficult to determine. It is something very private and in my search through the available forms of literature I could find no exact and explicit description. But I have been able to make reasonable deductions."

Garm shook his head. "Ridiculous. Budding is the holiest, most private function in the world. On tens of thousands of worlds it is the same. As the great photo-bard, Levuline, said, 'In budding time, in budding time, in sweet, delightful budding time; when . . .'"

"Captain, you don't understand. This cooperation between forms brings about somehow (and I am not certain exactly how) a mixture and recombination of genes. It is a device by which in every generation, new combinations of characteristics are brought into existence. Variations are multiplied; mutated genes hastened into expression almost at once where under the usual budding system, millennia might pass first."

"Are you trying to tell me that the genes from one individual can be combined with those of another? Do you know how completely ridiculous that is in the light of all the principles of cellular physiology?"

"It must be so," said Botax nervously under the other's pop-eyed glare. "Evolution *is* hastened. This planet is a riot of species. There are supposed to be a million and a quarter different species of creatures."

"A dozen and a quarter more likely. Don't accept too completely what you read in the native literature."

"I've seen dozens of radically different species myself in just a small area. I tell you, Captain, give these creatures a short space of time and they will mutate into intellects powerful enough to overtake us and rule the Galaxy."

"Prove that this cooperation you speak of exists, Investigator, and I shall consider your contentions. If you cannot, I shall dismiss all your fancies as ridiculous and we will move on."

"I can prove it." Botax's color flashes turned intensely yellow-green. "The creatures of this world are unique in another way. They foresee advances they have not yet made, probably as a consequence of their belief in rapid change

18

which, after all, they constantly witness. They therefore indulge in a type of literature involving the space travel they have never developed. I have translated their term for the literature as 'science fiction.' Now I have dealt in my readings almost exclusively with science fiction, for there I thought, in their dreams and fancies, they would expose themselves and their danger to us. And it was from that science fiction that I deduced the method of their inter-form cooperation."

"How did you do that?"

"There is a periodical on this world which sometimes publishes science fiction which is, however, devoted almost entirely to the various aspects of the cooperation. It does not speak entirely freely, which is annoying, but persists in merely hinting. Its name as nearly as I can put it into flashes is 'Recreationlad.' The creature in charge, I deduce, is interested in nothing but inter-form cooperation and searches for it everywhere with a systematic and scientific intensity that has roused my awe. He has found instances of cooperation described in science fiction and I let material in his periodical guide me. From the stories he instanced I have learned how to bring it about.

"And Captain, I beg of you, when the cooperation is accomplished and the young are brought forth before your eyes, give orders not to leave an atom of this world in existence."

"Well," said Captain Garm, wearily, "bring them into full consciousness and do what you must do quickly."

Marge Skidmore was suddenly completely aware of her surroundings. She remembered very clearly the elevated station at the beginning of twilight. It had been almost empty, one man standing near her, another at the other end of the platform. The approaching train had just made itself known as a faint rumble in the distance.

There had then come the flash, a sense of turning inside out, the half-seen vision of a spindly creature, dripping mucus, a rushing upward, and now—

"Oh, God," she said, shuddering. "It's still here. And there's another one, too."

She felt a sick revulsion, but no fear. She was almost proud of herself for feeling no fear. The man next to her, standing quietly, but still wearing a battered fedora, was the one who had been near her on the platform.

"They got you, too?" she asked. "Who else?"

Charlie Grimwold, feeling flabby and paunchy, tried to lift his hand to remove his hat and smooth the thin hair that broke up but did not entirely cover the skin of his scalp and found that it moved only with difficulty against a rubbery but hardening resistance. He let his hand drop and looked morosely at the thin-faced woman facing him. She was in her middle thirties, he decided, and her hair was nice and her dress fit well, but at the moment he just wanted to be somewhere else and it did him no good at all that he had company; even female company.

He said, "I don't know, lady. I was just standing on the station platform."

"Me, too," Marge said quickly.

"And then I see a flash. Didn't hear nothing. Now here I am. Must be little men from Mars or Venus or one of them places."

Marge nodded vigorously, "That's what I figure. A flying saucer? You scared?"

"No. That's funny, you know. I think maybe I'm going nuts or I *would* be scared."

"Funny thing. I ain't scared, either. Oh, God, here comes one of them now. If he touches me, I'm going to scream. Look at those wiggly hands. And that wrinkled skin, all slimy; makes me nauseous."

Botax approached gingerly and said, in a voice at once rasping and screechy, this being the closest he could come to imitating the native timbre, "Creatures! We will not hurt you. But we must ask you if you would do us the favor of cooperating."

"Hey, it talks!" said Charlie. "What do you mean, co-operate?"

"Both of you. With each other," said Botax.

"Oh?" He looked at Marge. "You know what he means, lady?"

"Ain't got no idea whatsoever," she answered loftily.

Botax said, "What I mean—" and he used the short term he had once heard employed as a synonym for the process.

Marge turned red and said, "What!" in the loudest scream she could manage. Both Botax and Captain Garm put their hands over their mid-regions to cover the auditory patches that trembled painfully with the decibels.

Marge went on rapidly, and nearly incoherently. "Of all things. I'm a married woman, you. If my Ed was here, you'd hear from *him*. And you, wise guy," she twisted toward

Charlie against rubbery resistance, "Whoever you are, if you think—"

"Lady, lady," said Charlie in uncomfortable desperation. "It ain't my idea. I mean, far be it from me, you know, to turn down some lady, you know; but me, I'm married, too. I got three kids. Listen—"

Captain Garm said, "What's happening, Investigator Botax? These cacophonous sounds are awful."

"Well," Botax flashed a short purple patch of embarrassment. "This forms a complicated ritual. They are supposed to be reluctant at first. It heightens the subsequent result. After that initial stage, the skins must be removed."

"They have to be *skinned?*"

"Not really skinned. Those are artificial skins that can be removed painlessly, and must be. Particularly in the smaller form."

"All right, then. Tell it to remove the skins. Really, Botax, I don't find this pleasant."

"I don't think I had better tell the smaller form to remove the skins. I think we had better follow the ritual closely. I have here sections of those space-travel tales which the man from the 'Recreationlad' periodical spoke highly of. In those tales the skins are removed forcibly. Here is a description of an accident, for instance, 'which played havoc with the girl's dress, ripping it nearly off her slim body. For a second, he felt the warm firmness of her half-bared bosom against his cheek—' It goes on that way. You see, the ripping, the forcible removal, acts as a stimulus."

"Bosom?" said the Captain. "I don't recognize the flash."

"I invented that to cover the meaning. It refers to the bulges on the upper ventral region of the smaller form."

"I see. Well, tell the larger one to rip the skins off the smaller one. —What a dismal thing this is."

Botax turned to Charlie. "Sir," he said, "rip the girl's dress nearly off her slim body, will you? I will release you for the purpose."

Marge's eyes widened and she twisted toward Charlie in instant outrage. "Don't you dare do that, you. Don't you *dast* touch me, you sex maniac."

"Me?" said Charlie plaintively. "It ain't my idea. You think I go around ripping dresses? Listen," he turned to Botax, "I got a wife and three kids. She finds out I go around ripping dresses, I get clobbered. You know what my wife does when I just look at some dame. *Listen—*"

21

"Is he still reluctant?" said the Captain, impatiently.

"Apparently," said Botax. "The strange surroundings, you know, may be extending that stage of the cooperation. Since I know this is unpleasant for you, I will perform this stage of the ritual myself. It is frequently written in the space-travel tales that an outer-world species performs the task. For instance, here," and he riffled through his notes finding the one he wanted, "they describe a very awful such species. The creatures on the planet have foolish notions, you understand. It never occurs to them to imagine handsome individuals such as ourselves, with a fine mucous cover."

"Go on! Go on! Don't take all day," said the Captain.

"Yes, Captain. It says here that the extraterrestrial 'came forward to where the girl stood. Shrieking hysterically, she was cradled in the monster's embrace. Talons ripped blindly at her body, tearing the kirtle away in rags.' You see, the native creature is shrieking with stimulation as her skins are removed."

"Then go ahead, Botax, remove it. But please, allow no shrieking. I'm trembling all over with the sound waves."

Botax said politely to Marge, "If you don't mind—"

One spatulate finger made as though to hook on to the neck of the dress.

Marge wiggled desperately. "Don't touch. Don't touch! You'll get slime on it. Listen, this dress cost $24.95 at Ohrbach's. Stay away, you monster. Look at those eyes on him." She was panting in her desperate efforts to dodge the groping, extraterrestrial hand. "A slimy, bug-eyed monster, that's what he is. Listen, I'll take it off myself. Just don't touch it with slime, for God's sake."

She fumbled at the zipper, and said in a hot aside to Charlie, "Don't you dast look."

Charlie closed his eyes and shrugged in resignation.

She stepped out of the dress. "All right? You satisfied?"

Captain Garm's fingers twitched with unhappiness. "Is that the bosom? Why does the other creature keep its head turned away?"

"Reluctance. Reluctance," said Botax. "Besides, the bosom is still covered. Other skins must be removed. When bared, the bosom is a very strong stimulus. It is constantly described as ivory globes, or white spheres, or otherwise after that fashion. I have here drawings, visual picturizations, that come from the outer covers of the space-travel magazines. If you will inspect them, you will see that upon every one of them a creature is present with a bosom more or less exposed."

The Captain looked thoughtfully from the illustrations to Marge and back. "What is ivory?"

"That is another made-up flash of my own. It represents the tusky material of one of the large sub-intelligent creatures on the planet."

"Ah," and Captain Garm went into a pastel green of satisfaction. "That explains it. This small creature is one of a warrior sect and those are tusks with which to smash the enemy."

"No, no. They are quite soft, I understand." Botax's small brown hand flicked outward in the general direction of the objects under discussion and Marge screamed and shrank away.

"Then what other purpose do they have?"

"I think," said Botax with considerable hesitation, "that they are used to feed the young."

"The young eat them?" asked the Captain with every evidence of deep distress.

"Not exactly. The objects produce a fluid which the young consume."

"Consume a fluid from a living body? Yech-h-h." The Captain covered his head with all three of his arms, calling the central supernumerary into use for the purpose, slipping it out of its sheath so rapidly as almost to knock Botax over.

"A three-armed, slimy, bug-eyed monster," said Marge.

"Yeah," said Charlie.

"All right you, just watch those eyes. Keep them to yourself."

"Listen, lady. I'm trying not to look."

Botax approached again. "Madam, would you remove the rest?"

Marge drew herself up as well as she could against the pinioning field. "Never!"

"I'll remove it, if you wish."

"Don't touch! For God's sake, don't touch. Look at the slime on him, will you? All right, I'll take it off." She was muttering under her breath and looking hotly in Charlie's direction as she did so.

"Nothing is happening," said the Captain, in deep dissatisfaction, "and this seems an imperfect specimen."

Botax felt the slur on his own efficiency. "I brought you two perfect specimens. What's wrong with the creature?"

"The bosom does not consist of globes or spheres. I know

23

what globes or spheres are and in these pictures you have shown me, they are so depicted. Those are large globes. On this creature, though, what we have are nothing but small flaps of dry tissue. And they're discolored, too, partly."

"Nonsense," said Botax. "you must allow room for natural variation. I will put it to the creature herself."

He turned to Marge, "Madam, is your bosom imperfect?"

Marge's eyes opened wide and she struggled vainly for moments without doing anything more than gasp loudly. *"Really!"* she finally managed. "Maybe I'm no Gina Lollobrigida or Anita Ekberg, but I'm perfectly all right, thank you. Oh, boy, if my Ed were only here." She turned to Charlie. "Listen, you, you tell this bug-eyed slimy thing here, there ain't nothing wrong with my development."

"Lady," said Charlie, softly. "I ain't looking, remember?"

"Oh, sure, you ain't looking. You been peeking enough, so you might as well just open your crummy eyes and stick up for a lady, if you're the least bit of a gentleman, which you probably ain't."

"Well," said Charlie, looking sideways at Marge, who seized the opportunity to inhale and throw her shoulders back, "I don't like to get mixed up in a kind of delicate matter like this, but you're all right—I guess."

"You *guess?* You blind or something? I was once runner-up for Miss Brooklyn, in case you don't happen to know and where I missed out was on waistline, *not* on—"

Charlie said, "All right, all right. They're fine. Honest." He nodded vigorously in Botax's direction. "They're okay. I ain't that much of an expert, you understand, but they're okay by me."

Marge relaxed.

Botax felt relieved. He turned to Garm. "The bigger form expresses interest, Captain. The stimulus is working. Now for the final step."

"And what is that?"

"There is no flash for it, Captain. Essentially, it consists of placing the speaking-and-eating apparatus of one against the equivalent apparatus of the other. I have made up a flash for the process, thus: kiss."

"Will nausea never cease?" groaned the Captain.

"It is the climax. In all the tales, after the skins are removed by force, they clasp each other with limbs and indulge madly in burning kisses, to translate as nearly as possible the phrase most frequently used. Here is one example,

24

just one, taken at random: 'He held the girl, his mouth avid on her lips.' "

"Maybe one creature was devouring the other," said the Captain.

"Not at all," said Botax impatiently. "Those were burning kisses."

"How do you mean, burning? Combustion takes place?"

"I don't think literally so. I imagine it is a way of expressing the fact that the temperature goes up. The higher the temperature, I suppose, the more successful the production of young. Now that the big form is properly stimulated, he need only place his mouth against hers to produce young. The young will not be produced without that step. It is the co-operation I have been speaking of."

"That's all? Just this—" The Captain's hands made motions of coming together, but he could not bear to put the thought into flash form.

"That's all," said Botax. "In none of the tales, not even in 'Recreationlad,' have I found a description of any further physical activity in connection with young-bearing. Sometimes after the kissing, they write a line of symbols like little stars, but I suppose that merely means more kissing; one kiss for each star, when they wish to produce a multitude of young."

"Just one, please, right now."

"Certainly, Captain."

Botax said with grave distinctness, "Sir, would you kiss the lady?"

Charlie said, "Listen, I can't move."

"I will free you, of course."

"The lady might not like it."

Marge glowered. "You bet your damn boots, I won't like it. You just stay away."

"I would like to, lady, but what do they do if I don't? Look, I don't want to get them mad. We can just—you know —make like a little peck."

She hesitated, seeing the justice of the caution. "All right. No funny stuff, though. I ain't in the habit of standing around like this in front of every Tom, Dick and Harry, you know."

"I know that, lady. It was none of my doing. You got to admit that."

Marge muttered angrily, "Regular slimy monsters. Must think they're some kind of gods or something, the way they order people around. Slime gods is what they are!"

Charlie approached her. "If it's okay now, lady." He made a vague motion as though to tip his hat. Then he put his hands awkwardly on her bare shoulders and leaned over in a gingerly pucker.

Marge's head stiffened so that lines appeared in her neck. Their lips met.

Captain Garm flashed fretfully. "I sense no rise in temperature." His heat-detecting tendril had risen to full extension at the top of his head and remained quivering there.

"I don't either," said Botax, rather at a loss, "but we're doing it just as the space-travel stories tell us to. I think his limbs should be more extended— Ah, like that. See, it's working."

Almost absently, Charlie's arm had slid around Marge's soft, nude torso. For a moment, Marge seemed to yield against him and then she suddenly writhed hard against the pinioning field that still held her with fair firmness.

"Let go." The words were muffled against the pressure of Charlie's lips. She bit suddenly, and Charlie leaped away with a wild cry, holding his lower lip, then looking at his fingers for blood.

"What's the idea, lady?" he demanded plaintively.

She said, "We agreed just a peck, is all. What were you starting there? What's going on around here? First these slimy creatures make like they're gods and now this. You some kind of playboy or something?"

Captain Garm flashed rapid alternations of blue and yellow. "Is it done? How long do we wait now?"

"It seems to me it must happen at once. Throughout all the universe, when you have to bud, you bud, you know. There's no waiting."

"Yes? After thinking of the foul habits you have been describing, I don't think I'll ever bud again. —Please get this over with."

"Just a moment, Captain."

But the moments passed and the Captain's flashes turned slowly to a brooding orange, while Botax's nearly dimmed out altogether.

Botax finally asked hesitantly, "Pardon me, madam, but when will you bud?"

"When will I *what*?"

"Bear young?"

"I've got a kid."

"I mean bear young now."

"I should say not. I ain't ready for another kid yet."

26

"What? What?" demanded the Captain. "What's she saying?"

"It seems," said Botax, weakly, "she does not intend to have young at the moment."

The Captain's color patch blazed brightly. "Do you know what I think, Investigator? I think you have a sick, perverted mind. Nothing's happening to these creatures. There is no cooperation between them, and no young to be borne. I think they're two different species and that you're playing some kind of foolish game with me."

"But Captain—" said Botax.

"Don't 'but Captain' me," said Garm, "I've had enough. You've upset me, turned my stomach, nauseated me, disgusted me with the whole notion of budding and wasted my time. You're just looking for headlines and personal glory and I'll see to it that you don't get them. Get rid of these creatures now. Give that one its skins back and put them back where you found them. I ought to take the expense of maintaining Time-stasis all this time out of your salary."

"But, Captain—"

"Back, I say. Put them back in the same place and at the same instant of time. I want this planet untouched, and I'll see to it that it stays untouched." He cast one more furious glance at Botax. "One species, two forms, bosoms, kisses, cooperation, BAH—. You are a fool, Investigator, a dolt as well and, most of all, a sick, sick, sick creature."

There was no arguing. Botax, limbs trembling, set about returning the creatures.

They stood there at the elevated station, looking around wildly. It was twilight over them, and the approaching train was just making itself known as a faint rumble in the distance.

Marge said, hesitantly, "Mister, did it really happen?"

Charlie nodded. "I remember it. Listen. I'm sorry you was embarrassed. It was none of my doing. I mean, you know, lady, you wasn't really bad. In fact, you looked good, but I was kind of embarrassed to say that."

She smiled. "It's all right."

"You want maybe to have a cup of coffee with me just to relax you. My wife, she's not really expecting me for a while."

"Oh? Well, Ed's out of town and my little boy is visiting at my mother's. I don't have to rush home."

"Come on, then. We been kind of introduced."

"I'll say." She laughed.

They had a couple of cocktails and then Charlie couldn't let her go home in the dark alone, so he saw her to her door. Marge was bound to invite him in for a few moments.

Meanwhile, back in the spaceship, the crushed Botax was making a final effort to prove his case. While Garm prepared the ship for departure Botax hastily set up the tight-beam visi-screen for a last look at his specimens. He focused in on Charlie and Marge in her apartment. His tendril stiffened and he began flashing in a coruscating rainbow of colors.

"Captain Garm! Captain! Look what they're doing now!"

But at that very instant the ship winked out of Time-stasis.

Callahan and the Wheelies

STEPHEN BARR

It is often said by sociologists of science and by similar pundits that the days of the garret or cellar inventor are long since past. Today, they say, science and invention are matters for giant laboratories, group-think, management controls, market research, and all that.

However, science fiction still gives space to such oddballs as the scientific loner, and the Callahan of this slap-happy tale is a prime example of such a character. Also an example, to say the least, is what happened as a result of his efforts—an example for the world to see, indeed, proving that today, as in the past, invention can be dangerous. Perhaps, after all, scientific activities should be undertaken only in the confines of a maximum-security corporate laboratory. Ask Amantha! Ask the Callahans' friendly power company!

"If I'd only *known*," Amantha said, "if someone had only *cautioned* me—if my mother'd just had the sense to *warn* me to . . . to . . ."

"What's all this leading up to?" Callahan asked uneasily.

"Why, then I'd have known better than to marry a mad inventor, is what!" Amantha said, picking up the wastebasket and retrieving its scattered contents. "Look at this room! Look at the whole house, for that matter! Why can't they be kept in the lab where they belong, I should like to know? Tell me that?" She blinked her black eyes angrily.

"I'm not an inventor," Callahan said, going over to where the little three-wheeled mechanism was now attempting to pull a book out of the bottom shelf. He turned it around to face the room. "I'm a research cybernetician. Inventors—"

"Well, whatever you are, you're mad as a hatter." Amantha glared at the little object on wheels—it was about the size of a roller skate and it seemed to be considering what to do

29

next. It turned its photoelectric scanners this way and that, waving its jointed grappling arms about. Then it appeared to make up its mind, and trundled over to a wall socket in the baseboard, plugged itself in and proceeded to recharge itself. Amantha turned in exasperation as another one came rolling in at the door with a faint clicking sound. It went to the first and waited patiently until it was through recharging and had disengaged itself from the outlet; then it took its place. The recharged one made for the door and, turning to the right, disappeared along the corridor.

"No you don't!" Amantha said, and ran after it. "Not in my study you don't go!"

Callahan followed and found his wife standing with her back to the door of her study, defensively facing the little machine, which looked frustrated. "It's bad enough," she said, "when they get into the closet and hide my shoes, God knows, but I'll not have any wheely going into my study, and that's flat!" The wheely—although it had no auditory equipment—seemed to understand, and turning neatly around, it went clicking down the corridor in the direction of the lab.

In the Callahans' big one-story house on the edge of a village in upstate New York there was one room kept inviolate, and that was Amantha's study where she did her writing—mostly stories about children. These stories were totally lacking in sentimentality, and had, in fact, a faintly sardonic tinge, which may have accounted for their popularity among the young.

When the wheely had disappeared into the lab, she looked Callahan in the eye. This could be alarming, because Amantha had an Irish father and a mother who was a French Gypsy. Callahan felt he could handle the Irish part but he wasn't so sure about the other.

"Callahan," she said, "the time has come to have this out. When you started in on this . . . this project of yours, the understanding was the writing would be done in my study and the inventing would be going on in the lab— you'd stay in your shop and I'd stay in my shop. And now what happens? The wheelies have got the run of the whole shebeen! Do you remember what that one did to my stockings? The little one that had the four wheels?"

"It's not around any more," Callahan said. "It shorted itself and blew its circuits. You can keep the bedroom door closed, can't you?"

"They get in the kitchen," she said, "and open the oven

30

door. You can't go opening the oven door on a soufflé! There's no lock on the oven and I don't want to shut up the kitchen—how would I keep an eye on the roast save I could smell it when I'm in the study?"

"What's wrong with using the timer on the stove?"

"Clocks are no good for food: they've not got the feel for it. You've just got to keep those chaps of yours in the lab, *miri rom,* or else teach them to mind. Let 'em run in the garden—it's a nice fine day."

"The last time they were in the garden," Callahan said, "one of them went out onto the highway and got flattened by a truck. And anyway they're not supposed to *mind:* they're supposed to have complete freedom of choice. I want their graphite-gel circuits to experience anything that—"

"Well, I hope you gave the poor little flattened-out thing a decent burial," Amantha said.

"I did not," Callahan said. "They're not *animals,* Amantha, dammit! They're machines—with flexible memory-circuits and feedback controls, and they're very impressionable."

"Hmph!" Amantha said. "I'd call it nosy!"

"They are not! That's not curiosity—they're motivated first by a random device and then they learn. The lines of connection in the graphite-gel that turn out the most successful remain like a printed circuit, and then if occasion arises, they *over*print them. My whole idea is to get away from a machine with a set of prearranged instructions, and let them teach themselves by trial and error. You might call it the survival element."

"Darwin's theory of devil take the hindmost, is what you mean," said Amantha. There was a sound of banging from the kitchen and she gave him a severe look and they went to investigate. A wheely was next to the treadle-operated garbage pail, raising the lid and letting it fall in an aimless way. Its scanners followed the movement, and an arm kept time with it.

"Now what!" Amantha said, and bent down to stop the clatter.

"No, leave it alone: it's getting a correlation between the movement of the treadle and the cover. It'll stop when it finds it doesn't help it move forward or get anywhere."

"Is *that* all the poor mite wants to do?"

"Well, that, and keep recharged—I had to start them with something. And I put in a couple of don'ts, like the heat detector, so they won't go and set us on fire. That's why they don't stick around when they open the oven door. They're quite simple, essentially, Amantha." The essentially simple wheely gave up the banging and butted the garbage pail, but it was too heavy to be moved that way. After another try it stopped and went into a corner where it came to a standstill.

"I think you're dotty," Amantha said. "I wish you'd stayed with computers. Computers aren't forever running around under foot."

"That's the whole point," Callahan said, sitting on the edge of the kitchen table with a lecturer's air. "A computer just sits back on its big can and never experiences anything that results from its own activities! It gets a mass of information fed into it, but that's not the same thing. Those big computers don't move around and *do* anything—if they did, and if they had some sort of goal like the wheelies recharging themselves, they'd be thinking instead of just calculating. True thought starts with operational response to environment!"

"That's a fine, fancy, twopence-colored phrase!" Amantha said. "You ought to take up writing, Callahan, and that's a fact."

"Well, I've got to get to work," he said, and got up.

"Dust yourself off, then," Amantha said. "You've got flour all over *your* big . . . yourself."

When he got to the lab, Callahan found two wheelies engaged in a shoving match. He watched with interest—this was a new phase. After a while one of them gave it up and turned aside, letting the other have the right of way. Callahan decided it had been a matter of chance—he did not feel that rivalry had been involved, it was whether an enduring or viable engram had been produced in their nearly amorphous "brains." Of course in the actual living animal brain, the whole system of neurons, synapses and connecting fibres was there to start with, and repeated activity would eventually produce useful patterns, but with the wheelies' undifferentiated mass of semi-conducting graphite-gel it was more like the lining up of polarized particles in a magnetic field. "What I want to try," he had said to Amantha, "is giving a small computer a *purpose*—and arms and legs. Well, wheels, anyway."

"I think you're dotty," she said.

He went back to work—attempting to take an electroencephalogram of a wheely. This had become increasingly difficult as they reacted more and more fractiously to being held still, and it was hard not to think of this as resentment. If one of them happened to be for the moment inactive, the electroencephalograph showed nothing but the basic Alpha-pulsation—its particular resonance—whereas when confined it would go into what Amantha called the dithers. The day wore on rather frustratingly. At five o'clock he went to the fuse box and opened a switch that supplied all the base-plugs available to the wheelies. The others—the ones in use for floor lamps—could not be got at without a special tool, and were on a separate circuit. This arrangement had become necessary when the wheelies had achieved their present adventuresomeness; without it, there would be no sleep for anybody. With their current off the wheelies would run out of power and come to rest until he recharged them in the morning.

At dinner he said, "You know, Amantha, they may get to associate me with stopping their power supply. Since they're not in perceptual working order when I recharge them, I don't get credit for it. They're getting a one-sided view—I hope they don't develop aggressive patterns."

"Well, watch out they don't *drab* you," she said. Callahan thought this over, and decided it meant poisoned—he wasn't much good at understanding the Romany *jib*, though.

"Underwood called up this afternoon," he said. "You were in the study. That man's a dolt. . . ."

"He's that," Amantha said. "What did he have to say for himself?"

"Oh, he wanted to remind me of the symposium tomorrow night. Since I'm the principal speaker I'm not likely to forget it. I'm reading a paper on my experiments. Then he maundered on about dendrite fibres—he's one of those over-informed skeptics. He doesn't seem to realise that graphite—"

"Come on," Amantha broke in. "We'll miss the TV."

"What's on? Not a western, I hope: I'm sick of cowboys and Indians."

"No, it's an eastern: policemen and miscreants."

He followed her down the corridor, but he was concerned with his thoughts about the coming symposium, and failed to notice a small shape that dodged around a far corner. Since all wheelies by this time had presumably run out of power, it was as well for his peace of mind that he did not see it.

When Callahan woke the next morning he saw that his wife was already dressed. She seemed to be having trouble with the bedroom door. "That's a funny thing," she said, with a frown. "The door's locked . . . and on the outside. . . ."

He got up and went to her and tried the handle, but the door wouldn't open. "For God's sake!" he said.

"I warned you. They're locking us in, now."

"But they can't *reach* the lock!" He started for the window. "Besides I turned off the base plugs. . . ." He climbed out and entered the house by the front door. He let Amantha out, and there was a silence. Then a wheely went clicking by into the living room.

"Well, you did forget the switch, Callahan."

"I did not, dammit! Come; I'll show you." They went to the lab and he opened the fuse box. "There: I told you it was off, and they couldn't have reached the bedroom key anyway."

"Yes?" she said. "Well, look at that."

He turned and saw a pile of books that had been arranged in a crude staircase from the floor to the work bench. "Well, I'll be. . . ." He stood staring.

"But, Callahan, dear, how could they manage the steps with their wheels?"

"Sponge-rubber tires," he said absently. "But their power should have run out last night . . . Oh, *ho!*" He pointed to the wall at the back of the bench where there was a wall socket at working level—not on the circuit with the disconnected base plugs. Next to it a test-tube rack had been knocked over. "This is the damnedest thing I've ever seen! But the bedroom lock. . . . There weren't any books piled up there!"

"Maybe they put 'em back," said Amantha. They went to the living room and found the books scattered on the floor. They watched as a wheely fiddled with them, finally putting one on top of the other. Then it sighted Callahan's foot, and it turned and strolled out into the hall at top speed.

"It's afraid of you, Callahan," she said. "And no wonder, with all the shouting."

"I wasn't shouting! And besides, it has no hearing!"

Amantha tossed her dark head. "*I* think you hurt its feelings."

"For Pete's sakes, the whole thing's just luck! Trial and error!"

"*I* think it was clever."

He went and got dressed, and then around the house collecting the inert wheelies—only the one had contrived to recharge itself—and he plugged them into the bench outlet for a few minutes each. Then he turned them loose for the day and reconnected the base-plugs. He realized he had forgotten to notice the identity of the one that had been so ingenious—or, rather, lucky—they all had number plates screwed into their tops. He went to ask Amantha if she had noticed.

"Thirteen, of course," she said. "Who else? He's the wily one."

"Ridiculous!" he said, and returned to the lab. He took the books back to the living room and worked for the next couple of hours rewiring all the outlets he had previously assumed to be out of wheely-reach, so that they could be turned off with the base-plugs. Then he considered putting a lock on the fuse box, but the wheelies would scarcely recognize the significance of a line switch he hoped. He went into the hall and saw his neighbor's eleven-year-old son, Peter Brown, coming in at the front door. He had a gleam in his eye, and Callahan led him away from the lab into the living room. Peter's widowed mother, Jessica Brown, had been in a few days back and she had seen a wheely. Report of this had probably got to Peter.

"Say, Mr. Callahan! Mother says you've got a model locomotive that runs around without any—" He broke off as two wheelies rolled in and raced for the nearest base-plug. "Oh boy! Look at that, will you! *Two* of 'em! What are they doing?" They were contesting electric-power rights and Peter went down on hands and knees to watch while the successful one recharged: he was fascinated. When the wheely was through it started away across the rug and Peter put out his hand, but it made a detour and went rapidly through the open French window.

"Damn!" Callahan said, and started after it.

"Why, it's just like it was alive!" Peter said delightedly, as he followed Callahan out onto the terrace. "Did you see the way it *dodged?* How did it see my hand, Mr. Callahan?"

"Photoelectric scanners. And they're not alive, Peter, but they might just as well be. . . . Oh, for Pete's sakes!" The wheely had crossed the lawn and was now on the cement apron of their small swimming pool. He began to run, but too late—the wheely, without a moment's hesitation, ran over the edge and disappeared with a faint splash. When they got there they could see it lying motionless on the blue tile bottom.

"Gee! It's drowned!"

"No, it's just shorted itself—it'll be all right when it dries out."

35

"Gee, aren't you going to get it out? Want *me* to, Mr. Callahan?" Peter was already pulling off his T-shirt.

"Sure," Callahan began, and Amantha appeared at the French windows.

"You've blown the fuse!" she called out. "My typewriter's off!"

"No, I haven't," he muttered distractedly, and walked back to the house. As he went in he heard Peter dive. When he looked in the fuse box he found the one for the rear section blown—there was a smell of hot oil in the air. After a short search he discovered the cause: a wheely—not Thirteen, he was oddly relieved to see—was in a corner behind some boxes with smoke coming from it. It had evidently found some thin nails and thrust them behind the guard that covered a floor plug, and the full voltage had gone through the grapplers and shorted in the graphite-gel.

He picked it up—and dropped it hurriedly: it was still hot. Well, now there were seven wheelies left—numbers one to six were experimental and had been scrapped. All the current models had a built-in response to any weakening in their batteries, which made them immediately seek out a base-plug and recharge, and he had found it advantageous to keep their batteries small so that they would be forced into frequent repetitions of the action. It was the equivalent of seeking food, and he hoped it would lead to a kind of survival of the fittest—not as between one wheely and another, but of the more useful engrams.

These in turn were the result of some enduring change produced in the cortex by previous activity—a form of memory. The wheely encountering the problems imposed by its environment would learn, and the problems, as R. W. Gerard had put it in reference to the living cerebrum, somehow whip into existence a brain capable of solving them. Callahan's thoughts were interrupted by Peter, who came into the lab, dripping and wearing nothing but shorts. He held out the wheely—also wet. "Think it'll be all right, Mr. Callahan?"

"Sure. Thanks a lot, Peter," Callahan said. "You'd better go on home and get into dry clothes." He put the wheely on the bench. Amantha came to the door to let him know the current was on again. He decided to take the blame for its interruption.

After Peter had been sent home to change, the rescued wheely began to make jerky, indecisive movements as its servo-circuits dried, and Callahan put it on the floor. Amantha

36

and he followed it as it went into the living room and had another try at the French windows—now shut. "Let's have an experiment," Callahan said, and picked it up and put it on the dinner table. It rolled to the edge, where it stopped— its scanners directed at the void. "See! It's learned from one lesson—that's amazing!"

"Number Thirteen, again," Amantha said. "I tell you, Callahan, he's the clever one." For once Callahan was in- clined to agree with her. "What time's your symposium to be at?" she asked.

"We're having the dinner first—that starts at seven. The yapping afterwards will probably keep up till all hours, so I'll put up at a hotel. I'll be back for lunch—don't forget to shut off the base-plugs, Amantha."

"I'll not. You better go pack your bag if you have to find a hotel: it's a four-hour drive, so you'd best leave here at two."

"Right. I'm going to take Thirteen with me for the demon- stration."

"Well, keep him out of mischief."

Callahan had a special carrier for the wheelies—it allowed a certain freedom of movement so that they would not get the "dithers"—but when the time came he could not find Thirteen anywhere.

"D'you think he's maybe crawled in behind the books in the living room?" Amantha said, after they had searched fruitlessly.

"There isn't room enough," Callahan said. "This is damned annoying, but I can't wait—I'll take Nine instead. Damn: I wanted to show them how Thirteen avoids the edge of the table!"

"Maybe he told Nine to watch out for edges."

"Oh, for Pete's sakes, Amantha! They can't *communicate!*"

"Well, I'll keep an eye out for Thirteen. Perhaps he'll com- municate his whereabouts."

Callahan nodded and went in search of Nine. The disap- pearance of his star wheely was unprecedented—none of them had ever hidden before. It occurred to him that it might have gotten outside, but all the doors and window screens were secure. It was very puzzling. Just before he left, he said, "If I were you I'd pull that switch early. In fact right now— otherwise you'll have to keep an eye on them all afternoon. They'll run out of juice by four if you do it now, and you'll have a little peace and quiet."

"I'll do that," she said, and kissed him goodbye. He went to the garage to get out the little coupe they used for long trips, but there was no response to the starter switch. He had no time to check the battery or wiring, so he took the jeep. In ten minutes he had forgotten the matter.

The symposium got off to a fair start: Callahan's report on the progress of his experiments was greeted with enthusiastic interest by everyone except Underwood, who interrupted constantly. He seemed incapable of grasping the concept of a flexible, self-teaching, practically self-creating cortex, and acted as if Callahan were withholding pertinent information. This was the moment Callahan had been waiting for. He beckoned to the waiter, who brought in the wheely carrier. He put it down gingerly—the faint scrambling from inside was disconcerting, but since this was a group of scientists he was ready for anything. Callahan thanked him, took out Nine and put it on the table. "Here, Gentlemen, is one of them," he said. "It's not my most highly developed one, but—"

"How come you didn't bring *that?*" Underwood interrupted.

"I intended to, but I . . . er, couldn't find it."

"Couldn't *find* it?"

"Well, you see . . . it had hidden."

Underwood sneered. "And I suppose this one will be unable to prove your rather extraordinary claims," he said. "Hidden!"

"All right, Underwood," another member said. "Let's see what it can do." He reached out his hand, which Nine examined with its scanners. Then it backed away and scooted to the edge of the table—and came to an abrupt stop. "I'll be damned!" the man said, admiringly. Callahan felt the same way—it almost looked as though Amantha had been right.

"I think," Underwood said, "that anyone who is familiar with Dr. Monkton's photoelectric 'cat' which follows and catches an illuminated 'mouse,' will not find this either novel or impressive."

"Yes, but the table edge is not illuminated," the other man said.

"When I was a boy," Underwood said, loftily, "I had a mechanical toy that never fell off a table. It had feelers resting on the board which dropped when it came to an edge, causing the mechanism to turn."

"This one wasn't using its feelers," Callahan said. "It's learned to recognize the cortical image of an open space. Here: I'll show you." He put Nine on the floor and got the members to make a ring with their legs close together, but leaving a narrow gateway.

Nine scanned the fence of legs, and evidently decided they were too closely spaced to get through. When it spotted the gate, it made for it, but just before going through it, it made a detour and untied one of Underwood's shoelaces. Then it dashed out of the gateway. The members laughed, and one of them said, "Very cute!" But Underwood did not seem to share this view.

"All it did," he said, as he tied his shoe, "was to register the light area and go toward it. Mere phototropism." He did not mention shoelaces.

"Well, if you think so, we can try something else," Callahan said, and went to retrieve the wheely. It was slowly rolling parallel to the baseboard, and he realized that its battery was weakening, and it was looking for an outlet. He explained this to the others, and they watched as it located one, and tried to remove the plugged-in cord, but it was stuck. After yanking unsuccessfully it gave up and came back to the table under which lay a knife that had been dropped. It was obvious that it had seen and remembered it, for it went directly back to the outlet again, and using the knife as a lever, pried the plug loose. Then it calmly recharged itself. Even Underwood was impressed. But Callahan was a little worried. . . .

He was dog-tired when he got back to the hotel, and didn't wake up until the following noon. He tried to reach Amantha by phone to say he would be late, but there was no answer. Where on earth was she? He was expected for lunch; she ought to be home.

He drove upstate at top speed and made the trip in a little over two hours. He left the car in the drive and went to the door: it was locked. He called out and rang the bell, but nobody came. Then from inside the house he heard very faintly his wife's voice calling. To get in he had to break a pane of glass and, once inside, he could definitely hear Amantha at the back. He ran down the passageway to the lab—also locked—and her voice came from inside, but curiously muffled. He lunged and broke the lock, knocking over a pile of books, and now her voice was over him: "Get me *out* of here, Callahan!"

"For Heaven's sake, where are you?"

"I'm up in the attic, entirely!"

"But there isn't any attic, Amantha!"

"Well, just the same, that's where I am!"

39

It dawned on him that there was an air space—with ventilating louvers at either end, and accessible by a trap door set in the lab ceiling directly over the bench. He now saw that a crate had been placed on this, and a chair on the crate. The trap door had a spring catch, which explained why Amantha was imprisoned. "Just a minute!" he shouted, and climbed onto the bench. He was about to mount the chair when he saw that one of the legs was not on the crate. Setting it straight he climbed up and unlocked the trap door. Amantha was covered with dust and spider web. Her eyes were blazing.

"My God!" she said. "Just wait till I lay hands on that Thirteen! I'll *dook* him! I'll decontaminate him!"

"Now, calm down, Amantha, and tell me what happened. What on earth were you doing up there?"

"I was lured, is what!" she said indignantly. "Out of the goodness of my heart I was trying to help that misbegotten, deceitful contraption, and all the time it was fooling! It's become the ringleader, Callahan, and that's no lie!"

"Look: let's begin at the beginning," he said. "Did you turn off the base-plugs early, the way I said?"

"Well, to tell you the truth, I didn't like to do it. They wanted to play—it seemed a shame to make them go to bed at four, surely."

"But did you *eventually* turn off the juice?"

"Wait till I catch my breath, will you? I've been shouting up in here since who knows, but I couldn't make anyone hear. The Browns must be out. Well, I turned it off, but they're getting it somewhere on the Q.T. It all comes from when they discovered the keyhole saw: Thirteen cut a hole in the floor into the crawl-space and they've been gallivanting all over the house under it!" She pointed to a jagged hole near the door. "He's got one in every room and doors won't hold 'em. And they've got a new way of climbing: they pull themselves up with a bit of bent wire. That's how I got locked in."

"I thought you said you were lured?"

"And so I was. Thirteen gets up there somehow, and starts going tip-tap, tip-tap. I came to see what's up and think he's got himself caught, so I pile up the crate and the chair and climb up with merciful intentions—and Thirteen skitters past me and drops on the chair and bang! I'm in!"

"It's a lucky thing you weren't able to follow," Callahan said. "The chair had one leg off the edge and you'd have taken a tumble—over there." He pointed, and saw for the first time the bottom of a broken bottle standing, jagged points up, on the floor where she would have fallen if she had stepped on the insecure chair. "You say Thirteen dropped onto it?" She nodded, looking at the broken bottle incredulously. "They weigh over seven pounds, Amantha, and the way the chair was placed when I came in, Thirteen would have knocked it over. No: it *moved* it."

There was a silence. Callahan shook his head—the whole thing was preposterous. The experiment was working too well. The wheelies' speed of mental development would do credit to a human brain. There was not a wheely in sight. "Where the devil are they all?" he said.

"They're all under the house conferring what to do next."

"You know what, Amantha?"

"No," she said. "My mind's a total blank."

"That's where they're getting recharged! They've tapped a BX cable under the floor—God knows how—and I don't know how to stop them unless I throw the main switch. . . ."

"What'd we do for light?"

"If I do it now, they'll be deactivated in a couple of hours. We won't be needing the lights till this evening."

"I'm having myself an egg and whisky," Amantha said. "I'm dead altogether. How would they know about the BX cable, Callahan?"

"They must detect it by electromagnetic induction . . . a new sense!" He looked around and noticed that various things were missing: pliers, a wire cutter, a spool of flex—as well as the keyhole saw and an auger to start it. There was a slight noise and the scanners of a wheely appeared in the hole. On seeing Callahan it sank out of sight again, and they heard it land on the cement floor of the crawl-space. Callahan went to the fuse box and pulled the main switch. Amantha went out to the kitchen, and shortly afterwards called to him from the garden.

"Will you look at that?" she said when he joined her. There was a pile of fresh earth and beside it a small hole in the ground, big enough for a woodchuck—but there had never been signs of one before. . . .

"They've learned how to dig," she said. "The hellers."

"You know what that means, don't you? They'll be able to get at the power company's main out at the road. The line isn't on poles any more—they've got it underground, and my turning off our main switch won't do any good! It's going to be a race against time: if they can't make it in two hours they'll run out of juice. Otherwise . . ." He looked at his watch. "It's ten of five—by seven we'll know the worst."

"I think you ought to go down there in the crawl-space now," Amantha said, "and have it out with them. You can get in by the little door in the closet. Tell me first: why did you take the jeep yesterday?"

"The battery's dead—I'm glad you reminded me. I'll go and check it. . . ."

He went to the garage, but he was not able to check the battery because it wasn't in the car. He went back and told Amantha the news. "They've got it under the house, of course! They've apparently worked out a way of bypassing their transformers and charge direct from the battery voltage—it's just right for *their* batteries! I'll fix their wagon *now!*"

He took out a flash and went to the closet where the access door to the crawl-space was, but it was immovable. He fetched a screwdriver and removed the hinges—the door had been barricaded with some scrap lumber. In the low-ceilinged space he found the battery from the coupe, and some of the missing tools, but no wheelies. At one point a cinder block had been dislodged from the foundations by scratching away the mortar from around it, and next the hole it left was another pile of dirt. As Callahan watched, an additional small amount was flung out, almost getting him in the face. A wheely's scanners appeared—then it turned and scuttled away into the tunnel.

"They've dug a tunnel, all right," Callahan said when he emerged from the closet. He held out the battery and the keyhole saw. "Without these I think they'll leave us in peace for tonight. I don't think they've tapped the main yet—they had the battery; and I'm going to bottle 'em up." He went to the garage and returned with a thirty-pound flagstone which was meant for a new walk, and put it on the wheely-hole in the living room. It was far too heavy for them to lift, and he covered the other holes the same way.

The next morning was hot and overcast, and when Amantha went to the kitchen to make breakfast she found the icebox not running, and the toaster wouldn't work. "The lights are all off!" she told Callahan when he arrived.

"That does it!" he said. "They've cut our lead-in—they've got all the power they want! I'll have to call the company. . . ." He went to the phone, and the company promised to send a man out right away. He went under the house, but there were no wheelies in sight—they must still be in their tunnel, he thought, and wondered how fast they could dig. Peter came in after breakfast.

"Hello," he said cheerfully. "All our lights are off! I looked at the fuses, but they're okay."

"*Yours* too?"

"Yes. Mother called the company, but they haven't gotten here yet. And say, Mr. Callahan, one of your little machines was out by the road! It went and hid when it saw me—in a woodchuck hole. It's a new one—there's a pile of fresh earth, and another one on our lawn. I didn't know there were any woodchucks around here, Mr. Callahan."

"Neither did I." Callahan heard Amantha coming down the hall and swear as she tried, unsuccessfully, to turn on a light. She appeared at the door, looking distracted.

"When did they say the man'd be here?" she said. "We're *dooked!* Oh," she caught sight of Peter. "*Sarishan,* Peter, *miri pal!* Now, suppose you *jaw tasaulore* to your *di,* like a good *chavvy.*" Under duress she was inclined to revert to Gypsy speech. Peter enjoyed this, though he didn't understand more than its drift. "I suppose the wheelies are still in that tunnel of theirs, *rakkering* away—"

"I keep telling you they can't talk, Amantha!" Callahan said.

"Is there a tunnel here?" Peter was greatly intrigued.

" 'Tis not one you could crawl into, rightly. The little fellows made it, so run along with you."

"Here's the repair man," Callahan said, "so scram, will you, Peter?"

Reluctantly Peter left, and they saw him cross the lawn and stop to talk with the man who got out of the service truck. Some time later, after trying unsuccessfully to locate the break in their line, the repair man said to Callahan, "We'll have to get a crew here to dig up the road. The people next door are in the same fix—a disconnected lead-in. It's not in the main or this whole sector'd be out. I don't get it . . . Say." He looked speculatively at Callahan. "The kid says you've got some kind of a machine that digs into the ground—maybe that's what's causing the trouble!" He looked severe—company property must never be tampered with. "I gotta go, now. You better watch what you do with that machine of yours. The crew'll be over later and dig up the road. There's no manhole for a couple of hundred feet." Shaking his head disapprovingly, he left. In a few moments his truck snorted and whisked out onto the road.

43

Callahan returned to the lab where he tried to work. There was no sign of wheely activity, which he found more ominous and distracting than their busy presence. Thunder rumbled in the distance, but the storm held off, and after lunch a truck drove up and a team of men started digging up the road.

Callahan went out after a while and found they had made a long trench uncovering the main. Another group was performing a similiar task at the Browns'. "You can try your lights, now, Mister," the foreman said. "We found the break. There was a dead short next the main—looked like a rat chewed it." He looked accusingly at Callahan. "Jones said you had some kind of digging machine—is it one of them rotary sewer cleaners? Because you ought to know better'n to go making holes under the sidewalks!"

"No, no. He misunderstood. The kid next door was telling—"

"Hey, Willis!" One of the work crew was looking at a portable meter thoughtfully. "There's a big drop in potential, still. There must be another short around here. It's not the one next door—they fixed it."

"There's rat holes running all over," a second man said.

"Them ain't rats," the first man said. "They're too big."

Callahan left them discussing the problem, and went back to the house where he tried the lights. They glowed a dim orange—there was obviously a bad power leak in the vicinity.

"Will it run the icebox, Callahan?" Amantha asked.

"I doubt it."

"I say we pack up and take the week off in New York. It'll be a holiday for us and the wheelies. Maybe they'll come to their senses. . . ."

"I can't just go away, Amantha, and leave them on the loose! And stealing power whenever they want it, damn it."

The point was argued at dinner, and afterwards Callahan turned on their portable radio, as the TV wouldn't operate on the reduced current. They listened to the news, interrupted by static from the distant lightning. When the local news came on they learned that their village had had an insignificant but perplexing robbery.

The big hardware store on Main Street had been entered and a number of items were gone, but the owner who had gone back there after dinner claimed that no one had broken in, and the lock had not been forced. He had the only key. The local police were puzzled, and the announcer thought it

44

was very droll. Callahan glanced at Amantha—she seemed to think it was all very droll, too.

"You've just got to admit that they're terribly industrious," she said.

"But it *can't* be the wheelies! Why, Main Street's three or four blocks from here!"

The single lamp they had left on as an indicator winked and brightened to full strength. "Glory be, they've fixed it," Amantha said. "I'll go turn on the icebox."

She stood up and started for the door. "There's Thirteen!" she cried. "No—he's gone! Into the lab. . . ."

Callahan hurried in pursuit, wondering how Thirteen had managed to move the heavy flagstone, but arrived too late. Thirteen was out of sight. Entrance had been gained by the simple method of cutting a new hole in the floor—they had got themselves another keyhole saw.

Callahan went back and they watched TV.

During the next few days he saw no more of the wheelies, and he had abandoned all idea of recovering them by digging, as things—or rather, the wheelies—had gone too far for that. He installed a readily accessible electrical outlet in the crawl-space next to the mouth of their tunnel as a lure, and an alarm system that would ring in the bedroom if it were used. In front of the tunnel itself he arranged a form of portcullis that would trap anything that came through. There was no sound from the alarm that night and the next morning he went down-under to check the trap. It had been propped open and the alarm disconnected.

"I'm worried," he told Amantha. "They're getting too damn smart—if the cops get on to this, I may be held responsible for the thefts at the hardware store, and damage to the power line."

"Can't you disown them, Callahan? They're not rightly children, so you could put a notice in the paper: the wheelies've left my bed and board."

"That wouldn't do any good. It's like leaving your car on a hill—the brakes fail and it runs downhill and kills someone."

"They're too weak to harm a soul, surely?"

"Not if they act cooperatively—they might take it into their cortex boxes to do us in." This was the day the news of the second robbery came over the air—small metal-working tools taken but the cash untouched, to the perplexity of the police. And a tunnel was discovered under the showroom

45

but it was too small for a man to get through, and everyone was at a loss.

"I wish I'd never made the blasted things!" he said to Amantha.

"I expect that's what Frankenstein said," she remarked.

Callahan had uneasy dreams that night, and woke sweating shortly before dawn. He was totally unable to move, and since he couldn't reach the light, he couldn't see what was holding him. He called out to Amantha.

"I'm here," she said. "I'm wrapped up in a cocoon, so get me out!"

Dawn came through the windows before Callahan was able to wriggle free. He was held down like Gulliver by the Lilliputian army—yards and yards of string had been wound around the bed, and he was breathing heavily when he finally got loose and cut Amantha's bindings. Something nagged at his mind—some noise out of the nightmare—and he went directly to the lab. It was a shambles: everything pertaining to the construction of wheelies had been spirited away, including his entire supply of graphite-gel.

In the afternoon, news came that a small "mechanized object" had been seen carrying a Stillson wrench in a vacant lot, and a fast-moving boy had nabbed it before it could get away. Nobody could make head or tail of it. It had run out of power shortly after capture, and a garage mechanic was called in to take it apart and see what it was. He could make nothing of the inner workings beyond the servomotors and the photoelectric scanners, and it ended up in the lost-and-found items. Callahan debated admitting ownership, but was reluctant to do so. He felt it might not be traced to him if he kept quiet, but he didn't bargain for Peter. Peter came over immediately after the broadcast. "Hey, Mr. Callahan!" he said excitedly. "The radio says they found one of your machines in the village! It's at the police station—aren't you going for it?"

"I guess so, Peter," Callahan said.

At the station house they were expecting him—Jones, the repair man, was there. He had put two and two together, and given them a modified version of Peter's original account, but to Callahan's relief, no connection had been made with the thefts. Jones made some remarks about short circuits in the company lines, but the police weren't interested. The wheelies were apparently now getting their power without any detectable line loss. Then Callahan noticed that the inert wheely on the sergeant's desk had no number plate. He bent

46

for a closer look, and his scalp crawled—there were no screw holes for attaching it.

He had not made this wheely. . . .

He mumbled thanks, left a five dollar bill for the youthful finder, and drove home with his mind whirling. Amantha met him in the hall.

" 'Twas Thirteen, I bet," she said.

He shook his head and explained, and they went into the lab. He took the little mechanism apart—it was almost identical with the ones he had made himself. Amantha looked at him wide-eyed. "D'you think *they* made it, Callahan?"

"I . . . I don't know. . . ."

"I say now's the time to pack off for New York."

"We *can't*. This is serious, Amantha," he said. "I'll *have* to tell . . . to warn people: Lord knows what they'll do next!"

He reached up to turn on the overhead light to make a closer examination—and was felled like a pine.

When he came to, Amantha was bending over him with a white face. He had pins-and-needles in his right arm and a nasty burn on his fingers.

"What was it, Callahan, dear?"

"Six hundred volts, by the feel of it." His eyes went up past her face, and saw the new wire that ran across the ceiling and connected with the switch chain. "This would seem to be a declaration of war!"

There were footsteps, and Peter's voice said, "Hey! What happened?"

"I fell over my foot, Peter," Callahan said, and got up.

"Oh. Well, I was going to tell you there's two more holes with piles of dirt—one's in the pasture in back, and the other's just inside the woods beyond. Did you go for your little machine, Mr. Callahan?"

"Yes," Callahan said, getting suddenly interested in Peter's information. "Thanks for telling me. Now, d'you mind running along? I've got work to do." He didn't want Peter tagging along on his proposed exploration: he would be in the way—worse, he might be in actual danger. He would have trouble enough in keeping Amantha from coming.

"Well, I just thought I'd tell you," Peter said, and slowly left them. Callahan watched through the window as he crossed the lawn, then he turned to Amantha and said with un-convincing casualness. "Think I'll stroll over and take a gander at the new holes. . . ."

"We'll do that," she said, firmly.

47

Callahan started to object, but gave up. "Well, stay close, will you?"

"I'll be close, because we'll take the jeep," she said.

"Why on earth?"

"There's an old trail through there you can get on from the lane beyond Jessica Brown's house. 'Tis wide enough for the jeep, and besides it's all brambles behind here—it'd ruin my nylons."

Callahan looked at his watch. "It's getting late," he said, "and it may storm. I'll go tomorrow—anyway, isn't it time to fix dinner?"

"Dinner's fixed and it's in a slow oven," she said. "Come on: I want to see if there's any more of their little tunnels in the wood. I bet that's where they've got their factory!"

Callahan shrugged. It all sounded like Snow White and the Seven Wheelies—only there might be a lot more than seven by now.

They drove the jeep up the branch road and turned into a bumpy but not impassable lane that meandered among the trees. After a while they stopped and got out at a point that Callahan judged to be in a line with their house. Almost at once they found a pile of fresh earth, with its accompanying ten-inch hole, and, deeper into the woods, another.

"What would that be?" Amantha said. She was pointing ahead, and he saw a new pile of earth—not something the size of a molehill, but enough to make a load for a small truck. When they got to it they found a ragged hole, six feet across. Callahan peered down into it—it was on the side of a rise in the ground, and went down on a declivity into the darkness. Lying scattered about the opening were a dozen or so wheelies—several without number plates— and they had all been mashed flat.

"Great guns!" Callahan said. "Somebody got here ahead of us! Who in—"

"The poor little flattened-out things!" Amantha said.

Callahan was looking around—a wide trail of crushed branches and broken saplings led off among the trees. "Someone's driven a half-track in here and dug up their hideaway," he said. "Who in hell can it have been?"

"What makes you think they dug their way *in*, Callahan? It looks more to me as if they'd dug their way *out!*"

He looked again at the way the earth had been thrust aside, and decided she was right. . . . Amantha nudged him. "Whatever it was, it only just came out," she said. "I
48

just saw a twig straighten itself up. Over there." She pointed at the trail of destruction, and they went over to it. Callahan noticed a worm struggling to burrow back into the newly turned earth. Amantha's remark about Frankenstein came back to him—what if after killing its maker, the monster made *another* monster—which in turn killed it?

"I don't like this, Callahan," Amantha said.

"Neither do I."

"No, but I mean the way it took. It's leading to our house. . . ." She pointed again. "D'you think that if a lot of them were to travel in a bunch they might leave a trail like this, Callahan?"

"I do not. And they'd have come out of their burrow one at a time, not leaving a huge hole. Go and get in the jeep, Amantha—I'm going to follow the trail and see where it leads."

"I'm coming," she said. "The hell with my nylons!"

When they came to the pasture behind their house they lost the trail. Beyond the edge of the woods no mark was left on the dry ground. It was getting dark, and the lowering sun was obscured by threatening thunderheads. In the distance beside their house something small whisked out of sight.

"Did you see that?" Amantha said. "They're not all killed!"

"I know it. Only two of the kill—I mean destroyed ones had number plates. . . . But where's *it* got to?"

"Oh, my stew! I should be putting the wine in it!"

"Never mind the stew—where did it *go?*"

"Behind the garage, the moment it saw us."

"I mean the . . . thing that crushed the wheelies."

"That was clumsiness, most likely."

"I'd like to believe it!"

"You forgot the jeep—I think it's going to rain and lightning."

"Damn the jeep! Come on!" They crossed the field and approached the house from the back. Everything was quiet as they went in by the kitchen, and Amantha took the stew out of the oven and put a glass of Burgundy in it.

"I don't think the big chap's been here," she said, replacing the stew. "Why would he come? It's not his home." Callahan was looking out the door.

"Amantha! Come here—you were right about them communicating!"

She joined him and saw a row of four wheelies in single file come to a halt, and another one line itself up parallel

49

to them. After a moment the four went on their way and the single one disappeared into a hole.

"I didn't see him wave or anything," Amantha said.

"It was induction," Callahan said. There was a rumble of thunder.

"Will you go and close the windows?" she said. "I'm getting my notebook. I left it out on the porch."

"I wish you—" Callahan started, but she was already outside. He went down the corridor towards the living room and was about to go in when he saw a faint bluish light in the room, and realized the television had been turned on and the venetian blinds drawn. It occurred to him that Peter might have come over to watch their set, and he called out, but there was no answer. From the doorway he looked around the room but could see nothing out of the ordinary. A sense of caution prompted him to turn on a light before going in, and he was about to do so when something about the wall switch caught his eye, and he peered at it in the bad light without touching it.

Attached to the wall with friction tape was the upper end of a piece of flex that stretched across the floor from behind the TV set. The two bare wires projected in front of the switch. He remembered that a TV transformer produces fifteen thousand volts, and backed away. The trick with the overhead light had been improved.

The phone in the hall rang and he went to answer it. It was Jessica Brown. "Have you seen Peter?" she said.

"No, I haven't."

"Well, if you do, will you tell him to come right home? It's going to rain." He hung up and wondered why Amantha was taking so long getting her notebook. He looked out through the open front door, and saw her coming across the lawn with some letters in her hand. He realized they had forgotten to go to the mailbox that morning. She smiled happily and waved an open letter when she saw him at the door.

"Hey!" she called out. "I've sold my book to—" Then she was gone, a section of turf disappearing with her into a gaping hole in the lawn. Callahan started forward, and something thin and cold wrapped itself around his neck, and he was dragged back into the house. Then he was struck a heavy blow on the head, and he blacked out.

Callahan's first emotion, when he came to, was anger at himself. He was lying on the floor in the small room where the closet was that led to the crawl-space. The closet was open, as were the doors to the room. One of these led to the main hall and the other to his lab, where he could see the corner of the work bench and the fuse box on the wall beyond it. Thunder was rumbling continuously, and there was a smell of burned stew in the air.

He got to his feet and found that his head was surprisingly not aching—in retrospect he realized that it had in all probability hit the side of the front door. The thing that had pulled him back into the house had not meant to strike him. If it was what he suspected, it would have left him for dead—or thought his battery had run out.

As his mind cleared he remembered Amantha, and started forward, but even before he got to the door he heard her cry out—"Callahan! Callahan!" in an agonized voice.

When he saw her his mind froze. She was at the far end of the hall, face down on the floor, with her wrists and ankles bound together behind her with flex. And between him and her was the thing that the wheelies had made—in their own image, but with certain improvements.

It had not two but four grappling arms, and he could see that it did not intend to run out of power, for a length of wire ran from a wall outlet to a reel attached to its side-plates, a reel that kept the wire from tangling. But now that he saw it in actuality, it was its size that appalled him: it was six feet long at least. . . . It also had an extra scanner, which was directed backwards, and this saw him the moment he started forward. The giant wheely immediately turned and came toward him, and Callahan saw that it held outstretched the bare end of a heavy insulated cable—the rest of which ran back through the door to the living room, and, he was sure, the TV set and its fifteen thousand volts. One touch from the cable would be death.

He dashed back into the small room, which led to the lab and in turn to the hall—and Amantha. But as soon as he got to the door to the lab he saw that the giant had anticipated him. This was going to be tough: the thing was possibly as intelligent as he was. It was now advancing on him again, but as Callahan backed away to escape electrocution, it itself turned, and he realized that it knew that if he got to Amantha first and freed her, he and she could escape through the front door. On regaining the hall he saw that once more the giant was between him and his wife—if only he could get back to the lab in time, and to

51

the fuse box, he could pull the switch and thus cut off the current to the TV set.

He edged back through the door and ran, but too late: the giant was there ahead of him. It seemed to be a stalemate; if he went to save Amantha he would be killed and she would be too. He could not outlast the giant as it had unlimited power on tap, whereas he would eventually tire. If he escaped to save himself she would be killed.

He thought of the telephone, but it was beyond the great wheely and its cable of death. Shouting would do no good either—for one thing the thunder was now so loud and continuous that he would never be heard, even if anyone came near enough.

But what was preventing the giant from immediately electrocuting Amantha? Did it realize that if she were killed nothing would stand between him and escape—that the only thing that held him there was the threat of *her* death! It seemed incredible, but it was the only explanation of its action. The thing *was* as rational as he was!

Amantha had managed to turn over on her back, and was in a half-sitting position, watching the giant with a chalk-white face. "Get out the back way, Callahan!" she cried. "Quick, or it'll do you in!"

There was a loud crack of nearby lightning and the beat of rain increased. The bluish glow from the TV set dimmed momentarily, and Callahan prayed that there might be an interruption in the power, but his hopes faded as he remembered that with the new underground cable this was unlikely.

"Lie still, Amantha!" he called back to her. "I'll think of something!"

"Well, think hard, *miri rom!* I fell through into a cave and the little ones tied me up before I could gather my wits—then the big chap brought me up through the crawl-space. What's that he's holding?"

"It's . . ." Callahan began, but stopped. Why frighten her more?

The great wheely started to roll very slowly towards him again, and he backed into the doorway of the little room—and at once came out. But the wheely had not been fooled—it was still coming. Once more he backed, only this time he kept going . . . and the wheely was waiting for him by the fuse box. It was not to be taken in by a thing so elementary as a double feint. Callahan felt that there was something in Game Theory that might help—if he could think of it. But the giant probably knew it, or would work it out without hesitation. Was there such a thing as a triple feint?

He turned and ran back towards the hall, and then immediately back: the wheely had not budged. He was desperate—the thing could out-think him no matter what he did. And what was a triple feint after all but a single one by another name? It was like playing odd-and-even, but with some superrational being.

Already he was beginning to tire, and with a side compartment of his mind he wondered where the little wheelies were. In retrospect they seemed very harmless . . . yet they had made this monster of rationality. If only there were some way to make a temporary barrier that would hold it back, if only for a minute—then he could get to Amantha, or the switch: either would do. But the only key was to their bedroom, and there was no way to jam or block the other doors. The room with the closet had no movable furniture except a flimsy chair, and there was nothing in the hall that he could get to ahead of the giant, which would unquestionably deduce his maneuver at once.

Perhaps there was something in the kitchen . . . no, the giant would merely go back and guard the switch, and Amantha. Could he not then get as far as the door to the living room—not to go in, for he would be bottled up and the wheely could kill him there before he could get to the window and escape—but long enough to yank the cable loose from the TV set? It was worth a try: but then he remembered that his reasoning about being bottled up was cockeyed because the wheely would be unable to kill him if, instead of trying for the window, he merely turned off the TV switch. But how could he be sure that the switch was still operative?

It was too big a gamble—he would have to try pulling the cable loose, and if that failed, he would at least not be trapped in a cul-de-sac. They'd merely be back where they started.

The giant was at the moment out of sight, at a point halfway between Amantha and the fuse box in the lab, and Callahan tiptoed into the hall. Not that the giant could hear him—but for all he knew it could interpret vibrations in the floor. He waited, and in a few moments a scanner appeared at the far door to the hall. The giant would of course have to keep up a constant sentry duty to guard both lines of approach. The door to the living room was nearer to him than

53

to the giant, but was the difference great enough? Well, he'd give it a try.

He decided that a single feint would give him the optimum start, and backed quickly into the door and out again. The scanner was gone, and he raced for the cable. Just before reaching it, the giant came around the corner, and he grabbed and pulled—starting backwards as he did so. But it held fast: the giant had taken precautions. He dropped the cable—they were back again at a deadlock.

The rain was coming down in a loud torrent, intermittently accompanied by splitting thunder and brilliant flashes of lightning. Amantha was staring straight ahead of her, frightened, he suspected, for the first time in her life. She must have deduced from his actions that the cable was what prevented him from going to her at once. How could he think his way out of this ghastly game of chess? An idea began to form in his mind—but how was he going to get the time to put it into operation, in the face of perfect logic and flawless rationality?

Flawless? Maybe that was the giant's Achilles heel—something utterly *non*-rational might be beyond its powers of analysis! He checked over the plan: it might just possibly work, given a little luck, and he set his mind to the task of choosing the right red herring—it must not be too irrational or the giant would dismiss it as a vagary. A haze of greasy acrid smoke was beginning to come from the ruined stew in the kitchen, and he wondered if he could find something with the right degree of foolishness to do there to give the right effect—he was going to have to go through the kitchen afterwards to achieve his ultimate purpose. But what? The door of the closet and, through it, the smaller one to the crawl-space caught his eye, and he realized he had the perfect solution.

He drew the giant away from the line of sight by going towards the hall. Then he went back, reached in and very quietly closed the little, inner door, and afterwards, the outer one—but slamming it hard enough to make sure its vibration would be felt. Then he dashed out and through the kitchen, where he grabbed a heavy cleaver—and out into the garden.

He was taking a terrible chance—he had not waited to see the success of his diversion—but he was gambling on the wheely puzzling over the closed door to the closet. It must reason that Callahan would be a complete fool to hide in

54

there, for his chances of being caught were much greater, and yet it would have to investigate, and all this would take time.

Outside, next to the kitchen door was a ground wire running down the side of the house from the lightning arrester on the television mast—and with a single blow of the cleaver he severed it. He was back in the house at once, and found that the giant had not bothered to open the closet door—but it *had* paused to determine the meaning of this absurd act, and now they were back in their original state of a stand-off.

But there was a difference—a hope, a faint chance that lightning would strike the aerial. It had before, but harmlessly because of the ground wire, and being in this exposed position there was a fair possibility of its happening again. Certainly there had never been a storm like this in his memory—he had something to wait for now . . . perhaps. After all, the Empire State Building was struck many times in every electrical storm in the city—not necessarily a bolt that was visible to the eye, but a huge surge of potential that made the dials of the weather indicators jump.

No, he thought, I'm a fool—the gamble wasn't going to pay off. He would wait and wait, and the storm would go, and he would eventually become exhausted . . . and that would be it. From the far end of the hall he heard a curious chanting sound, and recognized his wife's voice.

He went and looked from the door, and saw Amantha sitting with her face raised—her eyes were closed and she had a look of withdrawn concentration. She was reciting something—in the Romany *jib*—and he wondered if she was praying . . . but he thought the Gypsies did not pray. It was getting darker, and already his knees were feeling weak from tension, and then it happened.

There was a premonitory hissing *CLICK*, and the whole house shook with the crash and glare of what must have been a direct hit on their TV mast. The blue light from the living room went out as the set was blown, and part of the charge jumped through the insulation of the cable, and sparks crackled around the giant wheely. It came to a halt and dropped the cable, smoke coming from its joints.

There was now a glow of red from the living room where the shock had started a fire, but Callahan went to Amantha first and rapidly undid the flex bindings. The giant was completely inert, and leaving Amantha rubbing her ankles and wrists, he ran to the kitchen and got a pail of water, which he took into the living room.

The flames were confined to the wooden case of the TV set, and after disconnecting it, he doused the fire.

A little while later he and Amantha were having a drink in the kitchen. The burned stew had been dumped and the windows opened to clear the smoke. They both felt a bit light-headed.

"I didn't have much more than a hope," he was saying. "But lightning comes in various sizes: sometimes it's no more than a sort of reverse brush-discharge and most people don't even know it's happened—unless they happen to get in the way. They come with fair frequency—especially if there's a conductor sticking up from a flat area, like our aerial. But we got the full treatment, or rather the big fellow did, and I don't think he can even be repaired. I guess," he looked a little embarrassed, "I was praying, the same as you—after I'd cut the ground-wire. . . ."

"Yes," Amantha said, "I guessed that's what you were up to. But *I* wasn't praying, Callahan, dear."

"Then what were you reciting?"

She looked sly, and then shrugged and smiled. "Oh, *that*. That's a spell like. My mother taught it to me—it calls down the lightnings on your enemy. . . . Well, I've *rakkered* enough." She got up briskly. "It'll take forever to get the oven clean again. You'd better get the big chap out of the hall, Callahan."

He was looking at her with a thoughtful expression. Then he shook his head. "Say, that reminds me; where the hell are the little wheelies? I haven't seen them around. There were a few left when we—"

"Oh, they're all down in that cave of theirs—under the lawn. Peter's with them. . . ."

"Great God!" Callahan said, starting for the door, "I must help—"

"Calm yourself, Callahan," Amantha said. "They left all the dirty work to the big chap. They're sitting round in a circle, watching."

"Watching what, in God's name?"

"Watching Peter and Thirteen playing checkers. When I got myself tied up and dragged out of there—and it happened so quick I couldn't get my breath to sing out—Peter was so absorbed he didn't turn his head. And no wonder: Thirteen was beating him, I bet!"

Mrs. Poppledore's Id

R. BRETNOR

After you read this, I am sure you will agree that Mrs. Poppledore ranks as one of The Most Unforgettable Characters You Have Ever Met—and not only because of her peculiar Talent. Indeed, no! As heroine of a thoroughly nutty story, she is magnificent; as an example of the Irrepressible Female Goof, she is unsurpassed.

Along with her, as a sort of bonus, you get some brilliant satire on psychoanalysis, parapsychology, suburban religiosity, medieval exorcism in the Twentieth Century, book publishing, and reversed-collar soothers who write inspirational best sellers, all in one hilarious package. Is it Science Fiction? Who cares?

"Names," said Constance Poppledore. "People's names." Her large brown eyes regarded Dr. Vole. She asked herself why ugly, hairy little men so often were attracted to psychiatry. She sighed. "I think about them all the time," she said. "People's names, I mean. They're always like their hats. Why do you suppose Mildred Bunny's hats make her look as if she had long, floppy ears? Ugh!" She shivered. "Each time I see her, I think of nothing else for hours and hours."

Dr. Manfred Vole smoothed the fur on the back of his left hand, and made a soft professional noise. The garment which enveloped Mrs. Poppledore's rotundities was, like the *chaise longue* which supported them, chastely Hellenic. Hellenic, too, was the pear-shaped cluster of red grapes held in an antique attitude above her small red mouth. The balance of the Poppledore apartment was spare and angular with chrome and desiccated wood and zebra skin. The overall effect, thought Dr. Vole, was as though Isadora Duncan had been swallowed, young and whole, by some unpromising designer of svelte powder rooms.

"Now, Mrs. Poppledore," he suggested gently, "weren't we beginning to discuss the Id?"

Constance Poppledore ate a grape. "That's what's so sad about it," she informed him. "Poor Canon Bunny. She doesn't understand him, and people are always laughing at his name. But *I* think it's really rather nice. *V. Bede Bunny*. The Reverend Canon V. Bede Bunny. It has a Trollopey, Old English sort of sound. And it's only because his mother was a Venable, and his father was so clever and devout. And you can't name a little boy *Venerable*, now can you?"

Politely, Dr. Vole agreed that you could not. Mr. Julian Poppledore had urged upon him the problem of V. Bede Bunny's growing influence; and now, opening his notebook, he hastily scribbled *FF?* to remind himself that a father fixation might be worth looking into.

"Freud's concept of the Id," he stated with determination, "is something every really intelligent person should understand." He paused to let the flattery take effect; and Mrs. Poppledore reached out to him at once.

"Do have a grape," she said.

"No, thank you. Now, the Id—"

"That's what I mean! The things I feel about deep down inside. That's why I mentioned Canon Bunny, don't you see? It's so unfair! Especially with all those bishops so against him, and just when we're publishing his book. Why, if it hadn't been for that old Charles Laughton king with all the wives, *you* know, the whole thing might be different. Because *Peace Of Heart* is ever so much better than those other books. It's full of quotations from the Fathers, and from John Donne and Tristram Shandy and all sorts of people."

Dr. Vole experienced an emotion, instantly diagnosed it as acute annoyance, and applied a simple therapy, reminding himself that within six months his bill to Mr. Poppledore would more than meet the purchase price of a new Cadillac convertible, a yellow one. He saw himself driving up to the nurses' quarters at the Defective Children's Home and—

He shook himself. As the convertible dissolved, he remarked that Canon Bunny seemed to have a keen eye for a trend. "Freud was the same way," he said. "The concept of the Id—"

"Oh, was he? You must tell Canon Bunny all about it. He'll be so interested. But really, isn't it unfair? *They* have them all the time. I mean, they had one just a week ago. And in the *Bronx!*" She pouted. "It's quite absurd!"

"*They?*" asked Dr. Vole. "I don't seem to recall—"

"Of course you do! A week ago. It happened to some little Polish child. The picture wept real tears when she said her

58

prayers, even on television. Naturally, the Cardinal wouldn't say whether it was or wasn't, but then they never do."

It came to Dr. Vole that she was speaking of the Roman Church—and that miracles, through some grave error of the Reformation, were denied to Canon Bunny.

"I think about it all the time!" said Constance Poppledore. "Why couldn't Mildred be cured of her neuralgia, even though she does wear those hats? Or maybe some old leper? That would be better yet. *That* might mean half a million extra copies—and think of all the *good* they'd do! Besides, it would be nice for Rummage House, and dear Henry Rummage, and of course Julian. Publishing is such a dreadful gamble nowadays." She took a final grape, lowered her head, allowed her eyes to close. "But I suppose there's nothing we can do," she said resignedly. "Now you can tell me all about the Id."

Dr. Vole's bemused mental mechanism whirred into action. A gleam came to his eye. "Yes, Mrs. Poppledore. Yes, indeed. The Id—"

He broke off sharply—the door had opened. He turned his head.

"I'm sorry," said Constance Poppledore's maid, "but Canon Bunny's here."

V. Bede Bunny was portly but very pale. He hesitated at the door, one finger touching diffidently his pectoral cross. "I am so sorry, Mrs. Poppledore!" He glanced apology at Dr. Vole. "Surely I intrude?"

"Why, Canon Bunny!" Constance Poppledore swept up to greet him. "You? Intrude?" Laughing, she took his arm. "This is a dear new friend of mine and Julian's, Dr. Manfred Vole. He's my psychiatrist."

Dr. Vole rose reluctantly and shook a big white hand.

"Doctor, it's very good of you, allowing me to interrupt like this. I won't be long." As Constance Poppledore resumed her couch, he sat down comfortably. "A painful situation has come up," he told her. "A most important convert from Bombay is here, and I must entertain him tomorrow. The invitations have gone out; it's all prepared. And now poor Mildred—"

Mrs. Poppledore gave him a long and understanding look.

"—feels her neuralgia coming on again. So *she* suggested that you might be my hostess in her stead."

"How sweet of her! I'd love to, naturally. That is, if Dr. Vole thinks it won't hurt my Id."

"Your—*Id?*"

"He says my Id needs mending—that something horrible happened to it when I was small, in a dramatic episode."

"*Trau*matic," objected Dr. Vole.

She dismissed the technicality. "He says that if I think and think maybe I can remember just what happened, and then my Id will be all together again."

"That isn't quite correct—"

"Like Humpty-Dumpty," she persisted. "And the only thing I can remember is how I had the poltergeist when I was thirteen, and it threw stones and the furniture, and I was *so* annoyed."

"You should have told me!" Dr. Vole was irritated.

"John Wesley," put in Canon Bunny, uneasily, "wrote of his troubles with a poltergeist. I mention it in *Peace Of Heart,* as an example of how the wayward intellect can lead the soul astray."

"Well," said Constance Poppledore, "I'm sure his wasn't half as good as mine. And I wasn't led astray either, because mine started in right after Papa had been so mean to me—"

"Ah-h!" murmured Dr. Vole.

"—and afterwards he treated me ever so much better— Papa, I mean. He even let me ride with him Saturdays when he drove into Sioux Falls."

"I'm sure there was no parallel." The Canon flushed. "On the one hand, we have a misfit, a dissenter; on the other, the pretty innocence of a pink-cheeked country girl." He rose and made a bow at Mrs. Poppledore. "Dear me, it's *very* late, and I must run along. At four tomorrow, then? Good, good. Doctor, I trust we'll meet again, and—ha-ha!—discuss the *cure of souls* at greater length. No, don't get up. I'll find my way very nicely, thank you. Goodbye, goodbye."

The door closed behind him—and Dr. Vole turned to his patient testily. "It is significant," he told her, "that your hatred for your father produced hallucinations in your adolescence."

"I didn't *hate* him. It's only that he was horrid all the time, and mean to me. And it wasn't an hallucination!"

Dr. Vole thought of the Cadillac, and regained a measure of his self-possession. "How was he mean to you?"

"That's what I can't remember."

"Oh, but you must." His voice assumed a note of calm authority. "We must retrieve these dark experiences in order to deprive them of their power. Now we will try. Lie back— that's better. And close your eyes. Imagine that you're a little girl again, on the farm. There's your nasty father, just as he was. It's that same day. Now, think back—"

"I *am*. Only—"

"Try, *try*. He's getting ready to be mean to you! But don't get scared. He can't really hurt you anymore. He can't be-cause—"

A sudden inspiration came to Dr. Vole.

"—*because Canon Bunny's right there by your side*. Now! What is your father doing?"

"Why, I *remember*," cried Constance Poppledore. "He's—"

And just then, without any warning whatsoever, Dr. Man-fred Vole was lifted, chair and all, and hurled violently through the air to land with a crash on a zebra-skin rug some yards away.

"Did something fall?" she asked. "How strange! And I feel so much better! Do you suppose my Id is all right now?"

There was a silence. After a moment, dreamily, she said, "I'm sure that we could find a leper somewhere, couldn't we, if we tried hard?"

Dr. Vole could never quite recall his farewell to Mrs. Pop-pledore. Something had pelted him with two cubistic ash-trays, an old copy of *Flair*, and a table lamp that looked like a toadstool with the bends; yet even this assault left only a blurred impression on his memory.

Blind instinct turned him to the nearest bar. He entered, staggered to a stool, and tried to think of something alco-holic. Finally—

"A—a double Muscatel," he squeaked.

Administering this dose, he ordered another. When that was gone, he said, "Now I shall have some whisky," decisively.

"Scotch—" The bartender winced. "—or rye?"

"Both!" said Dr. Vole.

Presently he looked up from the contemplation of his empty glass, and, handling each word with great delicacy, said, *"There are . . . more things . . . under heaven and earth . . . Ho-Horatio . . . than are . . . than are . . .* I can't seem to remember the next line. *For—for you shall stand . . . at my right hand . . . and keep the bridge with me?"*

"That's right!" affirmed the bartender. "Horatio On The Bridge. It's about a Limey admiral."

"Thank you," said Dr. Vole. He descended, walked very carefully to the telephone, and called Mr. Poppledore's num-ber at Rummage House.

"This is Dr. Vole. V-O-L-E. I want to talk—"

"*I* want to talk to *you!*" shouted the telephone. "What's all this nonsense you've been giving Connie? About lepers. Yes, dammit, *lepers!* She just got through calling me. Wants *me* to find a leper! You think we can afford to let the Press catch on this whacky Bunny character is trying to heal lepers? His bishop's already trying to unfrock him!"

Dr. Vole held the instrument at a safe distance. "That's not important! The polter—"

"NOT IMPORTANT? How much to you suppose we've sunk in *Peace of Heart?* Now you get busy, Vole, and get her psycho'ed out of this, you hear me? What do you think I'm paying you for?"

There was an angry click, and Dr. Vole abruptly saw that Mr. Poppledore had no intention of holding the bridge with him.

He rang up Canon Bunny—who listened politely until he was informed that the poltergeist transferred the case of Constance Poppledore from the doctor's own mundane province to his more ghostly one.

"*My* province?" he exclaimed. "Oh, dear me, no! I feel that there must be some perfectly natural explanation—Exorcism? Doctor, this isn't the Sixteenth Century! Really, you sound a little overwrought. Can you have just imagined—? No? Well, take my advice; discuss it with some good psychia—Why, so you are! Of *course!* . . . The strain of modern life; it tells on all of us! There's a whole chapter on it in *Peace Of Heart*. I'll have a copy sent to you, inscribed. Goodness, now there's the bell! I do hope you'll feel better. Goodbye."

Dr. Vole peered sadly at the telephone. He saw that it was fuzzing at the edges and trying to waver off into a new dimension—as though it had no further reason for existence now that the connection with the Canon had been broken.

The circumstance disturbed and angered him. "I'll show you!" he exploded, grabbing the dial with both hands. "There *are* more things in—h-heaven and earth—H-Horazhio—"

Immediately, a flash of inspiration gave him the inner meaning of the words. How clearly they referred to the multiplicity of clergymen—here, there, everywhere—most of them probably eager to stand at his right hand!

He leaned against the wall. "Pes-bry-terians," he murmured happily, "Luther-ans, B-B-Baptists, Southern-fried Methodists, all sorts of other Prot—Ah-*ha!*"

Before his eyes swam the remembered countenance of Winton Furnwillie, Doctor of Divinity, consulting editor for Rummage House, author of *Satan: A Case History,* and pastor of a decorously prosperous North Side congregation.

"I'll take a cab!" declared Dr. Vole. He made a futile effort to retrieve his dime; then left the booth and tacked around the bar. "A Bunnyphone—tha's what you've got!" he called. "Long floppy ears. I saw 'em."

"Uh-huh—" The bartender was unperturbed. "—it's Easter. Bye-bye, Horatio."

Some moments later, Dr. Vole rode away wrapped in a rosy dream—of Mrs. Poppledore rising, purged and pure of Id, from the remains of her vanquished poltergeist, which lay, much like a wilted lettuce, at his feet.

Seated at his desk, penning the rough draft of some future sermon, the Reverend Winton Furnwillie looked like a carefully expurgated version of Bertrand Russell. When Dr. Vole appeared, he showed almost no surprise. He appraised him for the space of half a second. Then, with a quiet sigh, he motioned to his panting secretary to release the doctor's sleeve.

"Won't you sit down?" he said.

The chemical reactions in Dr. Vole had progressed somewhat. He bowed, lost his balance, caught at the edge of the desk, and lowered himself delicately to the floor. "F-Furnwillie," he giggled. "The Reveren' Doctor Winton F-F-Furnwillie. 'Stoo long. I'll call you Revdoc. Cincpac, Ingsoc, Revdoc—get it?" He composed his features. "The boy—stood—at my burning bridge," he began sonorously.

"Ah?" Dr. Furnwillie lifted a fine white brow.

"Yes," said Dr. Vole, "but doesn' soun' right. Try again." Closing one eye, he held a mock spyglass to it with both hands. " 'Sbetter. Uh—England expec's more things in heaven and earth, H-Horazhio—than every man—"

"The *correct* reading," interrupted Dr. Furnwillie, "is, 'There are more things in heaven and earth, Horatio, than are dreamt of in your philosophy.' Hamlet, Act 1, Scene V."

"Ph'losophy!" remarked Dr. Vole, wide-eyed. "Ol' William Shagespeare!"

Dr. Furnwillie beamed. "Excuse me for a moment." He rose and left the room, and there was a sound of running water. When he returned, he gave a brimming glass to Dr. Vole. "Drink this," he said, "and you'll feel ever so much better."

Dr. Vole did as he was told. He drained the glass. He

63

gasped. His eyes glazed. Dreadful things started happening to his midriff.

"A mild restorative," observed Dr. Furnwillie, seating himself again. "Water and spirits of ammonia. And now—" He lifted his hands in a gesture of commiseration. "—I see that you are troubled?"

"Gug!" said Dr. Vole emphatically.

"I understand. And you shall have my sympathy, my spiritual support, my counsel."

"Gug-splut!"

"Now, now! You mustn't thank me. And don't explain. The burden of even the most wretched sinner is mine to share. Nor does its nature matter. Our troubles and concerns proceed from Satan, whom I have analyzed quite thoroughly. We shall be practical. I will explain to you how Satan works, how best to thwart him. You will go forth thrice-armed. Satan, you see—"

Dr. Vole clutched the top of his head, which suddenly was threatening to come off. He wanted desperately to tell of his dilemma. His mind formed sentences. He forced words to his lips—

They came out as, *"Ooh-blug!"*

"Satan—" Dr. Furnwillie's tone became rather firmer than before. "—frightens too many people. It's been the propaganda—Faust and that sort of thing. It lends him stature. It hides his basic motives. Believe me, Dr. Vole, Satan is a social climber and nothing more. Incredible? Yes, to the old theologians. But I have proved it. He tries to curry favor, to worm or buy his way into our midst, to draw attention to himself. How shall we handle him? Well, how do we usually handle *hoi polloi?* We turn our backs on them. We refuse to admit that they exist. In short, we snub them—and they go away."

Dr. Furnwillie, his eyes flashing enthusiasm and good will, stood up and came to Dr. Vole, who was distinctly blue around the gills. He helped him to his feet, and steered him tenderly toward the door. "You must snub Satan, Dr. Vole," he said. "Ignore your worries, and they will go away. Yes, and read Emerson. How simple it all is!"

"B-bu—"

"My secretary will show you out. Don't forget, now—E-M-E-R-S-O-N. And do come by again—"

Dr. Vole stumbled down a corridor and out into the street. Feeling himself alone and friendless, he sat down and wept. But presently, perhaps as a result of Dr. Furnwillie's therapeutic potion, he happened to recall a high school playmate whom he had not seen for several years. Hope flickered faintly in his breast. "Ol' frien's, bes' frien's," he thought sentimentally. "Why not? *They* have them all the time!"

He hailed another cab. And twenty minutes later, clammily sober, he entered the gymnasium of one of the many colleges named after St. Ignatius of Loyola. There he found his friend, appropriately garbed, working out with Indian clubs.

"Hi, Spike!" moaned Dr. Vole.

His friend lifted a bushy brow. "Hi, Jitters," he replied coldly. "How's atheism?"

Uncomfortably, Dr. Vole recalled that certain statements of his own had caused a protracted rupture of relations. He sat down on a convenient bench, hiccupped humbly, and addressed Horatio in the most dismal tones.

His friend promptly dropped the clubs.

"Spike—I mean, Father Crabtree—I need your help."

Father Crabtree surveyed him doubtfully. He beheld the clear evidences of despair. He frowned—Jitters had been a pretty good kid back in his innocent pre-Freudian days. Perhaps—Abruptly, a picture came to him of Dr. Manfred Vole, attired in the rough habiliments of the Trappist order, piously hoeing turnips in the Wyoming wilderness.

He came over, and sat beside the doctor, and said, "Tell me about it, Jitters," in the voice he had heard his superiors use on roughly similar occasions.

After half an hour, Dr. Vole left the college, his head erect, a new spring in his walk. But his own hopes for his personal future were not at all like Father Crabtree's. For the first time since the appearance of the poltergeist, he was thinking of the Cadillac.

The happenings of the next few days were mildly puzzling to Constance Poppledore. She now remembered how that horrid man, her father, had tweaked her pigtails by way of punishment; and sometimes, when she considered the insolence of this mistreatment, the piano would start joggling up and down, or maybe a phone book would fly across the room. She had retrieved the dark experience—and the poltergeist. But was that anything to get upset about?

First there was that funny Dr. Vole, returning the same evening with all his talk about the Roman Church and someone named Horatio, and a petition to the Archbishop to exorcise the poltergeist. Not that it wasn't nice to have *them* on her side—but she certainly wouldn't have signed the petition if the doctor hadn't promised to use his medical connections to find a leper.

Then, at the party, that convert from Bombay came right out and insulted her! He told her how his fellow Hindus suffered, and that they had lots and lots of lepers there. And, when she asked if he would send her one by plane, he lost his temper—even though she offered to pay the fare both ways.

Ever since, there had been just one thing after another. Just for fun, she had shown off the poltergeist to Canon Bunny, and he'd been almost as upset as Dr. Vole—but more polite about it, naturally. The newspapers had started calling her to ask if it was true that something startling was going to happen at the Canon's Sunday services, and they hadn't believed her when she denied it, and they hadn't given her the least bit of help in trying to find a leper. Finally, on Tuesday, Dr. Vole had phoned to tell her that the Archbishop's investigator was coming on Thursday afternoon.

Excitedly, Constance Poppledore spent Thursday morning selecting her apparel for the visitation. Out of deference to the Archbishop, she finally chose a lavender *peignoir* expensively contrived to suggest a friar's habit complete with cowl and cord. Congratulating herself on the felicity of this chance purchase, she brought a copy of Flaubert's *Temptation Of St. Anthony* from Julian's bookcase, and placed it with a dish of grapes and a pair of studious spectacles beside her couch.

It was thus that, shortly after luncheon, she greeted the Reverend Mathias Gansfleisch, O.F.M.

She was disappointed. She had expected a Savonarola, tall and terrible and burning-eyed, with bell, book, candle, and stoup of holy water. Instead, she saw a very thick old man with a bald, pear-shaped head, who walked as though his shoes pinched. He was accompanied by Dr. Vole, who performed the introductions, and by two middle-aged clerics bearing brief cases—and it was immediately apparent that he disapproved of her.

"Father Gansfleisch," asserted the awed Dr. Vole, "is Visitor General of the Order of Friars Minor. He is an Exorcist. He holds a Doctorate of Sacred Theology and *three* Ph.D.'s."

"It is correct," said the Franciscan.

"Canon Bunny," boasted Constance Poppledore, "almost got to be a Rhodes scholar."

There was no response.

"He's an honorary canon—of a cathedral, I think. He doesn't spend much time at it, bcause he's the Rector of St. Ethelred's-at-Sea, and everybody just adores him. I'm sure you'd love him too, in spite of Mildred. Of course, he's not a *Roman* Catholic, but he always says that after all he is a fellow traveller."

There was a frigid silence.

"Besides," she persisted, heedless of the faces Dr. Vole was making, "it's not as if he and Mildred were, well, *really* married. I mean, when you see the poor old thing in one of her dreadful hats, you simply can't imagine——" Still silence.

She extended the dish of grapes; and the Exorcist drew back as though an ingratiating serpent had offered him an apple.

"Do you make a mockery?" he snapped at Dr. Vole. "You told me an innocent soul was in grave danger. Bah! I can see nothing to investigate!"

"P-p-possession!" stammered Dr. Vole.

Constance Poppledore clapped her hands. "It's nine points of the law, isn't it? But really I'm not worried about my poltergeist, Father. You see, I'm sure it's just my Id!"

And then, before the doctor could think of a reply—

"It's Canon Bunny, ma'am," announced the maid. "He's brought a friend."

The pastor of St. Ethelred's-at-Sea pumped Father Gansfleisch's unresponsive hand, greeted Dr. Vole like a long-lost brother, and smiled a nervous benediction at Constance Poppledore.

"Dear me! I've worried so—and now I see I needn't have at all!" He glowed. "Such reinforcements of sanctity and learning! Our little differences forgotten in adversity! I wish it weren't too late to mention it in *Peace Of Heart*. Perhaps the next edition—"

"He'll put your name in and everything!" cried Constance Poppledore. "Won't that be splendid, Father Gansfleisch?"

"No. It will not."

"Well—" Canon Bunny coughed. "—we're all up against something we don't understand, aren't we? That's why I thought I'd do my little bit—ha-ha!—to arm the bastions of the Spirit with the guns of Science." He beckoned to a small man shifting his feet uneasily at the door. "This is Dr. Espey of Duke University, where they study all these things. He'll be a great help to us, I'm sure."

Dr. Espey mumbled that hadn't he better—er—well—come back tomorrow?

"No, no, no!" protested Mrs. Poppledore. "Why, it'll be such *fun!* All of you after my poor little poltergeist at once! Father Gansfleisch can ring his bell, and Professor Espey can take photographs or something. And Canon Bunny can read the Song Of Solomon aloud—he does it beautifully!"

V. Bede Bunny reddened. "Only—only in sermons."

"And then, on Saturday, you must *all* come to our party for *Peace Of Heart*, and we can tell everybody how you chased my poltergeist away!"

Deliberately, Father Gansfleisch turned to the man from Duke. "I should like to ask—do you, a man of science, have an hypothesis about the poltergeist?"

"I shall assume," said Dr. Espey, "that you refer to poltergeists in general, and not necessarily to any specific specimen which may be present locally. In that sense, I consider *poltergeist* simply a term for whatever it is that causes otherwise unexplainable manifestations of a senseless nature —stone-throwing, bed-shaking, and so on. It is usually associated with an adolescent of—of retarded intellect."

They both regarded the thirtyish Mrs. Poppledore.

"The phenomena persist for a few weeks and then die down. There seems to be no serious malice behind them, and no great harm is done."

"You do not think that there can be danger to an immortal soul?"

"Well—frankly, no. I don't think that any exterior agent is responsible. Perhaps some latent psychokinetic faculty emerges—"

"That's what I tried to tell you!" put in Constance Poppledore. "It's my Id."

"In a manner of speaking, yes. Some submerged part of— well, her mentality."

"An interesting theory," declared Father Gansfleisch. "Perhaps we can observe together. However—" He glanced at Canon Bunny. "—it will not be necessary to read aloud the Canticle."

"I had no intention, sir," puffed the Canon, "of doing so!"

Father Gansfleisch waved a peremptory hand. "Let us proceed!"

"Is there something *I* can do?" sniffed Constance Poppledore sarcastically.

"Think of your papa being mean to you," coaxed Dr. Vole.

"Oh, well. I'll try." She removed the spectacles, pulled the cowl forward over her head, and ate a grape.

After a minute, she ate another; then, a third. Nothing stirred. Nothing flew.

They waited, Father Gansfleisch stolid in his chair, Dr. Espey acutely observant, Canon Bunny fidgeting. Several additional grapes disappeared.

When half an hour had passed, the Exorcist pulled out a large steel watch. *"Well?"* he said.

"Please, Mrs. Poppledore," begged Dr. Vole, "do try!"

"I *am.* I'm trying hard!" She sulked. "If you think you can do any better, go get your own old poltergeists!"

Father Gansfleisch rose. "I have seen enough," he proclaimed. "I shall report to the Archbishop this absurdity. I can only hope that Dr. Vole has been deluded, without a part in planning this. As for you, Mrs. Poppledore—"

His two clerics ranged themselves beside him.

"—you should have shame!"

Constance Poppledore turned over lazily, letting a golden sandal dangle from a pale pink toe. "Well, I think you're a horrid old man!" she tossed back over her shoulder. "And anyhow you can't heal lepers like Canon Bunny can!"

Father Gansfleisch gasped. So did the clerics. So did Canon Bunny.

"Oh!" Her hand flew to her mouth. "I shouldn't have said that!"

"Indeed!" blurted the Canon. *"Indeed*—!" His eyes darted from Father Gansfleisch, striding out, to Dr. Espey. "I'm afraid that we must go!" he croaked. "We really must!"

A moment later, Constance Poppledore was alone with Dr. Vole. She turned to him, all smiles. "That awful man! Do you think I'd let him watch my poltergeist after he was so mean to Canon Bunny? I simply lay there and thought of flowers and birds, and of how maybe we could find a leper after all. I never thought of Papa even once!"

A floor lamp hopped up and down. A driftwood book-end thumped against the wall.

"I guess I can do what I want with my own poltergeist!" said Constance Poppledore.

Though Julian Poppledore's office overlooked the Rummage House roof garden, the gay clatter from *Peace Of Heart's* pre-publication party tempted him not at all.

"Damn the poltergeist!" he shouted, across the executive expanses of his desk. "It's lepers I'm losing sleep about! Get a load of this!" He shoved a newspaper at Dr. Vole.

The doctor blinked at a page-two headline. BISHOP TO PROBE MIRACLE PUBLICITY, he read. *Peace Of Heart Author Denies Loaves-Fishes Rumor.*

"Look, Vole! The Bunny book is strictly for the *high*-class trade. This stuff'll ruin it! Two bishops came to see me yesterday. The papers are phoning every fifteen minutes. Winchell has started talking about Lazarus. Furnwillie keeps telling me to ignore the whole business. And you—you sit there doing nothing!" He snatched the paper back. "Well, get this! You straighten Connie out before tomorrow—or else!"

"Or—what?"

"Or no Cadillac!"

Flushing, Dr. Vole assumed the dignity of his diploma. "The purpose of psychiatry," he said, "is not merely to extract an idea like a tooth, but to adjust the entire personality. Mrs. Poppledore's innocent affection for Canon Bunny, her desire for a miracle—there are only two strands in a dark pattern which still requires patient exploration and sympathetic therapy."

Mr. Poppledore made a rude noise. "Any more of that stuff, and I turn you and your spook-hunter over to the A.M.A. No fee, No Cadillac. Maybe no license."

Dr. Vole realized that the threat against his license was a strategic exaggeration, but the possibility of publicizing his momentary lapse from Freudian grace did not appeal to him.

More reasonably, he said, "I shall do what I can, Mr. Poppledore. But you mustn't expect miracles."

"I don't. That's why I'm making damn sure nobody with as much as a pimple gets in that church tomorrow. I've hired the best detective agency in town. Their men are going to be at every door. Otherwise, I'm holding you responsible."

Mr. Poppledore relaxed his frown, displaying the forehead which made his pictures look so intellectual in *The Saturday Review*. He rose. "Shall we join the party?" he suggested pleasantly.

"Er—yes," replied Dr. Vole.

And they walked out together, almost arm in arm, into the throng of critics, clerics, purveyors of literary merchandise, and friends. Immediately, two intense Communists accosted them, exhibited a volume piquantly entitled *Collectivistic Peace Of Conditioned Reaction In The Workers' And Peasants' Socialistic State*, and, before they managed to escape, shouted that it had been translated from the Russian long before anyone ever heard of the war-mongering Rabbi Liebman.

"Where is Canon Bunny?" panted Mr. Poppledore at a middle-aged lady.

"The Vulnerable Bede? Mrs. Poppledore's right behind me,

so he must be 'way over there. He's been acting funny ever since she came—like maybe she'd got leprosy or something."

Mr. Poppledore winced. "Take care of Connie," he hissed at Dr. Vole, and vanished in the crowd.

The doctor found Constance Poppledore talking to the Archimandrite Pyotru, of the Near-Eastern Semi-Orthodox Church, who consisted of a square black hat, an enormous red robe, and a big black beard with lots of teeth in it.

". . . so whenever I think of Papa, things start flying all by themselves, but I'm not afraid of it, not any more, now that I know it's just my—" She broke off, catching sight of Dr. Vole. "Why, here he is now!" she exclaimed. "If it hadn't been for him I wouldn't have a poltergeist at all."

The Archimandrite, who was ambidextrously depleting a platter of *hors d'oeuvres,* grinned at the doctor between two anchovies, and roared, "O-ho-ho-ho! Thinks vly yin ehr!"

"Exactly!" cried Constance Poppledore. "Look—"

The table, the *hors d'oeuvres,* and an advance copy of *Peace Of Heart* rose three feet in the air, hovered for a moment, and came down again.

"Ya!" boomed the Archimandrite, helping himself to the salami. "Vine Amerigun mazhine vor delefission! Thinks vly!"

"Mrs. Poppledore," said Dr. Vole. "I hate to interrupt, but are you still determined to find yourself a leper?"

"A leper?" murmured Constance Poppledore. "Oh, dear me, no! I realized this morning that scrofula would be every bit as good—and now I've an idea that's even better yet."

"Make vly!" The Archimandrite waved a pickle violently. "More, more!"

Somebody's handbag thumped into the lap of an astonished swami—and Constance Poppledore giggled girlishly. "That's nothing! Weight doesn't mean anything at all. Watch this!"

Some yards away, an Australian tea tree grew in a huge porcelain tub. She gestured at it. It began to rise. The Archimandrite applauded gleefully.

The potted tree rose six inches in the air. It tipped first one way, then the other. Then—

Suddenly she squealed. The roof shook as the tree came crashing down. There was a silence.

"Mazhine vus bruk?" exclaimed the Archimandrite. "Zum dube blows out?"

"*There* she is!" Constance Poppledore, all rigid, was pointing at a small round woman who clung to Canon Bunny's arm in the far corner; and Dr. Vole saw that the woman was wearing a flat and unremarkable straw hat.

"*Ugh!*" whispered Mrs. Poppledore with venom. "Can't you just see her ears *wiggle*? And now my Id won't work again for hours!" She stamped her foot. "Well, anyhow—" surprisingly, she smiled "—she doesn't know about my big surprise tomorrow. When he's famous, he'll owe it all to me."

Dr. Manfred Vole, after endeavoring vainly to cajole Constance Poppledore into disclosing her secret, spent an almost sleepless night, his imagination presenting him, alternately, with a panorama of the loathsome maladies more readily obtainable, and with a foretaste of the rigors of a Cadillacless existence. He entered St. Ethelred's-at-Sea, next morning, in poor spirits.

Mr. Poppledore, accompanied by Dr. Furnwillie and by two ominously muscular men with beady eyes, intercepted him at the door, warned him to stay right next to Connie, and delayed him just long enough to prevent his doing so. He found the front pew full, and barely managed to squeeze himself into the one behind it.

At first, craning his neck and squirming, he irritated the spinster to his left and evoked angry grunts from a bulky, egg-bald gentleman who pressed against him from the right.

Presently, though, he started to relax, reassured by the clear complexions of the congregation and by the absence of strangers in the pew ahead. Mrs. Poppledore sat on the aisle, with Mr. and Mrs. Henry Rummage close beside her. Then came the pale horse, the Archimandrite Pyotru in full canonicals, the heads of several Rummage House departments, and—almost immediately in front of him—Mildred Bunny, flanked by two little Bunnies, male, aged eight and twelve respectively.

He sighed, rubbed his red-rimmed eyes, and settled back. After a while, his last remaining shred of apprehension disappeared. Half dozing, half awake, he dreamed about the Cadillac convertible. Even the sight of Canon Bunny, splendidly attired (as a sharp feminine voice behind him pointed out) in everything but the Triple Crown, did not disturb his reveries. And it was only when the sermon was about to start that he was jerked cruelly out of them.

"W-what's *that*?" gasped the spinster suddenly.

Dr. Vole sat up, all his fears returning. He could see nothing. No one exhibited a ravaged face or mutilated member. The aisles were empty. The lame, the halt, the blind were absent.

Canon Bunny was just entering the carven eminence of his pulpit—

"*There!*" cried the spinster. "I *knew* I saw it move!"

She pointed, her finger trembling—and, as she did so, a crimson faldstool slowly rose six inches, moved nimbly to the left, and came down again. An instant later, as though experimentally, it rose again and resumed its place.

Full realization hit Dr. Manfred Vole between the eyes. All thought of physical afflictions vanished from his mind. The yellow Cadillac popped like a bubble and disappeared in limbo.

The Canon cleared his throat. "Dearly beloved—" he began, benignly.

The doctor saw that Constance Poppledore was leaning forward tensely. Then, in a flash, the memory of what had happened to the potted tea tree came back to him. Constance Poppledore, obviously, had not seen Mildred Bunny. There was a chance. A chance to salvage all!

He darted a covert glance to either side. His neighbors seemed to be ignoring him. Unobtrusively, his hand stole forward—toward the narrow aperture where Mrs. Bunny's plump posterior pressed against the pew—

"Dearly beloved, by a strange coincidence, many months ago I chose for my text today these words out of Ecclesiastes—" The Canon beamed. " '—To the making of many books there is no end—' "

Three inches from their vulnerable objective, the doctor's forefinger and thumb poised threateningly. An instant—and the Canon's wife would scream, would leap erect. Her hat's long, floppy ears would wiggle for Mrs. Poppledore—

A huge hand clamped his wrist.

"A pincher, eh?" whispered the bulky person in his ear. "Oh, no you don't! Not in a church! You ought to be asham—"

He did not finish. There was a dreadful hush.

Slowly, with all the dignity of a well-filled balloon, the Reverend Canon V. Bede Bunny was rising in the air. Two feet, five feet, ten—

At first, he seemed surprised. But, having been taken up, he was, if nothing else, quick on the uptake. At fifteen feet, his countenance composed itself in sweet humility. At twenty, he brought his hands together as though in prayer. At thirty-five, picking up forward speed, he leaned a little forward, in the attitude of the more accomplished seraphim.

Mildred Bunny writhed—and, momentarily, a tiny ray of hope gleamed in the doctor's heart. Then it, too, died. Her offspring were standing in their seats, waving ecstatically at their airborne parent. But she had fainted.

"O-ho-ho-ho!" the Archimandrite roared. "Zo clefer delefission! Iss vly!"

Somebody screamed. Batteries of flash-bulbs opened fire. And Dr. Vole, following the Canon's progress in despair, caught Constance Poppledore's eye.

She waved at him. She smiled excitedly. Her mouth formed words. They were inaudible, but he saw what they were. *"Don't worry, dear Dr. Vole,"* she said. *"It's just my Id!"*

Triumphantly, she put the Canon through his paces. He dipped and soared. He banked and swerved. Climbing suddenly, he performed a perfect Immelman turn. With a *whoosh*, he dived and, flying backwards, hedge-hopped the bobbing bonnets of his congregation—

And it was then, just as he levelled off, that the elder of Mildred Bunny's children accomplished that which Dr. Vole had tried to do in vain. He clutched his mother's arm. He shook it violently. "Gee, Mama, *look!*" he yelled. "Daddy's got *anti-gravl!*"

Mildred Bunny regained consciousness. She shook herself. She staggered to her feet. *"Venable!"* she called hysterically. "You come right *down* from there!"

Dr. Vole saw Mrs. Poppledore turn her head. He saw her fix her gaze on Mildred Bunny's hat. Instinctively, he ducked—

For an instant, the Canon stayed suspended—but only for an instant. He started folding in the middle. Abruptly, with a frightened squawk, he fell.

Fortunately, the Archimandrite's well-upholstered lap was immediately under him.

Dr. Manfred Vole played no part in resolving the pandemonium which, at the Canon's landing, engulfed St. Ethelred's-at-Sea. In a daze, he watched his bulky neighbor vanish in the throng. Still in a daze, he watched him reappear with Mr. Poppledore's detectives at his heels, and take command. He found himself pushed, shoved, prodded forward. Finally, in a corner, surrounded by the occupants of the front pew, he was corralled. Not until several minutes later, when the last protesting worshippers and reporters had been herded out, did he realize that the net of the Law had enmeshed them all.

Deliberately, the bulky man locked the great doors of St. Ethelred's. Deliberately, he pocketed the key and strode across the church. As he faced them, his eyes were hard; his jaw was grim.

"He's from the *FBI!*" whispered the pale horse right into Dr. Vole's left ear.

"Ooh, Secret Service!" bleated Mrs. Henry Rummage, in his right.

"An oudraitch!" Wildly, the Archimandrite waved his arms. "You zecret bolice! Me, who is un-American citizen, you could nod arrest! I call my Gonsul! I—"

Mr. Julian Poppledore perspired and puffed. "What is the meaning of this?" he demanded. "Release us instantly, I say! My congressman shall hear of it! My senator shall—"

"Sit down," said the bulky man.

Mr. Poppledore sat.

"All right." The man opened his billfold and showed them a large card. "That's who I am. It ought to be enough, but I'll explain. Reverend Bunny here—" He indicated the rumpled Canon, huddling with his small family some distance from the rest. "—was seen to rise into the air without any visible means of propulsion or support, and to fly successfully for a considerable period of time. The natural assumption—supported by the remark of his own son—is that some anti-gravity device has been employed. If that is the case, the present state of international affairs will make it necessary to apply full security measures, and—"

"Why, how *exciting!*" gasped Constance Poppledore. "We'll all be classified Top Secret, like—like a bomb or something. Although it really isn't anything like *that*. It's purely spiritual, and dear Canon Bunny tells all about it in *Peace Of Heart*. That's his book, you know, the one we're bringing out this week."

The bulky man made a brief note. "I'm afraid," he said, "that it may be necessary to defer the publication of that book indefinitely—"

Julian Poppledore uttered a hollow groan.

"As for you people—well, we'll have to wait until we hear from Washington, except for this man here." He glared down his nose at Dr. Vole. "He's just a pincher. We'll turn him over to the city police."

"I'm not!" The doctor flushed. "I'm a psychiatrist. I came to be beside my patient, Mrs. Poppledore."

Julian Poppledore gave him a look of utter loathing. "We never saw the man before in my life," he stated flatly.

"Oh, that's not *true!* Julian's just being mean. If it hadn't been for Dr. Vole, and how he fixed my Id, there would not have been a miracle at all!"

The Archimandrite was spitting foreign objurgations through his beard. The staff of Rummage House was twittering nervously. Mildred Bunny was snuffling into her sodden handkerchief. And the Canon, ignoring the awed questions of his progeny, was staring fearfully at Constance Poppledore and muttering something about Babylon. Of the assemblage, only the Reverend Winton Furnwillie appeared quite self-possessed. He now looked up from a small volume of Emerson, which he habitually carried with him, smiled gravely, and in a loud, clear voice said, *"Nonsense!"*

"Huh?" said the bulky man.

"I said the word, 'Nonsense.' It was a comment on the foregoing conversation. I am, if I may say so, an authority on Satan, who seems to have been busy here today—"

"For Pete's sake, Furnwillie," breathed Julian Poppledore, "haven't we lost enough sales already? Do you have to go putting your big foot in it too?"

"Shush," said Dr. Furnwillie reprovingly. "We must be practical. It is quite obvious that there has been no miracle." He peered significantly at the Canon. "I can assure you of *that.* And I can also say that nothing of a scientific nature is involved. If it were, the instrument could not be spirited away. It still would be about the person of one of us, where a brief search would certainly reveal it. Do you not find that very simple and very logical?"

Reluctantly, the bulky man conceded that Dr. Furnwillie might have a point. "But all the same," he said, "I did see him fly myself. How about that?"

"You did not see him *fly.* You saw him rise some distance in the air. There is a difference." Dr. Furnwillie pointed at the ceiling. "There, sir, is your explanation. Like so many too-ostentatious churches, St. Ethelred's-at-Sea is carelessly designed and poorly situated. It is surrounded by tall buildings. Its vast, high windows are scarcely suitable for proper ventilation. Under such circumstances, curious and powerful currents of air come into being—up-drafts they're called. And with the obvious lifting power of our dear friend's capacious vestments—Well, need I say more?"

Oh, good boy, Furnwillie, thought Mr. Poppledore fervently *Let's get in there and pitch!*

76

"All right, all right, I'll search them." The bulky man sounded a little frantic. "But being picked up by air currents—that's pretty hard to take!"

"It does sound just a bit improbable," commented Dr. Vole.

Dr. Furnwillie smiled at the psychiatrist. "There are more things in heaven and earth, Horatio," he quoted gently, "than are dreamt of in your philosophy."

And the search commenced. Not one of them had said a word about the poltergeist.

Constance Poppledore left the church two hours later, arm in arm with Dr. Manfred Vole, and in fine fettle. Julian Poppledore followed two paces to the rear, making disgruntled noises.

"Dear Dr. Vole," she murmured as they reached the car, "it was *so* nice of that big man to let you go, although I'm sure he couldn't prove a thing. And now let's celebrate! Julian can drive, and you can sit behind with me." She paused to waggle a flirtatious finger. "But promise me you won't pinch!"

Dr. Vole stood on his dignity, making no reply. He followed Constance Poppledore into the car, ruefully noted that it was a Cadillac, and edged himself into his corner, as far away from her as he could get.

Julian Poppledore gnashed his teeth and then the gears, and they were on their way.

His wife sighed dreamily. "Well, it was *almost* perfect, anyhow," she said, after a while. "At least he didn't fall so very far, and I can't help feeling that I've done him good. Wasn't it noble of him to resign his pastorate, right there and then, and tell us he was going to be a missionary in Basutoland? He'll be so happy there, among the heathens. *They* won't mind Mildred's hats—that is, unless they're cannibals, of course."

"Well?" grated their driver. "Where do we drop you, Vole?"

"Oh, but we won't!" she cried. "We'll take him home! He's the only one who understands my poltergeist—and he's going to write a book!"

"Who, me?" croaked Dr. Vole.

She stretched luxuriously. She closed her eyes. "Yes, you," she sang. "It's all arranged. I thought of it this very minute, because I feel so—well, so *at rest*, and so serene. I even have the title for it—"

A horrible premonition came to Dr. Vole. "W-what?" he said.

"*Peace*—" purred Constance Poppledore. "*Peace Of Id.*"

The Teeth of Despair

AVRAM DAVIDSON AND SIDNEY KLEIN

Are TV quiz programs obsolete? Do all professors get $15,000 a year and up? These are common suppositions of the Man in the Street; and while he may be at least partly right about quiz programs,* he is definitely wrong about professors, at least those in the unsung smaller colleges of America's hinterland. The plague of poverty (genteel variety) among the faculties of Backwoods University is definitely a real one.

Therefore, although the parts of this story that deal with television may smack more of literary archeology than of science fiction, the rest of it is the real stuff—including, of course, Herman Grackl's Magic Molars.

The full import of the singular series of events involving the groves of Academe with the jungles of television, and culminating, perhaps significantly, on a certain April Fool's Day not so very long ago, has remained until now unknown to the American public. From a nation which went into something resembling a state of shock following the disclosure of corruption, nepotism, and anarcho-syndicalist infiltrations into one of its most cherished institutions, much, of necessity, had to be concealed.

It is only now that we are able to disclose this piece of history which, unknown to the protagonists themselves at the time, was eventually to result in the application to transtellurian satellite communications of that revolutionary principle whose name is now known to all the world. But at the beginning . . .

It was on a Sunday night in late February. The family of

*At least all the vulgarly rich ones of the fifties are defunct as of the mid-sixties, though some piddling little ones—up to, say, $15,000—still are around.

Dr. Thomas Grew, Professor of Physics at Ryland University, had some hours ago finished a supper consisting of the remains of the previous day's hamburger, hashed with potatoes. The meal had been eaten thoroughly, if not enthusiastically. After doing the dishes, Mrs. Grew and her elder daughter, Juanita, went out baby-sitting—not together—as they did several evenings a week. By this means they contrived to earn enough to buy Juanita's clothes. What Juanita discarded her mother wore, and after that they were cut down and passed into a second avatar for the use of Isabel, the younger Grew daughter. Isabel, an ungainly child with acne, ill-adjusted to her peer-group, objected stridently to this arrangement, which was the best that could be managed on her father's salary.

For some weeks, fortunately, Isabel had contented herself with being merely sullen, and at eight o'clock that evening she joined her brother Dudley, the Grews' only son, in fitting bobby pins onto fan-shaped cards—an arrangement in violation of child labor laws, connived at by a Mr. Calman, a drugs-and-sundries wholesaler in a small way of business, whose establishment was located on the ground floor of the run-down apartment house in which the Grews lived. Kindly Mr. Calman paid seventy-five cents per hundred cards, and supplied all materials. The children were allowed by their parents to keep the money in lieu of allowance.

Dr. Grew had recently been replaced in his part-time job as bus boy in a chow mein restaurant, owing to the arrival from Hong Kong (on a fraudulently obtained passport) of the proprietor's third cousin, a former lt. colonel in the nationalist army who had been living very quietly since the fall of Canton. As he had not yet been able to secure other employ, and as he had marked all his class papers that morning during the hour or so respite afforded by the attendance of his children at an Ethical Society Sunday school, Dr. Thomas Grew found himself momentarily with some spare time. He employed it in tinkering with a piece of electronic equipment he had pieced together for his amusement over a period of years by smuggling out a resistor here, a capacitor there, from the university lab. The fingers of his children dipped mechanically into the box of bobby pins. Their eyes were fixed immovably to the screen of the television set.

The presence of a television was absolutely against every principle which Dr. Grew held culturally dear, and its cost was astronomically beyond his own means. But it had been presented to them, second-hand, with much flourish, by the wealthy widow of a master plumber, a friend of his mother-in-law's. Dr. Grew did not wish to offend this woman, a Mrs. Novack, because she turned over to him the boxes of cigars which still came her way as gifts from various plumbing equipment manufacturers (she retained an interest in the business); and these cigars he traded off to Mr. Calman for a cheaper brand at the rate of one for one and a half, shredding them and smoking them in his pipe. He had been unable to afford pipe tobacco proper since his marriage, which had occurred during the latter part of the vice-presidency of John Nance Garner.

First the children spent half an hour in flaccid delight watching a mixed bag of trained dogs, ventriloquists, acrobats, and fancy roller skaters; then they watched a patriotic drama concerning the actions of a heroic female Confederate spy against the foul ploys of an evil and lecherous Union general. From time to time Grew said, "Please make that a weeny bit softer, kiddies"; but they paid him no mind, nor did he expect they would. After a while he ceased to notice the noise as he tenderly soldered in place the diode which was his latest acquisition.

And then, finally, it was time for *Get It While You Can*, a program during which even Dr. Grew attended carefully, only pretending from time to time to make a ritual and face-saving clatter with his wire-stripper.

Last week Robby Rheinhart, the lovable M.C., had faced the cameras with a little girl in a wheel chair, and the week before that it had been a war veteran on crutches. *This* week, however, he had with him a sturdy old man with a white cane, as the shapely female assistants, beaming vacantly, wheeled out a table on which were two huge bowls filled with large, opaque capsules. After the applause died down, Robby introduced This Week's Guest of Honor, Mr. Edward Palumbo of the Calabrese Home for the Blind. Then there was a commercial. Mr. Palumbo was induced to say a few words and answer a few questions. Then there was another commercial, in which a wistful young man in a bath towel sprayed his armpits with something from a squeeze-bottle. Then they dollied in once more on the oleaginous Rheinhart and on honest, rugged old Palumbo. While the orchestra played the theme music, the old guy took off his coat, rolled up his sleeves, held up both hands. The music played slower, he dipped his hand in the starboard goldfish bowl, and pulled out a capsule.

The music stopped.

"Inside this capsule which our dear old Pal, Eddie Palumbo, has just selected at random," Robby said, breathlessly, "is inscribed the name of one of our wonderful *stoodio* audience. Every one of their names, as you all know, is inside one of those capsules, but only one at a time can be chosen. And NOW." He broke open the capsule, stared at the slip of paper. The cameras played over the faces in the audience, some tense, some picking their noses, some breaking into shy gestures as they caught their faces in the monitor. Robby milked the moment, then, in a high, breathless voice, declaimed, "Mis-ter . . . Herman . . . GRACKL!!!"

The camera panned in on the name on the slip, then a view of the audience again, finally focusing on someone who had just realized that *he* was Mr. Herman Grackl. Hesitantly, and in sections, like a telescope, he rose in his seat.

"Mr. Grackl?" burbled Robby. "Well, for gosh sakes, aren't *you* the lucky one! Come on *up* here, time's a-wasting, and— *Get it while you can!*"

The lucky man shambled forward, smirking and blinking and mumbling his jaws, while the music played a rapid tempo. After he had shaken hands with the M.C. and been turned—by main force—*away* from the shapely female assistants and *towards* the audience, he played with the buttons on his shabby coat while Robby asked him a few questions.

"Where are you *from,* Mr. Grackl?"

"Uh, I live right here in town."

"Right here in town! And what do you do for a living, Herman?"

"Um, I'm retired."

"Retired! Well, aren't *you* the lucky one! I wish I were— What am I *saying?*" Robby Rheinhart screamed, clutching his own throat with both hands and bulging his eyes. "The *sponsor* may be listening!" The audience roared. "Well. What did you *used* to do for a living, Herm?"

"I git socia' securidy," said Herm, sucking in his lips and cheeks, then expelling them.

The Grew children giggled. "Dope," said Isabel. "Dope yourself," Dudley said, promptly. Isabel dropped her card of bobby pins and struck at him. Their screams finally attracted the attention of their father, to whom had suddenly occurred a solution to the problem of proper RF shielding. It was a full minute before he succeeded in wedging the kids apart and getting them reasonably quiet again. With a few deft twists of his long-nose pliers he then made the necessary adjustments.

"—in nineteen thirty-six?!" Robby Rheinhart was screaming. "*And out of oatmeal boxes!?* Well, isn't *that* something? Isn't that *some*-thing?"

"There, see," muttered Isabel petulantly, "and we missed what he said."

Perhaps the possibility again occurred to the M.C. that his *padrone* might be watching—conceivably with a stop watch—because he suddenly became less strident and more business-like. Old Mr. Palumbo, in return for $500 which the sponsors (Robby had already announced four times) were going to donate to the Calabrese Home for the Blind, thrust his big, gnarled hand into the other glass bowl and came up with another capsule, which Robby took from him and opened with pinch-lipped concentration. A glance at the contents and he had another fit of convulsions, combined with renewed manifestation of exophthalmia.

"Thirty-three hundred *dollars!*" he screamed, holding up the slip for the camera. "Every question that you answer correctly will be worth *thir*-ty *three hun*-dred *dol*-lars! *How about that!*"

Professor Grew groaned. The butcher who supplied his family with hamburger (the only meat they could afford) was becoming importunate. An increase in faculty salaries was, as the President of Ryland had pointed out only a month earlier, quite impossible at this time. Owing to the lousy season at football, alumni contributions had dropped to almost zero.

Glumly he watched Herman Grackl, shambling and blinking and mumbling his jaws, being escorted up the thirty steps to the throne from which he would answer—or fail to answer —the questions. A curtain parted on the studio stage, revealing a huge vault. Two presidents of well-known banks came forward and, one after the other, concealing the combinations, twirled dials. The door swung open, revealing another door. Two presidents of theological seminaries, followed by the national directors of two veterans' organizations, proceeded in turn to open four more doors by means of keys in their possession and in their possession only. Finally, in the innermost recess of the vault was revealed an envelope approximately the length and width of an Ispahani rug, and sealed with seven seals.

"Are you ready, Herm?" Robby, once again serious, asked.

Herm sucked in his cheeks, thrust out his lower lip, pulled it in again, nodded. "Ee-yup. Ready," he said, and gave an imbecile grin.

Robby Rheinhart broke the seven seals solemnly.

"Very well. And here is your first question. For $3300, tell us —*Who designed the Brooklyn Bridge?*"

Mr. Grackl's grin faded. He rolled his eyes, breathed noisily into the microphone, and wiped his brow on his coat-sleeve.

"You have twenty seconds in which to answer. It's worth thirty-three hundred dollars—so-o-o—*Get it while you can!*"

Professor Grew said, "George Washington Roebling, if I'm not mistaken."

"George Washington Roebling, if I'm not mistaken," said Mr. Grackl.

Professor Grew, hearing his very words repeated, smiled. Dead pan, Robby Rheinhart asked, "Is that your answer?"

"Of course it is. Certainly," said Grew.

"Of course it is. Certainly," said Grackl.

Professor Grew smiled—somewhat uncertainly, this time. Robby Rheinhart leaped into the air, clicked his heels, flung wide his arms, and shrieked, *"You're RIGHT! For thir-ty three hundred dol-lars!"* The audience burst into applause, and the band into music. Herman Grackl clasped his hands above his head and beamed. ("Silly ass," said Grew. Grackl's face fell. So did his hands.)

"Will you go for a second thirty-three hundred dollars, Herm?" the M.C. asked, when the noise died down. Herm hesitated, gazed all around him, chewed his lips.

"Go ahead," urged Grew. "You'll never get another chance like this."

"I-I think I'll go ahead," said Herman Grackl. A swallowing movement was clearly visible the length of his long neck. "I'll never get another chance like this."

During the applause, and the commercial that followed, Grew bit his fingernails and pondered. Three times—oh, there wasn't any doubt about it—the contestant, Mr. Herman Grackl, had repeated the words of Thomas Grew. Could it be a coincidence? Could (here, almost automatically, he laughed scornfully) could that fellow Rhine be right? Telepathy? "Well, we'll see," he said.

He saw soon enough.

"Our next question," announced Robby, solemn as a Senate investigator, "deals with a man who was a great man in his own right and whose *father* was also a great man. Now, Herm, for sixty-six hundred dollars: tell us: *Who* was Secretary of War in the Cabinet of President Garfield, and *who* was his father?"

The music played. "Oh, Christ," muttered Dr. Grew. "Oh.

Oh. Oh. *Ahh!*" In a flash, the Paraclete descending, it came to him. History wasn't, never had been, his strong point; after all, he was a physicist, damn it! but this he'd learned somewhere, and—

The music stopped. Robby repeated the question. Determining to play it slow, play it cool, find out for certainsure, Grew said, "In the cabinet of President James A. Garfield—"

"In the Cabinet of President James A. Garfield—" said Herm Grackl.

"James *Abram* Garfield," Grew said.

"James *Abram* Garfield," Grackl said. The audience laughed a little bit. The M.C. picked it up, put on a wry grin of admiring surprise.

"The son of the Great Emancipator—" Grew's voice trembled.

"The son of the Great Emancipator—" Grackl's voice didn't. Grew could stand it no longer.

"Robert Todd Lincoln!" he said, very rapidly.

"Robert Tom Lincoln!" shot out Grackl.

Robby Rheinhart took a quick gander at his paper, then another one off stage, then his face cleared. "Well, you got the middle name slightly wrong, but we'll accept it—you're RIGHT! For six-ty six hun-dred DOL-lars!"

It wasn't till the band stopped its victory blast that Grew found his voice again. "Listen, you better not take any more on tonight," he said. "I don't think I can do it again right now. Tell him you'll come back next week. I'll be in touch with you after the show."

This is just what Herman did. His expression, as the two shapely female assistants led him away, was dazed, pleased, and haunted.

Everbright, the Professor of Zoroastrian Philology, was a small, scrannel man with rufous eyes. For the past twenty odd years (tap-tap on his little bench, like Dr. Manet), he had made and mended not only his only shoes and those of his wife, father, father-in-law, and six children, but in his cellar did clandestine cobbling for a fashionable bootmaker. "A preposterous tale, Grew," said Professor Everbright, now.

Yeoville, Professor of Provençal prose, who (being a bachelor, and feeling he could not spare from his studies the time for an outside job) lived mostly on canned spaghetti, shook his pale and pendulous cheeks. "Not to be credited, my dear Tom," he said.

Wearing the turtleneck sweater and puffing the bulldog pipe, both of which had been obligatory equipment for chaplains at non-denominational colleges when he had first come to Ryland in the choppy wake of the Dayton Monkey Trial, De Wet (Comparative Religion) sighed. His burning eyes and deep pallor were due not so much to ascetic zeal as to his playing a set of skins in various crowded and ill-ventilated jazz joints at nonunion rates. "I don't dig this bit," he said. "Where *is* that cat? I'm buzzed for time, man, I've got a jam session in the Biblical Chaldee in an hour."

There were noises of approval from other Ryland faculty members—English, Chemistry, Teutonic Languages (Per-Gunnar Maelstrom, the Ibsen expert, trimming his frayed cuffs with a small pair of scissors borrowed from Goldberg of Botany), and all the rest.

"Very well," said Grew. "We will demonstrate the fact as any other fact is demonstrated." He opened the door of the Faculty Lounge—cautiously, for it had only one hinge. "Herman, will you come in, please?"

Herman Grackl entered, nodding bashfully right and left. "I've told them and they don't believe me," said Professor Grew. "So suppose you tell them."

"Jeeze, maybe I should of taken the money and quit, huh?" said Grackl, apprehensively. "Well, I kind of like don't blame you professors. But it's a fact. Why me? Why not say a hundred other people? I dunno. Maybe it's a gift. It comes and it goes. Rudy Vallee, in the old days it use to be Rudy Vallee more than anyone else. Sometimes—whatever they had like playing at the old Steel Pier in Atlantic Cidy. Couple a weeks ago it was a drunken woman she was takin off alla her clothes down at—"

"What in the Hell are you talking about?" demanded Pighafetti, the biochemist, the envy of all the rest: kept all his family rosy-cheeked and warmly clad on his after-school-hours earnings as a pizza baker. The strain told, however, in the deep circles under his eyes.

Herman Grackl made haste to oblige. "First of all, as a result of an industrial accident incurred at sea during the Prohibition Era, I got like a plate in my head and it comes down—" he traced its descent with a large finger, "—in ta the jore, right around *here*." He paused. Dr. Grew nodded encouragement. "But nothing happen as a result a that, except I use to get a headache, off and on. Until I got this now pyorrhea condition and I lose haffa my teeth. There was a dennis in them days, maybe you heard of him? Dr.

Goldpepper? Dr. Morris Goldpepper? Well, he made me this plate and he told me it had no less than two different metallic substances in it—"

Professor Everbright raised a thin, semi-translucent hand. "One moment," he said, in a voice like the rustle of falling leaves at Vallambrosa. "Are we to understand that you receive communications through your false teeth via the Marconi waves?"

"Your technical terms are a little archaic, Elmer," said Dr. Grew; "but in substance—well, yes."

"You stick to your Department and I'll stick to mine," Everbright said, with unexpected fire. "I'd like to see how *you'd* make out on a Pahlevi palimpsest with Kufic superscriptions all over it!"

Grew hastily signalled to Grackl, who had been listening with mingled incomprehension and respect, to continue. "So that's it," said Herm. "*How* it happens, Ida know. *When* it's going to happen, I never use to be able to predick. It'd fade in—'High-ho, everybody'—fade out again. Sometimes a short innerlude of organ music. Sometimes, if it's inny immediate neighborhood, I get a police call. Once inna while: TV. But I *never* got anything as what I mean *clear* until I got Professor Grew's message the other night. All them creck answers! And then, afterwards, he told me to come over to his house, so I come; he says to come here, so I'm here. And that's it."

There was silence. Then—"Demonstration, I promised a demonstration," said Dr. Grew, bustling around with slips of torn-up examinations (the university providing no scrap paper for faculty use) and pencils which students had from time to time imprudently left behind in class or lab. Half of the assembled savants he sent outside with Herman Grackl, the other half remained with him. And he then and there proceeded to send such messages and other data ($E_- = MC^2$, for example), via his little black box, through the dental prosthesis of Mr. Herman Grackl, as demonstrated conclusively the absolute truth of his account thereof.

However, there were no shouts of exultation. Dr. Yeoville sighed heavily and said, "Very well, we are convinced. Now what? Is it your intention to attempt to market this curious engine with monies raised from the Ryland Faculty? If so, here is fifty cents: I shall go without lunch for three days."

Grew smiled crookedly. He then spoke (Busztromowicz of the English Department later declared) as never man spoke to man before. With burning words that blazed and crackled in the ambient air he sketched their poverty—deep, of ancient duration, the scars of it beyond cure. He spoke of the utter contempt in which they were held; the vast sums spent annually in the United States on bubble gum, Tom Collins mixer, and pinball equipment, he compared with the pittances devoted to higher education. . . .

They listened, their eyes burned hotly, they made little growling noises in their throats and chests; shuffled their cracked shoes.

Finally, "All that you say is true," acknowledged Maelstrom. "Painfully, agonizingly true. But—as my students too often ask me—'So what?' "

"So this: Colleagues, I but state a simple fact when I say that we have here among us an accumulation of knowledge in no way inferior to that possessed by the sponsors of *Get It While You Can*. It is impossible that a question should be asked which at least one of our number could not answer. We have been poor long enough. Riches now lie within our grasp."

The University Poet-in-Residence, his lungs weakened by the steamy fumes of the dog laundry in which he toiled after hours, coughed fitfully. "Your proposal, Dr. Grew," he said in a thin voice, "is quite obvious. It is also dishonest, unethical, and meretricious. I am in favor of accepting it."

When the applause died away one single head was seen to shake. It was grey, and belonged to the Professor of Hellenic Civilization. "I fear me," he muttered. "I fear me. Beware of *hubris,* the sin of overweening pride, lest it destroy us. Is not poverty as becoming to scholars as a scarlet bridle to a white horse?"

"If Homer said that," roared Professor Maelstrom, "no wonder they threw him off a cliff!"

An unexpected touch of color glowed in the other's cheeks. "That was Hesiod, you Gothic oaf!" he snapped. Then the fight went out of him and he slumped in his seat, waved his hand in feeble surrender. "yeypaod, yeypaod," he whispered. "Do what you will: I shall be with you."

The faculty made the acquaintance of Herman's lady friend, a Mrs. Doll Moomaw, who had accompanied him and had waited in an outer room.

"Well-preserved," conceded Grew, in a whisper.

"And pneumatic," observed Everbright.

"I told Doll that you professors are, now, trying to find me a job," said Grackl, winking ponderously over her shoulder.

"I be damned and go-to-Hell," said Doll, briskly, "if I can figure out what Herman could do at a college besides sweeping out the can: but listen: as long's he makes some money. I think he's had this same suit on since the six-day bicycle races."

"Aw, now, *Doll*," said Herman, smirking bashfully.

"The late *Mr*. Moomaw, rest his soul, was of a short, stocky built; otherwise—"

But here Herman grabbed ahold and pulled her out, still explaining why the deceased's suits were of no use to his successor-apparent.

Professor Yeoville shook his head and dewlaps. "That woman worries me," he said.

But Grew, sanguine, clapped him on the back. "Ho, ho, you old bachelor!" he chuckled. Yeoville winced, fell silent.

The following Sunday night the Faculty of Ryland University (excluding, of course, the Professor of Athletic Science, who was known to be a fink for the Board of Trustees and the Alumni Association, and had therefore been omitted from the cabal) assembled behind the locked doors of their Lounge. Dr. Grew, speaking into his mechanism and gazing at the television set smuggled up, said, "If you receive me okay, Herman, stroke your right cheek twice."

Herman Grackl stroked his right cheek twice. ("Hot diggetty!" exclaimed an excited pedagogue—and was stricken silent by the warning glares of the others.)

That night Herman answered questions involving the tributaries of the Sepik Watershed, the more obscure poems of Fulke Greville, the Eleventh Mihir Yast, and the Presidents of the U. S. Congress under the Articles of the Confederation (in chronological order). He answered them all correctly; after which, by a show of hands, he was advised to retire until the following week. He had won, the previous week's score included, $19,800.

"Oughtn't we to have stopped right there?" the Professor of Hellenic Civilization asked.

"Why, it would come to less than a thousand dollars apiece," Grew objected.

"A thousand dollars!" repeated the Professor of Zoroastrian Philology, in tremulous tones.

"We must learn to think big," pointed out the Professor of Provençal prose. "*I* think we should wait until we have at least *two* thousand dollars apiece!"

In the month which followed, Herman Grackl, by naming

the Mayors of the Palace, twenty-three dwarf stars in order of magnitude, all the vessels involved in the Battle of Lepanto, the Dodecanese Islands with their principal cities and populations and chief exports, all the steps involved in the Activated Sludge method of sewage disposal and descriptions thereof; by explaining the systems of proportional representation obtaining in four Scandinavian countries and Switzerland, Frenet's formulas for a space curve, the Twenty-Four Traditional Measures of Welsh Poetry, and the meaning of thirty-two symbols from the Popol Voh; and by correctly identifying twelve Proto-Etruscan artifacts, paintings by Murillo, Winterhalter, and Rembrandt Peale, as well as musical pieces by Arne, Bartok, Pietro Yon, and Henry VIII . . . became a national figure.

He was featured on the covers of *Time* and *Life* magazines.

The then President of the United States, being asked in press conference about a clause in the tariff bill he was urging on Congress, replied, "Well, you are informing me of something about which the precise particulars I am not aware of. After all, I am not Herman Grackl." (Laughter.)

It was a merry group of scholars which assembled in the Faculty Lounge the evening of Herman's sixth appearance on *Get It While You Can.* Dr. Grew passed around the latest box of cigars which Chromo-Bright Tube and Pipe had presented to Mrs. Novack, and she to him; as one who was shortly to cut up a kitty in excess of $957,000 (for all concerned had determined that this would be the last evening), he felt he could well afford the gesture. The Professor of Levantine Archaeology declared that he had been pricing Jaguars. The Poet-In-Residence argued the claims of the Ferrari. Dr. Maelstrom announced a certain method he intended to recommend to the President of the University to relieve his (the President's) prostate condition. And then all conversation died down as they closed in to watch their protégé engage in preliminary banter with Robby Rheinhart, the genial M.C. of the program.

"Herm, there seem to be a few changes in your appearance," Robby said.

"Hey, you know, man, he's right," observed the Professor of Comparative Religion. "Like he looks different, somehow "

Herman Grackl smirked. "Well, Robby, when you're in love it *does* make a change."

Robby did a double take. "Did you say—*in love?*"

Another smirk. "Ee-yup. T'tell the truth—I'm engaged!"

Grew exclaimed, "He didn't say anything to us about—But I suppose it was inevitable—"

Robby inquired, "Well, Herm, is your fiancée by any chance *here* tonight?"

With a dip of his knees and a bob of his head, Herm allowed as how she was, and, with much palaver, coyness, applause, laughter, and hoo-hah, the camera showed the fiancée to all America. Mrs. Moomaw beamed, bowed, bridled, and displayed her superabundant charms to the ambient air.

"—so she says, 'Honey,' she says, 'the whole country is lookin' at you so why don't you get yerself fancied up?' So I says, 'You are right, Doll.' "

"*That's* what's like new about him," the Professor of Comparative Religion exclaimed. "Dig those crazy threads, man!"

And, after more persiflage, the refurbished Herman mounted the steps to the throne. The ceremony of opening the vault and removing the questions was gone through, and, as Robby Rheinhart broke the seventh seal, a certain amount of tension gripped those present in the Faculty Lounge.

"*Now*. Following the death of Alexander the Great—" ("Hah!" snorted the Professor of Hellenic Civilization, rubbing his hands.) "—there arose in the East a dynasty known as the Sassanian, or New Persian, Dynasty." (The Hellenicist bit his lip and ignored the glance of ill-concealed triumph thrown his way by the Professor of Zoroastrian Philology.) "There were twenty-eight members of this dynasty. For Thirty-three hundred dollars a point, Herm, name all twenty-eight members of the Sassanian, or New Persian, Dynasty. You have already won nine hundred and fifty-seven thousand dollars. If you name all twenty-eight correctly you will win ninety-two thousand four hundred dollars, which will make a total OF." He paused. "One *million*. Forty-nine thousand . . . four-hundred DOLLARS! Good luck, Herm. You have twenty seconds to think of your answer. Should you miss, of course," he concluded, cheerfully, "you lose everything."

The music began to play. "All right," asked Grew, flipping the switch on his hootenanny, "what's the first one?"

"Artaxerxes I," said Professor Everbright.

"Artaxerxes I," repeated Grew. "Got that, Herman?"

The music stopped. "Sapor, Hormisdas, Vahrahan, Narses," mumbled Everbright, counting on his fingers.

"All right, Herm," burbled Robby. "Your twenty seconds are up."

"He actually looks worried," chuckled Maelstrom. "What an actor!"

90

"For three thousand, three hundred dollars, tell us the name of the first Sassanid King of Persia."

Herman said nothing. "Artaxerxes I," repeated Grew. Herman cast an agonized look around him.

"I'll have to call for an answer, Herm," said Robby.

"*He's not acting!*" shouted Professor Maelstrom. "He doesn't hear you! The transmitter isn't working!"

"The transmitter is in perfect order!" Grew insisted. "ARTAXERXES I!" he yelled at the top of his voice. Herman's face broke out in sweat. He suddenly clapped his hand to his mouth, then began to slap, pat, prod, and poke his pockets, one after the other. Again and again. And then the hideous truth came to Professor Grew. "He's looking for his old teeth!" he wailed. "That blowsy old bitch he shacked up with —she's hypnotized him or something—she not only made him get a new suit of clothes, *but she made him get a new set of teeth, too!*"

The Poet-In-Residence uttered a hoarse scream and fell senseless to the floor. Pandemonium raged in the Faculty Lounge, while (unheard) on the screen Robby Rheinhart slowly shook his head.

"Hubris," whispered the Professor of Hellenic Civilization, as tears rolled down his seamed, emaciated face. "Hubris. Whom the gods would destroy—"

The proprietor of the chow mein restaurant where Dr. Thomas Grew had formerly worked passed him on the street the week following. Having a Confucian respect for scholarship, and being struck by the Professor's threadbare condition, he rehired him on the spot as supernumerary bus boy. Grew works there three nights a week, and though the pay is minimal and the tips scant, he is frequently able to bring home nourishing scraps of food.

It was there one night, whilst surreptitiously slipping into his greatcoat pocket the contents of a bowl of leftover wontons which the ex-general had earmarked for his Peke, that there occurred to the foreign-devil busboy in a blaze of illumination the practical application of what has since become known to all the world as the Grew-Grackl-Goldpepper Principle of Bimetallic Coupling which has made such revolutionary changes in satellite communications.

Under the circumstances it would be pointless to cavil at the fact that the overriding needs of the national security preclude the possibility of a patent; and that, hence, none of the three men has been able to realize any financial profits whatsoever.

The Galactic Calabash

G. C. EDMONDSON

Things do happen down south of the border! Chicken
factories extracted by financially obscure means from
the *gringo*; a deep-freezer room in the middle of a
desert-like Mexican ranch; a TV set with a peculiarly
rhythmic distortion to its picture; and then that weird
"edible" "gourd"! And all strictly non-science fiction except for the latter, about which let the tale tell. . . .

The affair of the galactic calabash began one Sunday almost
a year ago when, after much wheedling, I had induced my
mad friend to abstain from suppressing coastal carpetbaggers
for one weekend. We were bruising tires and nerves slightly
south of the place where U.S. 101 becomes *Carretera Federal
Número 2*, when he applied brakes with soul-shattering sud-
denness.

The cow gazed at us with the equanimity of a Methodist
bishop while my friend applied the horn. At imminent risk
of impacting a sinus, he lowered the window and shouted
raucous Arabic into the damp, maritime air. It sounded like
something an Arab might say to a Jew.

But the cow took no offense until my mad friend nudged
her gently with the grill. As she trotted away a turgid udder
swung, and I was struck with the resemblance to a Wagnerian
soprano we had once known, and said so. My mad friend
laughed uproariously.

"What's so funny?" a wife asked from the rear seat.

"A play on words," I explained.

"You'd have to speak Gaelic to understand it," my friend
added.

The wives returned to their discussion of whatever it is
that wives discuss.

"You'll find him interesting." I referred to the man we
were going to visit. I went on to explain how the meteor-

92

stricken Señor Galindo had arrived ten years ago from some pauperous tropic. He had brought little, save an immensely fertile wife, to this brawling, wide-open land of opportunity and inflation far up in the northwest corner of the republic. And now he was a power to be considered.

My mad friend placed his forefinger stiffly to one side of his nose and inhaled with difficulty through the other. "Serves me right for leaving Arizona," he muttered.

"If you're immune to Neo-synephrine I have some Scotch snuff."

He shook his head and continued driving. There was a tremendous bump where rain had undermined a bridge approach. My friend registered suffering as he thought of martyred tires.

"Back to the subject," he continued; "man is a theomorph. Therefore, any intelligent being is sure to be anthropomorphic. And please can, if you will, any hoopla about binary planets with tides being necessary before an air-breather climbs out of his tidal pool. We still haven't made peace with Darwin."

"But you will concede that dogma is not overthrown by admitting these possibilities?"

"We outlived Galileo."

"Turn here," I interrupted. We hurdled a culvert. Yesterday's cloudburst had removed all the topsoil, so we crept with agonizing slowness over a jumble of head-sized boulders for the next kilometer. Just over the rise of the hill we came to *La Granja Galindo*.

"Thank God he doesn't call it *hacienda*," my mad friend muttered, "but what's the difference between *granja* and *rancho?*"

"All same: farm and ranch."

The central core of Sr. Galindo's house was a marvel of decrepitude and slipshod construction. Surrounding it concentrically were the additions which fertility and increasing opulence had forced him to. Though he fully intended someday to erect a palace more in keeping with his present station in life, so far every peso had gone into more of the narrow, corrugated iron edifices which covered the downwind portion of his *granja*.

As I alighted from the car, Sr. Galindo detached himself from the sons, daughters, and employees who were unloading and tallying a truck. He was a large, bald-headed man, much whiter than I or my mad friend, and made a perfect picture of a jovial, Irish bartender until he opened his mouth to shout, "¡Hola! ¿What is new in the *platívolo* factory?"

"We've converted to cups," I said.

"I thought flying saucers were *platos voladores*," my mad friend muttered.

"Newspaper jargon," I explained. The Saucer Works gag referred to the place where I work—about which no more. We passed a bare, grave-like mound adjoining the kitchen garden and once more I admired the Mexican's practicality. How many men would let a meteorite do the spade-work for a new septic tank?

I presented my mad friend and his wife to Sr. Galindo, whose own wife arrived, wearing knee-length rubber boots and carrying a clipboard. She favored us with a grin and took our wives in tow toward the kitchen where they could supervise a young *tortillera* and discuss the new botch look which none dared as yet to wear.

"Thank God you speak Spanish," Sr. Galindo said to my friend. "I dislike to inflict my English on persons of discernment."

Galindo's English was fully as bad as he described it. It had been learned mostly during hours spent puzzling over bulletins from the U.S. Department of Agriculture.

After outfitting us with specially disinfected galoshes, he took us on a tour of the long, sheet-iron buildings and explained with loving thoroughness the workings of his fully automated factory. Conveyor belts brought compounded feeds directly from the mill to galleries where seven kilograms of feed plus measured amounts of antibiotics and water could be counted upon to produce three kilograms of dressed fryer at the end of eight weeks. But there was a slightly careworn look about the fryers' beady eyes, also little trilling noises and ruffled plumage. I wondered if my mad friend's aura was incompatible with avian contentment. Sr. Galindo disembarrassed me. "Since that accursed aerolith fell," he muttered.

I pressed him for particulars.

"For the past few months they've been a little slow making weight."

"Genetic difficulties?"

Galindo shrugged. "Maybe the strain's playing out. So far it's not serious."

We passed to another gallery where fertile eggs rolled gently from hens to another conveyor, through grading and candling machinery to incubators whence, twenty-one days later, they would be recycled into the eighth week grain-to-meat process.

"All this I owe to the *gringos*," Sr. Galindo said expansively. He was a great admirer of Americans with their beautiful machinery and assembly-line processes.

"Horse manure!" I spoke with the familiarity of long friendship.

Sr. Galindo glanced at me with a slight, quizzical smile. "I imagine some small part of it can be laid to Yankee ingenuity," my mad friend said placatingly.

"Damn small," I said, for I remembered the long bouts of legal skirmishing which had built Señor Galindo's business. Before his time, every chicken and egg consumed in this territory had been imported from Yankeeland. When the government, in misguided eagerness to protect and promote local industry, had forbidden the importation of eggs and chicken feed, Sr. Galindo had been close to ruin.

But by paying the fantastic interest rates prevalent in an unregulated economy, he had floated and juggled stock issues with an abandon far wilder than any blue-sky railroad pirate's. By dint of frantic prestidigitation and prevarication, Sr. Galindo bought out his American suppliers and transported their equipment to his own side of the border.

Thanks to a total absence of income tax, the Americans were now almost paid off and Sr. Galindo would soon be in the black. Though he admired American efficiency and often talked of emigrating, the jovial Mexican was never quite fool enough to do it.

"What's the new building?" I asked.

"Ah, this you must see." We waded through trays of disinfectant and took off the galoshes. On the way, we passed through the *sacrificadora* where fryers were placed on the hooks of a chain, which delivered them via scalding tank to a revolving drum with dozens of rubber fingers, which plucked feathers and rapped the unwary knuckle which came too near.

Farther down was a table where the fryer's less appetizing portions were removed to ride another conveyor to the cooker, which sterilized them before relaying to a far corner of the *granja*.

Señor Galindo's unbelievably handsome son gave me a smile of recognition as his cleaver did things worthy of a Samoan sword dancer. A daughter and another girl I did not recognize were stuffing dismembered fryers into plastic bags which they shrunk tight with the aid of a vacuum

95

cleaner. A third girl snapped a rubber band over each bag and packed it in a square stacking carton.

A smaller son followed us, plucking periodically at Galindo's sleeve and whispering.

Galindo led us into the new building which was, of course, a freezer. "Let's see those cuckolds"—*cabrónes* was the word he used—"try it again." He was referring to the time a conspiracy had been organized to down the price just when he had thirty-thousand fryers ready to kill and gobbling tons of feed each day.

"What's that thing?" my mad friend asked, pointing at a frost-rimed sphere in one corner of the vast freezing compartment.

Sr. Galindo picked it up with a puzzled air. He juggled it gingerly from hand to hand as we hurried from 60° below out into the watery February sunshine. He placed the sphere atop a bird bath he'd started two years ago and never had time to finish. While he clapped his hands and blew on them, the frost began melting. "Ah," he said with a sudden smile, "now I remember. *Es una calabaza.*" Which, owing to a linguistic peculiarity, could mean pumpkin or several kinds of squash, but not calabash.

"Last summer just before the *aerolito* fell," Galindo explained, "my wife planted some. When the freezer room was finished I needed something for a trial. I saw this magnificent *calabaza* had come unconnected from its vine. 'It will spoil,' I thought, so I put it in the freezer. ¿You like *calabaza?*"

I don't, and I'm sure my mad friend doesn't, but we both assured him we did.

"Tell your mother to put it in the oven," Sr. Galindo said to his offspring who followed us.

"I never heard of baking one whole," I protested.

"You'd need a hacksaw to slice it," my mad friend laughed.

"We always bake them whole where I come from," Galindo explained. "They burst and the seeds fall out. With grated cheese and *salsa picante*—" He raised his eyebrows and kissed his fingertips.

I knew the rest of the meal would be good anyhow. We had progressed by this time to the hammermill where Sr. Galindo compounded a mash of seeds ranging from rye to kaffir corn, with exact amounts of oyster shell, bone meal, fish meal, and vitamins. Some of the latter came from Germany by routes more devious than a shipment of heroin but their presence spelled the difference between profit and loss for Sr. Galindo's grain-to-meat conversion.

I wondered aloud what the small boy had wanted.

Galindo showed some embarrassment. "You know how hard it is to get anything fixed in this country. The TV's been acting up." He looked at me hopefully. I promised to do what I could—which, without tools, would probably be very little.

We were admiring a microtome and staining apparatus which augmented the microscope I had donated some years ago. Galindo was explaining to my mad friend the auguries performed over sliced liver in his constant war against the diseases which could wipe him out overnight.

My stomach had finally reached the conclusion that my throat was cut when the small boy who had taken the *calabaza* returned with the news that dinner and the ladies awaited.

But as usual, dinner and the ladies needed several finishing touches, so I glanced into the front room where the Galindo brood was acquiring its English in painless, Lone-Ranger-sized doses, and immediately knew I was off the hook.

"There's nothing wrong with your TV," I told Galindo. "See how the picture tears and the sound razzes in perfect unison? Something around here's setting up interference."

"The refrigeration—" Galindo began hopefully.

I shook my head. There were no neon signs within 10 km. I wondered what could be causing the pulsation. But dinner was finally served so I forgot about it.

Dinner was indeed delicious—young fryers barbecued and drenched in a sauce not so fiery as might be expected from Señora de Galindo's native state of Tabasco. Galindo ate much bread and salad. He ignored the chicken with an intensity which brought to mind the bitter days when he must have eaten little else. The meal was nearly over when he suddenly remembered and asked, "*¿y la calabaza?*"

Galindo's wife shrugged. "Like a rock," she said.

"¿After two hours in the oven? ¡How strange!"

Galindo was buttering a final *birote*, that Mexican creation which looks like a roll and tastes like bread used to taste, when it happened: There was a muffled explosion, more felt than heard, and the oven door flew open.

"*¡La calabaza!*" my wife shrieked. "¡We forgot to turn off the oven!"

"Those seeds and pulp will stick like glue," Mrs. Galindo moaned. She turned off the oven and we settled down for a final round of coffee, still twittering slightly, like poultry after a fox has been flushed from the henhouse.

The gentlemen retired to another room and discussed the

role of the Church in Mexican history. This was interesting, for Sr. Galindo was a Mason, while my mad friend was an apologist of such brilliance that I suspected he might someday follow the path of Giordano Bruno. They were nearing the gauntlet-and-card-exchanging stage when we were interrupted from the kitchen.

"¿What kind of *calabaza* was that?" Galindo's wife asked. We followed her to the now cool oven.

There were spatters of melted plastic, shattered bits of ceramic, and some extremely miniaturized devices at whose function I could only guess. Intermixed with the whole, were rent sections of the covering which had resembled some sort of *calabaza*. I began to wish I'd seen it after the frost melted away.

"¡Aja!" Galindo said with something of a twinkle. "You Americans and your fantastic new weapons."

I started to protest, but I knew Sr. Galindo's faith in the American Way would permit no other explanation.

One of the older children came from the front room. *"La televisión funciona perfectamente,"* he reported.

I had a sudden suspicion that I knew the exact moment when it had started functioning perfectly. "Do you mind if I take two or three of those little things that look like they're not broken?" I asked.

"It's yours." Galindo smiled. He didn't have to clean the oven.

Wishing they were mine, I slipped two of the small things into my pocket.

Late that night as we retraced our path over *Carretera Federal Número* 2 to the border, our wives again discussed the botch look, and what effect it would have on eye make-up.

"I can see where Galindo owes something of a debt to the U.S.," my mad friend said.

"Not half what the world owes him," I muttered.

"How come?"

"You know how in those science fiction yarns you hate so much, some mad scientist always saves the world from destruction?"

My friend made an interrogatory noise.

"Sr. Galindo just did."

"Did what?"

"Saved us from invasion."

"You write so much of that jazz you're beginning to believe it."

I remembered the unhappy condition of Sr. Galindo's fryers. "Wasn't it established several years ago that UHF radiation seems to foul up the compass arrangements in homing pigeons?" I asked.

"Not in the kind of stuff I read," my mad friend said.

"I don't know much about telemetering," I said, "but I've seen enough around the Saucer Works to know this isn't ours." I handed him something scraped from Galindo's oven. "It isn't Russian either."

"So?"

"Funny about you mentioning that tide-pool evolution bit today," I said. "I wonder," I wondered, "just how often a binary system like Earth and Moon occurs? It might pose all sorts of conjectures about climatic conditions for anyone unfamiliar with such a system."

"What *are* you running on about?" my mad friend inquired. Green eyes flared suddenly on the roadway and he braked just in time to miss a cow.

"Let me put it this way: If you dumped a weather station on an unknown planet and got a normal reading for several days, then a sudden drop to 60° below for six months, then in a matter of minutes the temperature climbed into a range that melted your transmitter, wouldn't you decide that planet wasn't worth invading?"

My mad friend placed a stiff forefinger to one nostril and inhaled noisily through the other. But he was very quiet all the way home.

Space-Crime Continuum

H. F. ELLIS

There is one specialized science fiction anthology that
I have never edited, and that I probably never will. Its
title is "Great Science Fiction Stories About Detectives";
and if you want to know why I have not done it, the
following luridly gleaming gem from the depths of London's fogs will tell you.

Frankly, I find that most science fiction detective
stories (except Isaac Asimov's, and an all-Asimov anthology would be silly, wouldn't it? *Wouldn't it?*) are
not my dish. So I will leave *that* collection for someone
else to do.

Meanwhile, we have this squirmy bit from Mr. Ellis
to serve as a Horrible Example of the genre. Treat it
gently; it is marked "fragile. . . ."

*"He was killed," grunted Dr. Polycarp, wearily stuffing
his Geiger counter into his bag, "by epsilon rays, or some
similar agency, fired from behind at a distance of not more
than two light years. Tell you more when we've had him
disintegrated."*

"Hmph!" snapped Philip Strong.

I quote this brief passage from my forthcoming interplanetary crime novel, *The Space Case,* to indicate the kind of
difficulty that faces an author who tries to have the best of
both worlds by combining detection and space travel in one
book. Alibis are the very devil. With the public demanding
ever more up-to-date and powerful weapons—the old short-
range uranium pistol cuts no ice nowadays—it is useless
for the chief suspect to produce the stub of a cinema ticket
as proof that he was on another planet at the material time.
What of it? says the reader; the man could have bombarded

his victim with beta particles at twice the distance, without even bothering to leave his seat. And so he could. That's what Philip Strong had in mind when he went on to say, *"So, on the evidence thus far, we can't exclude* ANYONE *who has been within twelve billion miles of this place during the last two years!"**

I'm solving this alibi problem, as a matter of fact, by the later discovery of indentations made by a meat chopper on the back of the victim's head (they were put there deliberately, after death of course, by the murderer, in order to throw suspicion on an old-fashioned and rather earthbound Egyptologist); but the device is a little thin, and involves some tricky space-time adjustments as the plot unfolds. Nor is this the only, nor even the most difficult, hurdle that has to be surmounted. The whole science of interplanetary detection, as Strong often says, is in its infancy.

There is also the difficulty of ascertaining whether death has, in fact, taken place. The body of Sir George Trevose, the astrophysicist, is discovered slumped sideways in a Venusian deck chair, with the uncompleted equation "$\log (-x) + (\cos v^2 s)^{2\pi n} = Rd\theta^3 \ldots$" scrawled in the meteoric dust at its feet. So far all is plain sailing. But what is Strong going to do to make sure that life is extinct? Rip open the front of Sir George's space suit—and kill him for certain by letting in the carbon dioxide for which the atmosphere of Venus is notorious? The point, however, is elementary and need not detain us.

In the matter of suspects I strongly advise newcomers to this field of fiction to retain at least some of the traditional figures of Earthly crime. With the whole Universe to pick from there is a temptation, as I well know, to look for the murderer among such characters as Krool, renegade son of the Hepat of Mars, Tchah his radioactive butler, Coreopsis, Queen of Madusia, and the sinister Obal Trug, self-styled Gookwar of Bom. The temptation ought to be resisted. Readers lose their grip if all the suspects are eighteen feet tall and have antennæ growing out of their heads, and tend eventually not to care *which* of them did it. Also it is difficult, without a certain artificiality, to assemble the whole lot in the detective's room in Albany, W.I, for the final showdown.

---

* Strong spoke loosely. See, in due course, my *Murder on Alpha Centauri*, where the whole case turns on an error in the speed of light made by a blundering local inspector.

It is better, I think, to adopt some sort of compromise between the old and the new:—

THE SPACE CASE — A Philip Strong Story

Synopsis of Opening Chapters

The Author, uncertain whether there is more money in interplanetary or detective fiction, has decided to combine the two and accordingly attaches himself, in the guise of TONY BLACK, a typical first-person stooge, to the house party of LADY TREVOSE, wife of SIR GEORGE TREVOSE, the notorious millionaire astrophysicist and owner of the spaceship *Hermione*. Included in the house party at the Trevoses' gloomy Shropshire seat are:

HUGH TREVOSE, Sir George's spendthrift son, threatened by his father with summary disinheritance if he does not immediately renounce his engagement to

SEMOLINA, an unspoilt Venusian priestess, who is being blackmailed by a syndicate of former admirers and has to raise 10,000 *krim*, or the equivalent in terrestrial money, by Monday;

SIMON WARWICK, confidential secretary to Sir George and an ex-Olympic javelin thrower, now under notice for stealing his employer's marijuana cigarettes;

PROFESSOR EIGG, a left-wing selenographer, whose plan to repopulate the Moon is being secretly encouraged by Lady Trevose. He is a gifted mimic, but his frequent threats against Sir George's life should not be taken too seriously according to

OOMPH, the half-crazed robot who acts as valet to the Professor and is subject to fits of homicidal rage if a rare South American lubricant, unknown to Western mechanical engineering, is poured into his gearbox.

When, late on Friday night, this likely lot is joined by PHILIP STRONG, a detective so well-bred as to be practically indistinguishable from a racehorse, the Author's sole remaining anxiety is lest the murder of his host should take place before he has had time to manœuvre the whole party into surroundings less hackneyed than a Shropshire library. To obviate this risk he (or rather Tony Black) suggests that a midnight trip in the *Hermione* would be fun. "Venus is nice at this time of year," yawns Strong, and Lady Trevose, who has been stabbing absentmindedly with a stiletto at a photograph of a Martian

102

princess she has just found in her husband's desk, enthusiastically agrees. Nobody notices Semolina's preoccupied look. . . .

It will be seen that I have kept all these suspects, and their motives, well within the bounds of the average reader's credulity; and it is upon *their* movements, upon the discovery of blowpipes, cosmic ray projectors, etc., in *their* luggage, that the main interest of the story centers. Subsidiary characters—Venusians, the Scorpion-men from outer space, a comic Thwapa (or police sergeant) who falls in love with Lady Trevose—are used purely to give local color and relieve the tension. Their irruptions are not permitted to interfere with the development of the central theme, the solution of Philip Strong's problem:

Strong bent down and, carefully manipulating his hydraulically operated aluminum gloves, removed some object invisible to me from the back of the deck chair. His eyes, behind the thick perspex of his helmet, had a withdrawn look.

Three sharp pips in my right ear warned me that Simon Warwick was speaking on the intercom. "Quick!" he said. "To your right. WHAT ARE THEY? Over."

His voice was urgent, and turning in the direction he indicated I saw some two hundred dwarfish green creatures with hideously elongated glass heads advancing over the rim of a nearby crater.

"My God!" I cried hoarsely. "Roger out."

They were closer now, coming towards us at a curious loping run, and the utter silence of their approach combined with the tritium bombs that gleamed dully at their waists in the thin Venusian sunlight lent them an oddly menacing air. "Calling Strong," I breathed into my mouthpiece, and I confess that it was all I could do to keep my voice steady. "Have you seen them? Over."

Never have I admired the man more. With barely a glance at the intruders he continued his patient sifting of meteoric dust through a borrowed hair net. "Ask them what they want," was all he vouchsafed.

I took a pace forward and, putting on as bold a front as I could command, asked the Green Men by signs what we could do for them. Instantly they halted their ranks, and one who seemed by his dress and bearing to be their leader signed back as follows:

"Hear the word of Toom, Locum of Phut! We come in peace. Only render up unto us one amongst you, that the

portion of Minrah, Ruler of the Skies, may be accomplished. Else, all must perish."

When I had passed the grim message on to Philip Strong he made no comment, save to inquire idly why the sign language employed by these people was so quaintly archaic.

"I don't know," I told him, a little impatiently. "It is customary on many planets. The point is, what are we to do? Give them Hugh Trevose?"

"On no account," he said sharply, screwing a high-power magnifying glass on to the front of his helmet. "I have yet to ask that young man what he was doing between the hours of eight and nine, mean stellar time, this morning. Let them have Semolina."

"Semolina!" I gasped.

"Certainly. She is clearly innocent. She had nothing whatever to do with the murder of this unfortunate knight."

"But, Philip," I cried, with a gesture of my enormous gauntlets. . . .

The point will by this time be clear. Singleness of purpose, a steady, ruthless determination on the part of the detective to keep to the matter in hand, must be the guiding star for all who set their hands to the difficult task of interplanetary crime fiction. Had Philip Strong allowed one of his principal suspects to be handed over. . . . But I have said too much already. One does not want to give the whole thing away before publication.

The Chessplayers

CHARLES L. HARNESS

You have heard, I am sure, about those psychological experiments in which rats (and various other animals) learn how to thread a maze in order to get to the prize —a bit of cheese or something like it—at the proper exit. Well, here is one rat who learned what is probably the greatest "maze" the human mind has ever conceived—chess.

Impossible, you say? Not in science fiction—or, for that matter, not in Professor Schmidt's concentration camp, where Zeno the rat learned the game. In concentration camps, besides death *only* miracles can happen. . . .

No matter what you think about the hero of this story, read it for the thoroughly delightful picture it presents of life among the chess nuts. It is quite realistic, I am told by those who know about such things.

Now please understand this. I'm not saying that all chessplayers are lunatics. But I do claim that chronic chessplaying affects a man.

Let me tell you about the K Street Chess Club, of which I was once treasurer.

Our membership roll claimed a senator, the leader of a large labor union, the president of the A. & W. Railroad, and a few other big shots. But it seemed the more important they were *outside,* the rottener they were as chessplayers.

The senator and the rail magnate didn't know the Ruy Lopez from the Queen's Gambit, so of course they could only play the other fish, or hang around wistfully watching the games of the Class A players and wishing that they, too, amounted to something.

The club's champion was Bobby Baker, a little boy in the fourth grade at the Pestalozzi-Borstal Boarding School. Several of his end game compositions had been published in *Chess Review* and *Shakhmatny Russkji Zhurnal* before he could talk plainly.

Our second best was Pete Summers, a clerk for the A. & W. Railroad. He was the author of two very famous chess books. One book proved that white can always win, and the other proved that black can always draw. As you might suspect, the gap separating him from the president of his railroad was abysmal indeed.

The show position was held by Jim Bradley, a chronic idler whose dues were paid by his wife. The club's admiration for him was profound.

But experts don't make a club. You have to have some guiding spirit, a fairly good player, with a knack for organization and a true knowledge of values.

Such a gem we had in our secretary, Nottingham Jones.

It was really my interest in Nottingham that led me to join the K Street Chess Club. I wanted to see if he was an exception, or whether they were all alike.

After I tell you about their encounter with Zeno, you can judge for yourself.

In his unreal life Nottingham Jones was a statistician in a government bureau. He worked at a desk in a big room with many other desks, including mine, and he performed his duties blankly and without conscious effort. Many an afternoon, after the quitting bell had rung and I had strolled over to discuss club finances with him, he would be astonished to discover that he had already come to work and had turned out a creditable stack of forms.

I suppose that it was during these hours of his quasi-existence that the invisible Nottingham conceived those numerous events that had made him famous as a chess club emcee throughout the United States.

For it was Nottingham who organized the famous American-Soviet cable matches (in which the U.S. team had been so soundly trounced), refereed numerous U.S. match championships, and launched a dozen brilliant but impecunious foreign chess masters on exhibition tours in a hundred chess clubs from New York to Los Angeles.

But the achievements of which he was proudest were his bishop-knight tournaments.

Now the bishop is supposed to be slightly stronger than the knight, and this evaluation has become so ingrained in chess thinking today that no player will voluntarily exchange a bishop for an enemy knight. He may squander his life's savings on phony stock, talk back to traffic cops, and forget his wedding anniversary, but never, never, *never* will he exchange a bishop for a knight.

Nottingham suspected this fixation to be ill-founded; he had the idea that the knight was just as strong as the bishop, and to prove his point he held numerous intramural tournaments in the K Street Club, in which one player used six pawns and a bishop against the six pawns and a knight of his opponent.

Jones never did make up his mind as to whether the bishop was stronger than the knight, but at the end of a couple of years he did know that the K Street Club had more bishop-knight experts than any other club in the United States.

And it then occurred to him that American chess had a beautiful means of redeeming itself from its resounding defeat at the hands of the Russian cable team.

He sent his challenge to Stalin himself—the K Street Chess Club versus All the Russians—a dozen boards of bishop-knight games, to be played by cable.

The Soviet Recreation Bureau sent the customary six curt rejections and then promptly accepted.

And this leads us back to one afternoon at 5 o'clock when Nottingham Jones looked up from his desk and seemed startled to find me standing there.

"Don't get up yet," I said. "This is something you ought to take sitting down."

He stared at me owlishly. "Is the year's rent due again so soon?"

"Next week. This is something else."

"Oh?"

"A professor friend of mine," I said, "who lives in the garret over my apartment, wants to play the whole club at one sitting—a simultaneous exhibition."

"A simul, eh? Pretty good, is he?"

"It isn't exactly the professor who wants to play. It's really a friend of his."

"Is *he* good?"

"The professor says so. But that isn't exactly the point. To make it short, this professor, Dr. Schmidt, owns a pet rat. He wants the rat to play." I added: "And for the usual simul fee. The professor needs money. In fact, if he doesn't get a steady job pretty soon he may be deported."

Nottingham looked dubious. "I don't see how we can help him. Did you say *rat?*"

"I did."

"A chessplaying rat? A four-legged one?"

"Right. Quite a drawing card for the club, eh?"

Nottingham shrugged his shoulders. "We learn something every day. Will you believe it, I never heard they cared for the game. Women don't. However, I once read about an educated horse. . . . I suppose he's well known in Europe?"

"Very likely," I said. "The professor specializes in comparative psychology."

Nottingham shook his head impatiently. "I don't mean the professor. I'm talking about the rat. What's his name, anyway."

"Zeno."

"Never heard of him. What's his tournament score?"

"I don't think he ever played in any tournaments. The professor taught him the game in a concentration camp. How good he is I don't know, except that he can give the professor rook odds."

Nottingham smiled pityingly. "I can give you rook odds, but I'm not good enough to throw a simul."

A great light burst over me. "Hey, wait a minute. You're completely overlooking the fantastic fact that Zeno is a—"

"The only pertinent question," interrupted Nottingham, "is whether he's really in the *master* class. We've got half a dozen players in the club who can throw an 'inside' simul for free, but when we hire an outsider and charge the members a dollar each to play him, he's got to be good enough to tackle *our* best. And when the whole club's in training for the bishop-knight cable match with the Russians next month, I can't have them relaxing over a mediocre simul."

"But you're missing the whole point—"

"—which is, this Zeno needs money and you want me to throw a simul to help him. But I just can't do it. I have a duty to the members to maintain a high standard."

"But Zeno is a rat. He learned to play chess in a concentration camp. He—"

"That doesn't necessarily make him a good player."

It was all cockeyed. My voice trailed off. "Well, somehow it seemed like a good idea."

Nottingham saw that he had let me down too hard. "If you want to, you might arrange a game between Zeno and one of our top players—say, Jim Bradley. He has lots of time. If Jim says Zeno is good enough for a simul, we'll give him a simul."

So I invited Jim Bradley and the professor, including Zeno, to my apartment the next evening.

I had seen Zeno before, but that was when I thought he was just an ordinary pet rat. Viewed as a chessmaster he seemed to be a completely different creature. Both Jim and I studied him closely when the professor pulled him out of his coat pocket and placed him on the chess table.

You could tell, just by looking at the little animal, from the way his beady black eyes shone and the alert way he carried his head, that here was a super-rat, an Einstein among rodents.

"Chust let him get his bearings," said the professor, as he fixed a little piece of cheese to Bradley's king with a thumbtack. "And don't worry, he will make a good showing."

Zeno pitter-pattered around the board, sniffed with a bored delicacy at both his and Bradley's chess pieces, twitched his nose at Bradley's cheese-crowned king, and gave the impression that the only reason he didn't yawn was that he was too well bred. He returned to his side of the board and waited for Bradley to move.

Jim blinked, shook himself, and finally pushed his queen pawn two squares.

Zeno minced out, picked up his own queen pawn between his teeth, and moved it forward two squares. Then Jim moved out his queen bishop pawn, and the game was under way, a conventional Queen's Gambit Declined.

I got the professor off in a corner. "How did you teach him to play? You never did tell me."

"Was easy. Tied each chessman in succession to body and let Zeno run simple maze on the chessboard composed of movies of chessman, until reached king and got piece of bread stuck on crown. Next, ve—one moment, please."

We both looked at the board. Zeno had knocked over Jim's king and was tapping with his dainty forefoot in front of the fallen monarch.

Jim was counting the taps with silent lips. "He's announcing a mate in thirteen. And he's right."

Zeno was already nibbling at the little piece of cheese fixed to Jim's king.

When I reported the result to Nottingham the next day, he agreed to hold a simultaneous exhibition for Zeno. Since Zeno was an unknown, with no reputation and no drawing power, Jones naturally didn't notify the local papers, but merely sent post cards to the club members.

On the night of the simul, Nottingham set up 25 chess tables in an approximate circle around the club room. Here and there the professor pushed the tables a little closer together so that Zeno could jump easily from one to the other as he made his rounds. Then the professor made a circuit of all the tables and tacked a little piece of cheese to each king.

After that he mopped at his face, stepped outside the circle, and Zeno started his rounds.

And then we hit a snag.

A slow gray man emerged from a little group of spectators and approached the professor.

"Dr. Hans Schmidt?" he asked.

"Ya," said the professor, a little nervously. "I mean, yes sir."

The gray man pulled out his pocketbook and flashed something at the professor. "Immigration service. Do you have in your possession a renewed immigration visa?"

The professor wet his lips and shook his head wordlessly.

The other continued. "According to our records you don't have a job, haven't paid your rent for a month, and your credit has run out at the local delicatessen. I'm afraid I'll have to ask you to come along with me."

"You mean—*deportation?*"

"How do I know? Maybe, maybe not."

The professor looked as though a steam roller had just passed over him. "So it comes," he whispered. "I know I should not haf come out from hiding, but one needs money. . . ."

"Too bad," said the immigration man. "Of course, if you could post a $500 bond as surety for your self-support—"

"Had I $500, would I be behind at the delicatessen?"

"No, I guess not. That your hat and coat?"

The professor started sadly toward the coat racks.

I grabbed at his sleeve.

"Now hold on," I said hurriedly. "Look, mister, in two hours Dr. Schmidt will have a contract for a 52-week exhibition tour." I exclaimed to the professor: "Zeno will make you all the money you can spend! When the simul is over tonight, Nottingham Jones will recommend you to every chess club in the United States, Canada, and Mexico. Think of it! Zeno! History's only chess-playing rat!"

"Not so fast," said Nottingham, who had just walked up. "I've got to see how good this Zeno is before I back him."

"Don't worry," I said. "Why, the bare fact that he's a rat—"

The gray man interrupted. "You mean you want me to wait a couple of hours until we see whether the professor is going to get some sort of a contract?"

"That's right," I said eagerly. "After Zeno shows what he can do, the professor gets a chess exhibition tour."

The gray man was studying Zeno with distant distaste. "Well, okay. I'll wait."

The professor heaved a gigantic sigh and trotted off to watch his protégé.

"Say," said the gray man to me, "you people ought to keep a cat in this place. I was sure I saw a rat running around over there."

"That's Zeno," I said. "He's playing chess."

"Don't get sarcastic, Jack. I was just offering a suggestion." He wandered off to keep an eye on the professor.

The evening wore on, and the professor used up all his handkerchiefs and borrowed one of mine. But I couldn't see what he was worried about, because it was clear that Zeno was a marvel, right up there in the ranks of Lasker, Alekhine, and Botvinnik.

In every game, he entered into an orgy of complications. One by one his opponents teetered off the razor's edge, and had to resign. One by one the tables emptied, and the losers gathered around those who were still struggling. The clusters around Bobby Baker, Pete Summers, and Jim Bradley grew minute by minute.

But at the end of the second hour, when only the three club champions were still battling, I noticed that Zeno was slowing down.

"What's wrong, professor?" I whispered anxiously.

He groaned. "For supper he chenerally gets only two little pieces cheese.

And so far tonight Zeno had eaten twenty-three! He was so fat he could hardly waddle.

I groaned too, and thought of tiny stomach pumps.

We watched tensely as Zeno pulled himself slowly from Jim Bradley's board over to Pete Summers'. It seemed to take him an extraordinarily long time to analyze the position on Pete's board. At last he made his move and crawled across to Bobby Baker's table.

And it was there, chin resting on the pedestal of his king rook, that he collapsed into gentle rodent slumber.

The professor let out an almost inaudible but heart-rending moan.

"Don't just stand there!" I cried. "Wake him up!"

The professor prodded the little animal gingerly with his forefinger. *"Liebchen,"* he pleaded, *"wach' auf!"*

But Zeno just rolled comfortably over on his back.

A deathly silence had fallen over the room, and it was on account of this that we heard what we heard.

Zeno began to snore.

Everybody seemed to be looking in other directions when the professor lifted the little animal up and dropped him tenderly into his wrinkled coat pocket.

The gray man was the first to speak. "Well, Dr. Schmidt? No contract?"

"Don't be silly," I declared. "Of course he gets a tour. Nottingham, how soon can you get letters off to the other clubs?"

"But I really can't recommend him," demurred Nottingham. "After all, he defaulted three out of 25 games. He's only a *Kleinmeister*—not the kind of material to make a simul circuit."

"What if he *didn't* finish three measly games? He's a good player, all the same. All you have to do is say the word and every club secretary in North America will make a date with him—at an entrance fee of $5 per player. He'll take the country by storm!"

"I'm sorry," Nottingham said to the professor. "I have a certain standard, and your boy just doesn't make the grade."

The professor sighed. *"Ja, ich versteh'."*

"But this is crazy!" My voice sounded a little louder than I had intended. "You fellows don't agree with Nottingham, do you? How about you, Jim?"

Jim Bradley shrugged his shoulders. "Hard to say just how good Zeno is. It would take a week of close analysis to say definitely who has the upper hand in *my* game. He's a pawn down, but he has a wonderful position."

"But Jim," I protested. "That isn't the point at all. Can't you see it? Think of the publicity . . . a chess-playing rat . . .!"

"I wouldn't know about his personal life," said Jim curtly.

"Fellows!" I said desperately. "Is this the way all of you feel? Can't enough of us stick together to pass a club resolution recommending Zeno for a simul circuit? How about you, Bobby?"

Bobby looked uncomfortable. "I think the school station

wagon is waiting for me. I guess I ought to be getting back."

"Coming, doc?" asked the gray man.

"Yes," replied Dr. Schmidt heavily. "Good evening, chentlemen."

I just stood there, stunned.

"Here's Zeno's income for the evening, professor," said Nottingham, pressing an envelope into his hand. "I'm afraid it won't help much, though, especially since I didn't feel justified in charging the customary dollar fee."

The professor nodded, and in numb silence I watched him accompany the immigration officer to the doorway.

The professor and I versus the chessplayers. We had thrown our Sunday punches, but we hadn't even scratched their gambit.

Just then Pete Summers called out. "Hey, Dr. Schmidt!" He held up a sheet of paper covered with chess diagrams. "This fell out of your pocket when you were standing here."

The professor said something apologetic to the gray man and came back. "*Danke*," he said, reaching for the paper. "Is part of a manuscript."

"A *chess* manuscript, professor?" I was grasping at straws now. "Are you writing a chess book?"

"Ya, I guess."

"Well, well," said Pete Summers, who was studying the sheet carefully. "The bishop against the knight, eh?"

"Ya. Now if you excuse me—"

"The bishop versus the knight?" shrilled Bobby Baker, who had trotted back to the tables.

"The bishop and knight?" muttered Nottingham Jones. He demanded abruptly: "Have you studied the problem long, professor?"

"Many months. In camp . . . in attic. And now manuscript has reached 2,000 pages, and we look for publisher."

"*We . . . ?*" My voice may have trembled a little, because both Nottingham and the professor turned and looked at me sharply. "Professor"—my words spilled out in a rush—"did Zeno write that book?"

"Who else?" answered the professor in wonder.

"I don't see how he could hold a pen," said Nottingham doubtfully.

"Not necessary," said the professor. "He made moves, and I wrote down." He added with wistful pride: "Zenchen is probably world's greatest living authority on bishop-knight."

The room was suddenly very still again. For an overlong

113

moment the only sound was Zeno's muffled snoring spiraling up from the professor's pocket.

"Has he reached any conclusions?" breathed Nottingham.

The professor turned puzzled eyes to the intent faces about him. "Zeno believes conflict cannot be cheneralized. However, has discovered 78 positions in which bishop superior to knight and 24 positions in which knight is better. Obviously, player mit bishop must try——"

"——for one of the winning bishop positions, of course, and ditto for the knight," finished Nottingham. "That's an extremely valuable manuscript."

All this time I had been getting my first free breath of the evening. It felt good. "It's too bad," I said casually, "that the professor can't stay here long enough for you sharks to study Zeno's book and pick up some pointers for the great bishop-knight cable match next month. It's too bad, too, that Zeno won't be here to take a board against the Russians. He'd give us a sure point on the score."

"Yeah," said Jim Bradley. "He would."

Nottingham shot a question at the professor. "Would Zeno be willing to rent the manuscript to us for a month?"

The professor was about to agree when I interrupted. "That would be rather difficult, Nottingham. Zeno doesn't know where he'll be at the end of the month. Furthermore, as treasurer for the club, let me inform you that after we pay the annual rent next week, the treasury will be as flat as a pancake."

Nottingham's face fell.

"Of course," I continued carefully, "if you were willing to underwrite a tour for Zeno, I imagine he'd be willing to lend it to you for nothing. And then the professor wouldn't have to be deported, and Zeno could stay and coach our team, as well as take a board in the cable match."

Neither the professor nor I breathed as we watched Nottingham struggling over that game of solitaire chess with his soul. But finally his owlish face gathered itself into an austere stubbornness. "I still can't recommend Zeno for a tour. I have my standards."

Several of the other players nodded gloomily.

"I'm scheduled to play against Kereslov," said Pete Summers, looking sadly at the sheet of manuscript. "But I agree with you, Nottingham."

I knew about Kereslov. The Moscow Club had been holding intramural bishop-knight tournaments every week for the past six months, and Kereslov had won nearly all of them.

"And I have to play Botvinnik," said Jim Bradley. He added feebly, "But you're right, Nottingham. We can't ethically underwrite a tour for Zeno."

Botvinnik was merely chess champion of the world.

"What a shame," I said. "Professor, I'm afraid we'll have to make a deal with the Soviet Recreation Bureau." It was just a sudden screwy inspiration. I still wonder whether I would have gone through with it if Nottingham hadn't said what he said next.

"Mister," he asked the immigration official, "you want $500 put up for Dr. Schmidt?"

"That's the customary bond."

Nottingham beamed at me. "We have more than that in the treasury, haven't we?"

"Sure. We have exactly $500.14, of which $500 is for rent. Don't look at me like that."

"The directors of this club," declared Nottingham sonorously, "hereby authorize you to draw a check for $500 payable to Dr. Schmidt."

"Are you cuckoo?" I yelped. "Where do you think I'm going to get another $500 for the rent? You lunatics will wind up playing your cable match in the middle of K Street!"

"This," said Nottingham coldly, "is the greatest work on chess since Murray's *History*. After we're through with it, I'm sure we can find a publisher for Zeno. Would you stand in the way of such a magnificent contribution to chess literature?"

Pete Summers chimed in accusingly. "Even if you can't be a friend to Zeno, you could at least think about the good of the club and of American chess. You're taking a very funny attitude about this."

"But of course you aren't a real chessplayer," said Bobby Baker sympathetically. "We never had a treasurer who was."

Nottingham sighed. "I guess it's about time to elect another treasurer."

"All right," I said bleakly. "I'm just wondering what I'm going to tell the landlord next week. He isn't a chessplayer either." I told the gray man, "Come over here to the desk, and I'll make out a check."

He frowned. "A check? From a bunch of chessplayers? Not on your life! Let's go, professor."

Just then a remarkable thing happened. One of our most minor members spoke up.

"I'm Senator Brown, one of Mr. Jones's *fellow chessplayers*. I'll endorse that check, if you like."

And then there was a popping noise and a button flew by my ear. I turned quickly to see a vast blast of smoke terminated by three perfect smoke rings. Our rail magnate tapped at his cigar. "I'm Johnson, of the A. & W. *We chessplayers* stick together on these matters. I'll endorse that check, too. And Nottingham, don't worry about the rent. The senator and I will take care of that."

I stifled an indignant gasp. *I* was the one worrying about the rent, not Nottingham. But of course I was beneath their notice. I wasn't a *chessplayer*.

The gray man shrugged his shoulders. "Okay, I'll take the bond and recommend an indefinite renewal."

Five minutes later I was standing outside the building gulping in the fresh cold air when the immigration officer walked past me toward his car.

"Good night," I said.

He ducked a little, then looked up. When he answered, he seemed to be talking more to himself than to me. "It was the funniest thing. You got the impression there was a little rat running around on those boards and moving the pieces with his teeth. But of course rats don't play chess. Just human beings." He peered at me through the dusk, as though trying to get things in focus. "There wasn't really a rat playing chess in there, was there?"

"No," I said. "There wasn't any rat in there. And no human beings, either. Just chessplayers."

What's the Name of That Town?

R. A. LAFFERTY

Being no Greek scholar, I am unable to enlighten you
as to the meaning of Epiktistes, the name of the inani-
mate hero (if there is one) of this story. All I can tell
you is that he is a very minor invention compared to the
one that goes back to sleep again after being kicked at the
end of this tale. Now *there's* an invention that would
solve a lot of the world's problems in a hurry if someone
would only invent it!

Anyhow, hold on to your sanity as you read this
fable. It's unsettling!

"Epiktistes tells me that you are onto something big, Mr.
Smirnov," Valery said, turning to her companion.

"Epikt has the loudest mouth of any machine I was ever
associated with," Gregory Smirnov growled. "I never saw
one that could keep a secret. But this one goes to extremes.
Actually, we don't have a thing. We're just fiddling around
with an unborn idea."

"How about it, Epikt?" Valery asked.

"Big, real big," the machine issued.

"What are you doing now, Epikt?" Valery wanted to know.

"Talk to me, dammit! I'm the man, he's the machine,"
Smirnov cut in. "He's chewing encyclopedias and other references. It's all he ever does."

"I thought he went through them all long ago."

"Certainly, dozens of times. He has all the data that can
be fed into a machine, and every day we shovel in bales of
the new stuff. But he's chewing it now for a very different
purpose."

"What different purpose, Mr. Smirnov?"

"It's difficult to say because I haven't as yet been able to
state it to him. We're trying to set a problem where it seems
there ought to be one—and then answer it. We may find

the answer before the question. At first he rejected my request, later he accepted it—ironically. I doubt that he's sincere now. He can be quite a clown, as you should well know."

"I know that you two are onto something good," Valery said. "The more you deny it, the more I'm sure of it. Tell me the truth, Epikt."

"Big, real big," Epiktistes issued to Valery.

"Valery," said Smirnov. "You're a woman and you might be inclined to say something about this to the other Institute people. Please don't. We don't have anything yet and it makes me nervous to have hot little people breathing down my neck."

"I won't say a word," Valery swore with grave insincerity. She winked at the machine, and Epikt winked back at her with three tiers of eyes. Valery Mok and Epiktistes had a thing going with each other.

Valery was nearly as bad as a machine at not being able to keep a secret. She had the whole Institute staff excited about what Smirnov and Epiktistes were working on. The staff consisted of Charles Cogsworth, her own over-shadowed husband, Glasser, the stiff-necked inventor, and Aloysius Shiplap, the seminal genius.

They were all after Smirnov and his machine the next day.

"We've been together on every project," Glasser said. "Valery tells us that the problem hasn't been properly formulated, and that Epikt has only accepted it ironically. We're pretty good at formulating problems, Gregory, and a little sterner than you, when it comes to dealing with clownish machines."

"All right, this is the way it is, Glasser," Smirnov said reluctantly. "My first statement was, we should seek to discover something not known to exist, by a close study of the absence of evidence. When I put the problem to Epiktistes in this generalized form he just laughed at me."

"That would have been my first impulse too, Smirnov," said Shiplap. "Don't you have a better idea of what you're looking for?"

"Shiplap, I had the feeling of trying to remember something that I'd been compelled to forget. My second statement wasn't much better. 'Let us see,' I said to Epikt, 'if we cannot reconstruct something of which even the idea has been completely eradicated, let's see if we can't find it by considering the excessive evidence that it was never there.' In this form,

Epikt accepted it. Or else he decided to go along with me for the gag. I'm never quite sure how this clanking machine takes things."

"Well, no hole can be filled up perfectly," said Cogsworth. "There will either be too much or too little of whatever is being used as the filler, or it will be of a different texture. The difficulty is that you didn't give Epikt any clues. There will be a million things forgotten or repressed that will show an irregularity of fill. How will Epikt know which of them is the one that you are somehow trying to remember?"

"Item. The buried thing will have a buried tie with my boss man Smirnov," Epiktistes, the machine, issued.

"Yes, of course," said Glasser. "Has Epikt turned up anything?"

"Only a bushelful of things that seem to mean nothing," said Smirnov sadly.

"Item. Why, in Hungarian dictionary-encyclopedias of a certain period, is there padding between the words Sik and Sikamlos?" Epiktistes asked.

"I follow your thought, Epikt," Glasser agreed. "That could be a clue to something. If the idea and the name of something were expunged from every reference, then, in all original editions, other subjects on the same page would have to be padded slightly or another subject set in. This filling might be hurried, and therefore of an inferior quality. So, who knows a word that is no longer used and that comes between Sik and Sikamlos? If we knew the word would we know what it meant? And would it help us if we did?"

"Item. Why is the young of a bear now referred to as a pup when once it may have been known as a cube?" Epikt issued.

"I've never heard the young of a bear referred to as a cube," Shiplap protested.

"Epikt has come on that by our omission-appraisal method," Smirnov explained. "There is probably an imperfect erasure working. I believe that cube is a distortion of a word that has somehow been forced out of folk memory. Epikt has this clue from a ballad which I believe is far removed from the main suppression or it would not have survived in even this distorted form."

"Item. Why is the awkward word Coronal used for the simple doubling or return of a rope? Why is not a simpler word used?" Epikt asked.

"Has Epikt considered that seamen have always used odd

terms and that landsmen often adopt them?" Cogsworth asked.

"Naturally—Epikt always considers everything," Smirnov answered. "He has thousands of these items now, and he believes that he will be able to put them into a pattern."

"Item. Why is there a great hiatus in period jazz? It's as though a great hunk of it had been yanked out by the roots, in the words of one Benny B-Flat."

"Smirnov, I know that your machine has unusual talents," said Glasser, "but if he can tie these things together he's a concatenated genius."

"Or a cantankerous clown," Smirnov said. "I know that he has to have some emotional release from the stress of his work, but he often overdoes it with humor and drollery."

"Item. Why is reference to the Amerindian peace pipe avoided as though some obscenity were attached to it, and none is discoverable?"

"That's a new one while we're standing here," said Smirnov. "He's accumulating quite a few of them."

"Item. Why is—?" Epikt started.

"Oh, shut up and get back to work," Smirnov ordered his machine. "Let's leave him with it until tomorrow, folks. It may begin to pull together by then," said Smirnov, stalking off.

"Going to be real big," Epiktistes issued to them after his boss man had left. "Boys and girls, it's going to be real big."

The next day they combined the meeting around the machine with a party for Shiplap. Aloysius Shiplap had grown—for the first time ever, anywhere—left-handed grass. It was not called that because it whorled to the left, but because the organic constituents of it were reversed in their construction. Left-handed minerals had been constructed long since, and perhaps they also occurred in nature. Left-handed bacteria and broths were long known, but nobody else had ever grown anything as complex as left-handed grass.

"In everything, its effect is reversed," Shiplap explained. "Cattle pastured on this would lose rather than gain weight. If there ever develops a market for really skinny cattle I'll be waiting for it."

They tossed off a good bit of Tosher's Gin as they got into the celebration. Tosher's is the only drink that will buzz up both humans and Ktistec machines. There is a flavoring used in Tosher's that gets machines high. The alcohol in it sometimes has a similar effect on humans.

Epiktistes got as mellow as a Pottawattamie County pumpkin. Ktistec machines are like the Irish and the Indians. They start unwinding when the gin begins to flow. Their behavior could become quite wild unless carefully watched.

And the Institute people were also having a good time.

"I wouldn't have him any other way," said Smirnov. "When he relaxes, he relaxes all over the place. Hawkin's machine literally bites people when it's frustrated by a difficult problem. Drexel's smaller machine comes all apart throwing arc snuffers and solenoids and is mighty dangerous to be around. There are worse sorts than this clown of a machine I have—though he does get pretty slushy when he's in his cups."

Valery Mok had gathered up a bunch of Epiktistes' utterances and slipped them into cocktail cookies. Glasser, eating one, chewed on a bit of the metallic tape. He pulled it, slithering, off his tongue, and read—

"Item. What was the mysterious name written by a deaf moron on the wall of the men's room in an institution in Vinita, Oklahoma?"

Epiktistes giggled, though the item may have been serious when he issued it.

Cogsworth pulled one out of his mouth, stripping the crumbs from it with his tongue as it came.

"Item. Why does Petit Larousse take five lines too many to say almost nothing about the ancient Chibcha Indians of Columbia?"

At this point Valery went into her high laugh that would even make the alphabet sound funny.

Shiplap pulled one out of his grinning mouth, and it seemed an extension of his grin as it came.

"Item," he read. "What is there about the Great Blue Island Swamp that puzzles geologists? Or—in the old bylining manner—how recent is recent?"

Tosher's is giggle juice. Glasser's laughter sounded like a string of firecrackers going off.

Smirnov extracted the utterance from his cookie in the lordly manner. He read the utterance as though it were of extreme importance—and it was.

"Item. What peculiarity is almost revealed by the faded paint of old Rock Island and Pacific Railroad boxcars?"

"Oh, stop giggling, Epikt, it isn't as funny as that!"

"It is, it is!" bubbled Valery. Then she nearly choked bringing out from her own cookie a very long tape, and she read it with a very gay voice:

"Item. Why, when the gruesome Little Willy verses were

revived among sub-teen-agers in the early nineteen-eighties, were they concerned almost entirely with chewing gum? In their Australian and British homelands six decades before, they were concerned with everything. But here we have gruesome verses about forty-nine different flavors of gum. As for instance,

> Little Willy mixed his gum
> with bits of Baby's cerebrum
> and Papa's blood for Juicy
>   Fruit.
> Mother said, "Oh, Will, don't
>   duit."

"I'd think it would give too high a flavor to the gum," said Glasser.

It's a lot of fun to open cocktail cookies and read out utterances of a Ktistic machine. The Institute staff generated a bunch of what we can only call merriment. But they were busy people, and the party had to come to an end. Epiktistes issued a verse as they prepared to leave.

> When the world's last Tosher's
>   is drunken,
> and the world's last item has
>   flewn,
> and the Institute people are
>   stunken,
> and Epikt is high as the—

And there he stuck! Eight million billion billion memory contacts he had in him, and he couldn't come up with a rime for flewn.

"How many items have you really gathered, Epikt?" Glasser asked as they began to break up.

"Millions of them, bub, millions of them."

"No. Actually he has about three-quarters of a million that he believes he can tie together," Smirnov explained. "I feel that he'll bring them into a pattern, but I'm afraid that it will be a facetious one."

"Epikt, you cute cubicle, will you be able to give us any idea of what to look for by tomorrow?" Valery asked.

"Boys and girls, I'll have it all wrapped up and on display for you tomorrow," Epiktistes issued. "I'll even be able to tell you what the thing smelled like."

Expectation ran high among the people of the Institute. Epiktistes wanted to have the reporters in, but Smirnov said no. He didn't trust his machine. Epikt was a cube twenty meters on a side; and of his thousands of eyes, some of them always seemed to be laughing at his master.

"It won't be a hoax?" Smirnov asked his machine apprehensively.

"Boss, did I ever hoax you?" Epikt issued.

"Yes."

"Boss, some things are best presented in the guise of a hoax, but underneath this won't be one."

It was a crooked-tongued machine sometimes, and Smirnov was more apprehensive than ever.

The next day everyone gathered early to hear what Epikt had to say. They pulled up chairs and recording canisters and waited for the machine to begin.

"Ladies, gentlemen, associates," said Epikt solemnly, "we are gathered together to hear of an important matter. I will present it as well as I am able. There will be disbelief, I know, but I am sure of my facts. Make yourselves comfortable." He paused and then as an afterthought added— "You may smoke."

"You clanking cubicle, don't tell us what we may do," Smirnov screamed. "You're only a machine that I made."

"You and three thousand other workers," issued Epikt, without blinking an eye, "and in the final stages, the important stages, I directed my own assembly. I could not have happened otherwise. Only I know what is in me. As to my own abilities—"

"Get on with it, Epikt," Smirnov ordered, "and try to avoid the didactic manner."

"Then to get to the point—in the year 1980, the largest City of the American Midland was destroyed by an unnatural disaster."

"That was only twenty years ago," Glasser cut in. "It seems that someone would have heard of it."

"I wonder if St. Louis knew that she was destroyed," Valery ventured. "She acts as though she thought that she were still there."

"St. Louis was not the City," issued Epikt. "This destruction of a metropolitan area of seven million persons in much less than seven seconds was a great horror from the human viewpoint—come to think of it I now recall being a little disturbed by it myself. The thing was so fearful that it was decided to suppress the whole business and blissfully forget about it."

"Wouldn't that be a little difficult?" said Aloysius Shiplap sarcastically.

"It was very difficult to do," issued Epikt, "and yet it was done, completely, within twenty hours. And from that moment until this, nobody has remembered or thought about it at all."

"And if Your Whimsical Highness will just explain how this was done?" Smirnov challenged his machine.

"I'll explain as well as I can, good master. The project was put in charge of a master scientist who shall be nameless—but only for a few minutes."

"How were the written references of a metropolis of seven million persons obliterated?" asked Cogsworth.

"By a device then newly invented by our master scientist," Epikt answered. "It was known as the Tele-Pantographic Distorter. Even I from this distance of time and through the cloud of induced amnesia, cannot understand how it worked. But it *did* work, and it simultaneously destroyed all printed references to our subject. This left holes in the references, and the flow of matter to fill those holes was sometimes of inferior texture, as I have noted. Holographic—that is handwritten, for you, Valery—references were more difficult. Most were simply destroyed. In more important documents, the text was flowed in automatic writing to fill the hole, and in close imitation of the original handwriting. But these imitations were often imperfect. I have a few thousand instances of this. But the Tele-Pantographic Distorter was a truly remarkable machine, and I regret that it is now out of use."

"Kindly explain what happened to this remarkable machine," said Smirnov.

"Oh, it's still here in the Institute. You stumble into it a dozen times a day, good master, and you curse it as 'That Damnable Pile of Junk,' " issued Epikt. "But you have a block that will not allow you to remember what it is."

"I believe that I have been stumbling into such a pile of junk for many years," mused Smirnov. "Several times I have almost permitted myself to wonder what it was."

"And you invented it. The master scientist of the memory-obliteration was yourself, Gregory Smirnov."

"Hog hang it, Epikt! Your jug will leak!" protested Shiplap. "How of the human memories? The seven million inhabitants of the city would have had relatives of at least an equal number elsewhere. Didn't they wonder about their mothers or children or brothers and sisters?"

"They sorrowed, but they didn't wonder," issued Epikt. "It was a sorrow to which they could really give no name. Examine the period and see how many really sad songs were popular in the years 1980 and 1981. But broadcast euphoria soon masked it over. The human memory of the thing was blocked by induced world amnesia. This was done hypnotically over the broadcast waves, and over more subtle waves. Few escaped it. The deaf moron mentioned in one of my items was one of those few. He scrawled the name of the town on a wall once, but it meant nothing to anyone."

"But there would be a hundred million loose ends to clean up," Glasser protested.

"Raise that number several powers," issued Epikt. "There were very many loose ends, and most of them were taken care of. I gathered a million or so that remained in the process of this study, but they could not break through the induced amnesia. The door was bolted on the whole subject. Then it was double-locked. It was necessary to destroy not only the memory, but also the memory of that memory. Mr. Smirnov, in what was perhaps his greatest feat, put himself under the final hypnosis against it. It was his job to pull in the hole after them all. But it bothered him more than others because he was more involved in it. After this temporary explanation it will bother him no more. This time he will forget it with a clear conscience.

"He does not recognize or remember it even now. It was his intent and triumph that he never should. The city and its destruction are forgotten forever, but the *method* of that memory-obliteration has only been forced to a subliminal level. It will be resurrected and used again whenever there is a great unnatural disaster."

"And where in tarnation or the American Midlands was this city?" Cogsworth hollered.

"Its site is now known as the Great Blue Island Swamp," issued Epikt.

"Finish it, you goggle-eyed gadget!" Shiplap shrilled. "What's the name of that town?"

"Chicago," issued Epiktistes.

That broke it! That tore it clear up! It was a hoax after all. That clattering clown of a cubicle had led them into it with all eyes open. Valery went into her high laughter, and her good husband Cogsworth chortled like that gooney bird with the hiccups.

"Chicago! It sounds like a little zoo beaver sliding down a mud slide and hitting the water. Chicago!" It was the funniest word Valery had ever heard.

"Nobody but a machine gone comic could coin a name like that," laughed Glasser with his fire-cracker laugh. "Chicago!"

"I take my hat off to you, Epiktistes," said Aloysius Shiplap. "You are a cog-footed, tongue-in-cheek tall tale teller. People, this machine is ripe!"

"I'm a little disappointed," said Smirnov. "So the mountain labored and produced a mouse. But did it have to be a wall-eyed mouse in a clown suit, Epikt? It's too tall even for a tale. That a great city could be completely destroyed only twenty years ago and we know nothing about it—that's tall enough. But that it should have the impossible name of Chicago tops it all. If you weighed all possible sounds—and I'm sure that you did, Epikt—you could not come up with a more ridiculous sounding name than that."

"Good people, it is meant to be this way," issued Epiktistes. "You cannot remember it. You cannot recognize it. And when you leave this room you will not even be able to recall the funny name. You will have only the dim impression that the clownish machine played a clownish trick on you. The disasters—for I suspect that there were several such—are well forgotten. The world would lie down and die if it remembered them too well.

"And yet there really was a large city named Chicago. As Sikago it left a hole in one Hungarian dictionary-encyclopedia; and the Petit Larousse had to flow French froth about the Chibcha Indians into the place where Chicago had stood. Something, for which I find the tentative name of Chicago Hot, was pulled out of the jazz complex by the roots. The Calumet River had flowed about the City somewhere, so there came a reluctance to use that name of the old Indian peace pipe. Chicago was a great city. The heart of her downtown was known as the Loop, and one of her baseball teams was named the Cubs. For that reason those two words were forced out of use. They might be evocative."

"Loop? Cubs?" giggled Valery. "Those words are almost as funny as Chicago. How do you make them up, Epikt?"

"In popular capsule impression Chicago was the chewing-gum capital of the world. The leader in this manufacture was a man named—as well as I can reconstruct it—Wiggly. Children somehow found the echoes of the gruesome destruction of Chicago and tied it in with this capsule impression to produce the bloody Little Willy verses about chewing gum."

"Epikt, you top yourself," said Shiplap, "if anything could top an invention as funny as Chicago."

"Good people, it comes down over you like a curtain," issued Epiktistes. "You forget again—even my joke, even the funny name of the town. And, more to the point, I forget also.

"It's gone. Gone. All gone. How peculiar! It is a long blank tape you all stare at as though you were under hypnosis. I must have suffered a blackout. I never issued a blank tape before. Smirnov, I have the taste in my terminals of an experiment that didn't quite come off. Feed me another. I don't fail often."

"That is enough for today, Epiktistes. We are all sleepy for some reason. No it didn't work out—whatever it was. I forget what it was that we were working on. It doesn't matter. Our failures are well forgot. We'll hit on something else. We're working on a lot of things."

Then they all shuffled out sleepily and went back to their work. Smirnov's machine had busted on something or other, but it was a good machine and would hit the next time, of that they were sure.

In a corridor, Smirnov stumbled into his old Tele-Pantographic Distorter. He had been stumbling unseeing into it every day for twenty years.

The machine rolled nine banks of eyes at Smirnov and smiled willingly. Was it another of those disasters? Was there any deep work to be done? Tele-Pan was ready. But no. Smirnov passed on. The machine smiled again and went peacefully back to sleep.

"That damnable piece of junk," Smirnov growled, walking along and petting his sore shin. "I feel almost as if I were on the verge of wondering what it is."

Rump-Titty-Titty-Tum-TAH-Tee

FRITZ LEIBER

Is black magic scientific? Can an African witch doctor, a "five-greats-grandfather" of one of the protagonists in this story, infect our modern world with a sinister symbolic syndrome somewhat like, but much worse than, the dancing mania of the Middle Ages? Mr. Leiber says, "Yes, indeed!"—and in the process of saying so has written a sharp spoof on subliminal advertising, modern art, "happenings," and many other aspects of our mass-communication-crazed society.

Once upon a time, when just for an instant all the molecules in the world and in the collective unconscious mind got very slippery, so that just for an instant something could pop through from the past or the future or other places, six very important intellectual people were gathered together in the studio of Simon Grue, the accidental painter.

There was Tally B. Washington, the jazz drummer. He was beating softly on a gray hollow African log and thinking of a composition he would entitle "Duet for Water Hammer and Whistling Faucet."

There were Lafcadio Smits, the interior decorator, and Lester Phlegius, the industrial designer. They were talking very intellectually together, but underneath they were wishing very hard that they had, respectively, a really catchy design for modernistic wallpaper and a really new motif for industrial advertising.

There were Gorius James McIntosh, the clinical psychologist, and Norman Saylor, the cultural anthropologist. Gorius James McIntosh was drinking whisky and wishing there were a psychological test that would open up patients a lot wider than the Rorschach or the TAT, while Norman Saylor was smoking a pipe but not thinking or drinking anything especially.

It was a very long, very wide, very tall studio. It had to be, so there would be room on the floor to spread flat one of Simon Grue's canvases, which were always big enough to dominate any exhibition with yards to spare, and room under the ceiling for a very tall, very strong scaffold.

The present canvas hadn't a bit of paint on it, not a spot or a smudge or a smear, except for the bone-white ground. On top of the scaffold were Simon Grue and twenty-seven big pots of paint and nine clean brushes, each eight inches wide. Simon Grue was about to have a new accident—a semi-controlled accident, if you please. Any minute now he'd plunge a brush in one of the cans of paint and raise it over his right shoulder and bring it forward and down with a great loose-wristed snap, as if he were cracking a bullwhip, and a great fissioning gob of paint would go *splaaAAT* on the canvas in a random, chance, arbitrary, spontaneous and therefore quintuply accidental pattern which would constitute the core of the composition and determine the form and rhythm for many, many subsequent splatters and maybe even a few contact brush strokes and impulsive smearings.

As the rhythm of Simon Grue's bouncy footsteps quickened, Norman Saylor glanced up, though not apprehensively. True, Simon had been known to splatter his friends as well as his canvases, but in anticipation of this Norman was wearing a faded shirt, old sneakers and the frayed tweed suit he'd sported as assistant instructor, while his fishing hat was within easy reach. He and his armchair were crowded close to a wall, as were the other four intellectuals. This canvas was an especially large one, even for Simon.

As for Simon, pacing back and forth atop his scaffold, he was experiencing the glorious intoxication and expansion of vision known only to an accidental painter in the great tradition of Wassily Kandinsky, Robert Motherwell, and Jackson Pollock, when he is springily based a good twenty feet above a spotless, perfectly prepared canvas. At moments like this he was especially grateful for these weekly gatherings. Having his five especial friends on hand helped create the right intellectual milieu. He listened happily to the hollow rhythmic thrum of Tally's drumming, the multisyllabic rippling of Lester's and Lafcadio's conversation, the gurgle of Gorius' whisky bottle, and happily watched the mystic curls of Norman's pipe-smoke. His entire being, emotions as well as mind, was a blank tablet, ready for the kiss of the universe.

Meanwhile, the instant was coming closer and closer when

129

all the molecules in the world and in the collective unconscious mind would get very slippery.

Tally B. Washington, beating on his African log, had a feeling of oppression and anticipation, almost (but not quite) a feeling of apprehension. One of Tally's ancestors, seven generations back, had been a Dahomey witch doctor, which is the African equivalent of an intellectual with artistic and psychiatric leanings. According to a very private family tradition, half joking, half serious, this five-greats-grandfather of Tally had discovered a Jumbo Magic which could "lay holt" of the whole world and bring it under its spell, but he had perished before he could try the magic or transmit it to his sons. Tally himself was altogether skeptical about the Jumbo Magic, but he couldn't help wondering about it wistfully from time to time, especially when he was beating on his African log and hunting for a new rhythm. The wistful feeling came to him right now, building on the feeling of oppression and anticipation, and his mind became a tablet blank as Simon's.

The slippery instant arrived.

Simon seized a brush and plunged it deep in the pot of black paint. Usually he used black for a final splatter if he used it at all, but this time he had the impulse to reverse himself.

Of a sudden Tally's wrists lifted high, hands dangling loosely, almost like a marionette's. There was a dramatic pause. Then his hands came down and beat out a phrase on the log, loudly and with great authority.

*Rump-titty-titty-tum-*TAH*-tee!*

Simon's wrist snapped and the middle air was full of free-falling paint which hit the canvas in a fast series of *splaaAATs* which was an exact copy of Tally's phrase.

*Rump-titty-titty-tum-*TAH*-tee!*

Intrigued by the identity of the two sounds, and with their back hairs lifting a little for the same reason, the five intellectuals around the wall rose and stared, while Simon looked down from his scaffold like God after the first stroke of creation.

The big black splatter on the bone-white ground was itself an exact copy of Tally's phrase, sound made sight, music transposed into visual pattern. First there was a big roundish blot —that was the *rump*. Then two rather delicate, many-tongued splatters—those were the *titties*. Next a small *rump*, which was the *tum*. Following that, a big blot like a bent spearhead, not so big as the *rump* but even more emphatic—the TAH.

Last of all an indescribably curled and broken little splatter which somehow seemed exactly right for the *tee*.

The whole big splatter was as like the drummed phrase as an identical twin reared in a different environment and as fascinating as a primeval symbol found next to bison paintings in a Cro-Magnon cave. The six intellectuals could hardly stop looking at it and when they did, it was to do things in connection with it, while their minds were happily a-twitter with all sorts of exciting new projects.

Simon's wide-angle camera was brought into play on the scaffold and negatives were immediately developed and prints made in the darkroom adjoining the studio. Each of Simon's friends carried at least one print when he left. They smiled at each other like men who share a mysterious but powerful secret. More than one of them drew his print from under his coat on the way home and hungrily studied it.

At the gathering next week there was much to tell. Tally had introduced the phrase at a private jam session and on his live jazz broadcast. The jam session had improvised on and developed the phrase for two solid hours and the musicians had squeaked with delight when Tally finally showed them the photograph of what they had been playing, while the response from the broadcast had won Tally a new sponsor with a fat pocketbook.

Gorius McIntosh had got phenomenal results from using the splatter as a Rorschach inkblot. His star patient had seen her imagined incestuous baby in it and spilled more in one session than in the previous hundred and forty. Stubborn blocks in two analyses had been gloriously broken, while three catatonics at the state hospital had got up and danced.

Lester Phlegius rather hesitantly described how he was using "something like the splatter, really not too similar" (he said) as an attention-getter in a forthcoming series of Industrial-Design-for-Living advertisements.

Lafcadio Smits, who had an even longer and more flagrant history of stealing designs from Simon, brazenly announced that he had reproduced the splatter as a silk-screen pattern on linen. The pattern was already selling like hot-cakes at five arty gift shops, while at this very moment three girls were sweating in Lafcadio's loft turning out more. He braced himself for a blast from Simon, mentally rehearsing the attractive deal he was prepared to offer, one depending on percentages of percentages, but the accidental painter was strangely abstracted. He seemed to have something weighing on his mind.

The new painting hadn't progressed any further than the first splatter.

Norman Saylor quizzed him about it semi-privately.

"I've developed a sort of artist's block," Simon confessed to him with relief. "Whenever I pick up a brush I get afraid of spoiling that first tremendous effect and I don't go on." He paused. "Another thing—I put down papers and tried some small test-splatters. They all looked almost exactly like the big one. Seems my wrist won't give out with anything else." He laughed nervously. "How are you cashing in on the thing, Norm?"

The anthropologist shook his head. "Just studying it, trying to place it in the continuum of primitive signs and universal dream symbols. It goes very deep. But about this block and this . . . er . . . fancied limitation of yours—I'd just climb up there tomorrow morning and splatter away. The big one's been photographed, you can't lose that."

Simon nodded doubtfully and then looked down at his wrist and quickly grabbed it with his other hand, to still it. It had been twitching in a familiar rhythm.

If the tone of the gathering after the first week was enthusiastic, that after the second was euphoric. Tally's new drummed theme had given rise to a musical fad christened Drum 'n' Drag which promised to rival Rock 'n' Roll, while the drummer himself was in two days to appear as a guest artist on a network TV program. The only worry was that no new themes had appeared. All the Drum 'n' Drag pieces were based on duplications or, at most, developments of the original drummed phrase. Tally also mentioned with an odd reluctance that a few rabid cats had taken to greeting each other with a four-handed patty-cake that beat out *rump-titty-titty-tum*-TAH-*tee*.

Gorius McIntosh was causing a stir in psychiatric circles with his amazing successes in opening up recalcitrant cases, many of them hitherto thought fit for nothing but eventual lobotomy. Colleagues with M.D.'s quit emphasizing the lowly "Mister" in his name, while several spontaneously addressed him as "Doctor" as they begged him for copies of the McSPAT) McIntosh's Splatter Pattern Apperception Test). His name had been mentioned in connection with the assistant directorship of the clinic where he was a humble psychologist. In closing, he mentioned that some of the state patients had taken to pommeling each other playfully while happily spouting some gibberish variant of the original phrase, such as *"Bump-biddy-biddy-bum*-BAH-*bee!"* The resemblance in be-

132

havior to Tally's hepcats was noted and remarked on by the six intellectuals.

The first of Lester Phlegius' attention-getters (identical with the splatter, of course) had appeared and attracted the most favorable notice, meaning chiefly that his customer's front office had received at least a dozen curious phone calls from the directors and presidents of cognate firms. Lafcadio Smits reported that he had rented a second loft, was branching out into dress materials, silk neckties, lampshades and wallpaper, and was deep in royalty deals with several big manufacturers. Once again Simon Grue surprised him by not screaming robbery and demanding details and large simple percentages. The accidental painter seemed even more unhappily abstracted than the week before.

When he ushered them from his living quarters into the studio they understood why.

It was as if the original big splatter had whelped. Surrounding and overlaying it were scores of smaller splatters. They were all colors of a well-chosen artist's spectrum, blending with each other and pointing each other up superbly. But each and every one of them was a perfect copy, reduced to one half or less, of the original big splatter.

Lafcadio Smits wouldn't believe at first that Simon had done them free-wrist from the scaffold. Even when Simon showed him details proving they couldn't have been stenciled, Lafcadio was still unwilling to believe, for he was deeply versed in methods of copying designs which had all the effects of spontaneity.

But when Simon wearily climbed the scaffold and, hardly looking at what he was doing, flipped down a few splatters exactly like the rest, even Lafcadio had to admit that something miraculous and frightening had happened to Simon's wrist.

Gorius James McIntosh shook his head and muttered a remark about "stereotyped compulsive behavior at the artistic-creative level. Never heard of it getting *that* stereotyped, though."

Later during the gathering, Norman Saylor again consulted with Simon and also had a long confidential talk with Tally B. Washington, during which he coaxed out of the drummer the whole story of his five-greats-grandfather. When questioned about his own researches, the cultural anthropologist would merely say that they were "progressing." He did, however, have one piece of concrete advice, which he delivered to all the five others just before the gathering broke up.

"This splatter does have an obsessive quality, just as Gory said. It has that maddening feeling of incompleteness which cries for repetition. It would be a good thing if each of us, whenever he feels the thing getting too strong a hold of him, would instantly shift to some engrossing activity which has as little as possible to do with arbitrarily ordered sight and sound. Try to set up a countercompulsion. One of us might even hit on a counterformula—a specific antidote."

If the ominous note of warning in Norman's statement didn't register on all of them just then, it did at some time during the next seven days, for the frame of mind in which the six intellectuals came to the gathering after the third week was one of paranoid grandeur and hysterical desperation.

Tally's TV appearance had been a huge success. He'd taken to the TV station a copy of the big splatter and although he hadn't intended to (he said) he'd found himself showing it to the M.C. and the unseen audience after his drum solo. The immediate response by phone, telegram, and letter had been overwhelming but rather frightening, including a letter from a woman in Smallhills, Arkansas, thanking Tally for showing her the "wondrous picture of God."

Drum 'n' Drag had become a national and even international craze. The patty-cake greeting had become general among Tally's rapidly-growing horde of fans and it now included a staggering slap on the shoulder to mark the TAH. (Here Gorius McIntosh took a drink from his bottle and interrupted to tell of a spontaneous, rhythmic, lock-stepping procession at the state hospital with an even more violent TAH-blow. The mad march had been forcibly broken up by attendants and two of the patients treated at the infirmary for contusions.) *The New York Times* ran a dispatch from South Africa describing how police had dispersed a disorderly mob of University of Cape-town students who had been chanting, *"Shlump Shliddy Shliddy Shlump* SHLAH *Shlee!"*—which the correspondents had been told was an anti-apartheid cry phrased in pig-Afrikaans.

For both the drummed phrase and the big splatter had become a part of the news, either directly or by inferences that made Simon and his friends alternately wheeze and shudder. An Indiana town was fighting a juvenile phenomenon called Drum Saturday. A radio-TV columnist noted that Blotto Cards were the latest rage among studio personnel; carried in handbag or breast pocket, whence they could be quickly whipped out and stared at, the cards were claimed to be an infallible remedy against boredom or sudden attacks of anger and the blues. Reports of a penthouse burglary included among the objects listed as missing "a recently-purchased spotted linen wall-hanging"; the woman said she did not care about the other objects, but pleaded for the hanging's return, "as it was of great psychological comfort to my husband." Splatter-marked raincoats were a high school fad, the splattering being done ceremoniously at Drum 'n' Drag parties. An English prelate had preached a sermon inveighing against "this deafening new American craze with its overtones of mayhem." At a press interview Salvador Dali had refused to say anything to newsmen except the cryptic sentence, "The time has come."

In a halting, hiccupy voice Gorius McIntosh reported that things were pretty hot at the clinic. Twice during the past week he had been fired and triumphantly reinstated. Rather similarly at the state hospital Bump Parties had been alternately forbidden and then encouraged, mostly on the pleas of enthusiastic psychiatric aides. Copies of the McSPAT had come into the hands of general practitioners who, ignoring its original purpose, were using it as substitutes for electro-shock treatment and tranquilizing drugs. A group of progressive psychiatrists calling themselves the Young Turks were circulating a statement that the McSPAT constituted the worst threat to classical Freudian psychoanalysis since Alfred Adler, adding a grim scholarly reference to the Dancing Mania of the Middle Ages. Gorius finished his report by staring around almost frightenedly at his five friends and clutching the whisky bottle to his bosom.

Lafcadio Smits seemed equally shaken, even when telling about the profits of his pyramiding enterprises. One of his four lofts had been burglarized, and another invaded at high noon by a red-bearded Greenwich Village Satanist protesting that the splatter was an illicitly procured Taoist magic symbol of direst power. Lafcadio was also receiving anonymous threatening letters which he believed to be from a criminal drug syndicate that looked upon Blotto Cards as his creation and as competitive to heroin and lesser forms of dope. He shuddered visibly when Tally volunteered the information that his fans had taken to wearing Lafcadio's splatter-patterned ties and shirts.

Lester Phlegius said that further copies of the issue of the costly and staid industrial journal carrying his attention-getter were unprocurable and that many had vanished from private offices and wealthy homes or, more often, simply had the crucial page ripped out.

Norman Saylor's two photographs of the big splatter had

135

been pilfered from his locked third-floor office at the university, and a huge copy of the splatter, painted in a waterproof black substance, had appeared on the bottom of the swimming pool in the girls' gymnasium.

As they continued to share their experiences, it turned out that the six intellectuals were even more disturbed at the hold the drummed phrase and the big splatter had got on them individually and at their failure to cope with the obsession by following Norman's suggestion. Playing at a Sunday-afternoon bar concert, Tally had got snagged on the phrase for fully ten minutes, like a phonograph needle caught in one groove, before he could let go. What bothered him especially was that no one in the audience had seemed to notice and he had the conviction that if something hadn't stopped him (the drum skin ruptured) they would have sat frozen there, wrists flailing, until he died of exhaustion.

Norman himself, seeking escape in chess, had checkmated his opponent in a blitz game (where each player must move without hesitation) by banging down his pieces in the *rump-titty* rhythm—and his subconscious mind had timed it, he said, so that the last move came right on the *tee;* it was a little pawn-move after a big queen-check on the TAH. Lafcadio, turning to cooking, had found himself mixing salad with a *rump-titty* flourish. (". . . and a madman to mix it, as the old Spanish recipe says," he finished with a despairing giggle.) Lester Phlegius, seeking release from the obsession in the companionship of a lady spiritualist with whom he had been carrying on a strictly Platonic love affair for ten years, found himself enlivening with the *rump-titty* rhythm the one chaste embrace they permitted themselves at each meeting. Phoebe had torn herself away and slapped him full-arm across the face. What had horrified Lester was that the impact had coincided precisely with the TAH.

Simon Grue himself, who hadn't stirred out of his apartment all week but wandered shivering from window to window in a dirty old bathrobe, had dozed in a broken armchair and had a terrifying vision. He had imagined himself in the ruins of Manhattan, chained to the broken stones (perhaps because he had both wrists heavily wound with scarves and cloths to cushion the twitching), while across the dusty jagged landscape all humanity tramped in an endless horde screeching the accursed phrase and every so often came a group of them carrying a two-story-high poster (". . . like those Soviet parades," he said) with the big splatter staring blackly down from it. His nightmare had gone on to picture the dreadful infection spreading from the Earth by spaceship to planets revolving around other stars.

As Simon finished speaking, Gorius McIntosh rose slowly from his chair, groping ahead of himself with his whisky bottle.

"That's it!" he said from between bared clenched teeth, grinning horribly. "That's what's happening to all of us. Can't get it out of our minds. Can't get it out of our muscles. Psychosomatic bondage!" He stumbled slowly across the circle of intellectuals toward Lester, who was sitting opposite him. "It's happening to me. A patient sits down across the desk and says with his eyes dripping tears, 'Help me, Doctor McIntosh,' and I see his problems clearly and I know just how to help him and I get up and I go around the desk to him"—he was standing right over Lester now, bottle raised high—"and I lean down so that my face is close to his and then I shout RUMP-TITTY-TITTY-TUM-TAH-TEE!"

At this point Norman Saylor decided to take over, leaving to Tally and Lafcadio the restraining of Gorius, who indeed seemed quite docile and more dazed than anything else now that his seizure was spent, at least temporarily. The cultural anthropologist strode to the center of the circle, looking very reassuring with his pipe and his strong jaw and his smoky tweeds, though he kept his hands clasped tightly together behind him.

"Men," he said sharply, "my research on this thing isn't finished by a long shot, but I've carried it far enough to know that we are dealing with what may be called an ultimate symbol, a symbol that is the summation of all symbols. It has everything in it—birth, death, mating, murder, divine and demonic possession, the whole lot—to such a degree that after you've looked at it, or listened to it, or *made* it, for a time, you simply don't *need* life any more."

The studio was very quiet. The five other intellectuals looked at him. Norman rocked on his heels like any normal college professor, but his arms grew perceptibly more rigid as he clasped his hands even more tightly behind his back, fighting an exquisite compulsion.

"As I say, my studies aren't nearly conclusive, but there's clearly no time to carry them further—we must act on such conclusions as I have drawn from the evidence assembled to date. Here's briefly how it shapes up: We must assume that mankind possesses an actual collective unconscious mind stretching thousands of years into the past and, for all I know, into the future. This collective unconscious mind may

137

be pictured as a great dark space across which radio messages can sometimes pass with difficulty. We must also assume that the drummed phrase and with it the big splatter came to us by this inner radio from an individual living over a century in the past. We have good reason to believe that this individual is, or was, a direct male ancestor, in the seventh generation back, of Tally here. He was a witch doctor. He was acutely hungry for power. In fact, he spent his life seeking an incantation that would put a spell on the whole world. It appears that he found the incantation at the end, but died too soon to be able to use it—without ever being able to embody it in sound or sign. Think of his frustration!"

"Norm's right," Tally said, nodding somberly. "He was a mighty mean man, I'm told, and mighty persistent."

Norman's nod was quicker and also a plea for undivided attention. Beads of sweat were dripping down his forehead. "The thing came to us when it did—came to Tally specifically and through him to Simon—because our six minds, reinforcing each other powerfully, were momentarily open to receive transmissions through the collective unconscious, and because there is—was—this sender at the other end long desirous of getting his message through to one of his descendants. We cannot say precisely where this sender is—a scientifically oriented person might say that he is in a shadowed portion of the space-time continuum while a religiously oriented person might aver that he is in Heaven or Hell."

"I'd plump for the last-mentioned," Tally volunteered. "He was that kind of man."

"Please, Tally," Norman said. "Wherever he is, we must operate on the hope that there is a counter formula or negative symbol—yang to this yin—which he wants, or wanted, to transmit too—something that will stop this flood of madness we have loosed on the world."

"That's where I must differ with you, Norm," Tally broke in, shaking his head more somberly than he had nodded it. "If Old Five-Greats ever managed to start something bad, he'd never want to stop it, especially if he knew how. I tell you he was mighty mighty mean and—"

"*Please, Tally!* Your ancestor's character may have changed with his new environment, there may be greater forces at work on him—in any case, our only hope is that he possesses and will transmit to us the counter formula. To achieve that, we must try to recreate, by artificial means, the conditions that obtained in this studio at the time of the first transmission."

A look of acute pain crossed his face. He unclasped his hands and brought them in front of him. His pipe fell to the floor. He looked at the large blister the hot bowl had raised in one palm. Then clasping his hands together in front of him, palm to palm, with a twisting motion that made Lafcadio wince, he continued rapping out the words.

"Men, we must act at once, using only such materials as can be rapidly assembled. Each of you must trust me implicitly. Tally, I know you don't use it any more, but can you still get weed, the genuine crushed leaf? Good, we may need enough for two or three dozen sticks. Gory, I want you to fetch the self-hypnotism rigmarole that's so effective—no, I don't trust your memory and we may need copies. Lester, if you're quite through satisfying yourself that Gory didn't break your collarbone, you go with Gory and see that he drinks lots of coffee. On your way back buy several bunches of garlic, a couple of rolls of dimes, and a dozen red railway flares. Oh yes, and call up your mediumistic lady and do your damnedest to get her to join us here—her talents may prove invaluable. Laf, tear off to your home loft and get the luminous paint and the black velvet hangings you and your red-bearded ex-friend used—yes, I know about that association!—when you and he were dabbling with black magic. Simon and I will hold down the studio. All right, then—" A spasm crossed his face and the veins in his forehead and cords in his neck bulged and his arms were jerking with the struggle he was waging against the compulsion that threatened to overpower him. "All right, then—*Rump-titty-titty*-tum-GET-MOVING!"

An hour later the studio smelt like a fire in a eucalyptus grove. Such light from outside as got past the cabalistically figured hangings covering windows and skylight revealed the shadowy forms of Simon, atop the scaffold, and the other five intellectuals, crouched against the wall, all puffing their reefers, sipping the sour smoke industriously. Their marihuana-blanked minds were still reverberating to the last compelling words of Gory's rigmarole, read by Lester Phlegius in a sonorous bass.

Phoebe Saltonstall, who had refused reefers with a simple, "No thank you, I always carry my own peyote," had one wall all to herself. Eyes closed, she was lying along it on three small cushions, her pleated Grecian robe white as a winding sheet.

Round all four walls waist-high went a dimly luminous line with six obtuse angles in it besides the four corners; Norman said that made it the topological equivalent of a magician's pentalpha or pentagram. Barely visible were the bunches of garlic nailed to each door and the tiny silver disks scattered in front of them.

Norman flicked his lighter and the little blue flame added itself to the six glowing red points. In a cracked voice he cried, "The time approaches!" and he shambled about rapidly setting fire to the twelve railway flares spiked into the floor.

In the hellish red glow they looked to each other like so many devils. Phoebe moaned and tossed. Simon coughed once as the dense clouds of smoke billowed up around the scaffold and filled the ceiling.

Norman Saylor cried, *"This is it!"*

Phoebe screamed thinly and arched her back as if in electro-shock.

A look of sudden amazement came into the face of Taliaferro Booker Washington, as if he'd been jabbed from below with a pin or hot poker. He lifted his hands with great authority and beat out a short phrase on his gray African log.

A hand holding a brightly freighted eight-inch brush whipped out of the smoke clouds above and sent down a great fissioning gout of paint that landed on the canvas with a sound that was an exact copy of Tally's short phrase.

Immediately the studio became a hive of purposeful activity. Heavily-gloved hands jerked out the railway flares and plunged them into strategically located buckets of water. The hangings were ripped down and the windows thrown open. Two electric fans were turned on. Simon, half-fainting, slipped down the last feet of the ladder, was rushed to a window and lay across it gasping. Somewhat more carefully Phoebe Saltonstall was carried to a second window and laid in front of it. Gory checked her pulse and gave a reassuring nod.

Then the five intellectuals gathered around the big canvas and stared. After a while Simon joined them.

The new splatter, in Chinese red, was entirely different from the many ones under it and it was an identical twin of the new drummed phrase.

After a while the six intellectuals went about the business of photographing it. They worked systematically but rather listlessly. When their eyes chanced to move to the canvas they didn't even seem to see what was there. Nor did they bother to glance at the black-on-white prints (with the background of the last splatter touched out) as they shoved them under their coats.

Just then there was a rustle of draperies by one of the open windows. Phoebe Saltonstall, long forgotten, was sitting up. She looked around her with some distaste.

"Take me home, Lester," she said.

Tally, halfway through the door, stopped. "You know," he said puzzledly, "I still can't believe that Old Five-Greats had the public spirit to do what he did. I wonder if she found out what it was that made him—"

Norman put his hand on Tally's arm and laid a finger of the other on his own lips. They went out together, followed by Lafcadio, Gorius, Lester and Phoebe. Like Simon, all five men had the look of drunkards in a benign convalescent stupor, and probably dosed with paraldehyde, after a bout of DT's.

The same effect was apparent as the new splatter and drummed phrase branched out across the world, chasing and eventually overtaking the first one. Any person who saw or heard it proceeded to repeat it once (make it, show it, wear it, if it were that sort of thing, in any case pass it on) and then forget it—and at the same time forget the first drummed phrase and splatter. All sense of compulsion or obsession vanished utterly.

Drum 'n' Drag died a-borning. Blotto Cards vanished from handbags and pockets, the McSPATs I and II from doctors' offices and psychiatric clinics. Bump Parties no longer plagued and enlivened mental hospitals. Catatonics froze again. The Young Turks went back to denouncing tranquilizing drugs. A fad of green-and-purple barber-pole stripes covered up splattermarks on raincoats. Satanists and drug syndicates presumably continued their activities unhampered except by God and the Treasury Department. Capetown had such peace as it deserved. Spotted shirts, neckties, dresses, lampshades, wallpaper, and linen wall-hangings all became intensely passé. Drum Saturday was never heard of again. Lester Phlegius' second attention-getter got none.

Simon's big painting was eventually hung at one exhibition, but it got little attention even from critics, except for a few heavy sentences along the lines of "Simon Grue's latest elephantine effort fell with a thud as dull as that of the tubs of paint composing it." Visitors to the gallery seemed able only to give it one dazed look and then pass it by, as is not infrequently the case with modern paintings.

141

The reason for this was clear. On top of all the other identical splatters it carried one in Chinese red that was a negation of all symbols, a symbol that had nothing in it—the new splatter that was the identical twin of the new drummed phrase that was the negation and completion of the first, the phrase that had vibrated out from Tally's log through the red glare and come slapping down out of Simon's smoke cloud, the phrase that stilled and ended everything (and which obviously can only be stated here once): "Tah-*titty-titty-tee*-toe!"

The six intellectual people continued their weekly meetings almost as if nothing had happened, except that Simon substituted for splatterwork a method of applying the paint by handfuls with the eyes closed, later treading it in by foot. He sometimes asked his friends to join him in these impromptu marches, providing wooden shoes imported from Holland for the purpose.

One afternoon, several months later, Lester Phlegius brought a guest with him—Phoebe Saltonstall.

"Miss Saltonstall has been on a round-the-world cruise," he explained. "Her psyche was dangerously depleted by her experience in this apartment, she tells me, and a complete change was indicated. Happily now she's entirely recovered."

"Indeed I am," she said, answering their solicitous inquiries with a bright smile.

"By the way," Norman said, "did you receive any message at the time from Tally's ancestor?"

"Indeed I did," she said.

"Well, what did Old Five-Greats have to say?" Tally asked eagerly. "Whatever it was, I bet he was pretty crude about it!"

"Indeed he was," she said, blushing prettily. "So crude, in fact, that I wouldn't dare attempt to convey that aspect of his message. For that matter, I am sure that it was the utter fiendishness of his anger and the unspeakable visions in which his anger was clothed that so reduced my psyche." She paused.

"I don't know where he was sending from," she said thoughtfully. "I had the impression of a warm place, an intensely warm place, though of course I may have been reacting to the railway flares." Her frown cleared. "The actual message was short and simple enough:

" 'Dear Descendant, They *made* me stop it. It was beginning to catch on *down here*.' "

142

Rundown

ROBERT LORY

What Modern Science Hath Wrought! (Wrought, in this instance, being a newly invented past tense for the verb "to wreak.")

No one should even try to write any more of an introduction to this story than that!

The subway train announced its arrival with a screech of grating steel. The man was shoved from the car onto the platform by the eight P.M. crowd. The noise and the abrupt handling of his body brought him to awareness.

Not that he had been asleep or unconscious. Although he might have been. He didn't know for sure.

He found it hard to concentrate, but soon a sign over the platform came into focus:

WESTBORO

It meant nothing to him. The second thing he became aware of did.

Another train had replaced his, and directly in front of him was an army of people, dispassionate towards everything but its one objective—to get on.

They came at him all at once, forming a pushing, elbowing, cursing, jarring mass of humanity. He glanced off one to collide with another. He escaped the punishment by a lunge to one side which ended with a crash to the cold cement floor.

He regained some semblance of steadiness on his feet and looked at the sign. It was still Westboro. It still meant nothing to him.

He was lost.

What was worse, he couldn't remember where he was lost *from*.

He turned to walk, he didn't know exactly where, when he smashed into a little boy eating an apple.

The boy reacted in a strange manner.

"Leave me alone, you dirty man, you," the boy said. He dropped his apple and ran off. Scared.

The man flushed with embarrassment, but the boy's remark made him look down at himself.

He saw a dirty man. Filthy. His white shirt—it had been white once—was torn at the elbow and was covered with grime, his shoes at the toes were white where the black polish had worn completely off, his pants reflected no evidence of ever having been pressed and the right leg was ripped from the knee down.

Two girls in their teens passed and giggled.

He was aware that others had noticed him.

"Hey, lookit the bum," a fat jolly-rover called out to his three on-the-towning cronies.

"Bum," the man thought, and reached to his back pocket.

No wallet. But not long ago he had one, he was sure, because the feel of its absence was there. Somebody must have taken it, or he might have lost it. In that crowd or on the subway or before. . . . He couldn't remember where he had been before.

The feeling of not remembering seemed familiar, and he tried hard to think. But there was nothing static in his mind that he could hold on to. His mind wasn't blank anymore; it was a jumble. He somehow recalled he had been looking for his money. He fumbled through his other pockets.

He found a dirty handkerchief and two cents.

The feel of the coins brought everything back.

Quickly he felt his pulse. It was slower than he had ever known it to be. Sure, there were times before when . . . but then the doctor always had been nearby. And this time, the most serious time of all—he looked up at the Westboro sign —he was lost. Perhaps, up on the streets, he would recognize something.

He began to take the stairs at a run, but his breath came too hard, and he walked the rest of the way to the turnstile. The arm caught tight as he started to go through and a sharp pain went through his groin.

"That's the way you go *in,* pal," somebody offered, and the man winced at the few laughs he had drawn. He saw the exit sign and walked quickly toward it.

The night lights were just ahead as he collided with a woman loaded with bundles. They spilled. "Sorry," he said, leaving her to her indignation, and at a faster pace he walked outside into the cool night air.

He had stopped walking and was leaning against the door of the Inn of Six Horses, which proudly displayed its name and namesakes in blue and white neon.

He had recognized nothing.

He had tried getting to the doctor's by cab, but no driver would listen to him without first seeing the fare, even though he assured them all that he could get it from the doctor.

A policeman had told him to move along or suffer the consequences of a thick nightstick.

A drugstore proprietor had answered his request to use the phone by threatening to call the policeman with the thick nightstick.

A dime. One dime!

He remembered his Shakespeare.

My kingdom for a . . . horse? Six horses. Maybe, just maybe, at the Inn of Six Horses. . . .

A short man at the bar, composing one half of the clientele, was calling the bartender's attention to the fact that the six horses outside outnumbered the customers.

"Go to blazes," the bartender commented on the short man's observation.

"I should," said the short one. "Then George here would be Uncas, the last of the Mohicans, riding your six old white stallions."

"How do you know they're stallions?" George said. He was lean, mean and weary, looking as if he had just returned from a hard day of peddling vacuum cleaners.

The door banged shut and three pairs of eyes focused on a dirty man.

"Here comes a touch," said Pete.

"Please," said the man, his voice shaky and weak.

"Before you go into your act, pal," Pete said, "understand this: Nobody gets nothing free here, this ain't no mission or nothing. This is a business like any place else."

"A real thriving business," mocked Shorty.

"Please, a dime, I need a dime, that's all I—"

"A *dime?*" George laughed. "For what, a cup of coffee? This is a high-class place. Beer costs fifteen cents here."

Shorty joined in with a snort. "Maybe he wants to call his girl."

"I *need* the dime," the man said, leaning on the bar for support.

145

"A matter of real life and death, huh?" George said.

"Yes. Look . . . here, I have two cents, you take them."

Pete looked suspiciously at the two coins. "We don't sell nothing that costs two cents."

"You take the two cents, but give me a dime. *Please.*"

"Sharp businessman," noted George.

"This is rich," said Pete. "Do you really expect to *buy* a dime for two cents?"

Shorty said, "He just noticed how well you're doing. He figures you can afford the loss."

"Boy, it burns me up," said Pete. "These professional bums make more in a week than I see in a month."

"You keep talking that way, and this clown will want to buy your business for the two cents." Shorty said. "Ain't worth it," George said and banged his glass down. "Fill it," he directed Pete.

As Pete turned, the man made a lunge for George's change on the bar.

"Watch him," warned Shorty.

George needed no warning. He had seen the man eying his money, and he had hoped for just such a move. With a right fist to the side of the man's head, George took revenge for a bad day's work.

The man lay very still on the floor.

"What a paste," said Shorty, admiringly. "You could have killed him like that."

"He sure ain't doing much moving," said Pete, coming around the end of the bar. "I'd better take a look."

"Man, I didn't hit him that hard."

"Well, *man,* he sure asked for it," said Shorty. And me and Pete will be right here to tell the cops that the guy was a crook and tried to rob your money. Right, Pete?"

"George, this guy's got no pulse," Pete said.

"Watcha gonna do, George?" Shorty said.

"Just shut up and wait a minute," Pete said. "I think he's trying to say something."

The man's eyes pleaded with each of the three. His lips quietly formed their message:

"Dime."

"Wow, talk about persistence," said Shorty.

George looked at his change on the bar.

He picked up a dime.

"Hey," said Shorty, "what are you doing?"

"Shut up," said Pete. "George's money is George's money. What he does with it is his business."

"Look," George said, "I didn't mean to hit you so hard. I mean, I hit you so hard my whole hand hurts. So here, you can have the dime, I won't miss it."

He pressed the dime into the man's hand.

"Holy cow," said Shorty. It was the first sound any of the three had made after the man had left, fifteen minutes before.

George stared into the mirror behind the bar, seeking some mighty truth in his own reflection. "He says . . . he says *Unbutton my shirt,* and then . . ."

George fondled some coins in his hand. "Then he takes that crazy dime, a plain old, regular, crazy dime. . . ."

Pete poured himself a Scotch. "What kind of guy is it, anyway," he said, "who walks around with a slot in the middle of his chest that he puts dimes into?"

"Yeah," said George, "and who *ticks,* yet?"

The Trouble With H.A.R.R.I.

EDWARD MACKIN

Here, for a change of pace, is a British science fiction tale—including "gaol" for "jail" and "maths" for "math." However, the story itself is a universal one; it could have been written in Urdu, if that language only had the vocabulary, and the people who speak it had the technology.

It is the last word on the cybernetic—the really *thinking*—machine. And it is a last word we probably would not like if we ever did achieve it. Perhaps the research it tells of is a project against which there should be a law. . . .

Cybernetics is not what it was. The trouble is that there are far too many of us nowadays. What with the cut-throat competition and the self-repair jobs, I am ready for the bread line any day.

It must be three months since my last job, which was a lousy little fish-meal factory whose owner had found it cheaper to work everything to repair-or-bust point than to employ a full-time engineer. All I got out of that was a fortnight's keep.

So here I am, waiting, like Micawber, for something to turn up, in a very bare office indeed, and with everything sellable sold. In fact, all that remains is the telephone, which is resting on the floor. I have three days, and then *I* shall be gone, too. Possibly to gaol.

I am commiserating with myself while I pace up and down the carpetless floor, and at the same time thanking my semi-lucky stars that it is getting into summer time, so I shall not miss my overcoat for some months.

Then the doorbell rang. I stood perfectly still thinking it might be a creditor, or possibly the police. They are very hard on debtors these days.

When the bell rang again I crept over to the door and peeped through the keyhole. What I saw was another eye looking at me.

"You might as well open the door, Hek Belov," said a familiar voice. "I can hear you breathing."

I pulled the door open, and dragged the owner of the eye in. It was Meerschraft. Meerschraft the fat, the amiable, the *generous*. An angel from Heaven, and a damn fine cyberneticist, too.

"Come in, you devil!" I said. "Here, sit on this clean bit of floor. I have eaten all the furniture, although some of it wasn't mine. Meerschraft, old friend, are you in funds?"

"Well," he said, cautiously, "I have a job; but it doesn't pay too well. As a matter of fact, I am here to offer you a similar position, although perhaps only of a temporary nature. I told my boss that if any man can solve this problem it is you. I said: 'Belov may be a lousy engineer; but he has that something that you and I lack. He has that sympathetic touch that machines love. They tell all their secrets to him, and he knows their language.' You know Professor Ratoff, of course? He runs the cybernetics department at the Hilberry Research Station."

"I don't know the professor," I told him, sourly, "and I didn't know you were such a snake-in-the-grass! *A lousy engineer. . . !* Thank you, Meerschraft, for the buildup. And what did Professor Ratoff say then, you swine?"

Meerschraft grinned.

"He said, quote: 'He couldn't be any lousier than you. So get hold of him.' Unquote. He also said that if you were unsuccessful I would be out on my fat ear. So it is up to you, old friend. I have an air-taxi waiting."

"Wait a minute," I said. "What's the job? You might give me a few details."

Meerschraft made some vague movements with his hands and arms, as though he were trying to conjure something into our presence.

"It's a kind of computer," he explained, "but it's no ordinary computer. The thing has a mind of its own. At least, it did have."

"Clear as mud," I said. "Anyway, I must have five pounds on account. Otherwise I don't move a step from here. As your job appears to be at hazard . . ."

I left this sentence unfinished. Pure blackmail, of course. Meerschraft sighed, and pulled out his wallet.

"Here," he said. "You crook! Somehow I think I should

have known better than to recommend you. It always costs me money. And this time it may cost me my job."

"Not it, my dear friend," I told him, warmly. "Consider this thing as good as fixed—whatever it is. My friend, you are in line for promotion, and a substantial bonus. Your employer will have reason to be grateful to you."

"Ratoff," said Meerschraft, bitterly, "wouldn't give you a wink if he had an eye tremor."

On the way over to the research station Meerschraft explained the setup. Hilberry was established under the Williamson Trust Fund, and was concerned wholly with the science of communication. The machine I had to deal with was a homeostatic and reflective reasoning instrument, or HARRI, as it was fondly called.

HARRI had been constructed not to solve equations, but to deal with concepts and events. As it was an inductive logical machine it could learn from experience, and it had been provided with a simple vocabulary of 420 words. The man who built it was that great physicist, Dr. Gosse Williams. He had built it and died, leaving Dr. Ratoff, who knew nothing about computers, holding this somewhat cumbersome baby.

"It worked all right at first," said Meerschraft, "and even extended its own vocabulary to 5,000 words within the first week. Then something went wrong with it, and it hasn't worked since. If you fix it, Hek Belov, you can call yourself a genius plus."

He wasn't kidding. One glance at the machine and I realized I had been taken for a ride. Meerschraft had talked about variable circuit loops and arbitrary levels in a way that had left me thinking that they were all part and parcel of this monstrosity. Not that I knew much about these things. Higher maths always bogfound me, and Meerschraft had trotted out a whole string of equations that I had nodded yes to without understanding a blind one.

Damn it all, I'm a practical man! I know a digital computer when I see one. I'm that practical I could re-wire any one of half-a-dozen types blindfold. It's a gift. You either have it or you haven't, and a headful of symbols is no substitute.

One peek at this rig-up and I thought Heaven help my creditors!

"I'll give you twenty-four hours," said Ratoff nastily. "If you don't come up with a solution in that time you won't get paid, and Meerschraft will be fired for wasting my time."

He stalked out and Meerschraft followed him, with one shoulder lifted high and his hands spread. It spoke volumes. Ratoff was a mean man. He meant what he said. I took another look at the machine, and then I thought of what Ratoff had said about a *solution*. This was significant, and it reeked of something I couldn't put a name to; but which was distinctly fishy.

What had started out to be a simple repair job had become a major project. I was being taken for a ride all right, the loused-up circuits told me that. The thing wasn't even a computer. It had been once, perhaps; but it looked as though some novice had been at it. There were connections that ended in mid-air and there were components without connections.

The solution that Dr. Ratoff had spoken about was nothing less than building a genuine think-box from scratch. I was supposed to solve in twenty-four hours what someone had taken a lifetime to figure out.

For a moment I was tempted to re-wire it as a plain digital computer; but they didn't want a digital. They wanted a kind of super-brain. What they had, it seemed, was a heap of junk. At least, it would be if I put the switch in and no one could tell me any different.

It began to dawn on me what had been going on. They'd had the clever-clever lads in first, instead of sending for old Belov. I ground my teeth, and spat on the floor. Poor, I might be; but no one could insult me with impunity.

I went to the door and turned the handle. It was locked. I shook it and shouted for my friend at the top of my voice.

"Meerschraft!" I bellowed. "Meerschraft, you dog! Open this door, you fat snake, till I tear your liver out!"

I shook the heavy plastic door and rattled the knob; but no one answered. Then I saw the box. It was a plain, metal box, and it hadn't been there before. I was certain of that. You have to have sharp eyes for my job. It was a pity that I hadn't sharp hearing as well. Someone had opened that door while I was inspecting the computer, and shoved the box in.

I opened it warily. And then I laughed. I felt happy again. It was packed with food—including a big cherry pie. If ever I wake in Heaven the first thing to greet me will be the aroma of cherry pie. There was a large flask of coffee, too. At least they didn't intend that I should starve.

I sat down by a long bench littered with test gear and devoured every bit of food in the box. I hadn't eaten properly for days. It seemed that Meerschraft, the fox, hadn't forgotten! Feed me and I am a roaring genuis. Starve me and all I can think about is food. I lit a cigarette, and between swilling the coffee down and smoking I ruminated on variable loops and arbitrary circuits. To be quite frank, I wondered what the hell they could be!

I left this alone after a while and posed the question direct. What was the difference between thinking man and non-thinking, but lightning-fast computer? Then the answer hit me and the mind barrier was broken.

That's the way it is with me. I get flashes of inspiration in the same way as a poet, and they excite me because I know they're good. Not accurate, maybe, but as long as they work, who cares? Let the clever boys dress them up in maths. I think in terms of solid circuitry.

The general idea comes first, and then a bit of the circuit flashes on the inward eye, as Wordsworth once said in another connection. I am very fond of the poets. I might have been one myself; only the rake-off is worse than cybernetics.

Anyway, the answer to my problem lay in the question, as answers so often do. What was the difference between thinking man and non-thinking machine? Just that, of course. A machine didn't think. It just banged out the answer straight away. The *only* answer that had been fed into it.

With man it is different. Ask him a question, and you never knew how he might reply. He might know the right answer—but there were other near-answers and nagging little paradoxes and absolutely crazy notions, all simmering together under that pot-lid cranium. A thick stew of reason and unreason.

Sometimes a hitherto crazy notion ousted the reasonable answer, or posed a question itself, and a new idea or a great invention was born. Sometimes reason was submerged under a flood of unreason, and the result was insanity as the tortured mind dredged things up from the communal subconscious.

With the computer it was different. The computer was too reasonable; too one-track. You asked it what two and two were and it said *four*. Nine out of ten men would have said the same; but the tenth would have asked: "Two and two what? Two males and two females? Or two elephants, a button-stick, and the Empire State Building?"

That was the trouble with the computer. It was too thinly logical. Too mathematical. It needed a diversity of ideas. It needed a whole heap of nonsense feeding into it. It needed to be slightly crazy—like man!

Two hours later I had completed the hookup. I switched on and asked it one or two simple questions. I was using the binary number system which had been tailored to fit the alphabet on this machine. The crystal memory-valve indicator showed totality as zero and the answer strip was running out blank. So I started feeding in. First of all facts, facts, and more facts, and then whacky, and half-clever notions and bits of poetry, anything and everything that came to mind.

I must have worked at this for hours before I asked it anything else. Totality had crept up to one percent, so the memory banks were okay. The answer strip gave the answers I had expected. The ones I had fed in. It was obvious that the thing wasn't using those variable circuit loops. They had locked in one position.

I kept banging in the same question and getting the same answers. The question was: *What is darkness?* The answers it kept giving were: *Darkness is an absence of light,* and a conflicting concept, also supplied by Belov, *Light is an absence of darkness.* Neither of these concepts was strictly true. A blind man doesn't sense darkness, or light. He sees precisely what you see out of the back of your head.

Take a good squint at it, for you are looking on a mystery. You should experience horror and awe and reverence. From out of this, eons ago, we poked our snouts. Tell me, my friends, what is it? You don't know? Then let old Belov tell you. It is nothing and it is damn near everything. It is the rest of the infinite universe that lies beyond the range of our five senses. Sometimes I think that man is resented—an impertinent questioner with a three-dimensional foot in the door of a multi-dimensional universe.

As I saw it, the conflicting concept of darkness as a positive phenomenon kept nagging at the electronic brain because the vibration increased each time, and then it blew a fuse and went dead. The easy way out, of course. The thing was dodging.

Having tried first one set of concepts and then the others, and not being able to circuit any on a purely logical basis, it had taken refuge in its own protective mechanism and thrown a faint. It was the Victorian lady's trick to escape an embarrassing situation.

It wasn't escaping that way, though. Out came the fuses and in went thick wire connectors. I was risking everything now. "Go on, you dope," I told it, "start thinking on your own account or blow your top. Please yourself."

I hated to think what Ratoff would say if he knew. Have me thrown in gaol, I supposed. But it was worth the risk. I was certain that the thing could answer at the expense of a little painful effort. . . .

It vibrated, shrieked, and groaned while I stood and cursed it. A wisp of smoke rose from somewhere inside the tortured mechanism, but somehow it didn't quite burn up. Gradually, it dropped back to its old smooth purr. It had resolved the situation somehow. I waited for the answer.

The paper strip began to move. On it I read: *Darkness is from within. Light is from without. Darkness is a negative phenomenon. Not sufficient information to expound.*

This was it all right! I was not concerned with the validity of the statements. It was thinking for itself, that was the point. By discarding one item of information and co-relating two others, it had arrived at a new and rather odd conclusion. It had also handed me a gratuitous piece of information about light. Oh yes, it was thinking, all right. All we had to do now was to shovel in all the information available on every conceivable subject—plus a few more bugs—and then we could ask it some really important questions, such as: *What do you propose that man should do to extricate himself from his present social and economic anxieties?* That was the sixty-four-dollar question. A waste of time, really. It was even money that the thing would answer: *Drop dead!*

Anyway, Meerschraft's job was safe, and that swine Ratoff owed me some money, although I'd be lucky to get enough to pay what I owed Meerschraft. I knew his type.

At least, I thought I did; but I was wrong. The first thing I found was that the door wasn't locked at all. I had been turning the knob the wrong way. When I reported progress to Ratoff he seemed surprised and faintly amused. Not a bit like what I had taken to be his overbearing self.

We checked up on the machine and then called Meerschraft. My fat friend came bursting into the laboratory in a great state of excitement.

"Belov," he shouted, "you're a genius!"

He slammed me on the back. "I knew you could do it," he said. "You told me so yourself."

"Yes, I did, didn't I?" I said. "But never mind the kudos. Just let me have whatever you consider the job is worth and I'll be on my way."

"Can you carry away a million pounds?" asked my friend,

grinning. "Not that we are likely to give you that much; but that is only a percentage of what it is worth to us. Anyway, how did you turn the trick?"

I explained about shooting it full of bugs, while Professor Ratoff fed questions into the brain and conned the answers.

"It's learning rapidly," he said after a while. "We have at last what we thought might prove impossible. You might as well know that this is a Government project, and as such top secret."

"Oh, I can keep my mouth shut," I assured him. "Don't worry about me."

"There's something else," he added, and looked at Meerschraft in an odd way. "Perhaps you'd better tell him. It was your idea in the first place."

"Well," said Meerschraft, looking a bit sheepish. "To start a long way off—er—faith has been said to move mountains. What I mean is, if you believe something is possible it becomes possible of accomplishment. You see, you just proved it. It doesn't work with everyone, I know. Some men are natural sceptics. Others have rigid thought forms and patterns of behaviour. . . ."

"Are you trying to tell me that I am not the first to have a go at fixing this machine? If so, save your breath. I could see that for myself."

Meerschraft nodded his head.

"It was fairly obvious, I suppose. I believe you were the twenty-first. It was borne on us eventually that we needed someone with a somewhat chaotic mind. A man with a flair for the unusual. A try-anything Charlie with the bare minimum of knowledge. We felt all along that this was not, in the final analysis, an engineering job at all, but a method of feeding in the information."

"I see." I said, hotly. "So you turned to old Belov. A try-anything Charlie with the bare minimum of knowledge! Meerschraft, you are a low-down, dirty dog! The whole thing seems fishy to me. I don't believe that your job was ever in danger."

"It wasn't. But I apologize. You have something that most of us lack. It is the equivalent of the gardener's green fingers. The man who did most of the work on this machine died before he was able to crack the problem of how to give the brain the power of independent thought. We, all of us, I think, only half believed in its possibility. The way I figured it, the man who was most likely to succeed was the man who really believed that it could be done.

"How do you convince a man that a thing can be done? Simply by telling him that it has been done before. What has been done once can be done again—and even improved on. The classic example of this is the four-minute mile. It was thought to be impossible until someone did it, and then it became quite commonplace. You see, it is largely an attitude of mind. What I am trying to tell you is that this machine was hardly more than an ordinary computer until you, Belov, found a way to bridge the gulf between automation and independent action. You would never have done it if you had not believed that it had been done before—now would you?"

I didn't bother to answer. I was watching Professor Ratoff, who was making impatient noises and even swearing softly under his breath.

"Anything wrong, Professor?" I inquired, smiling to myself. I had been reading the answer strip.

"HARRI is not behaving himself," he told me. "Just read this strip."

I read it again. One answer had been repeated almost *ad nauseam,* and then the answer to what was obviously another question appeared, and then the first answer appeared again. I laughed. I couldn't help it. These clever fellows had forgotten just one thing, and it took old Belov to spot it—a try-anything Charlie with the bare minimum of knowledge. That hurt; but I was going to rub their noses in it before I was finished. Besides, they had no right to make a man invent something unawares.

"Gentlemen," I said, enjoying myself, "you wanted a thinking machine. You have one, thanks to old Belov. Now, if you'll just advance me something on account I'll be getting back to town."

"Not without ironing out this defect, or whatever it is that has just developed," said the Professor determinedly. "Come on, Belov, you must know what it is. After all, you fathered it."

"Let him go," urged Meerschraft. "He's done enough for one day. He can come back tomorrow and remedy it. Can't you, old friend?"

I looked from one to the other, and I gave them my sweetest smile.

"Neither tomorrow or ever," I said. "You wanted a thinking machine and that is precisely what you have. When the

thing is thinking its independent thoughts it just bangs out
the answer to any old question, perhaps absentmindedly. Now
and then it may answer one of your questions. When it has
nothing better to do. But mostly it will be answering its own
questions—and you won't even see the answers. Just consider
that, gentlemen. It will be thinking twenty-four hours a day,
seven days a week, getting smarter and smarter, until, finally,
it knows all the answers. The questions may be biological,
and the first thing you'll know about it is when it stretches out
a thought and grabs you."

Ratoff looked worried; but Meerschraft just smirked.

"We can always switch it off," he said.

It was the cue I was waiting for.

"Listen, you fat ape!" I said. "If you stop a man's heart
what happens? He dies! Shut HARRI down, and see what happens. You are dealing with an entity now, not a machine.
Switch him off and he's dead; but in a few weeks' time it is
my bet that he won't let you switch him off. I leave the problem with you."

I went out and slammed the door.

The Water Eater

WINSTON K. MARKS

The hobbyist inventor, whose inventions usually go haywire, is a not uncommon character in science fiction,
and he is represented in this book by the "hero" of
"Callahan and the Wheelies" (see page 29). The ex-
perimenter who "invents" by mistake, however, who
creates something absolutely novel—and quite terrifying
—while trying to do something quite harmless with
his various noxious substances, is more of a rarity. In
the story below we have a pristine example of the
breed: a man who, because of the possibly catastrophic
byproduct of his quite innocent efforts, is much, much
more to be pitied than censured.

But then, perhaps (if the story is true)—perhaps we
all are to be pitied? Only time—and strange events in
Lake Michigan—will tell!

I just lost a weekend. I ain't too anxious to find it. Instead,
I sure wish I had gone fishing with McCarthy and the boys
like I'd planned.

I drive a beer truck for a living, but here it is almost
noon Monday and I haven't turned a wheel. Sure, I get beer
wholesale, and I have been known to take some advantage
of my discount. But that wasn't what happened to this weekend.

Instead of fishing or bowling or poker or taking the kids
down to the amusement park over Saturday and Sunday, I've
been losing sleep over an experiment.

Down at the Elks' Club, the boys say that for a working stiff
I have a very inquiring mind. I guess that's because they
always see me reading *Popular Science* and *Scientific American* and such, instead of heading for the stack of *Esquires*
that are piled a foot deep in the middle of the big table in
the reading room, like the rest of them do.

Well, it was my inquiring mind that lost me my wife, the skin of my right hand, a lot of fun and sleep—yeah, not a wink of sleep for two days now! Which is the main reason I'm writing this down now. I've read somewheres that if you wrote down your troubles, you could get them out of your system.

I thought I had troubles Friday night when I pulled into the driveway and Lottie yelled at me from the porch, "The fire's out! And it's flooded. Hurry up!"

Trouble, hah! That was just the beginning.

Lottie is as cute a little exwaitress as ever flipped the suds off a glass of beer, but she just ain't mechanically minded. The day Uncle Alphonse died and left us $2500 and I went out and bought a kitchen and shed full of appliances for her, that was a sad day, all right. She has lived a fearful life ever since, too proud of her dishwasher and automatic this and that to consider selling them, but scared stiff of the noises they make and the vibrations and all the mysterious dials and lights, etc.

So this Friday afternoon when the oil burner blew out from the high wind, she got terrified, sent the kids over to their grandmother's in a cab and sat for two hours trying to make up her mind whether to call the fire department or the plumber.

Meanwhile, this blasted oil stove was overflowing into the fire pot.

"Well, turn it off!" I yelled. "I'll be in right away!"

I ducked into the garage and got a big handful of rags and a hunk of string and a short stick. This I have been through before. I went in and kissed her pretty white face, and a couple of worry lines disappeared.

"Get me a pan or something," I said and started dismantling the front of the heater.

These gravity-flow oil heaters weren't built to make it easy to drain off excess oil. There's a brass plug at the inlet, but no one in history has been able to stir one, the oil man told me. I weigh 200 pounds stripped, but all I ever did was ruin a tool trying.

The only way to get out the oil was to open the front, stuff rags down through the narrow fire slot, sop up the stuff and fish out the rags with the string tied around one end of the bundle. Then you wring out the rags with your bare hands into a pan.

"Hey, Lottie," I yelled, "this is your roaster! It'll be hard to clean out the oil smell!"

But, of course, it was too late. I had squeezed a half-pint of oil into it already. So I went on dunking and wringing and thinking how lousy my cigarettes were going to taste all evening and feeling glad that I delivered beer instead of oil for a living.

I got the stove bailed out and lit with only one serious blast of soot out the "Light Here" hole. Then I dumped the oil out in the alley and set the roaster pan in the sink. Lottie was peeling potatoes for dinner, and she snuggled her yellow curls on my shoulder kind of apologetically for the mess she had caused me. I scrubbed the soot and oil off my hands and told her it was all right, only next time, for gosh sakes, please turn the stove off at least.

The water I was splashing into the roaster gathered up in little shrinking drops and reminded me that the pig hocks I brought home for Sunday dinner were going to rate throwing out unless we got the oil smell out of the pan.

"Tell you what you do," I said to Lottie. "Get me all your cleaning soaps and stuff and let's see what we got."

Lottie is always trying out some new handy-dandy little kitchen helper compound, so she hefted up quite an armload. Now, when I was in high school, I really liked chemistry. "Charlie, Boy Scientist," my pals used to sneer at me. But I was pretty good at it, and I been reading the science magazines right along ever since. So I know what a detergent is supposed to do, and all about how soaps act, and stuff that most people take the advertisers' word for.

"This one," I told Lottie, "has a lot of caustic in it, see?"

She nodded and said that's the one that ruined her aluminum coffee pot. She remembered it specially.

I poured some very hot tap water into the roaster and shook in the strong soap powder. "This is to saponify the oil," I explained.

"What's saponify?" Lottie asked.

"That means to make soap. Soap is mainly a mixture of some caustic with fat or oil. It makes sudsy soap."

"But we got soap," she said. "Why don't you just use the soap we got?"

We went into the business of soap-making pretty deep. Meanwhile, I read some more labels and added pinches of this and that detergent and a few squirts of liquid "wonder-cleaners" that didn't say what was in them.

160

In her crisp Scotch way, Lottie got across to me that she thought I was wasting soap powder and my time and cluttering up the sink while she was busy there, so I wound up with half a cup of Doozey soap flakes, filled the pan to the brim and set the concoction at the back of the drain board to do its business.

When dinner was over, I was in the living room reading the paper when I heard Lottie muttering at the sink. Lottie doesn't usually mutter, so I went out to see what was wrong.

"Nice mess," she said and pointed at the roaster. The stuff had cooled and jelled into a half-solid condition.

"Hah!" I said. "We had a supersaturated solution. When it cooled off, it coagulated."

Lottie scowled. It makes her nervous when I use big words which I only do when I'm talking about chemistry and the like.

"Well, uncoogalate it and dump it out of my roaster," she told me.

My scientific inquiring mind was stirred as I lifted the pan over to the table under the center light. We had here a gelatin of various cleaners, and every one of them claiming to be best ever. What would this new combination do?

I grabbed a pan off the stove that had a mess of scorched carrot-leavings in the bottom. Lottie had been soaking it with about a half inch of water. As I reached for a tablespoon, Lottie objected. "Look, now, if you are going to start another *experiment,* dump that mess out first and let me work on the roaster."

I saved about a cupful of the slimy gunk and she went back to her dishes.

"You'll be sorry," I said under my breath, "if this turns out to be the only batch of the finest cleaner in the whole world. And us with only a cupful."

A minute later, I was glad she hadn't heard me. When I dropped a little glob of the stuff into the carrot pan and stirred it around a bit, instead of dissolving and diluting in the extra water, the mixture seemed to stay the same density after swallowing up the water.

"Give me a pie tin," I demanded.

Lottie sighed, but she got a shallow pan out of the pantry and handed it to me. Then I poured the jelly out of the carrot pan and I made my first important discovery.

The stuff was not good for cleaning out scorched carrots. The pot was bone-dry. So were the carrots. They had a desiccated look and were stuck worse than ever to the bottom. I brushed them with my finger and the top layers powdered to dust. Then I noticed that not a droplet or smidgin of the jelly remained in the pot. When I had poured it out, it had gone out all at the same time, as if it was trying to hang together.

The carbonized carrots at the very bottom were hard and dry, too. A scrape job if I ever saw one.

The pie tin was now full almost to the rim. The globby stuff sort of rolled around, trying to find a flat condition, which it finally did. The motion was not as startling as the sudden quiet that settled over the surface after a last ripple.

The stuff looked like it was waiting.

The temptation was worse than a park bench labeled "wet paint," so I stuck my finger in it. Right in the middle of it.

A ripple flashed out from the center like when you drop a pebble in a pool, and the ripple hit the brim and converged back to my finger. When it hit, the surface climbed up my finger about an eighth of an inch. Another ripple, another eighth of an inch, and about now I felt something like a gentle sucking sensation. Also, another feeling I can only tell you was "unclammy."

I jerked away fast and shook my finger hard over the pan, but it wasn't necessary. None of the stuff had stayed with me. In fact, my finger was dry—powdery dry!

Then I got the feeling that someone was staring over my shoulder. There was. It was Lottie, and she had a look of horror on her face that didn't help my nerves a bit.

"Get rid of it, Charlie!" she cried. "Get rid of it! Please throw it out!"

"Now, now, honey," I said. "It ain't alive."

"It is!" she insisted.

Lottie chatters quite a bit and pretty well speaks her mind. But she doesn't go around making assertions. When she does come out flat-footed with a serious statement, it is always from the bottom of her 22-carat womanly intuition, and she is practically always right.

"How could it be alive?" I argued. I often argue when I know I'm wrong. This time I argued because I wanted to wipe that awful look off my wife's face. "Come on in the living room and relax," I said.

And then sweet-natured, honey-haired little Lottie did a violent thing. Still staring over my shoulder at the pie tin, she screamed wide-open and ran out of the house. A second later, I heard her start the car out the driveway at 30 miles an hour in reverse. She burned rubber out in front and was gone.

I hadn't moved an inch. Because when she screamed, I looked back at the jelly to see why, and the stuff had oozed over the edge and was flowing slowly toward me.

I know a little about Korzybski and how he wanted everybody to make what he called a cortico-thalamic pause whenever they get scared as hell. So I was making this cortico-thalamic pause, which is really counting to ten before you do anything, while Lottie was leaving the house. When I got through with my pause, I jumped backward over my kitchen chair so hard that I must have knocked my head on the tile sink-board.

When I came to, it was after midnight. The kitchen light was still on. Lottie was still gone. I knew it. If she was here, she'd have had me in bed. No matter how much of my employer's product I have sampled, never has Lottie let me sleep it off on the kitchen floor. Her 110 pounds is a match for my 200 in more ways than one, and she takes good care of her man.

Then I realized that this was not a stag beer-bust. There was something about a pot of soap jelly.

It was still there. A long slug of the half-transparent stuff had strung down off the edge of the table and still hung there like a nasty-looking icicle.

The knob on the back of my head throbbed so much that at first I couldn't figure what was wrong with the air. Then my aching dry throat told me what the matter was. The air was dry like the summer we spent at a dude ranch in Arizona. It made my nostrils crimp, and my tongue felt like a mouthful of wrinkled pepperoni.

When I got to my feet and looked at the top of the kitchen table, I almost panicked again. But this time the pause worked and I got better results.

Alive or dead, the gunk was the most powerful desiccant I'd ever heard of. It had drunk up the water in the carrot pot, sucked the surface moisture from my finger, and then spent the past few hours feeding on the humidity in the air.

It was thirsty. Like alcohol has affinity for water, this stuff was the same way, only more so. In fact, it even reached out toward anything that had water in it—like me.

That's why it had oozed over the pan the way it did.

What's so frightening about that, I asked myself. Plants grow toward water.

But plants are alive!

That's what Lottie had said—before she screamed.

"So you're thirsty?" I asked it out loud. "Okay, we'll give you a *real* drink!"

I got a bucket from the service porch and took the pancake turner to scrape the gooey nightmare into it. I even caught the drip off the edge, and it seemed quietly grateful to sink back to the parent glob in the pail, which by now amounted to about a quart.

I set the pail in the laundry tray and turned on the faucet hard. In about a second and a half, I almost sprained my wrist turning it off. Not only did the jelly drink up the water without dissolving, but it started creeping up the stream in a column about three inches in diameter, with the water pouring down its middle.

When I got the water shut off, the unholy jelly spout slopped back disappointedly.

And now the bucket was over half full of the stuff.

I dropped in an ice cube as an experiment. It didn't even splash. The surface pulled away, letting the cube make a pretty good dent in it, but then only gradually did the displaced goo creep back around it as if to sample it cautiously.

I couldn't stand the dry air any more, so I threw open the doors and windows and let the cool, damp night air come in. The ice cube had disappeared without even a surface puddle. Now, as the humidity came back, I thought I noticed a restless shimmering in the jelly.

The phone rang. It was Lottie's mother wanting to know why Lottie had come over there in hysterics, and where had I been since seven o'clock. I don't remember what I answered, but it served the purpose. Lottie hasn't returned and they haven't called up any more.

When I returned to the bucket, it seemed that the stuff was deeper yet, but I couldn't tell because I hadn't marked the level. I got Lottie's fever thermometer out of the medicine chest and took the jelly's temperature. It read 58 degrees F. The wall thermometer read 58 degrees, too. Room temperature, with the windows open. What kind of "life" could this be that had no temperature of its own?

But then what kind of a fancy-pants metabolism could you expect out of an organism that fed on nothing but Lake Michigan water, right out of the reservoir?

I got a pencil and notebook out of Lottie's neat little desk and started making notes.

I wondered about the density of the stuff. Ice floated in it and the bucket seemed heavy. I broke the thermometer and tapped a drop of mercury onto the restless surface. The droplet sank slowly to the bottom with no apparent effect either way.

Heavier than water. Lighter than mercury.

I took a beer out of the refrigerator and swallowed it. The last drops I sprinkled into the pail. The drippings sizzled across the surface until only a fine dust was left. A tiny ripple flipped this dust over to the edge of the pail as if clearing the thirsty decks for action. But this drew my eyes to the rim of the liquid. There was no meniscus, either up or down.

Remembering back, I figured this meant there was no surface tension, which reminded me that part of this mixture was made of detergent.

But had I created a new form of life? Like Lottie said, was it really alive? Certainly it could reproduce itself. It had brains enough to know the direction of more water, like when it took off after me on the table.

Not long ago, there was this important physicist who wrote about how life probably got started away back when the Earth was just forming. He argued that special creation was more or less a lot of hogwash, and that what actually took place was that as the Earth cooled, all the hot chemicals mixing around sort of stumbled onto a combination or two that took on the first characteristics of life.

In other words, this guy left off where Mr. Darwin began his theory of evolution.

Now me, I don't know. Lottie makes me go to church with the kids every Sunday and I like it. If this chemical theory about life getting started is right—well, then, a lot of people got the wrong idea about things, I always figured.

But how would I or this physicist explain this quivering mess of protoplasm I got on my hands by accident this particular Friday night?

I experimented some more. I got out the kids' junior encyclopedia and looked up some things I'd forgot, and some I had never learned in the first place.

So it got to be Saturday morning. Fred and Claude phoned about the fishing trip and I made an excuse. No one else bothered me. All day Saturday, I studied. And all Saturday night and Sunday. But I couldn't figure out any sensible answers that would make peace with my minister.

It looked like I had created some form of life. Either that or some life-form in the stove oil that had been asleep a billion years had suddenly found a condition to its liking and had decided to give up hibernating in favor of reproduction.

What drove me on was the thought that I must have something here that was commercially important—a new culture of something that would revolutionize some branch of chemistry or biology. I wouldn't even stop to fry an egg. I chewed up some crackers and drank a few more bottles of beer when my stomach got too noisy. I wasn't sleepy, although my eyes felt like they were pushed four inches into my skull.

Junior's little chemistry set didn't tell me very much when I made the few tests I knew how. Litmus paper remained either red or blue when stuck into the jelly. This surprised me a little because this whole mass of de-sudsed washing compound mixture had started out with a pretty good shot of lye in it.

So my notes grew, but my useful information didn't. By midnight Sunday, it appeared that my jelly invention had only one important talent: the ability to drink endlessly anything containing water. And only the water was used, it seemed. Dissolved solids were cast aside in the form of variously colored dusts.

By now, the goop had outgrown the pail and was two-thirds up in the laundry tub. A slow drip from the faucet kept the surface of my monster in a constant state of frenzy, like feeding a rumpot beer by the thimbleful.

It was fascinating to watch the little curleycues of jelly flip up after each drop, reaching for more, and then falling back with a cranky little lash.

At two o'clock this morning, I began to get a little sense in me. Or maybe it was just the fear finally catching up again.

There was danger here.

I was too fuzzy to know exactly what the danger was, but I began to develop a husky hate for the whole project.

"Kill it!" came into my mind. "Get rid of it, Charlie!"

Lottie's scream shrilled back into my ears, and this command became very important to me. I became angry.

"Want a drink, do you?" I shouted out loud. I put on the

166

tea kettle and when it was to full steam, I took it back to the tub. "I'll give you a drink with a kick in it!"

What happened, I would like to forget. Ten times as fast as it had climbed up the cold water spout, it ran up the boiling water stream, into the tea kettle, blew off the lid and swarmed over my hand with a scalding-dry slither that made me drop the kettle into the tub and scream with pain.

The jelly steamed and stuck to my flesh long enough to sear it half to the bone. Then it slopped back with the rest and left me grabbing my wrist and tearing at the flesh with my fingernails to stop the pain.

Then I got insane mad. I got my big blowtorch I use for peeling paint, and I lit it and pumped it up as high as it would go and aimed it down into that tub.

Not too much happened. The jelly shrank away from the roaring blast, but it didn't climb over the edge of the tub. It shrank some more and I poured the flame on.

It didn't burn. It just got to be less and less, and what was left began to get cloudy. And when I hit the bottom of the tub, the last glob moved around pretty active, trying to escape the heat, but I got it. Every damned last shred of it, and I was laughing and crying when I dropped the torch into the tub. I had been holding it with my scalded hand and I guess I fainted.

I wasn't out long. I got up and dressed my hand with lard, and it felt pretty good. Took a couple of aspirins and sat down at Lottie's typewriter. I know I won't sleep until I get this off my mind in about the way it happened, because I probably won't believe all of it myself when I get back to normal.

I just now went out and fished the blowtorch out of the laundry tub. All there was left in the bottom of the tub was maybe half a pound of singed-looking—soap flakes?

There, I've finished writing this all down. But I'm still not sleepy. I'm not worried about patching things up with Lottie. She's the most wonderful, understanding wife a guy ever had.

My hand feels real good now. I got it wrapped in lard and gauze, and I could drive the truck if I wanted to.

I'm not afraid of getting fired or bawled out for not coming to work on time this morning.

No, the reason I haven't turned a wheel on my beer truck today is something else.

Friday night, when Lottie wanted to wash the roaster, I

saved only a cup of the jelly for my experiments. The rest she washed down the drain.

The sewer empties into Lake Michigan.

The brewery where I load up is right on the shore of Lake Michigan.

I'm afraid to drive down there and look.

A Pride of Carrots

ROBERT NATHAN

In the 1959 introductory note which preceded this play by one of this country's best known and most beloved fantasists, on the occasion of its original appearance in the *Magazine of Fantasy and Science Fiction*, the editor referred to Mr. Nathan's little masterpiece of spoofing as science fiction.

Now that editor was—and is—a good man, who has never been known to tell a lie except when it was esthetically advisable. And since technological rather than artistic values are involved in the question of the categorizing of "A Pride of Carrots," I must herewith aver that this drama of life among the alien vegetables is, in very sooth, science fiction.

However, if you choose to judge it differently, you may. Should you want to think of it more as a blithe satire on almost everything from television to tyranny, from Victorian romances to space opera, you have my willing permission.

It really doesn't make any difference, does it?

ACT ONE: *Scene 1*

(*The scene is a blank plain on a distant planet. Could it be Venus? Who knows? But on the other hand, why not? In the background there is an appropriate, mysterious scene of hills or mountains, rocks or grottoes, done by an imaginative scenic-designer. The set is simple; the wings of angels must not be clipped, producers must be comforted; High School auditoriums and summer theatres must be kept in mind. We go forward from there.*

(*A moment after the curtain rises, two space-travelers float slowly downward, attached to parachutes. They are from Earth, and suitably attired; one of them holds a ray-gun in his hands, the other carries a walkie-talkie. They land, gaze about them, and at each other. They are alert, alarmed, and ready for anything. One of them bends down, and picks a daisy. As he does so, it gives a squeak of agony. He doesn't notice the squeak; he studies the daisy. Then he takes his helmet off.)*

1ST VISITOR (*Taking a deep breath*): Flora. So there's air. (*Breathing*) Quite good air, as a matter of fact.

(*The second man takes off his helmet. We now meet the two visitors—first, U. S. Navy Air Force Commander* BRIAN POTTER, *and second, the well-known news commentator,* ALFRED CAUDLE. *It is* CAUDLE *who carries the walkie-talkie.*)

CAUDLE: Where are we, do you think?

POTTER (*With firm satisfaction*): On Venus, obviously. The air is pure, wind moderate, w. to s.w., visibility good.

CAUDLE (*Into his walkie-talkie*): Calling NBC, Earth. Calling NBC, Earth. Come in, Earth.

POTTER (*Unwrapping small American Flag, and naval ensign*): I now claim this planet for the United States of America, and the Fifth Fleet.

CAUDLE: Wait a minute—wait a minute. I have to make my own claim. (*He unrolls the flag of the State of Texas.*) In the name of the sovereign state of Texas (that's in case we find anything submerged) and my sponsors, Southwest Oil, Surely White Tooth Paste, Heidelberg (Wisconsin) Beer, and Bar B-Q-Dog Food. Calling NBC. Come in, Earth.

(*Both men plant their flags in the ground. They are much moved. They look at each other; then they gravely shake hands.*)

CAUDLE: This is a solemn moment, Commander.

POTTER: It is, Caudle. The first men on Venus.

CAUDLE: It's a curious thing; I thought I heard a squeak when you picked that daisy.

POTTER (*troubled*): Did you? . . . To tell you the truth, I did too. I thought it was static in my ear-phone.

CAUDLE: Come in, NBC. What sort of people do you think we'll find, Commander?

POTTER: I don't know. Could be very like ourselves. Not a naval community, I fancy.

CAUDLE: It's a funny thing. I can't raise Earth.

POTTER: Probably hit a dead spot somewhere.

CAUDLE: Oh, fine. I'm on a coast-to-coast hookup in less than two hours. With seven new sponsors—and I can't get NBC!

POTTER: They can't blame you for that. The main thing is —we got here! Well—*I'm* going to explore. I think perhaps you'd better stay here so as not to lose each other. I'll just take a look around—see what's over those low hills.

CAUDLE (*Seating himself on a rock*): Don't be too long, Commander. I confess, I feel a little nervous . . . not knowing what might come out of the bushes.

POTTER: You can have my ray-gun, if you like.

CAUDLE: What will *you* do?

POTTER (*calmly*): Run like hell. (*He tosses the ray-gun to* CAUDLE, *and walks off.*)

(CAUDLE, *after gazing about him uneasily, sets himself to adjust his walkie-talkie. A gryphon enters quietly, R. He is a combination of horse, rooster, and sabre-tooth tiger. He approaches* CAUDLE.)

GRYPHON (*Half clearing his throat*): Hrmm! (*It is a horrid sound.*)

(CAUDLE *leaps half off his rock. He turns to look at the gryphon, and all but swoons in terror.*)

CAUDLE: A . . . get away, you monster! Where's my gun? Potter! Help!

GRYPHON: I *beg* your pardon?

CAUDLE: Potter! Potter! How do you shoot the damn thing? Help . . . What?

GRYPHON: I said, I beg your pardon. Are you ill?

CAUDLE: You . . . you talk!

GRYPHON: Naturally. Why not? So do you. Haven't I seen you somewhere before?

CAUDLE: Certainly not!

GRYPHON (*thoughtfully*): I've seen you somewhere . . . I have it! On NBC—the Cradle Hour.

CAUDLE: But . . . that's television! That's my program.

GRYPHON: Exactly. That's where I've seen you. You're Caudle.

CAUDLE: Do you mean to say that our television reaches to . . . that you have . . . that . . . that there's television on Venus? (*Into the walkie-talkie*) Come in NBC—for heaven's sake!

GRYPHON: Venus? What do you mean, Venus? You're from Venus. Up there. (*He points.*)

CAUDLE: But that's Earth. Come in, Earth!

GRYPHON: Nonsense . . . *this* is Earth. At least . . . we call it Earth. And we call that Venus. Apparently you call *that* Earth, and *this* Venus. Well . . . that's semantics for you. Silly, isn't it. What is your word for . . . for miscegenation?

CAUDLE: Why . . . inter-marriage, I suppose. *Mésalliance.*

GRYPHON: We call it cross-pollination. And what would you call a group of carrots?

CAUDLE: A bunch?

GRYPHON: Good heavens! A bunch? A pride of carrots! That is, of course, on this side of the border. And a gaggle of onions. But if you were on the other side . . . it would be an exaltation of onions, and a deceit of carrots. Semantics, you see.

CAUDLE (*bemused*): I see. I see.

GRYPHON (*modestly*): A charm of gryphons.

CAUDLE: You are a . . . gryphon, I take it?

GRYPHON: Of course. Rather highly placed, as a matter of fact. You see the gold collar? (*He shows* CAUDLE *his collar.*) I belong to the Secretary of the Interior. My name is Fido.

CAUDLE: And he . . . ?

GRYPHON: A very able carrot. Quite famous . . . for his wife's tassel. You've seen ordinary carrots, no doubt . . . with their tops? But this is a most unusual tassel. Blue. Everyone is copying it.

CAUDLE (*slowly*): A female carrot, with a blue tassel. And you have television?

GRYPHON: Oh, yes, indeed. The Secretary's entire family tunes you in every Sunday night. They never miss a program. That's where I saw you . . . I have no set of my own, of course.

CAUDLE: I can't get NBC . . . How does it happen that you, an animal, are bound as a sort of servant to a . . . a vegetable?

GRYPHON (*simply*): One has to eat.

CAUDLE (*With a shudder*): Vegetables?

GRYPHON: Lord, no! Dried seeds . . . truffles, marzipan . . . you look a little like marzipan yourself. Do you mind if I try . . . ? (*He takes a nip out of Caudle's rear.*)

CAUDLE: Ow!

GRYPHON: Mm. Delicious. But definitely not marzipan. What is it?

CAUDLE: Meat, you fool!

GRYPHON: You don't say! Meat? I never saw meat before.

CAUDLE: You're meat yourself.

GRYPHON: I am? No! Splendid. (*He takes a bite out of his own arm.*) Ow! That hurt!

CAUDLE: Of course it hurt. Now stop it. And go find your master, and—tell him I'm here. You say he's a carrot?

GRYPHON: Naturally. What else *could* he be?

CAUDLE: I want to meet him.

GRYPHON: He'll want to meet you, too. There are one or two things that puzzle us—

(*He goes away, and* POTTER *returns.*)

POTTER: I say, Caudle . . . there's a whole field of wild flowers . . . anemones, I think . . . just over that rise . . . singing like birds!

CAUDLE (*glumly*): I know.

POTTER: You know?

CAUDLE: We had a visitor. It seems . . . we're in some kind of vegetable world . . .

POTTER: A vegetable world? . . . Good heavens! I say, Caudle—you're not a vegetarian by any chance, are you?

CAUDLE: No . . . Thank heavens. I can take them or leave them alone. Still . . . in a sense . . . you're right, of course. When I think of vegetable soup . . .

POTTER (*sharply*): Forget it! Don't think of it! And when we meet these . . . onions—or carrots—or whatever they are . . . remember . . . we've never eaten anything but . . . air . . . in our lives.

CAUDLE: They probably wouldn't mind our having eaten caterpillars . . .

POTTER: Air, Caudle, air. It's safer. Till we look around us.

CAUDLE: They've looked at *us* already, I'm afraid.

POTTER: The devil you say!

CAUDLE: They've seen me on television.

POTTER (*startled*): They have? Then we *can* get through to Earth. . . .

CAUDLE (*disconsolately*): Sure. How?

POTTER: Ask somebody!

CAUDLE: How do you ask a carrot?

POTTER: Cheer up, old man. It could be worse. In the navy you meet all kinds of people. I've met vegetables before.

(*There is a choral-like sound of women's voices, and a middle-sized carrot enters L., carrying a water-dowser's hazel twig, all in gold. He comes up to* CAUDLE, *and pushes him gently out of the way.*)

CARROT: Pardon me, sir.

(*The wand bends down; at which the carrot gives a whistle, and an oversized market basket is wheeled in by two other carrots. In the basket is a large male carrot, with a fine green tassel on his head, and an attractive female carrot, with a blue tassel. The dowser points to the spot; the two servant carrots wheel the basket over, and then stand back; and the large male carrot gets out by opening a wicker in the side.*)

THE LARGE CARROT: Good earth beneath me . . . ? Moist?

DOWSER: Yes, sir.

CARROT (*Giving his hand to the blue tassled carrot*): Come, my dear. (*She steps down, beside him.*)

(*The two servant carrots reach into the basket, and bring out a bowl of water which they place carefully near their master, and two thorn bushes in pots which they place on either side of him. Then, and then only, he turns toward* CAUDLE *and* POTTER.)

CARROT: Welcome; to our planet. (*He bows; the lady curtseys; and* CAUDLE *and* POTTER *both bow.*)

CAUDLE: Thank you.

POTTER: In the name of the United States Navy . . .

CAUDLE (*hurriedly*): Later, Commander, later. Your Majesty . . . that is, Your Majesties . . . ?

BLUE TOP (*She has a lovely voice*): We're not majesties. There are none here. This is a republic; like Texas. My husband is Secretary of the Interior; his name is Edwin and I'm his wife, Edwina. And you're the famous news commentator, Alfred Caudle; and you're Commander Potter. We saw your take-off, and we watched your trip . . . though we lost you when you rounded Mars. Otherwise, we should have been here to greet you.

CAUDLE: Madam, you can perhaps conceive the feelings with which Commander Potter and myself gaze for the first time at this unfamiliar scene . . . the first mortal eyes to . . . glimpse these mountains, distant not only in space, but . . .

EDWIN: We are perhaps immortal?

CAUDLE (*confused*): No, no . . . I meant . . . I mean to say . . . the first travelers in space . . . The first . . . the first men.

EDWIN: No insult meant, no umbrage taken. Continue.

CAUDLE (*unhappily*): I find myself somewhat at a loss, Your Excellency.

EDWINA (*gently*): You must be weary, Mr. Caudle . . . and you, Commander. And hungry, perhaps. What food would please you? That is . . . if we have it. What do you like to eat?

CAUDLE: Air.

EDWINA (*puzzled*): Air? Well . . . there is plenty of that. Are you thirsty? For what?

POTTER: Water will do very nicely, madam.

EDWIN (*surprised*): Water! My dear . . . the man wants water.

174

EDWINA: Does he want it over him . . . or would he like to stand in it?

POTTER: I'll just drink it, if you don't mind.

EDWINA (*uncertainly*): Of course. (*She motions to one of the servants.*) Adalbert . . . Bring the gentlemen a cup of water . . .

(ADALBERT *reaches into the basket for a cup, fills it from the water pot, and hands it to* POTTER, *who takes a swallow, and looks surprised.*)

POTTER: It has a kind of taste . . . not unpleasant.

EDWINA (*cheerfully*): We've been . . . ah . . . sitting in it, I'm afraid. . . .

POTTER (*smiling*): To your health . . . both of you. (*He drinks the remainder.*)

CAUDLE: Mysterious are the ways of the Lord. Having made man in His own image . . .

EDWIN: What?

CAUDLE: I said . . . The Lord having made man in His own image . . .

EDWIN: Why man, in particular?

CAUDLE: It says so. In Genesis 1-26.

EDWIN: Ah? But surely . . . the Lord, of whom you speak . . . and by whom, I imagine, you mean the Creator . . . must Himself be the root of all things—No?

CAUDLE: In a sense, of course. . . .

EDWIN: Exactly. God is a root. *You* don't look in the least like a root. (*Turning to his wife.*) Does he, my dear? Do they?

EDWINA: Not at all. He has no stalk. (*Brightly to* POTTER.) Did you think you did?

POTTER: I'm afraid I never gave it much thought, ma'am.

EDWINA (*gently*): You should think about it. We're very down-to-earth people here, I'm afraid. Very literal. We have to be. The rabbits would have had us, otherwise . . . long ago.

CAUDLE: How did you prevent it? . . . If you don't mind my asking.

EDWIN: I don't mind telling you it was touch and go, for a while. But then we managed to drop a few seeds inside a thorn bush. After a while we moved out . . . and took the thorn bush with us. That was long ago, of course . . . when we had only the rudiments of a brain. But it was more than the rabbits had. From the tufts of rabbit wool left hanging on the briars, we made our first clothes. That fooled them completely. We left them to polish off the lettuces, and began

175

our development. As you can see, we use the thorn as a badge of authority.

EDWINA: How did *you* develop?

CAUDLE: I think we hid in trees.

POTTER: Nonsense. We evolved from the sea. The mammal, or milk-secreting vertebrate . . .

EDWIN: Er . . . pardon me, Commander . . . Later, perhaps? There are certain rules of hospitality—The leaders of the nation, the carrot-tops themselves, are waiting to greet you, with appropriate exercises. There will be entertainment by some very well-known vegetables; and speeches by the Heads of State, including myself. My speech is being written for me at this very moment, by a talented young parsnip in the Bureau of Agriculture. So—with your permission . . .

EDWINA: Just a moment, Edwin. Your daughter . . .

EDWIN (*sharply*): What about my daughter?

EDWINA: She is on her way here.

EDWIN: Damn.

(*A sound of galloping is heard and a moment later the gryphon comes trotting on L.—with a charming young female carrot on his back. She slips to the ground, and greets the travelers with a wave of her hand. Her name is* ALICE.)

ALICE: Hi!

(CAUDLE *and* POTTER *bow.* EDWIN *sighs heavily.*)

EDWINA (*graciously*): This is our daughter, gentlemen; Alice, allow me to present you to our visitors from space, Mr. Caudle and the Commander Potter.

ALICE: I know all about them, Mother. Welcome to Carrotania, gentlemen.

EDWIN: I have already welcomed them, my dear.

ALICE: You don't understand the animal kingdom, Father. They'd much rather be welcomed by a young girl.

EDWINA (*shocked*): Really, Alice! Where do you learn such things?

ALICE (*calmly*): At school. It's all in Zoology One.
'Spring, the sweet Spring, is the year's pleasant king;
Then blooms each thing, then maids dance in a ring,
Cold doth not sting, the pretty birds do sing
Cuckoo, jug-jug, pu-we, to-wit-ta-woo!'

EDWIN: For heaven's sake, Edwina . . . !

CAUDLE: Well, Well!

ALICE: I know another one, too . . .
'The blessed Damozel lean'd out
From the gold bar of Heaven.
Her blue grave eyes were deeper much

176

Than a deep water, even.
She had three lilies in her hand,
And the stars in her hair were seven.'
They really do like young girls, Father. You claim to be
so realistic. . . .

EDWIN: Oh . . . all right, all right. . . .

EDWINA (*To Alice*): That's enough, dear. We were just
going to escort them back to town . . . you can go with us
if you like. But try to control your high spirits. We're all a
little edgy, I'm afraid—this last day of waiting has been—
well, after all, they could have landed in Onionapolis!

ALICE: But they didn't. The onions didn't get them—we
got them . . . I like the Commander. He's cute.

POTTER: Well—thank you very much!

EDWIN: Oh God! . . . Come on, Edwina! Gentlemen . . .

(EDWIN *steps back into the basket, followed by* EDWINA.
*The servants take up the bowl of water and the two pots
of briars, and wheel the basket off.*)

POTTER: I suppose we'd better follow . . . ?

CAUDLE: Lead the way, Commander. . . .

ALICE (*Coming between them, and linking her arm in both
of theirs*): My parents think I'm quite mad. I'm not really. I
watch television all the time. I should like to be a great
actress, and help to sell cigarettes. Do you think that's ab-
normal?

POTTER (*heartily*): Not where I come from.

ALICE: I like you, Potter. You interest me. (*To* CAUDLE
—*with charm.*) You too, of course . . . shall we go? Come
along, Fido.

(*They leave, arm in arm, followed by the gryphon.*)

ACT ONE: *Scene 2*

(*I have changed my mind about High School auditoriums;
this play will be too rich for them.*

(*The scene is the private office, or study-and-Star Council-
room of the Secretary General of the Party, in Onionapolis,
in the United Socialist Republic of the Leeks and Onions. Naturally, it is underground. The Secretary himself,* O'DOR, *a
very large white onion, is seated at his desk; while before
him sits, in humble mien, a leek.*)

O'DOR: You say they have landed. How do you know?

LEEK: We have it on the best authority, sir—the underground—

177

O'Dor: They have not landed in our own Onionland, or in the Republic of the Leeks.

Leek: No, sir.

O'Dor: They have dared to land near Carrotapolis. That is a grave oversight on the part of our security police.

Leek: Unfortunately, our side of the planet was turned away from the direction from which they came, and so they landed on the back side.

O'Dor: The back side. Hmmm. See what you can do with that, Spindle.

Leek (Spindle): Yes, Little Father.

O'Dor: However—exchanging insults with the carrots isn't going to bring these space-men over to our own side. And we must have them, Spindle. We must get hold of their technical skill; we must have their know-how—before the carrots get it. Or else . . . (*He makes a motion indicative of "it is finished—kaput."*)

Leek: Yes, Little Father.

O'Dor: It is ridiculous—is it not?—that we, who invented television, jet propulsion, the atom bomb, and the bicycle, should be deprived of these two men who could tell us how to use them—? That our marvelous studies in science, and our never-to-be-challenged will for peace, should be frustrated by the fact that two men, arriving from distant space, had the misfortune to land upon our planet's behind, and are now the guests of our mortal enemies, the carrots! (*He rises, and holds up his clenched fist.*) Death to carrots!

Leek (*Doing likewise*): Death to carrots!

(*They sit down peacefully again.*)

O'Dor: By the way—when you write to Carrotania again, ask Edwin to send us 20,000 more tons of bone meal, and ten of leaf mold for the spinach beds.

Leek: He writes that he'd like about fifteen carloads of ammonium sulphate.

O'Dor: At the usual price?

Leek: Yes. . . .

O'Dor: Hmm—ammonium sulphate is a war material, Spindle.

Leek: Are you sure, sir?

O'Dor: You could lose your head for that remark. I am *always* sure. The mere fact of my saying it, makes it so. If you do not understand this, Spindle, you do not understand the making of history. This great truth alone, within two generations, will conquer the world. To *create* truth, Spindle

—*that* is the great thing! Not merely to go looking for it—have we ever used this sulphate in a war?

LEEK: Not to my knowledge, sir.

O'DOR: Good. Good. Then we are the first to discover that it is war material. Add 20% to the price.

LEEK: Yes, Little Father.

O'DOR: And bring me those scientists from the planet they —erroneously—call Earth.

LEEK: How am I going to do that, Little Father?

O'DOR: This I leave entirely up to you. There are ways— of the shanghai, the kidnap, the finagle, the seduction. . . .

LEEK: With an onion?

O'DOR (*dangerously*): What is the matter with an onion? A sweet, Spanish onion . . . ?

LEEK (*floundering*): Well . . . it is only that . . .

O'DOR: This also could cost you your head, Spindle.

LEEK (*meekly*): Yes, Little Father. We will do it with an onion. . . . Unless—

O'DOR: Yes? Unless?

LEEK: Nothing . . . I had a thought, suddenly; but it is better if you don't know it—then you are innocent, no matter what.

O'DOR (*excitedly*): Of course I am innocent! Already I deny it! I deny it categorically! It is altogether the fault of Carrotania! . . . Did you suggest otherwise?

LEEK (*hurriedly*): No, Little Father—no indeed.

O'DOR: I do not dislike you, Spindle.

LEEK: Oh—thank you, sir—

O'DOR: Therefore you have a future. At least, for a while. But you still have things to learn. One: The head of the state is always right; he cannot, by his very nature, be anything else. A Secretary General who is wrong is unthinkable. It is the same as saying: an onion without his rings. So—since he cannot be wrong, and must be right, he must also be innocent. All of which comes under the heading of being right. Right?

LEEK: Right.

O'DOR: Two: The United Socialist Republic of Leeks and Onions is a land of peace and freedom, mother of the arts, and home of the sciences. We allow no difference of opinion; therefore there is freedom, for no one interferes with what is allowed. Our artists enjoy the happiest of lives, painting onions; and our scientists have already three times turned biology, zoology, and the entire metaphysics of the universe upside down, and back again. When you can understand all these points, and add them together, you can see how silly it is to argue about whether ammonium sulphate is war material . . . or had we gone on from there?

LEEK: Yes, Little Father. We were talking about a sweet Spanish onion. . . .

O'DOR: You know one?

LEEK: I do, Little Father.

O'DOR: A nice one, hey? With a silky skin? No wrinkles . . . ?

LEEK: Like ivory.

O'DOR: And very Spanish? You know what I mean. . . .

LEEK: Exactly. . . .

O'DOR: Hot and sweet. . . .

LEEK: Like a tamale—

O'DOR (*Clicking his fingers*): With those castanets—

LEEK: And what a dancer!

O'DOR: Very Spanish. Sweet and hot. Languorous, hey?

LEEK: Melting. . . .

O'DOR (*Suddenly coming to*): What are we talking about?

LEEK: I don't know, Little Father. Was it about the planet's behind?

O'DOR: N-o . . . .

LEEK: I know. It was about the space-men. The men from the planet they call Earth.

O'DOR: That's it. I knew it. Well, then—what are we waiting for? Off you go; and bring them back with you. Death to carrots!

LEEK (*rising*): And—the little Spanish number?

O'DOR: Send her in to me.

LEEK (*meekly*): Yes, sir. (*Lifting his fist*) Death to carrots.

(*He goes out. As he goes out, he is passed by* GENERAL SHALLOT, *who enters. The general wears a colorful uniform, and is much bemedalled. He lifts his fist in greeting, and is greeted by the General Secretary in return.*)

SHALLOT: Etcetera.

O'DOR: Etcetera. Come in, Shallot. Sit down. (SHALLOT *seats himself.*) What news from the front?

SHALLOT (*comfortably*): Which front, Comrade?

O'DOR (*He'd much rather be called Little Father*): Any of them. All of them.

SHALLOT: We are continuing our tactic of embarrassing the enemy at all points. So far, we have caught twenty-seven violators of our territory. Naturally, we have been obliged to cross the border; in some cases we were forced to go as far as fifteen miles inside carrot territory, in order to be violated.

O'DOR: Were these carrots armed?

SHALLOT: Who knows? *We* were.

O'DOR: Well—there it is—a clear case of provocation. We will send the usual protest.

SHALLOT: Exactly, Comrade.

O'DOR: You *could* call me Excellency. Or Little Father.

SHALLOT (*proudly*): I am a descendant of the garlics. A garlic does not call *any*thing Excellency.

O'DOR (*hastily*): I was only joking. Ha ha ha. Here we are all comrades! *All* excellencies . . . Little Fathers. Except Leeks. Now I will tell you something. As you know, the Earth-men landed today in Carrotania.

SHALLOT (*Lifting his fist*): Death to carrots!

O'DOR (*likewise*): Likewise. By the way, Shallot—what are you doing tonight?

SHALLOT: Imperialistic warmongers! Nothing.

O'DOR: Capitalist swine! Come to dinner.

SHALLOT: Love to. Continue, Comrade.

O'DOR: Should they not have landed here?

SHALLOT: Possibly.

O'DOR (*outraged*): What do you mean, possibly? We are going to bring them here!

SHALLOT (*gravely*): Hmm—that may not be so wise, Comrade.

O'DOR: And why not? Don't you want to learn how to set off guided missiles? How to fly a jet?

SHALLOT: That is not the point, Comrade; the point is—do we want to lose our right to make complaints? Such things are weapons, too—the very best weapons. They cost nothing. And they create an atmosphere—an odor—it is a real onion odor.

O'DOR (*slowly*): I see. Then you are opposed to the kidnapping of these Earth-men . . . ?

SHALLOT: Definitely.

O'DOR: Very well. I will think about it. You can go, General. (*As* SHALLOT *rises*) By the way, I have news for you. You have been promoted to Field Marshal.

(SHALLOT *clicks his heels, bows, lifts his fist, and gives a loud bellow.*)

SHALLOT: Strength to onions!

O'DOR: See you at dinner. Eight-thirty sharp.

(SHALLOT *goes out.* O'DOR *reaches into his desk, and brings out a phone. He dials.*)

O'DOR: Hello—Secret police? General Shallot has just left my office. Liquidate him.

ACT ONE: *Scene 3*

(*A garden in Carrotopolis. It is evening.* ALICE *and* HERBERT, *a young carrot captain, are discovered in each other's arms.*)

ALICE (*Breaking away*): Herbert . . . we're mad.

HERBERT: Angel!

ALICE (*Rather matter-of-factly*): Mad. Wildly, ecstatically mad. Do you love me?

HERBERT: Madly.

ALICE (*languidly*): Life is a bag of peat-moss . . . Haven't we done all this before?

HERBERT: Only once.

ALICE: And you enjoy it enough to do it again?

HERBERT (*uncertainly*): Ye-es . . . I think so.

ALICE: Life is so boring, Herbert. Love is so seasonal. I must ask Brian if it's seasonal where he comes from.

HERBERT (*jealously*): Brian?

ALICE: The navy man. Potter.

HERBERT: What would he know about love? He has no blossoms.

ALICE: He must have *something*. . . .Love is so dull, Herbert. All those flies, everywhere you go.

HERBERT: Bees, darling. Not flies—bees.

ALICE (*petulantly*): What's the difference? They have wings. Love has wings. Herbert—here today, and gone tomorrow. Brian has wings. He wears them on his uniform. He says they're Navy wings. Do you think the Navy is love, Herbert? Oh . . . but you wouldn't know; you're in the Army, aren't you?

HERBERT: Kiss me!

ALICE: If you like. (*They embrace.*) I think perhaps I'll dye my top. Blue, like Mother's. If I were blue, would you dye yourself blue, too, Herbert?

HERBERT (*hoarsely*): Anything. Anything at all.

ALICE: Would you love me if I were blue?

HERBERT: Any way. Any color at all.

ALICE (*regretfully*): It's hardly worth doing then, is it? I wish I could find something exciting to do!

HERBERT: You could marry me.

ALICE: You know Father would never allow it.

HERBERT (*sadly*): I know. That's what—would make it exciting.

ALICE: I want to live. Dangerously. Before we're all wiped out by some horrid blight—I want to taste the delights of ... Herbert!

HERBERT: Yes?

ALICE: What does meat taste like?

HERBERT: How do *I* know?

ALICE: Brian is meat. So is Mr. Caudle. Fido told me.

HERBERT: By Jove! The animal kingdom! So they are.

ALICE: (*dreamily*): He said they're very good.

HERBERT: Getting married would last longer.

ALICE: It's so comfortable here, at Mother's. Of course, I'm madly—wildly—in love with you ... (*They embrace.*) but I *do* like having somebody turn down my bed for me at night ... and bring me breakfast in the morning. ...

HERBERT: If only there were a war going on!

ALICE: That's the most selfish thing I ever heard! You haven't the least regard for anybody. ... Don't touch me. (*Turning to go*)

HERBERT: But Alice. ...

ALICE: I hate wars; they upset everything. (*Turning to him again ... with sudden passion*) Herbert! Promise me there won't be a war!

HERBERT: But darling. ...

ALICE: Promise!

HERBERT (*helplessly*): Well—it isn't up to me, you know. I'm only a captain. ...

ALICE (*Turning away indignantly*): So that's what all your talk of loving me amounts to!

HERBERT: Alice ... !

ALICE: Don't touch me! I'm going to find a nice cool moist sandy place, and sit in it.

(*She goes out; with a despairing gesture,* HERBERT *follows her. A moment later,* EDWIN *and* CAUDLE *enter.*)

CAUDLE: But I don't understand, Your Excellency—if the onions don't want your land—and you say they have plenty of their own—and don't want your oil, or your heavy industries ... what *do* they want?

EDWIN: They want us to be onions.

CAUDLE: But that's absurd.

EDWIN: Of course it's absurd.

CAUDLE: And they'd go to war for that?

EDWIN: No one actually knows. Of course, they don't say so. What they want is for everybody to be round, and white, and onions. When as a matter of fact, the only possible thing for everyone to be—if they're to have a decent kind

183

of life—is long and crisp and carrots. Now *that's* something worth fighting for! Liberty. Freedom. The good life. And private enterprise . . . with the proper controls, of course. We have to keep control of chlorophyl. Can't let *that* get into private hands!

CAUDLE: The planet is pretty well divided between yourselves—and them?

EDWIN: Just about.

CAUDLE: Evenly—would you say?

EDWIN: Oh . . . we're strong enough, if it comes to that. As a matter of fact, we've been experimenting with a new shallow oil fryer—though so far it's only in the drawing-board stage, because of not having an onion to try it on. But just the same, a war now, at this point, would be the worst thing in the world—for both of us. For one thing—neither of us could afford it; and before it was over, we carrots would have whiskers, and *they'd* be scallions. And besides . . . (*In a low grave voice*) I think they plan to use nematodes. It's a race suicide, of course.

CAUDLE: Nematodes . . . ? Let me think a minute—aren't those the tiny worms that all but ruined the citrus in California back in the forties?

EDWIN: I don't know about citrus—it isn't exactly my line. Down here—they eat vegetables. A kind of virus. Too small to see . . . we've tried to outlaw them, but—*they* won't agree to it. That's what makes me think that . . . Well, it's all a mess. We'll wipe each other out, and then the spiders can take over. But it's sort of sad to think that no one will even remember us. No mulch any more. No bone meal. No clothes made of rabbit's fur. No chlorophyl. . . . Just spider webs. All over.

CAUDLE: Ugh! You know—I think we had a way of fumigating for nematodes back in the States. I'm not sure if it worked. I could find out—if I could only get through to NBC.

EDWIN: You can't get through . . . ?

CAUDLE: No. And it's particularly strange because I understand there's good reception here.

EDWIN: Maybe you've been jammed.

CAUDLE: But why? Who would jam me?

EDWIN: Who knows? *They* might, I suppose. We could send you out ourselves, of course, on a planet-to-planet hook up. . . .

CAUDLE (*eagerly*): Could you? That would be terrific . . .

wait a minute. How come we've never had you on our screens at home?

EDWIN: We've never broadcast to you.

CAUDLE: But you get ours . . . ?

EDWIN: My dear Mr. Caudle, the vegetable world is, upon the whole, modest, and even shy. We are not aggressive. We broadcast to the insects, and even to the birds; but not, as a rule, to the animal kingdom. Our experience with the rabbits, you know. . . . Perhaps we overdo it a little. Consider it an idiosyncrasy. I should be delighted to arrange a broadcast for you. Particularly, if you could find out anything about fumigating. . . .

CAUDLE: 'Good evening Mr. and Mrs. North and South America, and all the slips at sea.' . . . (*He laughs happily.*)

(POTTER *and* EDWINA *enter.*)

CAUDLE: Mr. Potter—Commander! We're going to broadcast!

POTTER: No! Splendid. I'll get to work on my report right away—or are we going to ad lib?

CAUDLE: Better type the report. You can ad lib to your wife.

EDWINA: You have a wife, Commander?

POTTER: Yes, ma'am. Every Navy man, over a full Lieutenant, has one.

EDWINA: A woman, I suppose?

POTTER: Oh, yes, ma'am. Definitely. She has to be.

EDWINA: What is your wife like, Mr. Potter?

POTTER: Why . . . er . . . she's a female. . . .

(*He tries to explain with gestures.* EDWINA *repeats his gestures with bewilderment.*)

EDWINA: You mean . . . like this? How very . . . odd. Bumpy.

POTTER (*embarrassed*): Yes, ma'am.

EDWINA: *You're* not bumpy.

POTTER: No, ma'am.

EDWINA (*thoughtfully*): I see. Is that how you tell your own from the others?

POTTER: How do you tell one carrot from another?

EDWINA: No two carrots are alike. There are a thousand differences . . .

POTTER: To a carrot. It's the same with us.

EDWINA: Of course, my dear! Remember the rabbits? They all looked exactly the same—but they did seem able to recognize one another. And onions! They're just a faceless mob, as far as I'm concerned.

185

CAUDLE (*hopefully*): To get back to the broadcast. . . .

POTTER: Right! What about it?

CAUDLE: If you ask *me,* I think it calls for a bit of a cele-bration—our landing the way we did. . . .

POTTER: And being received so kindly—

(*All bow.*)

CAUDLE: It's a pity we have no champagne.

EDWINA: Champagne? What's that?

CAUDLE: A kind of bubbly wine.

EDWIN (*frowning*): Wine is from grapes, isn't it? Friends of ours. Relatives.

EDWINA: I'm not sure I like this at all!

POTTER: We could break out our emergency rations.

CAUDLE: The very thing!

EDWINA: Cousin Muscat! Aunt Malaga! Uncle Zinfandel!

(*POTTER reaches into his pocket and brings out a tin box. He opens it, and extracts a can.*)

POTTER: Here you are. A can opener?

CAUDLE (*Bringing one from his pocket*): Right. . . . (*He takes the can, and reads the label.*) For emergency only. U. S. Navy. Concentrated carrot juice.

EDWIN (*thundering*): What?

POTTER: Oh—oh. . . .

EDWINA: I think I'm going to faint.

EDWIN: Carrot juice? Guards! Seize those men! They're onions!

(*The guards rush in.*)

ACT TWO: *Scene 1*

(*The library in* EDWIN'S *place in Carrotopolis—which is, not unreasonably, the capital of Carrotania. What will a carrot's library look like? There would be paintings of vegetables —ancestors and friends—on the walls; and the head of a large rabbit over the fireplace. The usual thorn bushes, and an ornamental pot of water. Beyond that, I am not pre-pared to go.*)

(*EDWINA is sitting on a small couch, knitting.* EDWIN *is pac-ing up and down the floor. The gryphon lies in his bas-ket, near the fireplace.*)

EDWIN: I tell you, my dear, it's a most uncomfortable pickle. These—mean creatures—are dangerous. At the same time . . . they *could* be helpful to us. If—I say *if,* they were peacefully disposed. . . . But *are* they peacefully disposed?

EDWINA: From what I've seen on television, they do enjoy a great deal of shooting, Edwin. And one does get the suggestion of a certain amount of—shall we say coarseness? —in their literature. One wonders.

EDWIN: One does; one does indeed. Still . . . this thing about fumigating; it could turn out to be very helpful. Very embarrassing to the other side.

EDWINA: They *do* drink wine, dear. I didn't like that at all.

EDWIN: I know. And carrot juice. . . . It gave me a nasty turn. Of course—they don't look like onions. . . .

GRYPHON: They don't taste like them, either.

EDWIN: You—tasted one?

GRYPHON: I did.

EDWIN: What did he taste like?

EDWINA: Was it sharp? Did it sting your nose?

GRYPHON: No. It was rubbery, on the whole—no crackle to it. No crispy-crunchy quality at all.

EDWIN: You see, my dear—

EDWINA (*uncertainly*): Y-yes. Still . . .

EDWIN: Your daughter seems rather attracted to them.

EDWINA: To the naval one. He has a wife.

EDWIN (*puzzled*): So? What has that got to do with it?

EDWINA: With what, dear?

EDWIN: With—with . . . I mean to say, what has his having a wife got to do with—with what he is? Or isn't?

EDWINA (*placidly*): Nothing, darling. Nothing at all. It seems it's part of the regulations. I just thought I'd mention it.

EDWIN: Well, don't. All you do is confuse me. . . . I feel that we could learn a great deal from him. And the other one. That is—if they aren't onions.

EDWINA: I don't know what we could learn from the other one, dear—except, perhaps, why the little man on television tries to sell us toothpaste. Or do you think he could tell us why there are wars?

EDWIN: Who?

EDWINA: Why—Mr. Potter, of course.

EDWIN: Don't be silly, Edwina; *no*body can tell you why there are wars. There just are, that's all. They're a necessary part of the economic structure. They provide a—a sort of enzyme to the body politic. Besides, we have to sell our bone meal . . . which reminds me; I must make a note to raise the price again . . . what with the higher cost of living. No, my dear—please don't meddle in what doesn't concern you. As long as there's no actual fighting . . .

EDWINA: Then why are they in prison? The two men, I mean—

EDWIN (*simply*): Security. The first duty of a Minister of State is to make sure that his country is secure.

EDWINA: I see. And his daughter?

EDWIN: What the devil has his daughter got to do with it?

EDWINA: She's growing up, Edwin.

EDWIN (*testily*): Of course she's growing up. Why shouldn't she grow up? Is there anything wrong with that?

EDWINA: Really, Edwin—a person can hardly open her mouth these days, without your jumping down her throat.

EDWIN (*grumpily*): Well—I'm sorry. I'm a little edgy, I guess. Maybe I'd better take Fido out for a walk.

GRYPHON: Uh—uh. I did it before I came in.

(EDWIN *sits down, and passes his hand wearily over his forehead.*)

EDWIN: Besides—this broadcast—

EDWINA: I think it would be quite exciting. . . . Would we be asked to speak, do you think?

EDWIN: I don't know. We might. Possibly.

EDWINA: Will it be telecast?

EDWIN: I—suppose so.

EDWINA (*Glancing up at her blue top*): I think it should be done in color. . . . I'll have the dressmaker in tomorrow. Something in blue, perhaps. . . . I'm so glad that Alice had her teeth straightened. . . . You see, I was right: I *told* you the elocution lessons were a good idea.

EDWIN: Wait a minute . . . I'm not giving a show. I want information—on vital matters. Military, and economic. Social studies. Fumigation. What has that got to do with elocution lessons?

EDWINA: And all that poetry she learned . . . English. Very good. *Old* English. They say the old English is the best. Mr. Laughton, I think . . . a large gentleman. . . .

EDWIN: For heaven's sake, Edwina!

EDWINA (*calmly*): Yes, dear . . . I know. You want to find out about nematodes; and about your new shallow oil fryer. But we're *not* at war—not exactly; and I don't know why you give me so little credit for intelligence. Alice, as I have said, is growing up. She has few opportunities to meet what I would call eligible parties . . . already I have detected cer-

tain looks between herself and that young captain—Herbert,
I think his name is. Is there any harm in showing herself
over a planet-to-planet hookup? Who knows what might come
of it? Since her teeth have been straightened. . . .

EDWIN: Fido—I don't care whether you did or didn't—
you're going for a walk!

(*He stalks out, followed by a grumbling gryphon.*)

ACT TWO: *Scene 2*

(*A cell, at night. There is a little light, but not much.*
POTTER *and* CAUDLE *are lying on their cots.*)

POTTER: You shouldn't have read the label, old man.
That's what did it.

CAUDLE: How could *I* tell? I thought it would be chicken
consommé . . . and just when I had the greatest broadcast of the Ages lined up! If only I could get through to
NBC. . . .

POTTER: What good would that do?

CAUDLE: They'd think of something. They'd appeal to Edwin's better nature.

POTTER: What *is* the nature of a carrot, Caudle?

CAUDLE (*miserably*): I don't know.

(*The door of the cell is unlocked, and* HERBERT *enters.*
He carries a lantern, which he sets on the table.)

HERBERT (*morosely*): There is a lady to see you, gentlemen. . . .

(*He steps aside, to allow* ALICE *to enter.* CAUDLE *and* POT-
TER *both rise.*)

CAUDLE: Miss Alice!

ALICE (*With her fingers to her lips*): Sh! Not so loud.
(*To the captain.*) Thank you Herbert. You can leave us
now. . . .

HERBERT: Mind you, Alice—this is contrary to your father's orders, and against my better judgment. . . .

ALICE: I know, darling. It's divinely, utterly mad . . . run
along, pet.

HERBERT: I shall wait for you outside the door. All you
need do is scream.

(*He goes out, and closes the door after him.*)

ALICE (*gaily*): You wouldn't hurt me, would you?

POTTER: Glad to have you aboard, ma'am.

ALICE: I knew you wouldn't. (*She seats herself on one of
the stools.*) They say that you're dangerous vegetarians. That
you—*eat* carrots. (*She shudders.*) Do you really?

189

POTTER: Well . . . you see, ma'am . . .

ALICE: I don't believe it. Anyway, I sent the guard away; there's only Herbert. We're all alone . . . practically.

POTTER: And you're not afraid?

ALICE: You're much too nice to eat poor little me!

POTTER: Thank you, ma'am.

CAUDLE: You, yourself, are a vegetarian, Miss Alice.

ALICE (*indignant*): I'm not. I'm a vegetable. It's not the same thing at all!

CAUDLE: Just answer me this: What will happen to you when you die?

ALICE: I'll be buried—of course. In the National Compost Heap.

CAUDLE: From which the rich, steaming soil is taken to nourish the young carrots . . . right?

ALICE: Of course—

CAUDLE: Which then—which then, mind you—must of necessity feed upon your decayed flesh—from which, I might add, the spirit has long since fled—

ALICE (*bemused*): Why . . . of course. Why—how clever you are. I *am* a vegetarian, aren't I? Or, at least—I was. And of course, the new little carrots still are. . . .

CAUDLE: Not only that. Cannibals!

ALICE: How madly amusing! Cannibals. You're perfectly right. I really did eat my—my grandparents, didn't I? (*Her face falls.*) I missed mother and father, though.

POTTER: I should hope so!

ALICE: Oh—but don't you see—? The whole *point* lies in eating one's parents! Why—it solves *everything*. It would be so satisfying to a young girl's psyche to have her father under her belt . . . as it were . . . wouldn't it?

CAUDLE (*surprised*): Have you been through analysis?

ALICE: Of course. Haven't you?

CAUDLE: Yes. . . .

ALICE: It's so nice to be able to talk the same language, isn't it. . . . (*She rises, and begins to move restlessly around the cell.*) Whose parents *did* I eat, I wonder?

CAUDLE: An idea, merely. A parental symbol.

ALICE: *My* analyst says symbols don't satisfy. . . .

CAUDLE: We must look to the Oedipus. . . .

ALICE: My analyst says the trouble is my mother has a blue top.

CAUDLE: Exactly. The active competition of an adult parent. . . .

ALICE: It tends to make me aggressive.

190

CAUDLE: Naturally. Feeling that your mother has an unfair advantage. . . .

ALICE (*to* POTTER): Kiss me!

POTTER: Eh? What?

ALICE: Kiss me!

POTTER: Good Lord!—Really . . . I . . .

ALICE: Are you afraid? It isn't even Spring. I don't come into blossom till July.

POTTER: I know. But . . .

ALICE: Am I not beautiful? Am I not to be desired? By the Navy?

POTTER: Oh yes! Yes indeed! But . . .

ALICE: I could have your head, Potter. On a silver tray. Like Salome. I will kiss your mouth, Iokanaan . . . Potter.

POTTER: I know. But . . .

ALICE (*softly*): I could set you free. . . .

CAUDLE: For heaven's sake, kiss her, and get it over with.

POTTER: But . . .

(*She kisses him.* POTTER *draws back, and looks around dizzily. He turns, and kisses her again.*)

POTTER (*Drawing a deep breath*): Hmm. You smell so good. Like a grocery.

ALICE (*Also a little dizzy*): It feels like April. Is this love, Potter?

POTTER (*hoarsely*): How can I feel this way about a carrot?

ALICE: I feel a strange heat. Not like the sun. . . .

POTTER: Like a garden. In the summer.

ALICE: I don't feel at all like a vegetable. . . .

POTTER: I wouldn't have thought it possible.

CAUDLE (*indignantly*): Look. How about getting us out of here?

ALICE: Potter—say something! What has happened to us?

POTTER: I don't know. Wait.

(*He brings out a small book, and leafs through it rapidly.*)

ALICE: What is it, darling?

POTTER: Service Manual—

ALICE: Does it say something about us?

POTTER: Wait a minute—here it is (*reading*): 'They salute mutually, but in any case there should be no hesitation on the part of either, or delay in rendering the salute. . . .'

(*They are about to embrace each other again, when* HERBERT *sticks his head in at the door.*)

HERBERT: Time is up, folks.

ALICE: Oh? . . . Yes . . . Is it? I suppose so. Must I go?

HERBERT: What's the matter? Don't you feel good?

ALICE: Of course, I feel . . . wonderful. Divinely, madly wonderful . . . goodbye, my Potter. Goodbye, darling. I'll be back. I'll be back quickly . . . to set you free . . . Don't forget me . . . you'll see. . . .

(*She rushes out.* HERBERT *follows her more slowly, shutting the door after him.*)

HERBERT (*disgustedly*): Oh, for heaven's sake!

(CAUDLE *turns to* POTTER, *and looks him over with enthusiasm.*)

CAUDLE: Well—that's the Navy for you. What have you fellows got that I haven't got?

POTTER: Blossoms in our hair . . . I sure hope she gets us out of here.

CAUDLE: I have a broadcast to do. The biggest sponsor tie-up in history. Eleven hundred stations, including Liberia —and the State of Georgia. If I don't make it . . . (*He shakes his head gloomily.*)

POTTER: Cheer up, old man. You'll be there. You'll make it. She'll get us out all right—

CAUDLE: You really—like the girl, don't you?

POTTER: Yes.

CAUDLE: Well—it's none of my business, of course—but— what about Mrs. Potter?

POTTER: What about her?

CAUDLE: She isn't going to like this pretty vegetable of yours.

POTTER: Caudle—could you be jealous of a—a stalk of celery?

CAUDLE: I'm not married—

POTTER: But suppose you were?

CAUDLE: I don't know. Could be. If I found my wife in bed with it—

POTTER (*hotly*): We're not in bed yet!

CAUDLE: She doesn't blossom till July. It's only February.

POTTER: I wish we were safe at home. There's something frightening—about being in love with a carrot!

CAUDLE (*sniffing*): Smell anything, Commander?

POTTER (*uncertainly*): N—no. . . .

CAUDLE: Funny. . . . (*sniffing*) I thought for a moment I smelled onions—

POTTER: That's not very likely. . . .

CAUDLE: Just an idea, I guess. . . . You know, it makes you think. Suppose God *is* a root?

POTTER: Then what are we?

CAUDLE: I don't know. (*Rubbing his eyes.*) My eyes are watering.

POTTER: Mine, too . . . You know I—*do* smell onions. . . .

(*The cell door opens, and* SPINDLE *and two other onions, disguised as carrots, appear.*)

SPINDLE: Gentlemen—

POTTER: Eh?—Who are you?—

SPINDLE (*bowing*): You are free, gentlemen—

CAUDLE: She *did* manage it, then!

SPINDLE: This way. Hurry, please—

POTTER (*Rubbing his eyes*): Where is she? I can't see, very well.

SPINDLE: She is waiting for you, sir—

POTTER: Come along, then—Dammit, I'm crying.

(*He strides out, followed by* CAUDLE. *As* CAUDLE *passes* SPINDLE, *he stops to sniff.*)

CAUDLE (*suspiciously*): That's funny—(*Calling*) Potter!

(*There is the sound of a blow beyond the door, and a groan. A leek steps up behind* CAUDLE, *and puts his hand over his mouth. At the same time,* SPINDLE *hits him over the head with a sap.* CAUDLE *goes limp; the leek supports him.*)

SPINDLE: Good. Splendid. Take them both down the back way—Our agent is waiting with a market wagon . . . what about the other one? The carrot?

(*The leek points;* SPINDLE *reaches outside the door, and drags into the cell the inert form of* HERBERT.)

SPINDLE: How fortunate that all the guards were withdrawn—except this gentleman. Run along, Comrade . . . I shall wait here. Who knows? Perhaps our snare will trap an even rarer prize. . . .

(*The leek leaves, carrying* CAUDLE *with him.* SPINDLE *closes the door, and sets himself to wait—a hunched and fateful figure. In a moment,* ALICE'S *voice, light and joyous, is heard outside the cell.*)

ALICE: Potter! Caudle! Everything's arranged . . . !

(*She bursts in—and stops short as she sees* SPINDLE.)

ALICE: What?—Where's Potter? Who are you? That odor! (*She puts her hands before her eyes.*) My eyes—

(*She sees* HERBERT *lying on the floor; she stares at him a moment, then turns to* SPINDLE, *who makes a motion to reveal himself.* ALICE *screams, and turns to run; it is too late.* SPINDLE *grasps her.*)

SPINDLE: Aha, my pretty little root—of the celery family . . .

ALICE (*In a feeble croak*): Help! Papa!

SPINDLE: It is useless to scream; there is no one to hear you. Or have you forgotten that you sent the guards home—yourself? Your Earth-men friends are already on their way to the Little Father in Onionapolis. In three days you will join them—in the dungeons of the Echalote.

ALICE: No. . . .

SPINDLE: But first—there is a little experiment, with a petite marmite . . .

ALICE: Papa!

SPINDLE: Without the leeks, of course. Simply, the marrowbone, and one carrot—

ALICE: Oh!

(*She swoons.* SPINDLE *stands looking down at her with relish, and rubbing his hands.*)

ACT TWO: *Scene 3*

(O'DOR's *office, in Onionapolis.* O'DOR *is seated at his desk, with* SPINDLE *beside him. Before him, with bandages around their heads, sit* POTTER *and* CAUDLE.)

O'DOR: So you see, gentlemen, we had no choice; the stakes were too high—being no less than war or peace. It was unlikely that the carrots would give you up of their own accord; and so, we simply—ah—took steps to expedite matters.

CAUDLE: (*Feeling his head*): With a piece of iron pipe?

(O'DOR *looks questioningly at* SPINDLE, *who shakes his head.*)

O'DOR: My dear Mr. Caudle, we do not use pipe of any kind. Besides, my agents tell me that you went with them willingly, and without remonstrance.

POTTER: We were out cold.

O'DOR: Exactly. You gave no sign of complaint. We were obliged to interpret your silence as best we could. . . . Besides—you had no business in Onion territory.

CAUDLE (*indignantly*): We weren't *in* Onion territory!

(O'DOR *looks at* SPINDLE *who shakes his head.*)

O'DOR: Come, come, my dear Mr. Caudle. In the first place your friend has just admitted that you were both of you unconscious; therefore, you couldn't possibly have known where you were. In the second place—where are you now? In Onion territory. Therefore, to argue about where you were, when you didn't know where you were, is unrealistic.

194

POTTER: All right; so now we know. What's all this about war and peace?

O'DOR (*Sitting back, and placing the tips of his fingers together*): Mr. Potter, it is a fact that of all the people of this planet, we onions are the most peaceful, the most freedom-loving, and the most cultured. Spindle—give Mr. Potter a sample.

SPINDLE (*Rises; singing*): 'On the Road to Mandalay, where the flying fishes play, and the dawn comes up like thunder over China cross the bay—'

O'DOR: That's enough. (SPINDLE *sits down again.*) So tell me, Mr. Potter of the U. S. Navy—how do you make war?

POTTER: How do we what?

O'DOR (*patiently*): Make war. How do you destroy whole armies—cities, countries with all their inhabitants? Without, at the same time, annihilating yourselves? Unfortunately, there is no blight that will make compost out of carrots without doing the same for onions. I have to think of my people.

SPINDLE: God bless you, Little Father.

O'DOR: Thank you. (*He sighs.*) We are still in the drawing-board stage. We need technicians.

POTTER: Don't look at *me*. Count me out of that one.

CAUDLE: There's a very good program every Sunday afternoon, called "Do It Yourself." You could tune in on it, and get your technical advice that way.

O'DOR: We do not allow reception from the outside. That way, we do not get any wrong ideas. We listen only to ourselves.

POTTER: You won't get any wrong ideas from me, either.

O'DOR: My dear Commander, you must understand that the terms Right and Wrong can only be used in reference to the destiny of our people, and must be always at the service of Didactic Materialism. The End justifies the Means: when onions rule the world, who would wish to be celery? I offer you an important place in history.

POTTER: The only place I want to be is next to a girl with a carrot top who smells like a garden after rain.

O'DOR (*surprised*): *That* I did not expect. However—let us not grow emotional. Perhaps you are closer to her than you think. . . . Will you teach us to make war, Commander? You see—I am giving you another chance. Opportunity rarely knocks so often.

POTTER: I will not.

O'DOR: You will not help us to detonate the hydrogen bomb?

POTTER: Good Lord! *Have* you the bomb?

O'DOR: We have invented it . . . but we haven't been able to make it go off yet. You won't help us?

POTTER: I should say not!

O'DOR: Very well; I am sorry. Perhaps we will find a way to make you change your mind. There is a little experiment we have in mind—with a pot of boiling water. You would not care to see your—shall we say girl-friend?—floating about with only a marrowbone for company? No? . . . Ah well. Think it over. Spindle—take these gentlemen to the solarium, and entertain them. Show them the vampire marigolds . . . and the lizard-eating oleander. They might be interested to watch the muerte vine digest its daily mouse. . . . And on the way, send in the other prisoner. And now, gentlemen—if you please. (*He rises.*) We shall meet again. A pot of hot water. (*The other three also rise.*) I believe it is called a petite marmite. Good day to you.

SPINDLE: Come.

(POTTER *and* CAULE *follow* SPINDLE *out.* O'DOR *takes down a large atomizer of perfume, and sprays himself liberally; then he arranges his uniform; after which he seats himself at his desk, and bends a stern but lofty gaze at the door. It opens, and* ALICE *enters. She is frightened and indignant. She stands in the doorway, silent and morose.*)

O'DOR: Well, well! Come in—come in, young lady. (*As* ALICE *hesitates.*) Don't be bashful—I won't eat you.

(*He rises, and walks toward her. As she moves out of his way, he circles behind her and shuts the door. She turns to look; then resigns herself to her fate, and moves toward the desk.*)

O'DOR (*Walking around behind her, looking her over*): Sit down, my dear, sit down. This is really a pleasure. (ALICE *seats herself reluctantly in front of the desk.*) So you are Edwin's daughter. How is my dear friend, the Secretary of the Interior? He hasn't answered my last note. . . . No doubt an oversight. I dare say he'll be glad to hear that you are in good health . . . still. But one never knows—does one? Here today, and gone tomorrow. Still, if one is smart . . .

ALICE: Why don't you say what you mean, and get it over with?

O'DOR: I am saying it, my dear. I am saying it. Give

me time. . . . But that's the way with you carrots—so impulsive. . . .

(ALICE *does not reply.*)

O'DOR (*After a moment's pause*): Of course—we know that you have been quietly mobilizing for months. . . . I can't imagine why. We ourselves have only one wish—to be at peace with all the world. I suppose you wouldn't care to tell me the present whereabouts of the Carrot Eighth Army? (*No answer.*) Or the air force? We have ways of finding out, of course. But it would be so much easier if you were to tell us.

(ALICE *sits in tight-lipped silence.*)

O'DOR (*carelessly*): By the way—your friend Mr. Potter was here. He just left.

(ALICE *is silent.*)

O'DOR: Young people are so stupid. Their silence gives them away. Do you think we don't know about your little affair? Mr. Potter, also, was singularly uncooperative. Too bad. We might have to . . .

ALICE: You wouldn't dare!

O'DOR: No? Why not? Do you think we are afraid? After the protests we are accustomed to get from your father, nothing can frighten us. However—speaking of your father —we have not received the 20,000 tons of bone meal which we ordered. Why is that? Nor has he agreed to the necessary slight rise in the price of ammonium sulphate.

ALICE: Mr. Potter had nothing to do with it.

O'DOR: Possibly . . . possibly. But I cannot help but associate Mr. Potter's sudden arrival in Carrotania with this new—shall I say?—unwillingness to cooperate. There are ways, of course, of making people more willing. My assistant is showing Mr. Potter the muerte vines.

ALICE (*horrified*): Not the meat-eaters!

O'DOR: Why not? Mr. Potter *is* meat—I believe? But of course . . . if *you* have something you would like to share with us . . .

ALICE: What do you mean? How? In what way?

O'DOR (*Coming close to her*): Hmmm. You have a lovely skin, my dear. So moist and tender. No wrinkles.

ALICE: Will you let him go, if I . . . if I . . . ?

O'DOR: Yes, yes . . . you smell good, too. Like a salad . . . very fragrant. But delicate.

ALICE: What do you want to know? Our army . . .

O'DOR: Yes, yes, the army. I have heard that you carrots

have ways of making love . . . is it true? . . . certain ways—
(*He caresses the back of her neck.*)

ALICE (*hurriedly*): The navy . . . the marines . . .

O'DOR: We could make such beautiful communion together.

ALICE: What are you doing?

O'DOR: What freshness! What youth! I love you.

ALICE: You're mad. . . .

O'DOR: It's too strong for me . . . I must have you!

ALICE: Don't touch me . . . the air force . . .

O'DOR: Please . . . no more statistics. They are published, anyway, every day in your newspapers. When we are ready, we will strike . . . First, we lull you to sleep. Then—when you are snoring—forward march! Kiss me.

ALICE: Never!

O'DOR: My blood is boiling!

ALICE: Odious onion!

(O'DOR *grabs her, they struggle for a moment, and she falls to her knees. He steps back.*)

ALICE (*weeping*): *Visi d'arte, visi d'amore.* I lived only for love, and for joy, and to do a little singing. . . . I harmed no one. Why has this happened to me?

O'DOR: I am suffocating. . . .

ALICE: Ah me—the happy gardens of my youth, the gentle showers, the warm sun of summer in which I grew, the scented air . . . my young heart trembling with delight at the first dandelion. . . . Was it for this I gave my blossoms to the breeze? What a way to treat me!

O'DOR: You are torturing me. Get up.

ALICE: Was it for this I spent my virtuous childhood in the company of the little celeries, my cousins? And played my girlish games among the cucumbers? To come to a breathless end in the arms of my enemy? The enemy of my country?

O'DOR: Stop crying! What has your country got to do with it? Be a little realistic.

ALICE: Oh, heaven!

O'DOR: You do not realize your situation. One word from me—and you are in the soup.

ALICE: I would a thousand times liefer—

O'DOR: Or—what is perhaps more to the point—your friend Mr. Potter is left alone with the marigolds . . .

ALICE: No! Oh no!

O'DOR: Ah—that fetches you. You really care for him, don't you?

ALICE: More than life.

O'DOR: All the better. It is much more exciting to make love to a woman already in love. It adds a kind of seasoning—a sauce, as it were. . . .

ALICE: You—you nettle! You noisome weed!

O'DOR: Splendid—splendid. So sweet, and so hot. Almost Spanish.

ALICE: Is this the way you make war? On helpless women and children?

O'DOR (*Taken aback*): War? Who is making war? I am paying you compliments!

ALICE: They are odious to me.

O'DOR: Very well . . . we will try Mr. Potter in the muerte vines. Have you ever seen them work? First they grasp their victim like this. (*He grasps hold of her.*) Then they twine about him; then, slowly, they shred the flesh into . . .

ALICE: No—No . . . I can't stand it. I can't fight any more.

O'DOR: You give up? You give in?

ALICE (*dully*): Will he have a safe conduct back to my father?

O'DOR: Yes, yes. . . .

ALICE: Will there be one for me? . . . Afterwards?

O'DOR: Afterwards.

ALICE: Write it out. . . .

O'DOR (*Going to his desk, and writing*): You do not trust me? Some day you will be ashamed of that. For Mr. Potter —a pass; also for Mr. Caudle. And now—for Miss Alice . . . (*He rings a buzzer; the door opens and* SPINDLE *enters.*) Spindle—you will let the Earth-men go. And later, you will see that this lady is returned to her own people—just like Palmieri.

SPINDLE: Mrs. Palmieri?

O'DOR: That's the one. *Just like Palmieri*—you understand?

SPINDLE (*Making a circle of his fingers*): I understand, Little Father.

O'DOR: Right?

SPINDLE: Right. Just like Palmieri. Mrs.

(*He goes out.*)

O'DOR: Now—oh most divine creature. . . .

(*He rises, and moves upon* ALICE. *She has backed against the desk; her hands, groping, have found a paper cutter; she clutches it.*)

O'DOR: At last—you are all mine. . . .

(*As he reaches for her, she stabs him.*)

ALICE: It is thus a carrot kisses!

(*He falls. She looks at the knife in horror, sniffs it, shudders, and throws it away. Then she takes two candles from the desk, lights them, and places one at the dead onion's head, and one at his feet. She backs slowly to the door, wipes her streaming eyes, blows her nose; and turning, goes swiftly out.*)

ACT TWO: *Scene 4*

(*The corridor outside* O'DOR's *office.* POTTER *and* CAUDLE *hurry up, while* ALICE *comes out of the door, still wiping her eyes, and shuts it behind her.*)

POTTER: Alice!

ALICE: Thank God you're safe!

(*She falls into his arms.*)

POTTER: You are crying?

ALICE: It's nothing. It's only onion juice. Here are your passes—go quickly—both of you!

POTTER: And you?

ALICE: My pass is for later. I must wait for a little while. It's better so. . . .

POTTER: But why?

ALICE: If I go with you now, they'll be suspicious. I must try to save you—

POTTER: No! If we have to die—then we'll die together!

ALICE: No, my dear. That wouldn't help my country—or this little world—or even me. You see—I've become very sensible; realistic they call it here. I'm not important—but *you* are; because you have the gift of peace. Think of all the wonderful things you can teach us . . . to keep the world safe for celery . . . the celery family. . . . Don't you see? It doesn't matter about *me;* I'm just a girl who had a good time in the world; and maybe it's over now . . . maybe that's all there is, there isn't any more. 'The leaves are falling, so am I . . .' Goodbye; think of me . . . and never ask the price of freedom. I'll try to catch up to you at the frontier. If I don't come—be kind to carrots—for my sake. Go now—and God bless you.

CAUDLE (*Looking at his watch*): I can just make my broadcast. . . .

ALICE: 'I strove with none, for none was worth my strife.

Nature I loved, and, after Nature, Art:
I warmed both hands before the fire of life. . . .'
(POTTER *takes her hands in his and gazes at her.*)
CAUDLE (*impatiently*): Come on—come on—
ALICE: 'It sinks, and I am ready to depart.'
CAUDLE: We'll only just make it.
ALICE: Go now; and hurry.
POTTER: Farewell!
(POTTER *and* CAUDLE *hurry off. A moment later six leeks enter, headed by* SPINDLE, *all dressed as chefs, each carrying a huge spoon. They pass* ALICE *without looking at her, and go into* O'DOR's *office. She flattens herself in terror against the wall. In the office there is a silence, broken by a sudden outcry. The door is flung open, and the chefs emerge. They see* ALICE, *and slowly, inexorably bear down on her. . . .*

(*In the darkness, a broadcast. There is the crackle of static; then* CAUDLE's *voice.*)
CAUDLE'S VOICE: Calling NBC. . . . Calling NBC. Come in, Earth. Come in. This is Caudle on Venus. Are you there, NBC? This is the historic moment, for which mankind has waited since the world began. You are about to hear the first voice from another planet . . . by courtesy of Southwest Oil, Heidelberg (Wisconsin) Beer. . . . (*As though to someone in the studio.*) What's that? I can't hear you. . . . (*Broadcasting again*) There's a certain amount of excitement here, folks—which you can easily understand under the circumstances. Stand by now. In a minute, across thirty million miles of darkness and empty space, you will hear the voice of . . . of . . . (*To someone in the studio*) What? She what? Alice? In a soup? . . .
(The static takes over.)

EPILOGUE

(*The cashier's desk at a Super Market.* MRS. POTTER *has brought a market basket up to be counted. The cashier is a middle-aged lady.* MRS. POTTER *is not unattractive.*)

MRS. POTTER: Let's see . . . one peas, one cauliflower . . .
CASHIER: You must be very happy to have your husband back again, Mrs. Potter. And all those write-ups in the papers! My goodness! Did he really get to Venus, like they said? I missed the broadcast.
MRS. POTTER: Yes, he did. One ketchup—

CASHIER: He looks a little thin, in his pictures. I guess maybe they didn't have much to eat up there.

MRS. POTTER: I guess not . . .

CASHIER: What was it like?

MRS. POTTER: He hasn't said much . . . and four dozen onions, please. . . .

CASHIER (*astonished*): Four dozen?

MRS. POTTER: That's right. He—he eats them. Raw.

CASHIER: Raw? They say onions are good for colds.

MRS. POTTER: I know.

CASHIER: There's lots of things like that. Like carrots make your hair curly.

MRS. POTTER: He won't touch carrots.

CASHIER: He won't? Not even cooked?

MRS. POTTER: Not even. I served a petite marmite the other night, and he got up and left the table.

CASHIER: No! Now isn't that something!

MRS. POTTER: One sack of peat moss.

CASHIER: What's that for?

MRS. POTTER: He says he's got blossoms in his hair.

CASHIER: Humph! . . . (*She looks at* MRS. POTTER, *then rings up the charges, with a slightly befuddled air.*) That'll be $3.47, Mrs. Potter. I'll have someone take them out to the car for you.

MRS. POTTER (*Paying her*): Thank you. . . .

(*She leaves.*)

CASHIER: Goodbye now. (*She takes hold of a lock of her own hair, and peers up at it. She lets it fall back into place, and shrugs her shoulders helplessly.*) Blossoms? . . . In February?

The Terra-Venusian War of 1979

GERARD E. NEYROUD

Another Venusian story—and from the same issue of
the same magazine that published the immediately pre-
ceding story at that. Sheer coincidence? Who knows—or
dares to tell?

In any event, there is no doubt but that this is science
fiction, while there was some doubt about the matter in
the case of Mr. Nathan's little play. Even the part
about the 1961 landings on the Moon by two United
States spacemen. So it didn't actually happen? That
does not make it any the less fun to read about!

As for the story's ending, we can only hope that the
year 1979 will find it becoming roseate fact, rather than
the science fiction which, today, it so indubitably is.

There are still a few stiff-minded people who refuse to admit
that Venus attacked the earth in 1979. People, mark you,
who lived through the war, heard the nuclear blasts shat-
tering the order of space, saw the golden legions of Venus
advancing relentlessly through the void, witnessed the prodigious aftermath of the invasion. Nothing but imagination,
the non-believers say; a world-wide hallucination instilled
into the minds of men by the frenzied shoutings of press,
television and radio. The skeptics cannot very well deny the
extraordinary effects of the Venusian incursion—those effects
still linger today, though fast fading—so they glibly ascribe
them to earthborn causes.

I am not an imaginative person; I am a retired businessman known to my family and friends as a confirmed cynic,
and I say that the skeptics are egregiously wrong. Furthermore, I deny that the press and the air-news people over-
played the momentous happenings of the spring of 1979.
There was no need for synthetic sensationalism; the genuine

article was wild enough. I should know; I was in on the Terra-Venusian affair from its very beginning.

Perhaps I should not have used the words "attack" and "war," but there are no other terms in any earth language to describe the happenings. "Extraterrestrial Intervention" would be nearer the mark, but it is a clumsy phrase and meaningless without the facts.

Here, then, are the facts:

The first inkling of the coming storm was a little story in the *Washington Starpost* of April 1, 1979. My clipping file (I collect clippings) is on my desk and I can quote the story in full:

VENUS SIGNALS
BAFFLE D.C. ASTRONOMER

The appearance of a large number of golden globes in the vicinity of the cloud-veiled planet Venus was reported here today by Carl Maxner, noted Washington astronomer. The globes, presumably of gaseous origin, appear to be emanating from the surface of the mystery planet at regularly spaced intervals, Maxner said.

Using an "astrophotonic scanner" of his own design and construction, the astronomer claims to have penetrated for the first time the dense atmospheric layer that hitherto has shrouded the actual surface of Venus from human observation. Maxner offers no explanation of the phenomenon, but thinks that the regularity with which the globes appear and their orderly dispersal could incate the presence on our sister planet of a high order of intelligence. The globes will be no threat to the earth, Maxner said. Venus, at its closest approach, is twenty-three million miles away, he pointed out, and no gas bubble, however huge, could traverse even a minute fraction of that distance without breaking up.

The inevitable refutation came the following day in an Associated Press despatch from the Palomar Observatory high in the Californian Sierras. It was headed SCIENTIST SCOFFS AT VENUS GLOBES, and quoted Professor Amos Higginbotham, astrophysicist at the Observatory, as declaring:

The Washington report that large golden globes were issuing from the planet Venus is completely nonsensical.

Our giant telescope, incidentally the largest in the world, has failed to disclose anything that would even remotely confirm the claims of this self-styled astronomer. The story is unworthy of serious consideration.

On the same day the *New York Daily Mirage,* true to type, invested the story with a sex angle:

SAYS VENUS BLOWING BUBBLES

Venus, shy damsel of the evening sky, is shrouding her lovely form with golden bubbles to ward off the naked eye of a Washington D. C. peeping tom. The naughty man who says he saw the lady in the bubble bath is Charles Mickser, amateur stargazer and lover of nature in the raw. Mackser told our inquiring reporter today that the bubbles are bright gold and very large, which is fortunate for Venus, who is quite a big girl herself. Muckser abruptly terminated the interview when it was suggested that the star in his eye might reside on the top floor of the Shoreham Hotel.

The Maxner report was given its coup-de-grace on April 4 by the *New York Tribune-Times* in this down-column story on page 7:

VENUS GLOBES SCHOOLBOY HOAX

The report that a Washington astronomer, Carl Maxner, had observed "golden globes" issuing from the surface of the planet Venus was an April Fool hoax perpetrated by a schoolboy, it was revealed last night. The Washington Bureau of the *Tribune-Times* has ascertained that Maxner, described by another newspaper as a "noted astronomer," is a fifteen year old pupil at Washington's Northwestern High School.

Jonas Higbee, Assistant Principal of Northwestern High, told a *Tribune-Times* representative that Maxner had shown some slight interest in astronomy and had been permitted to construct his "astrophotonic scanner" in the school workshop. "It was strictly a Rube Goldberg job," Higbee said, "made out of bits and pieces, and I doubt if it could pick up the full moon on a clear night. Washington High frowns on hoaxes of this kind and we have been considering disciplinary action. However, we understand the boy's father has already taken him in hand."

At the Maxner home on Kalorama Road, Mrs. Bruno Maxner, the boy's mother, refused to permit her son to be interviewed. "I have just sent Carl to bed," she told our reporter. "His father was much too rough with him." Replying to a further question, Mrs. Maxner said that the astrophotonic scanner had been broken.

Three days later, on April 7, the austere and unimpeachable *Manchester Guardian* resurrected the golden globe story in a new version that jolted the world. The *Guardian's* thunderclap was carried under a three-decker head on page 5 and my files, fortunately, enable me to quote it in full.

STRANGE MANIFESTATIONS
ON PLANET VENUS;
BRITISH ASTRONOMERS PUZZLED
IS EARTH MENACED?

Perplexed astrophysicists at the Jodrell Bank Observatory near Manchester confessed today that they were nonplussed by the appearance of a cluster of spheroids of immense size on the surface of the planet Venus. The spheroids, said to be pale gold in colour, were first picked up by the Observatory's astrophotonic scanner (incidentally, the first of its kind in the world) a fortnight ago, and have since been kept under close and constant observation.

At a hastily convoked press conference, Sir Hilary Biggleswade, K.C.B.E., F.R.A.S., President of the Royal Outer Space Society, told the assembled reporters that the mysterious spheroids are beginning to form—or, disturbing thought, are being formed into—a circle, and that the most recent observations seem to indicate that this circle is advancing steadily towards the earth.

"Our first hypothesis," Sir Hilary said, "was that the spheroids were of a gaseous nature—skinless balloons, you might say—but this theory is no longer tenable. The objects, whatever they may be, are now many thousands of miles from their mother planet and are moving earthward in a space vacuum in which any such concentrations of gas would have been instantly dispersed."

Sir Hilary answered in the affirmative when asked if an alternative theory had been formulated. "The spheroids could consist of captive light, or possibly captive sound, or even of a captive abstraction—though how such a phenomenon could be caused is beyond human comprehension."

Speaking with great solemnity and emphasis, the great scientist added: "The spheroids appear to be under some form of central control, and the methodic manner of their advance would seem to postulate the existence on the planet Venus of a high and very possibly malign intelligence."

He terminated the conference on a note of foreboding. "We can only wait and see, or hear—or both," he said, "and we shall not have to wait very long."

Thus Carl Maxner, the forgotten Washington boy, was vindicated.

America reacted calmly to the news from Jodrell Bank, and nowhere was there any evidence of panic. The general attitude was one of doubt of the validity of Sir Hilary Biggleswade's conclusions; it was best expressed by radio news analyst Gabriel Trumpeter, who said: "If there were anything to it we would have been told about it by our own scientists, admittedly the best in the world. We don't have to listen to foreigners."

Aging President Kenfeller, then in his fifth term, issued a brief, reassuring statement from the White House. There was absolutely no cause for alarm, the President said; he was advised that there was no evidence whatsoever of any hostile intent on the part of Venus. Our stockpile of interplanetary ballistic missiles was at its peak and the American Space Force could be depended upon to cope with any situation that might arise. "Americans may sleep peacefully in their beds."

At his Thursday press conference, Secretary of State Righteous W. Rath issued a stern hands-off warning to Venus. America will not tolerate aggression in any form or from any source, he said. Rath announced that he was flying to the Moon to investigate the situation on the spot. Reminded by a reporter that Venus was several million miles beyond the Moon, the Secretary replied curtly that distance meant nothing to him.

Newspaper comment reflected the national complacency. We may disregard the *Daily Mirage* which, in a story headed VENUS BLOWS AWAY BUBBLES SAYS SIR BIGGLESWADE, offered sympathy to Carl Maxner for the loss of his astrophotonic scanner at this propitious moment. The more stately *Wash-*

ington Starpost took a middle-of-the-road course. In an editorial written entirely in Greek, the Capital daily is believed to have castigated a pinchpenny administration for failing to establish a base on the Moon, which was the obvious place from which to ward off a Venusian attack. "Have we forgotten," the *Starpost* is thought to have said, "that the Moon became American territory as far back as 1961?"

The *Starpost* was referring, of course, to America's first and last attempts to set foot on the Moon. The first, in May 1961, was only partially successful, in that the manned rocket ship missed its target by the small margin of 6,000 miles. This spaceship is still in orbit, around the Sun, but has transmitted no signals for many years and it is feared that its batteries may be dead. A bipartisan attempt to land two men on the moon in August of the same year was brilliantly successful. The spacemen, Joel C. Tagliaferro (Dem.) of Lumberton, N. C. and Richard Roe (Rep.) of Albuquerque, N. Mex., landed their spaceship on the shores of the Mare Nectaris, issued forth briefly to plant our flag in lunar soil, and returned hastily to their ship and to earth. Interviewed on their arrival at the Patuxent River Base on Chesapeake Bay, Tagliaferro was quoted as saying "Let the Russians have it." His fellow traveler concurred.

It was exactly a month later that Congress declared the Moon to be American territory, thus opening the way to ultimate statehood. Russia protested vigorously, insisting that the United States was interfering in its internal affairs. "As is well known," the Kremlin spokesman said, "the brave Red Spaceforce has long occupied the far side of the Moon, and the entire planet is now properly known as the Lunar Socialist Soviet Republic."

There Congress decided to let the matter rest; in my opinion, wisely.

In contrast to America's complacency, Britain and Western Europe received Sir Hilary Biggleswade's warning with alarm and even consternation. Public tension mounted as the Jodrell Bank findings were confirmed by the famed Greenwich Observatory, from its new home at Gurstmonceux in Sussex, and by the scientists manning the skyscanners at Pic du Midi, ten thousand feet up in the French Pyrenees, who reported that "les globules Venusiennes" were now measurably closer to earth.

In London, the tocsin was sounded by Viscount Betelgeuse (better known as Space Marshal Sir Nigel Cosmore-Gore,

R.S.F., F.R.O.S.S.). From the plinth of the Nelson Column in Trafalgar Square, Lord Betelgeuse solemnly warned a sea of eighty-five thousand upturned faces (police estimate) that the hour of Britain's greatest ordeal was about to strike. "We do not know the nature of the peril that threatens us," he said, "but we do know that the Royal Spaceforce will not be found wanting. We will fight them in the stratosphere, we will fight them in the ionosphere, we will fight them in the troposphere. We will never surrender."

A thunderous roar of defiance mingled with cries of "good old Beetlejuice" and "oo's afraid of Venus" manifested once again the unconquerable spirit of the British.

There were similar demonstrations, less restrained for the most part, in Paris, Pampeluna, Hamburg, and other cities. Riots and looting were reported from Naples and Kephalonia. Moscow preserved an enigmatic silence.

The news of Europe's growing unease was received in America with tolerant amusement. Gabriel Trumpeter, as usual, struck the keynote with his statesmanlike broadcasts. "If," he declared, "foreigners want to go into a tizzy over the wacky ideas of their half-baked scientists, it is their affair; it is certainly not ours." He had personally telephoned not only Palomar but also the Naval Observatory in Washington and the Pentagon, and all three had assured him categorically that they had no comment. The moral was clear, he told his vast audience. If Palomar had seen no Venus Globes it was because there were no Venus Globes. Europe was having nightmares. These people must be told once and for all that this time America was not going to pull their chestnuts out of the fire.

And America, obeying the President's mandate, slept peacefully in its bed.

On the morning of April 16, America rose yawning from that same peaceful bed, retrieved the newspaper from the porch, turned its face skyward for a look at the weather—and felt the icy grip of apocalyptic fear. Overhead, shimmering in the bright sunlight, was an awesome circlet of golden globes.

For an eternal moment that morning there was no sound in America. All movement had ceased, the streets were empty of life, radio and television were hushed. It was as though all people everywhere were on their knees. Then, suddenly, the quiet sound came, an all-encompassing murmur compounded of the prayers of women and the deeper urgencies of men. Only the children were silent, wide-eyed and marveling, unafraid of the overwhelming glory above.

The radio returned to life and the people clustered around the little boxes as their forefathers had clustered around the hearth, reaping comfort from the radiation. "Do not panic," the little boxes were saying. "The situation is in hand. Stay Indoors. Close all doors and windows. Stay close to the inner walls. I repeat, do not panic. The Spaceforce is taking over. Trust our spacemen. DO NOT PANIC."

Listeners sensed wavering panic in the voice as it died, drowned out by the roaring fury of war. The Spaceforce screamed into the skies, jets howling, nuclears throbbing, rockets seeking out and blasting the unattainable and the unblastable. Bold watchers at the windows saw the spacecraft tear through the golden globes and turn to charge again. Then, at some unseen signal, the planes and rockets left the sky and silence again blanketed the world, and the golden globes of Venus, unharmed by the fury, floated serenely down and settled lightly on its continents and its oceans.

Television flickered into life and wavering patterns resolved into the face of the President. In every living room between Caribou and San Diego, between Seattle and Key West, Americans hungrily watched the little oblong of light and waited for guidance.

There was no anxiety in the face of the man in Washington. His lips were curled into a half-smile, the strong eyes were serene behind their eyebrow hedge. He opened his mouth to speak but no words came from the screen. Instead, the mouth remained open and twisted into a prodigious yawn. The President of the United States had yawned in the faces of his fellow citizens. It was masterly statecraft; it was the guidance they wanted.

Americans all over the country yawned back at the President and went to bed.

The Great Sleep held Americans unconscious for a day— or a year or a decade; nobody ever knew or will ever know for how long—and set them free in a world bathed in soft golden haze. There were no golden globes; it seemed now that the globes had never been.

The morning paper was waiting on the porch, slightly damp in the lambent air and printed on rose-pink stock, and nobody was surprised by the banner headline:

HAPPY NEW WORLD
TO ALL!

I still have a copy, browning at the edges now, of the *Washington Starpost* I picked up on my porch on that unforgettable morning. It is dated April 17, 1979 (there is a question mark after the date), and it makes fascinating reading today. It told, for instance, that all the world had experienced the golden globes, had shared America's experience. In England the Queen had yawned too, and abolished the income tax. The newly crowned King Charles XI of France, and the other heads, crowned and uncrowned, of Europe had yawned with equally gratifying effect. The Cham of Tartary (formerly China) had yawned to the extent of dislocating his jaw, with the result that China was again sleeping its age-long sleep. The Man in the Kremlin had done more than yawn. He had beaten the Iron Curtain into tractor parts, freed the satellites (including the Moon) and sent a message of brotherly love to the President and capitalists of the United States.

There were other news items of less import but equal significance. Arkansas reported the election, by unanimous vote, of a Negro governor. Reno and other separation centers told of a sensational decline in the number of divorce suits, and in Washington the Post Office Department announced with gratification that in all parts of the country dogs were fawning on mail carriers. From Ireland came the news that an heroic monument to Oliver Cromwell had been unveiled, to popular acclaim, in Dublin's Phoenix Park. And Hollywood let it be known that henceforth television shootings would be effected exclusively with cupid arrows.

It was wonderful and still is.

Over Washington the air is so clear that my son, Carl Maxner, Junior, has been making some interesting observations of the planet Venus by means of the powerful new astrophotonic scanner I gave him for Christmas. He has just told me they are fighting on Venus.

His theory, which I am inclined to accept, is that Venus sent the world its love, keeping none back for itself.

The Coffin Cure

ALAN E. NOURSE

Here is a science fiction tale of one of the true classic types—the medical catastrophe. Ever since H. G. Wells's "Food of the Gods" and before, we have had a series of vivid stories telling what might happen if some experiment involving the health and/or happiness of mankind went haywire. This is one of the best of the lot, and, furthermore, an ominously possible one.

Of course, "The Coffin Cure" is pure fiction thus far— for which let us be thankful—but it is also as scientific as all get-out, as it would have to be, considering its author's professional qualifications; he is a practicing M.D. There is no doubt that his narrative describes a scientifically very possible event. Let us just hope that the busy researchers in pharmaceutical laboratories throughout the land don't hit on this particular cure-all; or, if they do, let us pray that the Food and Drug Administration is on its toes and does not permit it to flood the land prematurely. Because, as you will gather as you read, it could easily do us all in!

When the discovery was announced, it was Dr. Chauncey Patrick Coffin who announced it. He had, of course, arranged with uncanny skill to take most of the credit for himself. If it turned out to be even greater than he had hoped, so much the better. His presentation was scheduled for the final night of the American College of Clinical Practitioners' annual meeting, and Coffin had fully intended it to be a bombshell.

It was. Its explosion exceeded even Dr. Coffin's wilder expectations, which took quite a bit of doing. In the end, he had waded through more newspaper reporters than medical doctors as he left the hall that night. It was a heady evening for Chauncey Patrick Coffin, M.D.

Certain others were not so delighted with Coffin's bomb-shell.

"It's idiocy!" young Dr. Phillip Dawson all but howled in the laboratory conference room the next morning. "Blind, screaming idiocy! You've gone out of your mind—that's all there is to it. Can't you see what you've done? Aside from selling your colleagues down the river, that is?"

He clenched the reprint of Coffin's address in his hand and brandished it like a broadsword. " 'Report on a Vaccine for the Treatment and Cure of the Common Cold,' by C. P. Coffin, *et al.* That's what it says—*et al. My* idea in the first place, Jake and I pounding our heads on the wall for eight solid months—and now you go sneak it into publication a full year before we have any business publishing a word about it—"

"Really, Phillip!" Dr. Chauncey Coffin ran a pudgy hand through his snowy hair. "How ungrateful! I thought for sure you'd be delighted. An excellent presentation, I must say— terse, succinct, unequivocal—" he raised his hand—"but *generously* unequivocal, you understand. You should have heard the ovation—they nearly went wild! And the look on Underwood's face! Worth waiting twenty years for. . . ."

"And the reporters," snapped Phillip. "Don't forget the reporters." He whirled on the small dark man sitting quietly in the corner. "How about that, Jake? Did you see the morning papers? This thief not only steals our work, he splashes it all over the countryside in red ink."

Dr. Jacob Miles coughed apologetically. "What Phillip is so stormed up about is the prematurity of it all," he said to Coffin. "After all, we've hardly had an acceptable period of clinical trial."

"Nonsense," said Coffin, glaring at Phillip. "Underwood and his men were ready to publish their discovery within another six weeks. Where would we be then? How much clinical testing do you want? Phillip, you had the worst cold of your life when you took the vaccine. Have you had any since?"

"No, of course not," said Phillip peevishly.

"Jacob, how about you? Any sniffles?"

"Oh, no. No colds."

"Well, what about those six hundred students from the University? Did I misread the reports on them?"

"No—98% cured of active symptoms within twenty-four hours. Not a single recurrence. The results were just short

213

of miraculous." Jake hesitated. "Of course, it's only been a month. . . ."

"Month, year, century! Look at them! Six hundred of the world's most luxuriant colds and now not even a sniffle." The chubby doctor sank down behind the desk, his ruddy face beaming. "Come now, gentlemen, be reasonable. Think positively! There's work to be done, a great deal of work. They'll be wanting me in Washington. Press conference in twenty minutes. Drug houses to consult with. How dare we stand in the path of Progress? We've won the greatest medical triumph of all times—the conquering of the Common Cold. We'll go down in history!"

And he was perfectly right on one point, at least.

They did go down in history.

The public response to the vaccine was little less than mass-scale. Of all the ailments that have tormented mankind throughout history, none was ever more universal, more tenacious, more uniformly miserable than the common cold.

It respected no barriers, boundaries, or classes; ambassadors and chambermaids snuffled and sneezed in drippynosed unanimity. The powers in the Kremlin sniffed and blew and wept genuine tears on drafty days, while Senatorial debates on earth-shaking issues paused reverently upon the blowing of a nose, the clearing of a rhinorrheic throat. True, other illnesses brought disability, even death in their wake, but the common cold brought torment to the millions, as it implacably resisted the most superhuman of efforts to curb it.

Until that rainy November day when the tidings broke to the world in four-inch banner heads:

COFFIN NAILS LID ON COMMON COLD!

"No More Coughin' "
States Co-Finder of Cure

SNIFFLES SNIPED; SINGLE SHOT TO SAVE SNEEZERS

In medical circles, it was called the Coffin Multicentric Upper Respiratory Virus-inhibiting Vaccine, but the newspapers could never stand for such high-sounding names and called it, instead, "The Coffin Cure."

Below the banner heads, world-renowned feature writers

expounded in awesome terms the story of the leviathan struggle of Dr. Chauncey Patrick Coffin, *et al.* in solving this riddle of the ages:

How, after years of failure, they ultimately succeeded in culturing the true causative agent of the common cold, identifying it not as a single virus or even a group of viruses, but rather as a multicentric virus complex invading the soft mucous linings of the nose, throat and eyes, capable of altering its basic molecular structure at any time to resist efforts of the body from within, or the physician from without, to attack and dispel it; how the hypothesis was set forth by Dr. Phillip Dawson that the virus could be destroyed only by an antibody which could "freeze" the virus-complex in one form long enough for normal body defenses to dispose of the offending invader; the exhausting search for such a "crippling agent" and the final crowning success, after injecting untold gallons of cold-virus material into the hides of a group of cooperative dogs (a species which had never suffered from colds and hence endured the whole business with an air of affectionate boredom).

And, finally, the testing. First, Coffin himself (who was suffering a particularly horrendous case of the affliction he sought to cure); then his assistants, Phillip Dawson and Jacob Miles; then a multitude of students from the University —carefully selected for the severity of their symptoms, the longevity of their colds, their tendency to acquire them on little or no provocation, and their utter inability to get rid of them with any known medical program.

They were a sorry spectacle, those students filing through the Coffin laboratory for three days in October: wheezing like steam shovels, snorting and sneezing and sniffling and blowing, coughing and squeaking, mute appeals glowing in their bloodshot eyes. The researchers dispensed the material —a single shot in the right arm, a sensitivity control in the left.

With growing delight, they then watched as the results came in. The sneezing stopped; the sniffling ceased. A great silence settled over the campus, in the classrooms, in the library, in classic halls. Dr. Coffin's voice returned (rather to the regret of his co-workers) and he began bouncing about the laboratory like a small boy at the fair. Students by the dozen trooped in for checkups with noses dry and eyes bright.

In a matter of days, there was no doubt left that the goal had been reached.

"But we have to be *sure*," Phillip Dawson had said emphatically. "This was only the pilot test. We need mass testing now on an entire community. We ought to go to the West Coast to run studies—they have a different breed of cold out there, I hear. We'll have to see how long the immunity lasts, make sure there are no unexpected side effects. . . ." And, muttering to himself, he fell to work with pad and pencil, calculating the program to be undertaken before publication.

But there were rumors. Underwood at Stanford, it was said, had already completed his tests and was preparing a paper for publication in a matter of months. Surely, with such dramatic results on the pilot tests, *something* could be put into print. It would be tragic to lose the race for the sake of a little unnecessary caution. . . .

Phillip Dawson, though adamant, was a voice crying in the wilderness, for Chauncey Coffin was boss.

Within a week, though, even Coffin was wondering if he had bitten off just a trifle too much. They had expected that the demand for the vaccine would be great—but even the grisly memory of the early days of the Salk vaccine had not prepared them for the mobs of sneezing, wheezing, red-eyed people bombarding them for the first fruits.

Clear-eyed young men from the Government Bureau pushed through crowds of local townspeople, lining the streets outside the Coffin laboratory, standing in pouring rain to raise insistent placards.

Seventeen pharmaceutical houses descended with production plans, cost estimates, colorful graphs demonstrating proposed yield and distribution programs.

Coffin was flown to Washington, where conferences labored far into the night as demands pounded their doors like a tidal wave.

One laboratory promised the vaccine in ten days; another guaranteed it in a week. The first actually appeared in three weeks and two days, to be soaked up in the space of three hours by the thirsty sponge of cold-weary humanity. Express planes were dispatched to Europe, to Asia, to Africa with the precious cargo, a million needles pierced a million hides, and with a huge, convulsive sneeze, mankind stepped forth into a new era.

There were abstainers, of course—there always are:

"It doesd't bake eddy differets how buch you talk," Ellie

Dawson cried hoarsely, shaking her blonde curls. "I dod't wadt eddy cold shots."

"You're being totally unreasonable," Phillip said, glowering at his wife in annoyance. She wasn't the sweet young thing he had married, not this evening. Her eyes were puffy, her nose red and sore. "You've had this cold for two solid months now and there just isn't any sense to it. It's making you miserable. You can't eat, you can't breathe, you can't sleep—"

"I dod't wadt eddy cold shots," she repeated stubbornly.

"But why not? Just one little needle. You'd hardly feel it—"

"But I dod't like deedles!" she cried, bursting into tears. "Why dod't you leave be alode? Go take your dasty old deedles ad stick theb id people that wadt theb."

"Aw, Ellie—"

"I dod't care, *I dod't like deedles!*" she wailed, burying her face in his shirt.

He held her close, kissing her ear and making comforting little noises. It was no use, he reflected sadly. Science just wasn't Ellie's long suit; she didn't know a cold vaccine from a case of smallpox, and no appeal to logic or common sense could surmount her irrational fear of hypodermics. "All right, sweet, nobody's going to make you do anything you don't want to."

"Ad eddyway, thik of the poor tissue badufacturers," she sniffled, wiping her nose with a pink facial tissue. "All their little childred starvig to death—"

"Say, you *have* got a cold," said Phillip, sniffing. "You're wearing enough perfume to fell an ox." He wiped away her tears and grinned at her. "Come on now, fix your face. Dinner at the Driftwood? I hear they have marvelous lamb chops."

It was a mellow evening. The lamb chops were delectable —far the best he had ever eaten, he thought, even with as good a cook as Ellie for a spouse. Ellie dripped and blew continuously, but refused to go home until they had taken in a movie and stopped by to dance a while.

"I hardly ever gedt to see you eddy bore," she wistfully explained. "All because of that dasty bedicide you're giving people."

It was true, of course. The work at the lab was endless. They danced, but came home early nevertheless. Phillip needed all the sleep he could get.

He awoke once during the night to a parade of sneezes

from his wife, and rolled over, frowning sleepily to himself. It was ignominious, in a way—the wife of one of the cold-cure discoverers refusing the fruit of all those months of work.

And cold or no cold, she surely was using a whale of a lot of perfume.

He awoke suddenly, began to stretch, and sat bolt upright in bed, looking wildly about the room. Pale morning sunlight drifted in the window. Downstairs, he heard Ellie stirring in the kitchen.

For a moment, he thought he was suffocating. He leaped out of bed, stared at the vanity table across the room. *"Somebody's spilled the whole damned bottle—"*

The heavy sick-sweet miasma hung like a cloud around him, drenching the room. With every breath, it grew thicker. He searched the vanity top frantically, but there were no open bottles.

His head began to spin from the emetic effluvium.

He blinked in confusion, his hand trembling as he lit a cigarette. No need to panic, he thought. She probably knocked a bottle over when she was dressing. He took a deep puff— and burst into a paroxysm of coughing as acrid fumes burned down his throat to his lungs.

"Ellie!" He rushed into the hall, still coughing. The match smell had given way to a caustic stench of burning weeds. He stared at his cigarette in horror and threw it into the sink. The odor grew worse. He threw open the hall closet, expecting smoke to come billowing out.

"Ellie! Somebody's burning down the house!"

"Whadtever are you talkig aboudt?" Ellie's voice came from the stair well. "It's just the toast I burned, silly."

He rushed down the stairs two at a time—and nearly gagged as he reached the bottom. The smell of hot, rancid grease struck him like a solid wall. It was intermingled with an overpowering oily smell of boiled and parboiled coffee. By the time he reached the kitchen, he was holding his nose, tears pouring from his eyes.

"Ellie, what are you doing in here?"

She stared at him. "I'b baking breakfast."

"But don't you *smell* it?"

On the stove, the automatic percolator made small, promising noises. Four sunnyside eggs were sizzling in the frying pan; half a dozen strips of bacon drained on a paper towel on the sideboard. It couldn't have looked more innocent.

218

Cautiously, Phillip released his nose, sniffed. The stench nearly strangled him. "You mean you don't smell anything *strange?*"

"I dod't sbell eddythig, period," said Ellie defensively.

"The coffee, the bacon—come here a minute!"

She reeked—of bacon, of coffee, of burned toast, but mostly of perfume.

"Did you put on fresh perfume this morning?"

"Before breakfast? Dod't be ridiculous."

"Not even a drop?" Phillip was turning very white.

"Dot a drop."

Phillip shook his head. "Now wait a minute. This must be all in my mind. I'm—just imagining things, that's all. Working too hard, hysterical reaction. In a minute, it'll all go away." He poured a cup of coffee, added cream and sugar.

He couldn't get it close enough to taste it. It smelled as if it had been boiling three weeks in a rancid pot. It was the smell of coffee, all right, but a smell that was fiendishly distorted, overpoweringly and nauseatingly magnified. It pervaded the room and burned his throat and brought tears gushing to his eyes.

Slowly, realization began to dawn. He spilled the coffee as he set the cup down. The perfume. The coffee. The cigarette. . . .

"My hat," he choked. "Get me my hat. I've got to get to the laboratory."

It grew worse all the way downtown. He fought down nausea as the smell of damp, rotting earth rose from his front yard in a gray cloud. The neighbor's dog dashed out to greet him, exuding the great-grandfather of all dog odors. While Phillip waited for the bus, every passing car fouled the air with noxious fumes, gagging him, doubling him up with coughing as he dabbed at his streaming eyes.

Nobody else seemed to notice anything wrong at all.

The bus ride was a nightmare. It was a damp, rainy day; the inside of the bus smelled like the locker room after a big game. A bleary-eyed man with three-days' stubble on his chin flopped down in the seat next to him, and Phillip reeled back in memory to the job he had held in his student days, cleaning vats in the brewery.

"It'sh a great morning," Bleary-eyes breathed at him. "Huh, Doc?"

Phillip blanched. To top it, the man had had a breakfast of salami. In the seat ahead, a fat gentleman held a dead cigar clamped in his mouth like a rank growth. Phillip's stomach began rolling; he sank his face into his hand, trying unobtrusively to clamp his nostrils. With a groan of deliverance, he lurched off the bus at the laboratory gate.

He met Jake Miles coming up the steps. Jake looked pale, too pale.

"Morning," Phillip said weakly. "Nice day. Looks like the sun might come through."

"Yeah," said Jake. "Nice day. You—uh—feel all right this morning?"

"Fine, fine." Phillip tossed his hat in the closet, opened the incubator on his culture tubes, trying to look busy. He slammed the door after one whiff and gripped the edge of the work table with whitening knuckles. "Why do you ask?"

"Oh, nothing. Thought you looked a little peaked, was all."

They stared at each other in silence. Then, as though by signal, their eyes turned to the office at the end of the lab.

"Coffin come in yet?"

Jake nodded. "He's in there. He's got the door locked."

"I think he's going to have to open it," said Phillip.

A gray-faced Dr. Coffin unlocked the door, backed quickly toward the wall. The room reeked of kitchen deodorant.

"Stay right where you are," Coffin squeaked. "Don't come a step closer. I can't see you now. I'm—I'm busy. I've got work that has to be done—"

"You're telling *me*," growled Phillip. He motioned Jake into the office and locked the door again carefully. Then he turned to Coffin. "When did it start for you?"

Coffin was trembling. "Right after supper last night. I thought I was going to suffocate. Got up and walked the streets all night. My God, what a stink!"

"Jake?"

Dr. Miles shook his head. "Sometime this morning. I woke up with it."

"That's when it hit me," said Phillip.

"But I don't understand," Coffin howled. "Nobody else seems to notice anything—"

"Yet," Phillip said. "We were the first three to take the Coffin Cure, remember? You and me and Jake. Two months ago."

Coffin's forehead was beaded with sweat. He stared at the two men in growing horror.

"But what about the others?"

"I think," said Phillip, "that we'd better find something

220

spectacular to do in a mighty big hurry. That's what I think."

Jake Miles said, "The most important thing right now is secrecy. We mustn't let a word get out—not until we're absolutely certain."

"But what's *happened?*" Coffin cried. "These foul smells everywhere. You, Phillip—you had a cigarette this morning. I can smell it clear over here and it's burning my eyes. If I didn't know better, I'd swear neither of you had had a bath in a week. Every odor in town has suddenly turned foul—"

"*Magnified,* you mean," said Jake. "Perfume still smells sweet—there's just too much of it. The same with cinnamon; I tried it. Cried for half an hour, but it still smelled like cinnamon. No, I don't think the *smells* have changed any."

"But what then?"

"Our noses have changed, obviously." Jake paced the floor in excitement. "Look at our dogs. They've never had colds—and they practically live by their noses. Other animals—all dependent on their senses of smell for survival—and none of them ever have anything even vaguely reminiscent of a common cold. The multicentric virus hits primates only—*and it reaches its fullest parasitic powers in Man alone!*"

Coffin shook his head miserably. "But why this horrible reek all of a sudden? I haven't had a cold in weeks—"

"Of course not! That's just what I'm saying," Jake persisted. "Look, why do we have any sense of smell at all? Because we have tiny olfactory nerve endings buried in the mucous membrane of our noses and throats. But we've always had the virus living there, too, colds or no colds, throughout our entire lifetime. It's *always* been there, anchored in the same cells, parasitizing the same sensitive tissues that carry our olfactory nerve endings, numbing them and crippling them, making them practically useless as sensory organs. No wonder we never smelled anything before! Those poor little nerve endings never had a chance!"

"Until we came along and destroyed the virus," said Phillip.

"Oh, we didn't destroy it. We merely stripped it of a very slippery protective mechanism it had against normal body defenses." Jake perched on the edge of the desk, his dark face intense. "These two months since we had our shots have witnessed a battle to the death between our bodies and the virus. With the help of the vaccine, our bodies have

221

won, that's all—stripped away the last strongholds of an invader that has been almost a part of our normal physiology since the beginning of primates. And now, for the first time, those crippled little nerve endings are just beginning to function."

Coffin groaned. "God help us. You think it'll get worse?"

"And worse. And still worse," said Jake.

"I wonder," said Phillip slowly, "what the anthropologists will say."

"What do you mean?"

"Maybe it was just a single mutation somewhere back in prehistory. Just a tiny change of metabolism that left one line of the primates vulnerable to an invader no other would harbor. Why else should Man have begun to flower and blossom intellectually—grow to depend so much on his brains instead of his brawn that he could rise above all others? What better reason than because, somewhere along the line, *he suddenly lost his sense of smell?*"

"Well, he's got it back again now," Coffin said despairingly, "and he's not going to like it a bit."

"No, he surely isn't," Jake agreed. "He's going to start hunting very quickly for someone to blame, I think."

They both looked at Coffin.

"Now don't be ridiculous, boys," said Coffin, beginning to shake. "We're in this together. Phillip, it was your idea in the first place—you said so yourself! You can't leave me now—"

The telephone jangled. The frightened voice of the secretary bleated, "Dr. Coffin? There was a student on the line just a moment ago. He—he said he was coming up to see you. Now, he said, not later—"

"I'm busy," Coffin sputtered. "I can't see anyone. And I can't take any calls—"

"But he's already on his way up," the girl burst out. "He was saying something about tearing you apart with his bare hands."

Coffin slammed down the receiver. His face was the color of clay. "They'll crucify me! Jake—Phillip—you've got to help me!"

Phillip sighed and unlocked the door. "Send a girl down to the freezer and have her bring up all the live cold virus she can find. Get us some inoculated monkeys and a few dozen dogs." He turned to Coffin. "And stop sniveling. You're the big publicity man around here—you're going to handle the screaming masses, whether you like it or not."

"But what are you going to do?"

"I haven't the faintest idea," said Phillip, "but whatever I do is going to cost you your shirt. We're going to find out how to catch cold again if we have to die trying."

It was an admirable struggle, and a futile one. They sprayed their noses and throats with enough pure culture of virulent live virus to have condemned an ordinary man to a lifetime of sneezing, watery-eyed misery. They didn't develop a sniffle among them.

They mixed six different strains of virus and gargled the extract, spraying themselves and every inoculated monkey they could get their hands on with the vile-smelling stuff. Not a sneeze.

They injected it hypodermically, intradermally, subcutaneously, intramuscularly and intravenously. They drank it. They bathed in it.

But they didn't catch a cold.

"Maybe it's the wrong approach," Jake said one morning. "Our body defenses are keyed up to top performance right now. Maybe if we break them down, we can get somewhere."

They plunged down that alley with grim abandon. They starved themselves. They forced themselves to stay awake for days on end, until exhaustion forced their eyes closed in spite of all they could do. They carefully devised vitamin-free, protein-free, mineral-free diets that tasted like library paste and smelled worse. They wore wet clothes and sopping shoes to work, turned off the heat and threw windows open to the raw winter air. Then they resprayed themselves with the live cold virus and waited prayerfully for the sneezing to begin.

It didn't. They stared at each other in gathering gloom. They'd never felt better in their lives.

Except for the smells, of course. They'd hoped that they might, presently, get used to them. They didn't. Every day it grew a little worse. They began smelling smells they never dreamed existed—noxious smells, cloying smells, smells that drove them gagging to the sinks. Their nose-plugs were rapidly losing their effectiveness. Mealtimes were nightmarish ordeals; they lost weight with alarming speed.

But they didn't catch cold.

"*I* think you should all be locked up," Ellie Dawson said severely as she dragged her husband, blue-faced and shivering, out of an icy shower one bitter morning. "You've lost your wits. You need to be protected against yourselves, that's what you need."

"You don't understand," Phillip moaned. "We've *got* to catch cold."

Ellie snapped angrily, "Why? Suppose you don't—what's going to happen?"

"We had three hundred students march on the laboratory today," Phillip explained patiently. "The smells were driving them crazy, they said. They couldn't even bear to be close to their best friends. They wanted something done about it, or else they wanted blood. Tomorrow we'll have them back and three hundred more. And they were just the pilot study! What's going to happen when fifteen million people find their noses suddenly turning on them?"

He shuddered. "Have you seen the papers? People are already going around sniffing like bloodhounds. And *now* we're finding out what a thorough job we did. We can't crack it, Ellie. We can't even get a toe hold. Those antibodies are just doing too good a job."

"Well, maybe you can find some unclebodies to take care of them," Ellie offered vaguely.

"Look, don't make bad jokes—"

"I'm not making jokes! I don't care *what* you do. All I want is a husband back who doesn't complain about how everything smells, and eats the dinners I cook, and doesn't stand around in cold showers at six in the morning."

"I know it's miserable," he said helplessly. "But I don't know how we can stop it."

He found Jake and Coffin in tight-lipped conference when he reached the lab.

"I can't do it any more," Coffin was saying. "I've begged them for time. I've promised them everything but my upper plate. I can't face them again. I just can't."

"We only have a few days left," Jake said grimly. "If we don't come up with something, we're goners."

Phillip's jaw suddenly sagged as he stared at them. "You know what I think?" he asked suddenly. "I think we've been prize idiots. We've gotten so rattled, we haven't used our heads. And all the time it's been sitting there blinking at us!"

"What are you talking about?" snapped Jake.

"Unclebodies," said Phillip.

"Great God!"

"No, I'm dead serious." Phillip's eyes were very bright.

"How many of those students do you think you can corral to help us?"

Coffin gulped. "Six hundred. They're out there in the street right now, a blood-seeking mob howling for a lynching."

"All right, I want them in here. And I want some monkeys. Monkeys with colds—the worse colds, the better."

"Do you have any idea what you're doing?" asked Jake.

"None in the least," said Phillip happily, "except that it's never been done before. But maybe it's time we tried following our noses for a while—"

The tidal wave began to break two days later . . . only a few people here, a dozen there, but enough to confirm the direst newspaper predictions. The boomerang was completing its circle.

At the laboratory, the doors were kept barred, the telephones disconnected. Within, there was a bustle of feverish —if odorous—activity. For the three researchers, the olfactory acuity had reached agonizing proportions. Even the small gas masks Phillip had devised could no longer shield them from the continuous barrage of violent odors.

But the work went on in spite of the smell. Truckloads of monkeys arrived at the lab—cold-ridden, sneezing, coughing, weeping, wheezing monkeys by the dozen. Culture trays bulged with tubes, overflowed the incubators and work tables. Each day six hundred angry students paraded through the lab, arms exposed, mouths open, grumbling but cooperating.

At the end of the first week, half the monkeys were cured of their colds and were unable to catch them back; the other half had new colds and couldn't get rid of them. Phillip observed this fact with grim satisfaction and went about the laboratory mumbling to himself.

Two days later, he burst forth jubilantly, lugging a sad-looking puppy under his arm. It was like no other puppy in the world. This one was sneezing and snuffling with a perfect howler of a cold.

The day came when they injected a tiny droplet of milky fluid beneath the skin of Phillip's arm and got the virus spray and gave his nose and throat a liberal application. Then they sat back and waited.

They were still waiting three days later.

"It was a great idea," Jake said morosely, flipping a bulging notebook closed with finality. "It just didn't work, was all."

"Where's Coffin?"

"He collapsed three days ago. Nervous prostration. He kept having dreams about hangings."

Phillip sighed. "Well, I suppose we'd better just face it. Nice knowing you, Jake. Pity it had to be this way."

"It was a great try, old man. A great try."

"Ah, yes. Nothing like going down in a blaze of—"

Phillip stopped dead, his eyes widening. His nose began to twitch. He took a gasp, a larger gasp, as a long-dead reflex came sleepily to life, shook its head, reared back. . . .

Phillip sneezed.

He sneezed for ten minutes without a pause, until he was blue-faced and gasping for air. He caught hold of Jake, wringing his hand as tears gushed from his eyes.

"It was a sibple edough pridciple," he said later to Ellie as she spread mustard on his chest and poured more warm water into his foot bath. "The Cure itself depedded upod it —the adtiged-adtibody reactiod. We had the adtibody agaidst the virus, all ridght; what we had to find was sobe kide of adtibody *agaidst* the adtibody." He sneezed violently and poured in nose drops with a happy grin.

"Will they be able to make it fast enough?"

"Just aboudt fast edough for people to get good ad eager to catch cold agaid," said Phillip. "There's odly wud little hitch . . ."

Ellie Dawson took the steaks from the grill and set them, still sizzling, on the dinner table.

"Hitch?" she said.

Phillip nodded as he chewed the steak with a pretense of enthusiasm. It tasted like slightly damp K-ration.

"This stuff we've bade does a real good job. Just a little too good." He wiped his nose and reached for a fresh tissue.

"I bay be wrog, but I thik I've got this cold for keeps," he said sadly. "Udless I cad fide ad adtibody agaidst the adtibody agaidst the adtibody—"

On Camera

JOHN NOVOTNY

There are times when I, as a late and reluctant comer (Spring 1966) to the idiot-box audience, could wish that the feat perpetrated by the anti-hero of this tale would actually happen, to relieve the tedium and homogenized vulgarity with which all glazed-eye TV watchers are drenched. On the other hand, I have to admit that the idea of seeing this raving maniac and his family on my picture tube is nothing to excite me, either. Better that it all remain just a story. . . .

I have no apologies for the fact that two or three of the programs mentioned hereinafter no longer grace the airwaves; *sic transit gloria C.B.S.* Obsolescence is an occupational hazard of science fiction tales that deal with such ephemerae as television. "On Camera" is still a delightful bit of foolery.

Robert Masters laughed derisively at his wife.

"How we do run on," he snorted, tugging at the television set. "It was I who walked home twenty-two years ago. You had nearly decapitated my ear lobe with your teeth and—"

"One cannot decapitate an ear lobe," Jane Masters interrupted.

"—you were after the other one when I leaped from the car, fortunately escaping with my honor," Robert continued calmly.

"An ear lobe may be severed, but not decapitated," Jane insisted.

"What a fool I was," Robert Masters mused. "If I had only stayed in the car that night. Heaven knows what might have happened."

"Nothing would have happened," Jane smiled, "except perhaps you might have appeared before my father without any ear lobes. What are you going to do?"

"Tape them tightly to my head, naturally," Robert said

227

easily. "Now that it's out in the open I don't intend to take any chances."

"I am referring to the television set."

"Oh." Robert grasped the set and pulled. "I'm going to fix it."

Mrs. Masters got up, walked to the writing cabinet, extracted a small notebook, and returned to the sofa. She opened the book and raised an eyebrow.

"On our first anniversary you fixed our Atwater Kent and put the entire neighborhood in darkness," she announced. "Since then you have annihilated three electric clocks, two radios, our daughter's record player, and one vacuum cleaner. You fought a draw with the front door lock and were beaten soundly by a three-way lamp. You average four fuses just warming up a soldering iron."

"Very funny," Robert observed.

"And now you intend to louse up the television set."

"My dear," Robert sighed. "I intend to fix the television. Borrowing our daughter's college-taught English does not become you."

"Nor does getting electrocuted become you," she answered. "Each time you approach an appliance I die a little."

Robert removed the back of the set.

"You are in good form tonight," he sighed, squinting at the arrangement of tubes and wires. "Will you hand me the screwdriver?"

Jane pushed it over with the toe of her shoe.

"I suppose this makes me an accessory," she observed.

"If you wish to see Ed Sullivan tonight you will continue with the helping hand. Is it turned to CBS?"

"Yes," said Jane. Robert reached in with the screwdriver.

At that moment Ed Sullivan shrugged his shoulders, rubbed his hands, and peered out at the studio audience.

"And now, ladies and gentlemen, here is someone else I would like you to meet."

With a shriek of pain and a wild grimace, Mr. Robert Masters joined Ed Sullivan on television screens across the country.

"Damn it to hell!" he roared, holding his arm and hopping around the living room. Mr. Sullivan stared with horror at the monitor. An engineer in the glassed-in control booth fainted dead away. Some television sets were snapped off quickly but a much larger number acquired new interest in their households. Mr. Sullivan moved not a muscle. This did not hold true for Mr. Masters. He moved every muscle which could be moved as he circled the living room. Once he kicked fretfully at the offending set. Another "damn!" spread over America. Jane frowned and reached out to slow him down on each trip. Robert glared at her.

"Don't you intend to use the telephone?" he asked angrily.

"I don't know if we can get a repairman at this time of—"

Robert Masters left the ground, giving many viewers the false impression that they were watching a profane, but skilful, acrobatic act.

"A doctor!" he shouted. "You could call a doctor!"

Jane looked disgusted.

"We always do," she said bluntly. "And what comes of it? Nothing. When he arrives you insist you know more than he. You fight with him. He leaves. We have all but exhausted our local supply, and I like the one we have now."

"I may be dying of electrical poisoning while you ramble on," he said hoarsely. CBS trembled, spun dials, checked circuits, and prayed. Ed Sullivan retired behind his big curtain.

"I don't think it works like that," Jane disagreed. "With electricity you go quick—*poof!*—or not at all."

"Cold-blooded," Robert moaned. Many Americans sprang to their desks to write concurring letters. Others leaped to Jane's defense and dusted off old physics books for reliable quotations. By this time CBS had a turntable spinning and a stack of records waiting in another studio. The order was given to abandon Ed Sullivan. An announcer cleared his throat.

"Because of operating difficulties the Ed Sullivan Show has been interrupted. Until this is cleared up we will entertain you with recorded music."

"Electricity can be quite lingering," Mr. Masters said firmly, refusing to be shunted aside by CBS.

"And so can you," muttered the chief engineer on duty, as he composed his resignation.

"Robert," Jane said softly. "You are an expert with money. As far as investments are concerned your knowledge and acumen are without equal. Why must you stoop to playing with appliances?"

"Do you really feel that way?" Robert asked, pleased. His anger began to diminish and, as it did, his image faded on television screens. Mrs. Masters gathered her husband into her arms.

"I've never joked about your work, Robert," she said. "You're the best investment councilor in New York."

Robert Masters smiled and deserted television as applause rang through homes across the nation.

"You're right about one thing, Jane," he said ruefully. "I really loused up the television. I wonder what Ed Sullivan had on for tonight?"

Two hours later they found out. Marie Masters drove home from her grandmother's house and flew into the living room.

"Why didn't you tell me?" she demanded. "We might have missed it."

"Missed what?" Jane asked. "And what are you doing home? I thought you were staying with Mother until tomorrow."

"How can you take it so calmly?" Marie exulted. "I thought you were wonderful. Gram thought Dad was overacting but I didn't agree with her. And why didn't you tell me?"

Robert Masters took his daughter's hand and led her to the sofa.

"Sit down," he said firmly. He waited while she sat. "Now please explain yourself coherently and without your usual modern-day expressions."

"Father," Marie smiled. "Stop being obtuse. Gram and I watched Ed Sullivan."

Jane and Robert looked at each other.

"That's nice," Jane said, hopefully.

"You should have told us you were going to be on," Marie insisted. "And your material could have been a little better."

"Material?" Robert asked. "Is this more of your school talk?"

"But the ending was wonderful," Marie said. "I almost cried when Mother said you were the most."

"I said what?" Jane asked, wonderingly.

"Sorry," Marie said. "When you said Dad was the best investment man in the business."

There were a few moments of silence and then Robert leaned forward.

"Are you trying to say that you thought you saw your mother and me on television?" he asked softly.

"I didn't think," Marie laughed. "I saw."

"Marie," Jane Masters said, patting her daughter's hand. "It must have been someone else. Your father and I have been home all evening."

"I told Gram it wasn't a set," Marie said. "I knew the room was real. They had the camera right here, didn't they?"

"It wasn't us," her father stated.

"Who else says 'Damn it to hell' like you, Father?"

"Marie!" Jane gasped.

"On television?" Robert demanded.

"And then you hopped around the room swearing," Marie said. Robert and Jane sank back in their chairs.

"Did I want your mother to call a doctor?" Robert asked faintly.

"Certainly," Marie said. "I laughed."

"Good Lord!" Robert cried. Jane slowly covered her mouth.

"You shouldn't have laughed," she said reprovingly to her daughter.

"That's not the point, my dear," Robert sighed. "Apparently I did something with that screwdriver and we were on television."

Marie stared at her parents.

"You're not joking? You didn't know?"

"Your father tried to fix the television set," Jane explained. "Oh."

Robert studied the two women in his life.

"It's that simple, is it?" he said sadly.

"Oh, Daddy," Marie said unhappily. "I didn't mean that. You were really very good."

Robert groaned.

"I imagine I was. Was it a clear picture?"

"I knew you almost immediately. But Gram kept fussing with the controls."

"Isn't that annoying?" Jane mused. "She always does that. —Oh my heavens!"

"What's the matter?" Robert asked quickly.

"This dress," Jane fretted. "I should have worn the taffeta. I look positively huge in this. I hope Mrs. Pembrooke wasn't watching."

"I've been thinking," Marie said. "Perhaps no one else recognized either of you. There were no credit lines and no announcements. If anyone asks, just deny everything."

A smile slowly formed on Robert Masters' face.

"There are times when I regret having sent you to Radcliffe, but this is not one of them," he beamed. "A man is fortunate to have a daughter with a good mind. And you did well by speeding home to warn us about all this."

"Could we discuss allowance?" Marie asked. Mr. Masters stretched and yawned.

"Now I think I'll go up to bed," he announced. He kissed his wife and daughter. "Goodnight all."

They watched him leave; then Jane turned to her daughter.

"Answer me truthfully. Did I look positively huge?"

There were a few remarks passed at the office Monday morning about the mix-up on the Ed Sullivan show. One partner mentioned that an actor looked startlingly like Robert but the programming was so poor you couldn't make sense out of the act. Beyond that nothing was said and the day passed easily. On Thursday evening the Masters visited Jane's mother and swore her to silence. All went well until the next Saturday evening. The Masters were having company and Robert was playing solitaire while waiting for the guests to arrive. A vital queen seemed to be missing. Robert lifted the edge of a card slowly.

"That's cheating," Jane called from the hall.

"I'm not playing against anyone," Robert muttered.

"Your honor is at stake," Jane said.

"Honor my foot," Robert snapped. "One queen and I'm certain this will come out."

The Masters' television set was off or they might have noticed a faint image beginning to form alongside Bud Collyer.

"Cheating at solitaire is a sign of no personal integrity," Jane insisted. Robert hurried through the pack again.

"I need that queen!" he said hotly. Bud Collyer leaned forward and studied the monitor. Then he looked around and examined the stage. He smiled and turned back to the contestants.

"Now for the hundred-dollar clock—" he began.

"Who's that?" the husband contestant asked, pointing at Robert Masters on the monitor.

"I haven't the faintest idea," Bud admitted. "And I suggest we just disregard him."

"It's not just to make us nervous?" the husband asked.

"You'd be surprised whom it's making nervous," Bud Collyer said. "For the hundred-dollar clock—"

Jane walked into the living room.

"You can't have the queen," she said. "It's covered."

Beat the Clock watchers were treated to the sight of a good forthright bit of cheating. Mr. Masters glared at his wife, seized the red queen, and slapped it face up.

"There!" he said.

"I think that stinks," Jane told him. Bud Collyer winced and inadvertently knocked over four paper cups just as the two contestants arrived with spoons held in each hand and a potato on each spoon. The husband looked down at the cups and then at Bud.

"Why did you do that?" he asked.

"Well—" Bud began.

"Ain't no way we can get the potatoes in them when you knocked 'em over," the husband complained.

"Well—" Bud tried again. The buzzer sounded.

"See? Now we didn't beat the clock," the husband pointed out. The wife began to cry.

"I'll tell you what we'll do," Bud said. "I was clumsy. We'll put you past the hundred-dollar clock and the two hundred-dollar clock. Right up to the Jackpot Clock. Okay?"

The man frowned.

"I suppose you'll be knocking the words off the board."

Bud wiped some perspiration away.

"We'll give you the television set," he said. The man and woman smiled.

"That sounds fair," the husband said. "We'll take it."

Robert went through the pack and slammed the cards to the table.

"What's wrong now?" Jane asked.

"I also need a jack."

"Cheating shows," Jane said airily. Robert stood up.

"That is an asinine statement," he shouted.

Bud Collyer swallowed.

"I think someone in Control should do something," he said hopefully. A door opened.

"What in hell do you think we're trying to do?" a frenzied voice boomed. The door slammed.

"Next contestants," Bud whispered.

Early Monday morning CBS Vice-President Maystrik's phone rang. He lifted it gingerly and found the Federal Communications Commission on the other end.

"Castleman speaking," the phone boomed.

"Hello, Neil," Maystrik said warily.

"You can't get away with this, you know," Neil Castleman told him. "Don't know why you even tried."

"Away with what?" Earle Maystrik asked.

"Come now, boy," Castleman laughed. "Superimposing on the *Beat the Time* program."

"Beat the Clock!" Vice-President Maystrik said clearly. "And we didn't superimpose. We didn't plan it. We don't know who the bird is."

"We do," Castleman said. "Robert Masters. Investment firm. How in the world did you talk him into it?"

"Neil," Maystrik said quietly. "Listen to me and believe what you hear. We had nothing to do with the man appearing during our program. We don't know how it happened or even if it's going to happen again."

The FCC pondered a moment and made its decision.

"I'm sending Dave Whitman up there to handle this matter," Castleman said crisply. "It's not going to happen again."

But it did happen again and the FCC had no one but itself to blame. Dave Whitman and Earle Maystrik called on Robert Masters at his office.

"Yes," Robert confessed. "It's happened twice and I'm at a loss to explain it."

Dave nodded politely.

"Naturally we can't permit it to continue," he smiled. Robert frowned.

"Then I suggest you tell CBS to stop it," he said warmly. Mr. Maystrik joined the conversation.

"And I suggest you stay the hell off our programs," he snapped. "Our viewers don't tune in to see you."

Arthur Godfrey leaned forward, examined the monitor, and grinned. He motioned for silence.

"I been hoping for this," he drawled. "If you people out there think I act up once in awhile, wait until you get a load of this fellow. All children under sixteen should be sent outdoors."

He leaned back and Mr. Masters obliged by leaping into furious focus.

"You can take your viewers and—" Robert Masters snarled. Dave interrupted him.

"Apparently the viewers do want to see him," he said. "NBC is quite concerned. In fact they tried to dummy up the same situation. Threw an image of a pretty girl in a bathing suit onto a few of their own programs."

"I certainly hope you took appropriate action," Maystrik said indignantly.

"We did," Dave Whitman said quietly. "And they insist we do the same with you."

"I'd like to see you try," Robert Masters sneered. His secretary entered.

"Excuse me," she announced, "but the receptionist called. She says you're on the television set out there. She says Arthur Godfrey is convulsed."

Earle Maystrik covered his face.

"What will the sponsors say?" he groaned.

"Arthur is not bothering with commercials while you people are on," the secretary informed them. They ran to the reception room and stared at themselves on the big screen. As embarrassment overcame anger the picture of Robert Masters faded and with him went Maystrik of CBS and Whitman of the FCC. Dave watched with interest and turned to Masters.

"You're no longer angry?" he asked.

"Why, no," Robert said. "But I can be very quickly."

"Let's see."

Robert grimaced and frowned. Nothing happened.

"Can't seem to make it," he smiled.

"You're a cheap fourflusher," Dave said.

"Here he comes again!" Godfrey shouted.

"Aha!" Dave gloated. He stood there smiling.

"Well?" Robert demanded.

"You told us that this began when you tried to fix your set," Dave said. Robert nodded and left Godfrey.

"You were tuned to CBS," Dave continued. "When you hit the current it looks like you charged yourself and now you're a sending station exactly like CBS. When you're angry you generate enough power to televise."

"So now I'm no cheap fourflusher," Robert said ruefully. "I'm a television station."

"I think we're going to sue," Mr. Maystrik announced.

"Easy. Easy," Dave cautioned. "We'll be back with Arthur."

"I beg your pardon," Maystrik said quickly. Robert pointed at him.

"I don't like you," he said, and then turned to Dave. "And I don't think I care for you either. I suppose you're good at fixing electric clocks."

"Well—I can do it, if necessary," Dave admitted.

"I knew it," Robert said disdainfully. "Now, gentlemen, we have used enough of the firm's time. If you have anything further to discuss, and I imagine you have, I suggest we meet at my home this evening. I do not enjoy the prospect but I wish to get this matter cleared up."

"We have all big shows tonight," Maystrik cried. Masters smiled.

"Just avoid making me angry."

Marie Masters found Dave Whitman charming.

"I'm very glad they sent you," she told him. "Up at Radcliffe we're one hundred percent in favor of the FCC."

"You don't say," Dave grinned. "That's wonderful. I'd like to tell you all about how we operate."

"Fast, I believe, would cover it," Robert said drily.

"Robert!" Jane called. "That's not polite."

"Watch your ear lobes," Robert muttered, walking across the room.

"Why did he say that?" Dave asked.

"I have no idea," Marie said as she smiled disarmingly. Maystrik motioned and Dave joined the CBS vice-president and Mr. Masters.

"Well?" Maystrik asked. "What are we going to do?"

"Capitalize on it," Dave said crisply.

"Capitalize on what?" Robert asked.

"On your ability," Dave explained. "I talked with Washington most of the afternoon and, while they're not too enthusiastic, they're willing to go along with a test."

"I refuse," Robert said.

"You don't even know what you're refusing," Dave said.

"Are you trying to irritate me?" Robert asked.

"Mr. Masters, you are in a position to help the government," Dave said.

"Republicans or Democrats?" Robert asked quickly.

"Both."

"I refuse."

"Mr. Masters, by both I mean everyone. If an attack knocks out our communications we cannot communicate with the public."

Robert Masters stared at the FCC man.

"What are you talking about?" he asked.

"I'm talking about using your ability in the event of war," Dave said firmly. "In the event of attack the public must be kept informed. Our plans are all set up to do this. But if the communications centers are disabled we're sunk. You will be our emergency station."

"I think that's wonderful," Marie said. "Father will make a terrific station."

"If you please, Marie," Robert said. "I would like to hear more about this ridiculous plan."

"Anyone tuned to CBS can receive you," Dave went on. "You televise yourself and those near you and the view is always on your face. Either you or someone next to you can read the instructions to the public. That's all there is. We'll run a test tomorrow from your office."

"Have you spoken to—?"

"The other partners of Mertons, Stoehr, Masters and Kohn were delighted with the idea," Dave said. Robert walked about the room slowly. Every so often he looked at Dave Whitman. Once he stopped in front of Dave.

"I'd much prefer broadcasting just to the Republicans," he said hopefully.

"Mr. Masters, how can the Democrats be restrained from watching?" Dave sighed.

"You're the FCC," Robert snapped. "You figure a way."

"It can't be done," Dave said flatly. Robert walked again. "What are you so quiet about?" he asked Maystrik. Maystrik shrugged.

"I don't know. CBS doesn't seem to have much to say about all this. I wonder if I should call Ed Murrow?"

Robert froze and his wife and daughter immediately leaped up. While Jane soothed him and led his thinking back to the test of the next morning, Marie explained to Maystrik and Dave.

"We are very fond of Mr. Murrow but a few weeks ago he said some things about taxes. Father has banned him for a month."

"Oh?"

"But if you tell him, please explain that Father has, at one time or another, banned John Daly and Mr. Swayze for lesser offenses."

Mr. Masters rejoined the conversation.

"I am agreed," he said. "Tomorrow morning. And now I'm sure you gentlemen will excuse us."

Mr. Maystrik quickly took the hint and Mr. Whitman followed him to the door.

"Good evening," Robert said, shaking their hands and ushering them into the night.

"Good evening, Father," Marie said, squeezing through the door after them.

"Where are you going?" he asked. Marie motioned for Dave to wait at the car.

"Dave is going to take me for a beer," she smiled, "and it sounds antiseptic but I may end up being kissed by the FCC. 'Night."

She hurried down the walk. Robert stalked back to the living room and confronted his wife.

"Why, in heaven's name, didn't we send her to NYU?" he demanded.

The group in Mr. Mertons' office was held to a minimum. Along with the four partners were Mr. Maystrik, two other CBS officials, Mr. Whitman, and a technician to handle the huge television set which had been installed.

"We go on at eleven thirty," Dave said. "CBS will go off the air. You'll be on your own."

"I'm getting nervous."

"Buck up, man," Mr. Stoehr said stoutly. "Imagine you're investing someone else's money."

"You'd better be as good as *Strike It Rich*," Mr. Maystrik warned. "This is their time."

"Oh, shut up," Mr. Mertons said. "This is patriotic."

"Get ready," Dave said.

"Where will I stand?" Robert asked.

"It doesn't make much difference," Dave smiled. "I'm reading the announcement so I'll stand next to you."

Mr. Masters stepped to the center of the office.

"How about here?"

"Fine," Dave agreed. He stepped to Mr. Masters' side. "Just a few seconds to go.—Get ready.—We're on!"

The screen of the big set faded and went blank. Everyone waited. Dave nudged Robert.

"I'm sweating," Robert whispered.

"Get angry," Dave said.

"I don't feel angry."

"Think of the Democrats," Mertons encouraged. Mr. Masters concentrated and then grinned sickly.

"I don't think I know any," he said. Dave nodded.

"I was afraid you'd make an ass of yourself," he said clearly.

"A what?" Robert asked.

"You heard me," Dave retorted. "If you had a little common courtesy and listened when someone spoke perhaps—"

"An ass of myself!" Masters shouted.

"You're on," the technician announced. Everyone looked at the screen except Mr. Masters who continued to glare at Dave.

"Ladies and gentlemen," Dave began. "You are now watching a test which is of grave importance to each of you. It is being sponsored by the United States government in association with the Columbia Broadcasting System."

"You're fading," the technician called. Dave brought his heel down on Robert's toes.

"That's better," the man called. Robert turned his head to glare at the technician and Dave found himself speaking with his back to the television audience. He pulled Mr. Masters roughly back in place.

"A full explanation of the irregularities and any unusual language—"

"He means me," Mr. Masters said nastily.

"—will be in tomorrow's newspapers," Dave continued. "This represents independently powered television which will bring you instructions in the event of enemy attack."

"And you all had better damn well listen," Mr. Masters stated, "because I can stand only so much of this boy."

"Should the occasion ever arise for use of this facility, please leave your sets tuned to CBS even if they seem to be blank," Dave continued. "Mr. Robert Masters and a qualified announcer will bring the necessary message to you."

"Fading," the technician called. Dave's elbow found Robert's stomach.

"Ugh!" Robert gasped. "Do that once more and you won't be around for any enemy attack."

"This test originated in the offices of Mertons, Stoehr, Masters and Kohn," Dave concluded. He stepped aside and Mr. Masters' partners crowded around him. In unison they sang.

"Your investment will be safe
Stocks, or bonds, or loan.
Hurry down and ask to see
Mertons, Stoehr, Masters or Kohn."

Robert Masters swallowed.

"Who in blazes thought of that?" he asked.

"Hello, Jimmy," Stoehr called out, waving. "Eat your lunch for mommy."

Robert looked around in alarm. The partners turned hurriedly to remain facing the unseen camera.

"I'm bringing Sam home for dinner, honey," Mertons announced for his wife's benefit.

"Gentlemen!" Dave called. "Personal messages are not permitted."

"I'm getting weary of this rubbish," Robert announced tiredly. "Are we off?"

"You're off," the man at the set said.

"Well done," Dave smiled. "I had to let your associates get in a plug. It won't happen again."

"I hope it never needs to happen again," Robert said. "The impact—the full meaning—just now struck home. I think it was that ridiculous commercial that did it."

"You did a good job," Dave said warmly. "I'm getting along now; but I'll see you tonight."

"Why?"

"Marie invited me for dinner," Dave smiled. "She's some girl." He waved and left.

"Antiseptic, my foot," Robert sneered. He turned to Maystrik. "Did you notice a Band-Aid on Whitman's ear?"

Dinner went far more smoothly than expected and Marie explained it to Dave in whispers.

"The experience sobered Father quite a bit. He realizes there are emotions much more important than anger."

"Like love?" Dave asked.

"No," Marie said. "Like fishing. Father considers that an emotion. He has decided to relax, enjoy himself more, and conserve his power for the war effort."

"That's very admirable," Dave agreed.

The remainder of the evening was pure light and laughter. Mr. Masters even confided his plan for an immediate vacation.

"—and we'll spend a number of weeks along the Mediterranean coast," he concluded. "Just the three of us."

"Oh, Father," Marie said sorrowfully. "I can't go."

"Why not? Radcliffe has released you."

"It's not that," Marie said. "It's Dave. We're in love. We're going to be married."

Robert Masters stood up slowly.

"You're in what?"

"Love," Marie said.

"With that?" Mr. Masters pointed a quivering finger at Dave. "Are you asking me to be father-in-law to the rudest, most self-centered creature I've ever met?"

His voice rose and Dave ran to the television set, snapped it on, and turned to CBS. Mr. Masters filled the screen. Dave turned quickly.

"Now, Dad—" he began.

"Dad!"

A few of the cheaper sets in the immediate neighborhood blew their picture tubes and minor tubes gave out all over the city.

"This little nincompoop has called me dirty names," Robert shouted.

"Conserve your energy," Dave pleaded.

"Stamped on my foot and hit me in the stomach," Robert ranted. Dave ran to stand beside him.

240

"Ladies and gentlemen," Dave pleaded. "What you are now watching is strictly a personal matter. I feel certain you will understand, and I ask that you switch immediately to NBC."

He turned back to Mr. Masters.

"Dad," he urged. "Let's talk this out in a democratic way."

Robert crouched ominously and pointed at Dave.

"He called me that again!" he shouted. "And he used that dirty word too!"

"Robert," Mrs. Masters observed with interest. "Look. You're coming over in color now. I didn't know we had a color set."

They stared at the picture tube where Robert Masters glowed in brilliant shades of red. Portions of the coaxial cable melted away in the Middle West. Robert placed his hand on his forehead and quickly pulled it away.

"I'm burning up," he gasped, falling back into a chair. "Get a thermometer." Jane hurried to do his bidding. Robert glared at the instrument and thrust it beneath his tongue.

Millions of viewers waited in silence for the required two minutes.

Dave Whitman studied the television set.

"I believe you're fading slightly, sir," he announced carefully. Robert removed the thermometer and squinted toward the normal mark. Slowly, with horror, his eye travelled up the tube; then he sank back and tossed it over his shoulder.

"You're gone," Dave said.

"I know," Robert sighed. "In the prime of life."

"I mean from television. You're off."

Robert shrugged and smiled a very small smile.

"What difference does it make, son?" he asked quietly. Marie gasped.

"Oh he's sick," she whispered.

"What about the defense plan, Mr. Masters?" Dave asked. Robert closed his eyes.

"I don't think I can get angry at anything."

"Edward R. Murrow," Dave said.

"A fine chap," Robert mused. "Smokes too much."

"Mother threw away your trout rod," Marie lied, watching her father carefully. He merely held out his hand and clasped his wife's.

"It was rather worn and I guess Jane really knows best," he sighed.

"He has blown his stack," Marie whispered to Dave. "Short-circuited himself clean out."

Dave whispered in Marie's ear. She nodded and leaned toward her father.

"I'm voting Democrat next November," she said clearly. Mr. Masters' eyebrows raised and one hand grasped the chair arm. Marie and Dave watched nervously. Robert relaxed again.

"You must make your own decisions, Marie," he said in a fatherly tone. Marie regarded him suspiciously and pulled Dave across the room.

"He's not finished yet," she said. "I'll bet he just used up all his anger. I'd say we have maybe three months."

"Time enough for a honeymoon," Dave smiled. "Then back to work. Perhaps this will tone him down and he'll conserve himself for emergencies."

"I wonder if I should ask for a raise in allowance," Marie mused. Dave frowned.

"Let's not chance that," he decided. "Besides we'll be married soon."

Mr. Masters watched as they kissed. He smiled approvingly.

"Lovely young couple," he murmured to his wife. Jane shook out the aspirins, arranged the ice pack neatly atop his head, and shook down the discarded thermometer.

"Open up," she ordered.

See No Evil

JOHN R. PIERCE

Here is an original, never-before-published science fiction jest in which Mr. Pierce, who is Executive Director, Research, Communications Science Division, Bell Telephone Laboratories, takes a swipe at television and the so-called code of morals under which it operates. He also passes some not-so-sly digs at the genus TV mogul, and does all this while describing one of the most elaborate hoaxes in "science fiction" literature.

It would be nice for the entertainment world's Powers That Be, I suppose, if Vic Thatcher's imitation machine really could be invented!—but then it would deprive the nation's millions of TV-watchers of an occasional unpremeditated pleasure during their viewings of the otherwise surgically sterile picture tube.

Incidentally, and for the information of those who are not sophisticated on electronic matters, the "I.R.E." referred to early in the story refers to the late and lamented Institute of Radio Engineers, which not so long ago was absorbed into the much larger Institute of Electrical and Electronics Engineers.

The story was originally written under the pseudonym "J. J. Coupling," a name which Mr. Pierce used in the past for some of his lighter science articles and an occasional story.

When Vic Thatcher and I were at Far Western, a lot of the graduate students of that less prosperous day supported themselves, but barely, by teaching undergraduate courses. Not Vic, though. He made a good deal more by building not only diathermy machines for legitimate doctors, but exotic, impressive and functionless gadgets with flashing lights and sound effects for successful quacks. I liked him then and I like him now. The fact that he acquired a little more of the world's goods than most of the rest of us pleased me. But some other classmates whom I have liked quite as much have always been less pleased with him than I. I chalked this up to envy or to excessively rigid standards.

So, always when I have been at Far Western, talking to Gregory and others, I have been rather annoyed when one of them mentioned Vic in the way some of them do, and I have said so. Last time, though, I was silent. I didn't want to think of my last encounter with Vic, let alone talk about it. I knew very well what my friends would say if I did, and I couldn't think just what to say in reply. Too, I didn't want to tell my part in the matter.

I happened to see Vic that time by sheer coincidence. He didn't know that I was coming out to give a paper on game-playing machines at the Pacific Coast I.R.E. Convention, and I didn't know that he was in California. My talk was written up in the papers, though, and Vic saw it and called me at my hotel. The morning after that, I found myself spending an unexpected and profitable day at a large studio in Culver City, a place which certainly beggars any description you might get from me. Megalith was just getting into television. Vic was Research Director for Special Projects, and I was an expert consultant on communication theory. The scene was a conference room.

I must say that it wasn't much different from any other conference room, except that the table, the chairs, and the rug were not only impressive and expensive, but they were good, too. The men around the table looked intelligent and business-like. Vic, tall, dark, and moustached, looked just the serious and dynamic technical leader. Mr. Braden, who sat at the head of the table, with a secretary slightly behind him, radiated authority and competence. The others are pretty much blanks as far as my memory goes. Vic started by introducing me.

"I was fortunate enough to persuade Dr. Coupling to come out to the Coast for a few days," he said. "I'd like to have brought out Norbert Wiener and Claude Shannon as well, but Norbert is in France right now, and of course, Bell Labs men don't do consulting work."

Vic smiled, and Mr. Braden smiled back at him, and inclusively at me.

"How is Dr. Shannon, Dr. Coupling?" Mr. Braden asked. "Vic has been telling me a lot about his work, and about yours, too."

I replied somewhat foggily that Claude was well, while I wondered just what I was supposed to be at this conference, and what Vic had been telling Mr. Braden about me.

"Of course, I haven't told Dr. Coupling the exact nature of our work," Vic explained. "You understand, John," he continued, "that important commercial interests are involved, and we must maintain a certain degree of secrecy."

At this, Mr. Braden nodded seriously and approvingly.

"But," Vic continued, "I think we should have Dr. Coupling's reassurance on certain basic points."

The half-hour that followed left me completely bewildered. As anyone who has read a recent article in one of our flossiest magazines knows, communication theory, or information theory as some call it, is chock full of erudite and glamorous terms and concepts which easily convey a sense of philosophical profundity. Entropy, ergodic source, multidimensional message space, bits, equivocation, Markoff process; all of these sound good in almost any order. If they are put in just the right order, they make sense of a theoretical sort. And a real expert can sometimes use them to solve everyday, useful problems.

Mr. Braden certainly knew all the terms, and he had mastered the trick of stringing them together right. What he said could be interpreted logically enough, but how it could be connected with any practical problem in the television industry, or in the movies either, I couldn't for the life of me imagine. However, as he framed his questions I managed to respond appropriately, wondering all the while whether we were saying something or merely engaging in a superior sort of logical double-talk.

Yes, I agreed, any electric signal could be represented as a point in a multi-dimensional message space. Yes, signals of a particular character would occupy only a restricted portion of such a message space. Voice signals of English speech would occupy one very restricted portion of the space, I said as an illustration. Voice signals of German speech would occupy another limited portion of the message space, probably near to that occupied by English voice signals—near in some way which could be defined by lattice theory.

Lattice theory is a branch of algebra.

Music would occupy another very restricted portion of such a message space. Noise would be spread randomly over the space.

Yes, in principle a device could be made which would transmit only a restricted set of signals, represented by a certain region in message space. I was about to add that a given sort of signal, such as music, or perhaps music by Beethoven, was probably spread loosely like tangled spaghetti, through a message space of billions of dimensions, and that I'd like to see a machine which could actually sort such signals out.

I think that Vic guessed what I might say at this point.

"Of course, Dr. Coupling knows how difficult that is, Mr. Braden," he said. "But you don't know our techniques, John," Vic told me, smiling assuredly.

Mr. Braden glanced around the room at all the others who were present.

"I'm afraid we must get on with other business," he said. "It's been very good of you to come and help us, Dr. Coupling," he added, rising and shaking hands with me. "Vic will be tied up for a while, but Larry Holt will show you around the lot."

A shortish, lean man with a rather pointed face sprang up from the opposite end of the table, and he and Vic conducted me to the door. As I was about to leave, Vic handed me a check and said to Larry:

"Dr. Coupling would like to cash this. He needs it for expenses on the trip back east."

I looked at the check; it was for two thousand dollars.

Larry drove me to the bank in a Cadillac convertible. "You have to have one," he told me when I admired it. At the bank he identified me, and I found myself in the entirely unreasonable position of carrying two thousand dollars in cash. On the way back, Larry discussed the studios that we passed, and, arriving back at Megalith, proceeded to show me around. I saw more than I can recall of the huge lot with its weathered towns, indoor tanks, and immense buildings like super-barns housing varied and domesticated civilizations. In the end I was so groggy with surprise that nothing registered very clearly, but Larry evidently knew everybody and everything, and I gather that what there is to see of the movies, I saw. We had lunch with a veritable star, too, though a small one, and I found that among people who think of science as sorcery rather than hard work, it is rather nice to be called Doctor.

A little after two, Larry took me over to one side of a huge building where a long, low, closed structure was built along the wall. It was plainly finished on the outside, with no openings except a few doors. He took me in through one of these, and there was Vic in a handsome office, smiling fit to kill. The intense leader was clean gone; his face seemed broader, and his eyes twinkled.

"Thanks, Larry," he said, waving my guide away. Then he leaned back and grinned across the table at me.

"Well, Johnny, what do you think of the movies?" he asked.

"What in the devil is it all about, Vic?" I demanded. "And thanks for the check, by the way."

"It's usual," Vic said. "After all, remember that you made a special trip to the Coast. You had to get someone to take over your classes, of course. And Braden wouldn't have taken you seriously if I'd given you less."

"But what is this all about, Vic?" I insisted.

"This," he announced, "is Special Developments. Megalith is getting into TV and we're stealing a jump on our competitors through the magic of research."

"But what does it have to do with communication theory and message space?" I asked.

"Wait and see, Johnny; wait and see. I've arranged a tour for Braden tomorrow, and you're going to get a preview."

Vic picked up the phone. "I'll be in the lab, Nelly," he said. Then he got up, opened another door from the office, and we were in the dream laboratory.

Nobody but the president of a company ever expects a laboratory to look that way. Usually, lab benches are built by someone who knows that people will pound on them, but who never imagines that people will look at them. The same goes for the rest of lab fixings. But this laboratory had been designed with an artist's eye. It was large and uncluttered. A few spic-and-span machine tools occupied one corner. The walls were lined with handsome apparatus, all of which had meters and handles galore and multitudes of flashing lights. In one corner at the far end, under the smooth glow of the fluorescent lights, stood a man in a white smock. Before him was a glittering array of equipment, and he gazed with rapt intensity on the soft, green face of an oscilloscope tube.

"Mr. Smith," Vic said. The man turned. "Mr. Coupling is visiting us today." Once more Vic was the dynamic leader. He turned toward me and explained, "We don't use titles in our laboratory. We try to maintain a friendly spirit."

Mr. Smith held out his hand and I shook it. He was a short, weedy-looking individual with cigarette-stained fingers. Vic proceeded, strictly in line with Braden's perfectly logical brand of double-talk.

"Smith," he said, "has been working on a digrammer. In order to explore message space, we must study a sequence of actual signals. Largely as a demonstration of how this can be done, Smith has constructed this device which records the statistics of signals in a two-dimensional space."

This went on, and I got a concise and complete description of the digrammer, without the slightest idea of why it had been built. I thanked Smith, and we went out.

"What's it all about?" I asked. "That's all old stuff—Bell Laboratories did it years ago. And who is Smith, anyway? He looks like a radio serviceman to me."

"That's what he is," said Vic. "It's a beautiful digrammer, though. And you should see the record player he made for my apartment. Here, though; you ought to see this next." We went into a small, uniformly lighted room, the walls of which were hung with what seemed at first to be completely abstract drawings. Vic resumed his executive manner.

"The purpose of this project, of course," he said, "is to provide mechanical, or, I should say, electronic protection against the transmission of matter not conforming to the code of decency.

"In the case of film, the print has always been carefully examined by experts before release. The intention of the director, of course, is, while never appearing prudish, always to observe the code most carefully. But of course sometimes an actress may lean over a bit too far, or a skirt may slip back too revealingly. Editing takes care of such matters in the case of film, but in the case of live telecast, matters are different. Careful tests show that no man is quite alert enough or quick enough to switch infallibly over to another camera when unfortunate incidents occur. We mean to do this electronically.

"Consider the advantage it will give Megalith," he continued, "to proceed with perfect freedom in sending anything not positively forbidden under the code, and to know that an electronic monitor, faster than the speed of thought or the glimpse of an eye, is ready to catch and avoid the slightest slipping over the line."

"But that's silly," I said. "In principle you can eliminate —filter out—set off alarms with—any prescribed set of signals. But—why, all the electronic computers in the country together couldn't do it in practice, even if we knew how to program them, which we don't."

Vic looked at me with mock seriousness.

"Do you think that Mr. Braden knows that?" he asked.

"Probably not," I said.

"He doesn't," Vic assured me. "Now, this room illustrates one line of research we are following."

I had completely forgotten where we were, and I turned to the drawings on the walls with interest.

"We must expect simple things from our circuits at first," Vic told me. "These drawings, as you see, are highly stylized and simplified. The Art Department has been very cooperative in working with us, and I believe that we are now able to indicate in just a few lines and marks certain things which are objectionable under the code."

It may have been merely suggestion, but as Vic spoke, the lines, whorls, and dots seemed slowly to take form and meaning, leaving me, figuratively, gasping. In a calm and detached voice of science-as-it-is-thought-to-be, Vic pointed out one objectionable feature after another, and told just which whorls suggested them. The patterns, which before had been seen by the eye only, became obscene to the mind as he spoke.

"And you will observe," he concluded, "the geometric simplicity and the distinctive differences of the patterns which our electronic circuits will sort out."

"Of course," he told me, as we went to the next room, "this material is useful only in our preliminary work with electronic circuits. The final device must distinguish among half-tone material. This problem we are approaching on two levels.

"Here," he said, conducting me to a small room with subdued lighting, "we are working on the problem of liminal units. Miss Anderson, this is Mr. Coupling. Could you show him the A-B test?"

Miss Anderson was a tall blond with an erect carriage and regular features. She seemed to miss beauty only through being a little frightening. She held a notebook and a pen in her left hand, and she wore a white nylon smock.

Miss Anderson seated me in a chair about five feet from a rectangular opening and put in my hand a push button attached to a cord.

"Any machine which exercises discrimination must be set to respond to some least difference," she explained. "If we are to conform to the code, such a difference should be as fine or finer than one limin. A limin," she added, "is of course the least change that a human being can detect. But I suppose you know all that, Mr. Coupling," she said, smiling at me.

I said yes and smiled back.

"In this experiment," she continued, "a bell will sound. When it does, the picture may or may not change. If you think that the picture has changed, push the button. The results are recorded automatically. Do you understand, Mr. Coupling?"

I smiled back and said that I did understand. Then a silvery bell sounded, and in front of me there appeared in vivid color the image of a redhead in a golden gown with extreme décolletage. The bell sounded again, and the décolletage dropped alarmingly; I faithfully pressed the button.

I must have concentrated rather a long time on the problem of whether or not the gown changed at a given stroke of the bell, for finally Vic broke in.

"I think we should see some of the other work, Mr. Coupling," he said. And, as I rose, "Could Miss Anderson explain anything else to you?"

"You've taken a good deal of data?" I asked.

"People around the studio have been very obliging," she said. "There's always a long line—that is, except when Dr. Thatcher has special guests," she added.

"Is this your whole work?" I asked.

She looked thoughtful.

"We've been considering cleavage as a separate problem," she replied. "And then, there is the work on form-fitting ballet costumes, especially tights. But I don't suppose that we'll really need to work on cleavage in connection with that," she added, looking me candidly and innocently straight in the eye.

Vic had opened a door and I followed him into a small projection room.

"Where did you get her?" I asked.

"Marta came from the stenographic pool," he said. "She did major in psychology, though. She can act, too. Maybe she'll get a chance after Braden and the others meet her."

But Vic was bent on giving me the whole tour.

"Of course," he told me, "we can't expect our first machines to have anything like the discrimination of one liminal unit. We must try at first merely to distinguish violent contrasts. For this purpose I have had some special films made. These each consist of a number of contrasting scenes. First, you will see a scene filmed in strict conformity with

250

the code. Then there will follow a somewhat similar scene filmed so as to be clearly unacceptable under the code in most if not all particulars."

As we seated ourselves, Vic in a chair with an impressive instrument panel before it, he pushed a button, the lights dimmed, and the film started. Each scene was preceded by a brief introduction and followed by a brief analysis in the calm, dispassionate voice of Miss Anderson. The pictures were not of such a nature as to calm anyone, however. My tour of the laboratory had been a completely downhill slide, and as the lights went on I felt that I had reached the bottom.

"Has Braden seen this at all?" I asked.

"Only the digrammer," Vic told me.

"You can't get away with it, Vic!" I said. "Not even in Hollywood."

Vic almost burst out laughing.

"You let me worry about that. You got your check cashed, though?"

I nodded.

"Come and have a drink, then," he said, "and tell me what you've been doing."

He had a man take my rented car back to the hotel, and we drove to Ciro's in a Porsche. This was clearly a cut above Larry's Cadillac, although I found it noisy and bouncy. *Taut* is, I believe, the sports-car men's word.

During a sometimes alcoholically happy and sometimes confused evening, we talked about old times, old friends and bygone encounters—about everything but what was on my mind. What was the explanation of Vic and his project? Did he have some deep-seated grudge against the movies? Had he talked big one alcoholic evening, only to find the next day that what he said had been remembered and taken seriously? Or, had he merely seen a chance to make an easy dollar, just as he had passed one on to me? Thinking of my two thousand dollars, I was sure that he had made plenty. Clearly, he had enjoyed himself and didn't take the matter very seriously. I was worried, though, both for him and for me. How did he propose to extricate himself from this situation? At the end of the evening, when we parted, I found out.

The next day, when I left for the east, Vic took off via Pan American for San Tratorio, where he is now special assistant to the Secretary of Interior, in charge of technical education. He had had the job sewed up for the couple of idle months he had spent in Hollywood, working for Megalith. I am sure that he is finding San Tratorio profitable.

I can't be quite sure how Mr. Braden took the trip through the laboratory in the morning of the day Vic left. Calmly, I imagine, in his role of the cool executive. I soon realized that he would be the last person in the world to want anyone else to know about what had happened. And I found out later that he was cannier than I could have imagined. I believe that he lost almost nothing by Vic's profitable deception. They used the laboratory as a set in "Terror from Space"; it looked swell. You may have seen the abstract designs on neckties. I even saw some of the movies in a dealer's room at a midwest electronics conference. Marta Anderson didn't get to act, though. Her name was with Vic's on the card I had from him last Christmas.

Punch

FREDERICK POHL

The introductory comment on this story by the editor
of the *second* magazine that published it ran to ten
words. Mine is even shorter:
Ouch!

The fellow was over seven feet tall and when he stepped on
Buffie's flagstone walk one of the stones split with a dust of
crushed rock. "Too bad," he said sadly, "I apologize very
much. Wait."

Buffie was glad to wait, because Buffie recognized his
visitor at once. The fellow flickered, disappeared and in a
moment was there again, now about five feet two. He blinked
with pink pupils. "I materialize so badly," he apologized.
"But I will make amends. May I? Let me see. Would you
like the secret of transmutation? A cure for simple virus
diseases? A list of twelve growth stocks with spectacular
growth certainties inherent in our development program for
your planet Earth?"

Buffie said he would take the list of growth stocks, hugging
himself and fighting terribly to keep a straight face. "My
name is Charlton Buffie," he said, extending a hand gladly.
The alien took it curiously, and shook it, and it was like
shaking hands with a shadow.

"You will call me 'Punch,' please," he said. "It is not my
name but it will do, because after all, this projection of my
real self is only a sort of puppet. Have you a pencil?" And
he rattled off the names of twelve issues Buffie had never
heard of.

That did not matter in the least. Buffie knew that when
the aliens gave you something it was money in the bank.
Look what they had given the human race. Faster-than-light
space ships, power sources from hitherto nonradioactive ele-

ments like silicon, weapons of great force and metal-working processes of great suppleness.

Buffie thought of ducking into the house for a quick phone call to his broker, but instead he invited Punch to look around his apple orchard. Make the most of every moment, he said to himself, every moment with one of these guys is worth ten thousand dollars. "I would enjoy your apples awfully," said Punch, but he seemed disappointed. "Do I have it wrong? Don't you and certain friends plan a sporting day, as Senator Wenzel advised me?"

"Oh, sure! Certainly. Good old Walt told you about it, did he? Yes." That was the thing about the aliens, they liked to poke around in human affairs. They said when they came to Earth that they wanted to help us, and all they asked of us in return was that they be permitted to study our ways. It was nice of them to be so interested, and it was nice of Walt Wenzel, Buffie thought, to send the alien to him. "We're going after mallard, down to Little Egg, some of the boys and me. There's Chuck—he's the mayor here, and Jer—Second National Bank, you know, and Padre—"

"That is it!" cried Punch. "To see you shoot the mallard." He pulled out an Esso road map, overtraced with golden raised lines, and asked Buffie to point out where Little Egg was. "I cannot focus well enough to stay in a moving vehicle," he said, blinking in a regretful way. "Still, I can meet you there. If, that is, you wish—"

"I do! I do! I do!" Buffie was painfully exact in pointing out the place. Punch's lips moved silently, translating the golden lines into polar space-time coordinates, and he vanished just as the station wagon with the rest of the boys came roaring into the carriage drive with a hydramatic spatter of gravel.

The boys were extremely impressed. Padre had seen one of the aliens once, at a distance, drawing pictures of the skaters in Rockefeller Center, but that was the closest any of them had come. "God! What luck." "Did you get a super-hairpin from him, Buffie?" "Or a recipe for a nyew, smyooth martini with dust on it?" "Not Buffie, fellows! He probably held out for something *real* good, like six new ways to—Oh, excuse me, Padre."

"But seriously, Buffie, these people are unpredictably generous. Look how they built that dam in Egypt! Has this Punch given you anything?"

Buffie grinned wisely as they drove along, their shotguns firmly held between their knees. "Damn it," he said mildly,

"I forgot to bring cigarettes. Let's stop at the Blue Jay Diner for a minute." The cigarette machine at the Blue Jay was out of sight of the parking lot, and so was the phone booth.

It was too bad, he reflected, to have to share everything with the boys, but on the other hand he already had his growth stocks. Anyway, there was plenty for everyone. Every nation on Earth had its silicon-drive spaceships now, fleets of them milling about on maneuvers all over the Solar System. With help from the star-people, an American expedition had staked out enormous radium beds on Callisto, the Venezuelans had a diamond mountain on Mercury, the Soviets owned a swamp of purest penicillin near the South Pole of Venus. And individuals had done very well, too. A ticket-taker at Steeplechase Park explained to the aliens why the air jets blew up ladies' skirts, and they tipped him with a design for a springless safety pin that was earning him a million dollars a month in royalties. An usherette at La Scala became the cosmetic queen of Europe for showing three of them to their seats. They gave her a simple painless eye dye, and now ninety-nine percent of Milan's women had bright blue eyes from her salon.

All they wanted to do was help. They said they came from a planet very far away and they were lonely and they wanted to help us make the jump into space. It would be fun, they promised, and would help to end poverty and war between nations, and they would have company in the void between the stars. Politely and deferentially they gave away secrets worth trillions, and humanity burst with a shower of gold into the age of plenty.

Punch was there before them, inspecting the case of bourbon hidden in their blind. "I am delighted to meet you, Chuck, Jer, Bud, Padre and of course Buffie," he said. "It is kind of you to take a stranger along on your fun. I regret I have only some eleven minutes to stay."

Eleven minutes! The boys scowled apprehensively at Buffie. Punch said, in his wistful voice, "If you will allow me to give you a memento, perhaps you would like to know that three grams of common table salt in a quart of Crisco, exposed for nine minutes to the radiations from one of our silicon reactors, will infallibly remove warts." They all scribbled, silently planning a partnership corporation, and Punch pointed out to the bay where some tiny dots rose and fell with the waves. "Are those not the mallards you wish to shoot?"

"That's right," said Buffie glumly. "Say, you know what

I was thinking? I was thinking—that transmutation you mentioned before—I wonder—"

"And are these the weapons with which you kill the birds?" He examined Padre's ancient over-and-under with the silver chasing. "Extremely lovely," he said. "Will you shoot?"

"Oh, not *now*," said Buffie, scandalized. "We can't do that. About that transmutation—"

"It is extremely fascinating," said the star-man, looking at them with his mild pink pupils and returning the gun. "Well, I may tell you, I think, what we have not announced. A surprise. We are soon to be present in the flesh, or near, at any rate."

"Near?" Buffie looked at the boys and the boys looked at him; there had been no suggestion of this in the papers and it almost took their minds off the fact that Punch was leaving. He nodded violently, like the flickering of a bad fluorescent lamp.

"Near indeed, in a relative way," he said. "Perhaps some hundreds of millions of miles. My true body, of which this is only a projection, is at present in one of our own interstellar ships now approaching the orbit of Pluto. The American fleet, together with those of Chile, New Zealand and Costa Rica, is there practicing with its silicon-ray weapons and we will shortly make contact with them for the first time in a physical way." He beamed. "But only six minutes remain," he said sadly.

"That transmutation secret you mentioned—" Buffie began.

"Please," said Punch, "may I not watch you hunt? It is a link between us."

"Oh, do you shoot?" asked Padre.

The star-man said modestly, "We have little game. But we love it. Won't you show me your ways?"

Buffie scowled. He could not help thinking that twelve growth stocks and a wart cure were small pickings from the star-men, who had given wealth, weapons and the secret of interstellar travel. "We can't," he growled, his voice harsher than he intended. "We don't shoot sitting birds."

Punch gasped with delight. "Another bond between us! But now I must go to our fleet for the . . . For the surprise." He began to shimmer like a candle.

"Neither do we," he said, and went out.